Our Noise

A Novel

JEFF GOMEZ

SCRIBNER PAPERBACK FICTION
Published by Simon & Schuster
New York   London   Toronto   Sydney   Tokyo   Singapore

SCRIBNER PAPERBACK FICTION
Simon & Schuster Inc.
Rockefeller Center
1230 Avenue of the Americas
New York, NY 10020

Cub, Further and Guided by Voices lyrics used by permission.

SCRIBNER PAPERBACK FICTION and design are trademarks of Simon & Schuster Inc.

Designed by Irving Perkins Associates

Manufactured in the United States of America

10 9 8 7 6 5 4 3 2 1

Library of Congress Cataloging-in-Publication Data
Gomez, Jeff.
    Our noise : a novel / Jeff Gomez.
      p. cm.
    I. Title.
PS3557.O456O93   1995
813'.54—dc20   95-16014
                                                            CIP

ISBN 0-684-80099-3

Acknowledgments

Many thanks, Heather at ICM,
Bob and Sarah at Simon & Schuster,
and also to Bret for all his help

for my mother

We are the people our parents warned us about.

—Brenda Kahn

Hello Kitty

1

CUB IS GODDESS.

Randy scrawls these three words in bold print with the blunt end of a thick piece of charcoal onto an extra-large white cotton T-shirt he bought earlier in the day in a pack of three for fifty cents.

Chipp notices his roommate carefully going over each letter, making it thicker until CUB stretches from armpit to armpit, IS covers the sternum area (and then some), and GODDESS travels from hip to hip. Randy's pink tongue is peeking out between rows of slightly crooked, cigarette-and-coffee-stained teeth. He squints crystal blue eyes, concentrating, and the dark rings around the sockets make him look older than twenty. Chipp pauses for a second from his own task of altering a green baseball hat with a yellow bill and a yellow K on the brim. He's adding a shield emblem around the lone letter in Wite-Out.

"Uh, shouldn't that be CUB ARE GODDESSES?"

"What?" Randy says a few seconds later, distracted.

"I said," Chipp repeats, setting down the bottle of Wite-Out which, after a half-hour of close and careful application, has started to get him high, "shouldn't the shirt read CUB ARE GODDESSES?"

"But . . ." Randy's thin voice cracks. He runs a bony hand over his large head covered (scarcely) with a short buzz cut. "That doesn't make sense." Randy again looks over the shirt, thickening the curve of the U in CUB before continuing. "CUB IS GODDESS. It's like a, uh, play on words of that whole CLAPTON IS GOD crap that those old fogies used to spray-paint every place. Which is bullshit because Clapton *sucks*. 'Layla' Unplugged? Give me a fucking break." Randy gets hold of his growing laughter and turns back to his roommate. "So now do you get it?"

"Well, *of course* Clapton sucks," Chipp says incredulously. "But it still doesn't make sense."

"What do you mean?" Randy points at the brown rectangular stereo speaker, its front covered in a beige fabric sparkling with glitter, vibrating back and forth. "Listen." He points his finger at the wooden cabinet as if to the song itself, as if he could lift the tune out of thin air the way he did the T-shirt earlier in the day, out of a pile of trash, drape it against his lean body, and announce to the world, "All right."

The glassy electric guitar is backed by a simple four-four drumbeat pounded out primitively, as if by fists, and the bass line hugs the melody being chirped out in a girl's childish voice: *"Hanging out at the motel six, hanging out just for kicks, hanging out at the motel six . . . with you . . ."*

"Cub rules!" Randy says.

"Of course." Chipp sighs. "That's not the point, idiot. It's just the phrase, CUB IS GODDESS, it . . . doesn't work."

"Huh?"

The song ends and another instantly takes its place, the jangly rhythm and sugar-coated harmonies hugging the corners of the nearly empty but still messy apartment.

"Look. There's three chicks in Cub, right?"

"Yeah, so?"

"Then it should read CUB *ARE* GODDESSES, not CUB *IS* GODDESS. You see?"

"No." Randy winces. "No, no, no. Then you don't get the joke as much. I mean, I don't care if it's grammatically correct. I want it to be *cool*."

"Whatever," Chipp mumbles, picking up the drying cap from an overturned orange crate that holds a stack of vinyl LPs.

"Hey, that doesn't look half-bad," Randy says, glancing over at the hat, the front of which has been turned into the K Records logo. "Is that from a real sports team? I can't think of a major league team that begins with a K."

"Well"—Chipp tries to place the hat on his head, though it

stops abruptly, way too small, covering only the back of his head like a yarmulke—"judging from the *size*, fuck, it's from some goddamn Little League team."

"Jesus, Chipp, didn't you even try that thing on?"

Chipp quickly takes the cap off to examine it.

"Well, no, not really. But hell, it was only a quarter, so I just figured . . . Besides, you didn't give me any time. You found your little packet of T-shirts, started humming that damn Cub song 'What the Water Gave Me' over and over again, came up with your little CUB IS *whatever* idea, and all of a sudden wanted to hurry home."

Chipp unclasps the plastic band at the back of the cap and attaches the first hole of one end to the last peg of the other end, giving him as much space as it possibly can. He tries it on again. This time the hat fits better, but only slightly. The band stops about a full inch above the top of his ear, the bill sticking comically up and a wild tuft of his sandy blond hair sprouting out of the hole in the back.

"Better," Randy says. "But just promise me you'll never wear that thing sideways."

"Or like those rappers."

"Yeah, backward." Randy laughs. "I hear you."

Chipp lies on his belly and stretches out on the stubby carpet that feels more like lightly textured concrete, a shabby pattern of only semi-soft fabric pellets stained every few inches to varying degrees. He rolls onto his side, kicking over the still open Wite-Out bottle, but the liquid is too thick even to trickle out.

"Walk down any street, and you may meet a stranger . . . someone who could love you, take you far away . . ."

Chipp takes off the hat, which he's convinced is cutting off the blood flow to his brain, giving him a tremendous headache.

Randy rises off the floor where he's been sitting cross-legged for the past forty-five minutes, waits a few seconds to regain feeling in his legs, bites his lower lip at the arrival of the piercing needlelike sensation, then grabs his T-shirt off the ground. He pulls his weathered Fred Perry polo over his head, replacing it with his do-it-yourself, albeit grammatically incorrect, CUB IS GODDESS T-shirt. He smiles.

The phone rings, and Randy and Chipp both stare at it. Then

they stare at each other. Then they stare at the ceiling, their fingernails, the walls. Meanwhile, the phone is still ringing.

"Why don't you get it?"

"Why don't *you* get it?"

"You're just like a three-year-old, you know that?"

"Yeah, well, so are you."

Three rings later Chipp moves from the floor, sits in a wooden chair, and grabs the receiver.

"Chipp? Hey, this is Heather."

Randy clutches his stomach for a second before leaving the room. Chipp hears one of the doors down the hall slam shut.

"Hey, Heather, what's up?"

"Nothing. I just got back from DISContent. I picked up some old records from the freebie bin—you know, that old cardboard box near the door where they give away that used stuff they can't even get rid of in the forty-nine-cent bin."

"Really?" Chipp asks, stretching to reach for his hat without pulling the phone off the arm of the chair. "What did you pick up?"

"Mostly junk, which is why they're giving it away, right? Some Simon and Garfunkel, *Frampton Comes Alive,* an old Oingo Boingo *ten*-inch. Jesus, remember them? Ouch! What was that noise?"

Chipp looks down at the white rotary telephone painted in Day-Glo colors, a black-and-white swirl painted over the round disc in the middle of the dial.

"Nothing. Dropped the phone. Keep going."

"Oh, and I got this record with that 'Oh Mickey' chick, Toni Basil, covering this old Devo song, 'Be Stiff.' Anyway, I thought it would sound good on the answering machine. I also picked up this cool New Order EP that's got that really great song 'Temptation' on it."

Randy reenters the room with a thick book in his hands, right after the sound of the toilet flushing.

"We're out of toilet paper," he whispers. Chipp just waves him off, concentrating on the phone conversation.

"Is it the new version or the old version?"

"It's old," her voice says matter-of-factly, as if Chipp's question was not only stupid but out of line as well. "I told you, it was *used.* Things don't get *used* unless they've been around for a while."

"I know it was *used,*" Chipp returns with a sigh, rolling his eyes even though Heather is not there to witness it. "It's an old record, sure, but what I'm asking is, *how* old."

"Huh?"

Chipp sits up in his stiff wooden chair and glances around their spare apartment that he described to Randy the other day as Japanese in the "less is more" style. In reality they're just too poor to afford anything other than a few thrift store nightstands and bookshelves made from cinder blocks and thin sheets of wood.

"It's either from around '87 or '82. Which is it?"

"I don't, uh . . . know." Heather pauses, fingering the gray record sleeve that sits in her hands. She looks up at the clock. 2:41. "It just says 'Temptation' on the cover, that's all."

"No, no, no," Chipp says as if the fact were an elementary truth any young person stopped on the street would know. "There's the first version and then the revamped second version that's not so good."

"What? Two versions? But I thought—"

"Look, Heather, what are the first couple words of the song?"

"Huh?"

Randy sits down on the floor and begins flipping through the book that Chipp can now tell is a dictionary. Randy keeps browsing through the volume, looking from his homemade T-shirt to the thin pages.

"Heather?" Chipp asks, yawning. "How does it begin?"

"Hang on a sec." She rises from her chair and puts the record on the turntable, stacking it on top of three others, and gently places the needle into the groove. The room is filled with a slight dance beat, a percolating synthesizer line, and a wash of electric guitar.

"Jeez, Chipp, there actually aren't any words. Bernard's just sort of, well, *cooing.*" She clears her throat for a moment before imitating the lead singer's sirenlike crooning. She does it once, then lowers her voice a bit. "Er, like that."

"No, the lyrics. Are the first words 'Oh, you've got green eyes, oh, you've got blue eyes, oh, you've got gray eyes,' that little bit? Or are they 'A heaven, a gateway, a home . . .'?"

"No, no, the 'A heaven, a gateway' part comes later. This one starts out with the bit about the eyes."

"Well then," Chipp says smugly, sitting back deep in his chair and confidently crossing his legs, "you've got the old version. New Order originally recorded that song as a twelve-inch single back in the early eighties when they sounded like Joy Division sans Ian Curtis. But, uh . . ." Chipp recoils at the sound of his voice as it dominates both the scarcely furnished room and the phone conversation. "Anyway . . ."

"Hmm, didn't know that."

"Yeah, well, just because we're young doesn't mean we shouldn't have some sense of history. After all, as soon as all these old people die, this is going to be our world."

Heather laughs on the other end of the phone, twirling the cord around the floor like a jump rope.

"But I didn't think we were going to live that long. Remember all that drunken talk about living fast, dying young, and leaving a good-looking corpse?"

"Well"—Chipp glances across the room at Randy, who's checking the spelling of GODDESS—"some of us won't even be able to get that right."

Heather laughs and calls something out to her roommate that Chipp can't hear, then returns to the phone.

"Listen, the reason I called is I wondered if you wanted to do something tonight. I thought maybe you could come over for a drink or"—she pauses for a second before adding—"something."

"Hang on a second." Chipp cups a hand over the mouthpiece as he whispers to Randy, "Hey, what are you doing later?"

"Going out. Sorry."

Chipp rolls the decision over in his head for a few seconds before answering.

"Sure, why not."

"Great. Come on over anytime past eight. Jen's got a date so we'll have the place to ourselves."

After a few more minutes of small talk, Heather ends the conversation when Jen picks up another extension and starts dialing as a subtle reminder that she needs the phone. After Chipp hangs up the receiver, he notices that Randy has discarded the CUB IS GODDESS T-shirt and has started all over again. Now he's going over the letters, carefully thickening each line, trading the blank space of cotton for his newest slogan that reads DON'T BLAME ME, I VOTED FOR VELOCITY GIRL.

2

Dave crosses the street carefully, looking both ways.

He smiles and pats the pocket of his moth-eaten secondhand blazer before skipping through the crosswalk. With his index finger and thumb he opens the jacket, peers inside, triple-checking that the check is still there. It is. He breezes into the bank, queues up, and alternately smiles at the guard and the video camera in the corner, unsure of who is the boss.

"Next!" a woman calls out to him, breaking his spell.

He saunters up to the counter and throws down the check. He signs his name with unreadable Picasso-like flair and then pushes it across the counter like a chess piece in the last stages of the game.

She picks it up as if it smells and looks queerly at the check, then back to Dave.

"Oh no, not again," he begs, taking a deep breath. "Look, *I'm* Violent Revolution Records. Me! I own it! This check is made out to Violent Revolution Records, see? So this money belongs in *my* account. See?" Dave jumps up and down in front of the teller, who's just sitting there, motionless.

The check is for twenty-seven dollars and is from a kid in Pennsylvania who wants the new seven-inch single by one of Dave's bands, Bottlecap, a CD by another, The Disappointed, as well as a Violent Revolution Records T-shirt, one of which Dave is wearing himself. The check came in the morning's mail to his post office box, and Dave's plan for the day was to cash the check, buy some greatly needed groceries, and have a decent meal, events that hadn't occurred in weeks.

"Sir, I'm sorry." The teller finally breaks her frozen glare. "We just can't cash this check."

"Why not?"

"Your name is David Rowland, correct?" Her tone is flat and ominous. She stands there waiting for Dave to respond lamely in the affirmative when it's pretty obvious who he is.

"Correct." He tosses back his dirty-blond hair in an attempt to sublimate the growing anger.

"Now, this check . . ." She picks it up again to examine it. The words are in a childlike scrawl, the *R* in Revolution printed backward. Dave is beginning to hope that the kid who sent it was just horsing around. He runs a hand across his heated brow. *Why didn't I stay in college?* he quickly thinks to himself. *Why didn't I get that damn degree? Why did I get into this damn business? Maybe my father was right.* "This check is made out to Violent Revolution. Now, what *is* Violent Revolution anyway?"

"It's my company." Dave is squirming like an uncomfortable child who has had enough and just wants to go home. "I sell records, T-shirts, CDs. You know, small shit. I tell people to send cash or, if they have to, a check, but to make it out in my name. But some people are so stupid. I even had *Maximum Rock and Roll* put it in bold print: PLEASE MAKE ALL CHECKS AND MONEY ORDERS PAYABLE TO DAVID ROWLAND! But you always get some pinhead who insists on making it out to Violent Revolution, and then I always get this hassle."

"I've never heard of that record company before. And how do I know you really own it? You could have gotten that check anywhere."

Dave pulls back the brown blazer he bought last month at the Love Is Christ thrift store for six bucks, revealing a black T-shirt with a smiley face, a lit bomb, and the words VIOLENT REVOLU-TION RECORDS, in vaguely '70s lettering.

"Well, why did you name it that? Why couldn't you have named it something nice, like . . . Capitol? Or RCA?"

He looks up wearily at the woman. Her skin is stretched so tight, he can see at least half a dozen veins through her cheese-cloth skin.

"Well, I don't know. I always thought the name Violent Revolution was kind of catchy," he says sarcastically.

"Now," she says, quickly running out of patience, "you show me a piece of identification with that name under your photo and I'll be more than glad to cash that check, but otherwise I am sorry."

"But it's my company."

"Well then, why don't you have a merchant account?"

"Because"—Dave sulks, leaning against the counter with all of his weight—"I really don't do that much business. I mean, my regular job is being a waiter, but you know, one of these days I hope to— Look, this snotty-nose kid wants to buy a few records, so just cash the fucking check so I can send him his goddamn shit!" Dave suddenly finds himself shouting. The bank becomes eerily quiet. Where are the violins plucking out a Muzak "Papa Don't Preach"? Where is the idle chatter of the customers that usually drives him insane? Instead there's only silence and every eye in the place on him. A few seconds later he hears the faint buzzing of the video camera hoisted in the corner as it swings to the left, fitting him into view.

A small bald man in a brown suit approaches him.

"Now, sir, if you'll just leave quietly."

"But I need my fucking money!"

A security guard appears and sternly grabs Dave's shoulder and begins forcing him toward the door. The cool air strikes Dave's face as he's shoved through the revolving plate glass door. He looks back just in time to see the ugly old woman behind the counter rip the check in two.

The Bradys never went to bed angry. Dave remembers this as he punches his time card on the ancient machine in the employee lounge of the Whales Fin that stamps the date and time with a hollow *ping*.

"It's a good thing I'm not a Brady," Dave mumbles, reaching for a stack of blank checks where they're kept between the rows of fresh pepper grinders and old salad dressing containers now filled with croutons for easy dispensing, "because at this rate I'd be up all night."

"You say something, Rowland?"

Dan, the manager, enters the break room and eyes his employee suspiciously. Glancing at his watch he notices that Dave is actually five minutes early for his shift rather than his recently habitual ten minutes late. "Clock out, Rowland. You don't go on for another five."

"But I was hoping to get started on my tables—you know, check out the salt and pepper left over from the lunch shift because sometimes the busboys will forget to. I mean . . . the lunch crew won't—" He tries to stall, but Dan cuts him off.

"Clock *out,* Rowland," he says as he glances around the room, looking for something else to criticize. Perturbed there is nothing else wrong, he turns on his heel and exits, but only after tapping his watch and saying, "Time is money, and that means minutes, too. It all adds up, Rowland."

As Dan disappears down the hallway to check on the soft-drink dispensers stored in cardboard cubes in the rear of the restaurant, Dave hears the manager's spiel continuing, "Minutes, Rowland. You may think it doesn't add up, but it does."

Dave steadies his time card, ready to clock back in for what now would be a measly three minutes, but instead places it back in its slot along with the others.

"Bad day, huh, Dave?" Carlos says, emerging from the bathroom sandwiched between Dan's office and the employee lounge.

"Yeah, you could say that." Dave picks up a starched white apron from the pile and wrestles with the knot, as he always does.

"How long you been working here? Eight months?"

"Six!"

"Whatever. And you still can't tie that fucking thing?"

"It's just I've got poor coordination. Get off my back." Dave tries a few more times as Carlos watches him. "So are you going to help me or not?"

"Don't I always?"

Carlos throws his cigarette into a big sink with dishes in it and puts his arms around Dave's waist to retrieve the loose ends of the apron strings.

"Well, well." Stacy walks in, wraps her purse up in its strap, and heads toward the lockers. "I'm not sure what's going on here, but I'll treat it like a UFO sighting. I know I saw some-thing, but I'm not sure what it was."

Carlos ties the knot tightly, causing Dave to gasp, and then leaves, shooting Stacy a look.

"That's real funny," Dave says, giving the knot some slack. "What, did you watch *Stripes* again last night?"

"Maybe I did. So what, it's a good movie."

"What's this obsession you have with Bill Murray anyway?"

"It's not an, uh, obsession." Stacy starts nervously scratching her pale face, running a hand through her strawberry blond hair. "I just think he's funny, that's all."

"How many times have you seen *Ghostbusters*?"

"Twenty. How many have you?"

"Twice. Now you see, that's a normal number. Twenty's an obsession."

Stacy lunges forward.

"But what about that scene where he's covered in all the goop and he has the cutest look on his face and he goes, 'I've been slimed!' I mean, that's classic!"

"Big deal." Dave positions his black folder filled with checks, wine lists, and specials in the small of his back, straightens his tie, and makes sure he has a few pens in his pocket. "It's not like he's Woody Allen or anything. He doesn't even write his own material."

"You're just jealous." Stacy brushes up close to Dave and then waltzes out of the room.

"Am not!" Dave shouts more than thirty seconds after Stacy has exited.

Before heading out onto the floor, Dave checks a diagram of the restaurant, which is divided into nine different sections. Tonight he is in station seven, which consists of a set of two tops and two booths.

"Not bad," he mumbles, making his way through the kitchen, "as long as I don't get triple-seated."

As Dave moves through the dining room that is slowly filling up, he can't help but imagine how many times this exact scene is being played out across the country. He thinks of all the restau-rants in the United States, from every five-star gourmet estab-lishment serving the latest in nouvelle cuisine to the greasy truck stops lining the freeways of the country (the far reaches where nobody in the joint can even *say* nouvelle cuisine). Dave thinks of all the other kids in his situation, doing what he's doing, and it makes him feel incredibly small.

Dave takes a deep breath before approaching his first table, which consists of a middle-aged couple with a young boy. He pretends he likes them, introduces himself and then the featured meals of the evening, and pretends even more that he likes what he's doing. Being a waiter is like being an actor, and Dave always feels as if he has a bad case of stage fright.

On his way back to the alley after taking their drink orders, he finds his limbs heavy, his movements slow and leaden with gloom. His sloping shoulders and arched back symbolize the "what's the point?" despair that is coursing through his body.

"There are others out there tonight smarter than I am," he thinks to himself as he fills a rocks glass with ice, Coke, and then a dash of grenadine and a cherry. "There are countless others winning the battle while I fall further behind."

He steadies the Roy Rogers on his tray and heads back to the dining room to deliver the drink to the small boy who is sitting in his chair, on his knees with elbows poised on the back-brace and eyes alert, waiting for it.

Carlos, who's in station eight, whizzes by Dave singing, *"And the train conductor said, take a break station eight, you've been on this shift too long, take a break, station eight."*

"More like *section* eight," Dave calls out to Carlos just as he's leaving the alley, balancing a large tray with a Maine lobster at each end, facing each other at the center.

Throughout the evening the food comes out of the window at a good rate, something rare for the kitchen on any night, and the bills in Dave's pocket, the tips he's accumulated, are turning into a pleasant wad that bumps his left thigh every time he moves.

"Phoebe Cates on five," Carlos rushes into the alley screaming. "Phoebe Cates on five," he repeats, setting down a tray full of dirty dishes and checking for his appetizers in the window.

"Is this like the time you saw Gregory Peck up in the smoking section?" Dave asks as he scoops out ice using a glass instead of the metal scoop as he's supposed to.

"Hey, don't bring that up again." Carlos tugs on a plate of fried zucchini and places it on a new tray. "Stoner, how about a bullet of red?" he calls through the window, then turns again to Dave. "It was dark, and I . . . got confused."

"That guy was Mexican!" Dave laughs. He notices a chip in the lip of his glass but fills it up with soda anyway.

"Yeah, yeah," Carlos grumbles, turning back to the window. "Stoner? Where's my fucking sauce?"

Dave places the soda along with a glass of sweet tea and another of regular tea (with a straw in one to tell the difference) and heads out onto the floor, consciously making a pass by table number five. Sitting there is an attractive, dark, slightly European-looking girl with brown eyes, jet black hair, and a cute smile, but definitely *not* Phoebe Cates. Dave drops off his drinks, takes an order, and checks on another table before heading back into the alley where Carlos is still waiting for his marinara sauce.

"Close"—Dave begins to punch in his order at the computer next to the bar—"but no cigar."

Carlos waves him off and finally completes his own order and heads out of the alley.

Stacy slides by with a pitcher of water, which means cheapskates are somewhere in her station, and says something like "What about *The Razor's Edge?* Now *that's* range!"

"That's a remake," Dave shoots back. "And not even a good one!"

Twenty minutes later she cozies up to him at the salad bar and whispers in his ear, "Come on over later. *Caddyshack*'s on TV. We'll have a few drinks. It'll be fun."

Dave nods, then notices that an elderly couple who had been sitting at his booth and had mumbled something about an anniversary have gone, leaving behind their doggy bag and a twenty-dollar bill.

"The boys are back in town, the boy-oise are bah-ee-ack in townnn . . ." Dave is singing, off-key, trying to give his thin voice some semblance of soul. *"The boys are back in town . . ."* He pauses for a second as a pile of vomit makes a rush at his throat, but he manages to keep it down. His mouth is filled with an acidy resi-

due, the reconnaissance unit of the vomit that never escaped. Sure that the moment of temporary sickness has passed, he drains the last of another beer and continues shouting, *"The boys are back in town!"*

"What in the fuck do you mean by that?" Stacy asks, taking a sip of her own drink, a wine cooler.

"The boys are, uh, back in town. Don't you remember that song from that movie *48 Hours?"*

"Sure. Not a bad flick. Would have been better with Bill Murray in either of those roles, but, yeah, what about it?"

"Well, that's what that song is from."

"Yeah, so? What's the significance?"

"The boys who are coming back to town," Dave says cleverly, proud of his song–subject matter link, "is my band Bottlecap."

"Oh, the ones who have been out on tour?" She takes another sip and looks at the damage Dave has already done to her apartment—records scattered over the floor as well as half a dozen beer cans in various crushed states. "When do they get back?"

"They should be here"—he glances at his wrist even though he is not wearing a watch—"in no time. Their final show was last night in Kentucky, so I'm sure they've been on the road all day and night, heading back home. I figure they'll be back in Kitty by the morning."

The beers tickle Dave's empty stomach and carry him further along faster than if he had eaten something before. Poised on the brink of a really good buzz, he feels his whole body start to go numb, his teeth go a little fuzzy, his vision become slightly blurred. He drains the last of the beer and then gets another.

"Jesus, Dave, that's a six pack already. You'd better slow down."

Dave stumbles toward the fridge and pulls out another beer. It's always funny to find out the things he can't do after drinking six or seven beers. He never knows beforehand. He always has to wait to do them, then sit back and see what worked and what didn't. Sitting on the couch, he could have sworn he would be able to make it to the kitchen okay, but once up, his legs begin to fail him, his kneecaps turn to Jell-O, and it seems as if he's negotiating the deck of a violently tossing ship. Stacy laughs and goes into the kitchen.

"You're really a work of art, you know that?"

Dave sits on the couch staring at a poster for the movie *Quick Change*, which Bill Murray actually directed, or at least co-directed. Dave wonders how someone does that. Would the other guy say, "Then the camera pulls back, swings left, and she gives her line," and then Bill would just nod approvingly?

"Look, that's it for the beer, and I'm all out of coolers. Here." Stacy sets down a teakwood tray with some crackers, a bottle of wine, and some sliced cheddar cheese.

Dave scoots off the couch and onto the cool hardwood floor.

"Ritz crackers? Ooh, now that's classy."

"Easy, buster. You almost got Saltines."

"And how are we going to end the evening? Making S'mores by the campfire?"

Dave's head falls forward onto Stacy's chest. She picks it up and tosses it back the other way, causing Dave to fall back against the couch with a thud.

"God, you're being grumpy. And you have no reason to be. I saw that wad of tips you were counting in the dry box. How much was it?"

"Fifty," Dave mumbles.

"Before or after tipping out?"

"After."

"Not bad. I only made thirty-five, and I had a bigger station. Of course, that huge table of campers didn't help anything."

"Yeah, it was a good night, actually." Dave regains a hold on things, thinking back to his disastrous afternoon at the bank. "If Dan hadn't called and begged me to take Amy's shift, I would have been having *Where's Waldo* SpaghettiOs for the fourth night in a row." Dave laughs and takes a sip of the wine, which is very good, along with a cracker. "Thank god Amy's such a fuckup."

"But what else? You seemed preoccupied." Stacy puts a slice of cheese delicately on a cracker and slips it carefully into her mouth. Then she picks up the glass of wine and takes a sip. "And not just tonight, I mean. But lately. You've been, sort of, I don't know, out of it, for the past couple of weeks."

"It's just . . . what the fuck am I doing with my life? Why didn't I stay in school? Why did I come back to Kitty?"

"I thought it was because of the record label. To be close to the bands."

"Ahh." Dave shrugs her off. "That was just an excuse probably. I mean, I was at the University of Virginia, and my diploma, I mean, it was in fucking sight! And I just freaked out." The small river of booze inside him is carrying him to a place he had long been avoiding. "Have you ever carried something that was just too heavy for you, and your arms just . . . gave out? They couldn't hold it anymore? That's what happened to me. And at the end it was like a building had collapsed. I just couldn't take it."

"But I still don't understand. Couldn't take what?"

"I don't know, really. It's just that every time I thought of graduation as being just around the corner, it freaked me out, because what was behind *that* corner? I knew I'd have to get a real job and that if I didn't, everyone would look at me like a loser. Like, what's this guy with a college degree doing peddling these seven inches and T-shirts by bands who eventually end up on the sides of milk cartons?"

Stacy laughs.

"You think that's funny? My life is turning into a club date that no one shows up for. I just don't know why I bother with anything these days."

"Well, how are the records selling?"

The question hits him right in his queasy gut.

"Not so good. My weak stab at self-distribution is getting me nowhere. I can't get my merchandise into any good stores or catalogs. I used to make a pretty good amount of change selling stuff wholesale to DISContent, but since the majors started leaning into Jim for selling used CDs, he's used that as an excuse to squeeze a lot of smaller labels off his shelves. He said he couldn't keep dealing with so many different small labels, so I can't even sell my stuff there unless I go through a distributor like Mordam or Revolver. Do you know how humiliating that is? To not even be able to go into a record store in my hometown and see my stuff on the shelves?"

"I'm sure it's just temporary," Stacy says, cozying up to him on the floor even though Dave doesn't register her presence.

"I hope so, because if I don't start moving some records,

they're going to bury me in a coffin made of vinyl with a flip-top jewel case lid."

Dave drains the wine and sets the glass carefully on the floor. He then puts his arm around Stacy's waist, as if he knows that's what she's been waiting for.

"And what about all this?" Stacy twirls her arms around, like Vanna White showing off a washer and dryer.

"What? You mean being here with you?"

"What do you think I mean?"

Dave looks into Stacy's eyes, which seem on the verge of something, either laughter or tears, but he's too drunk to tell. She's very good looking, and Dave has lusted after her for quite a long time. They've gotten together at a few parties but always seemed more like friends than lovers. He glances briefly at the TV screen where Bill (as Stacy refers to him) is dressed up in fatigues and is running around a golf course.

"Hello, Dave. Remember me?"

He leans in and puts his other arm around her.

"That's better."

Dave knows she feels about him the way he feels about her, which is nothing serious, but she's got this need to be held tonight—a need that Bill cannot fill from the TV screen.

"I like you, Stacy. I really do." He shuts his eyes and seems to just sort of float away, the warm sensation in his stomach cradling him like a blanket.

As he holds Stacy tighter and she nuzzles her warm nose past the flap on his shirt and begins lightly kissing his chest, he thinks back to earlier that day when he was standing in line at the bank, arguing with the teller. He remembers the bubbling hate, the rage, and that "not again" feeling of disappointment. But here in Stacy's comfortable apartment, holding this girl in his arms, he finally feels okay. Warm. How did McMurtry put it in that novel? *Snug.*

She was changing him, making the world a nice place to be. Dave just closes his eyes and smiles. In the back of his head he knows that the problems are still there: The dishes need to be done, Evatone won't return his calls, Ben Weasel wants his DAT tape back if Dave can't raise the money for the single. He knows that Stacy's arms are something real, but they won't stay around him for long. *Fuck it,* he thinks, *please fuck it and please go away. Please let me be. Give that stillborn diploma and my problems to somebody else, anyone, even Stacy.*

On the TV, Bill is in his bunker/apartment, surrounded by gardening equipment and a mound of plastic explosives. He cradles a rifle against his shoulder and pulls the trigger, garbling the words, "And that's all she wrote."

3

"You looking forward to going back?" Mark asks, seeking out Gary's bloodshot eyes from the rearview mirror.

Mark steers with one hand and with the other turns down the volume of the tape deck. Scrawl's *Velvet Hammer* cassette drops in volume like jumping off a step, Marcy May's voice dissipating into the far reaches of the dingy, dirty, off-white Ford Econoline 250 van.

"I'm relieved the tour's over," Gary finally says, scratching his belly, then his head, trying to scratch out a better answer, "but looking forward to going back? Uh . . . no."

"Why not?" prompts Steve, who is sitting just a few feet away in the middle of the van with his back against Mark's Fender Twin Reverb amp, his feet underneath a pair of rusted metal buckles in the floor where a bank of two seats can be installed. Right now the extra seats are gathering dust in Mark's father's garage, where they've been ever since Bottlecap commandeered the van for its three-month, ten-state tour. Now, on the way back, the van is dirtier than before, the tires seem flatter, and even the spirits of the three band members inside seem to be running low.

"Bllfff." Gary exhales a lungful of air as an initial response before adding, "It's just, go back to what? To being a fucking waiter? A telemarketer? Usher at the movie theater? Or whatever other job I'll be able to scrounge up six months from now?" He rubs his gray eyes and then runs a hand through his jet black hair that in some places refuses to part for him. His fingers get stuck in large unwashed clumps like a car on an off-ramp that suddenly dead-ends. He chews with his nails at his itchy scalp, which he is almost positive is littered with lice. He glances down at his arm, his pale skin even whiter than usual thanks to being cooped up in the van or else in clubs and bars during the depressing autumn with its cool breezes and shortened days. Gary can remember only one sunset in three months, and only to the extent that it pissed him off, that the sun got in his eyes and made him squint, honk at other drivers, and generally be crankier than usual. All it made him do was curse at Mark for talking him into swapping shifts at the wheel. And now, like some pirate on the verge of scurvy, Gary sucks in his hollowed cheeks and looks forward to a square meal. Indeed, his bowels haven't moved for nearly a week now while he was sure that Steve's ass was at the opposite point, rumbling every few hours like some sort of agitated California coastline, and this pissed Gary off, not because of envy but because it meant they were always having to pull off to a convenience store or the side of the road where Steve would jump out, relieve himself, and then jump back in quickly, causing the van to reek of shit.

"It's not like *I've* got a cushy new job waiting for me or anything." Gary sends the accusation flying into the front seat where it hits Mark in the back of the head.

"Hey!" Mark finds Gary's gaze again in the mirror, beyond which are a few trucks, light traffic, and the sun going down that he hadn't noticed before. "Don't make it sound like that. My dad only offered me the job, and who said I'm going to take it?"

"Shit, you'd be a fool not to." Steve says what Gary's thinking. Steve's blond cropped hair is standing on end, also the victim of inadequate rinses at various gas station bathrooms throughout the Southeast. "That cushy assistant librarian gig at the community college sounds like a dream. Well, maybe not a dream, but it sounds easy and it's killer money. Besides, a friend of mine said it'd be working for the state, so you'd get benefits and raises at, like, regular intervals, not when some old fart finally notices you. Man, you'd be set for life."

Set for life. The words ring in his ears the way the lyrics to

"Remember That Day" were ringing before. *Set for life*. His father had also used that phrase when trying to convince him to
take the job. Then, like now, it had the opposite effect. Where
his father was trying to instill in him some sense of security,
permanence, and responsibility, Mark had only seen stagnation,
capitulation, and atrophy. *Set for life*. Mark passes a battered
red Yugo that's sputtering in the slow lane with a YO-♡-JALISCO
bumper sticker and Nevada plates. *Yeah, but what kind of life?*
Mark thinks. *That's got to count for something*.

"It's like," Steve continues, "I'm in Gary's shoes. I don't have
a job to go back to." On a whim he actually glances at Gary's
shoes, only to find his feet in a pair of white socks, now gray,
black on the bottom, and solid with dust, grit, and grime all over
the ankle and shin area. "What I mean is, we're fucked. After
all, it's not like this tour made us rich or anything."

Gary slides over a few feet and rests his back on a brown
cardboard box that is still filled with various Bottlecap merchandise: CDs, seven-inch singles, stickers, T-shirts. The box was
supposed to be empty. In fact, the box shouldn't even have
been there. They should have ripped it into clean little strips in
Louisville the night before. Instead, the cargo was riding back
with them with only a small dent in the contents.

"Man," Gary says angrily, "I'm going to kill Dave for making
us lug all this shit around." He knocks his sock into the side of
the box, where it lands with a solid thud.

"Wait a second. Why is this Dave's fault?" Steve asks.

"Because it's his shitty record label. He pressed all these shitty
records, and he's the guy who booked all those shitty shows we
just played where practically no one showed up and it was his
idea to do this long tour anyway."

"Yeah," Mark calls out from the front seat, "except for that
string of shows you set up using that *Book Your Own Fucking Life*
booklet you bought at DISContent and your sister's calling card.
And actually the tour was your idea because you had just quit
your job and were bored, remember?"

"I don't want to split hairs." Gary waves off Mark's comments.
"The point is . . . I don't know how much longer we can continue like this."

Even though the cassette in the tape deck had been turned

down minutes ago and so had ceased to be heard, it clicks off when it runs out of space, the finality of it punctuating the tension in the van and startling everyone.

"What are you saying?" Steve says delicately, as if treading on thin ice.

"I'm saying . . ." Gary hesitates. He hadn't planned to bring this up so soon. He was planning to wait until a few weeks after the tour, after he saw how easy it was for him to get yet another job. If he happened to luck into something fairly secure, he was going to tell his old high school friends and bandmates adios. Gary's reasoning was, Sure, it was a long, strange trip, but enough is enough. "I'm saying that unless something big happens to us, that . . . that I'll want out."

"Big like what?" Mark asks, fumbling with the radio, trying to pop out the cassette, only it's stuck halfway in and halfway out.

"Like, you know, we talked about sending out our CD to some big record companies, maybe trying to land a deal with a major. Things like that. It's just I'm not looking forward to playing The Scene every Friday night with occasional trips down to Chapel Hill or up to Arlington. Being Kitty's hotshot bar band is not what I want out of life."

"Actually," Steve nervously ventures forth, "I agree with that last part. This tour didn't work out as well as I would have hoped either, and, well, I just don't want to go back to being some high school party band."

As the songwriter and de facto leader of the band, Mark feels like a parent trying to contend with two bawling kids on a tedious road trip. All he wants to do is pry out the cassette from the tape eating player and hear side one again.

"Guys, I'm with you when we're all talking about a career reassessment. And I know that if I take this job my dad's offering, it would drastically cut down on our practice time and also our ability to play out-of-town gigs. That kind of thing was easy when I was working at the bookstore, but this will be a strict nine-to-five shift. Besides, my dad's getting pissed off at all the mileage we're putting on this thing."

" 'Strict nine-to-five shift?' " Gary echoes the words Mark has just spoken in a whiny, effeminate voice. "Who in the fuck are you, Dolly Parton? Are you going to start growing tits and speaking in a twangy, fucking accent? Jesus, man, check your balls at the door, why don't you."

Steve laughs and leans across the space and holds out his reeking hand for a high five, which Gary is reluctant to return.

"You guys done picking on me?" Mark says as he finally gets a healthy amount of plastic between his index finger and thumb and yanks the cassette out of the player. He flips it over with a flick of his wrist and shoves it back in. A dim green arrow pointing toward the passenger door lights up, and Mark hears the clicking of the machine creaking into action, music filling the van.

"Your mother wants to know when you're coming home for a weekend."

Satisfied, Mark yawns, scoping out the darkening roadside for the icon of a thick fork set against the backdrop of a circle, representing a crude plate.

"Time to start looking for a place to eat," he announces to his crew who are still infused in a combination of laughter from making fun of Mark and a puddle of self-pity for their own misfortunes.

"You know," Mark calls out again as it gets harder and harder to find Gary's eyes in the waning light, "you still haven't answered my question. Are you looking forward to going back?"

Gary shrugs and tries to get comfortable on the cold steel floor, but after three months he should realize that it's an impossibility. He glances out the back windows and catches a glimpse of the setting sun until it's blocked by a billboard advertising Disney World. Then he sees the black limitless road, the interstate stretching out behind them to—he now believes after twelve weeks spent on it—eternity.

"Let's just say," Gary begins, his gaze still trailing out the filthy window, "that I'm looking back . . . to going forward."

Steve's eyes dart around the laminated Shoney's menu, trying to gauge the future temperature of his intestines. He places a hand on his nauseous, toxic stomach and thinks he can actually feel the tubes twisting around, still trying to work through the Egg McMuffin and hash browns he defiantly shoved down just a few hours ago.

"Uh, I think I'll just have a cheeseburger. Cheese is good for you, right?" Steve says cautiously.

"Oh, brother," Gary groans, trying to remind himself to steal some extra napkins before they pile into the van for the last leg of their journey.

"Say, guys," Mark begins as he slides his large menu, covered with garish photographs of various burger plates, tuna melts, and omelettes, into a wire holder behind the sugar, cream, and napkins, "I was just thinking. How's about using some of our petty cash and staying at that motel across the road for tonight?" He jerks his thumb over his shoulder to the large building behind them, across the freeway but visible through the large plate glass window. "You know, get a good night's rest and then head for Kitty first thing in the morning. Whaddya say?"

It takes the boys only a millisecond to react.

"Oh no you don't, Pellion. You're not pulling that shit," Steve says quickly.

"Yeah," Gary says, hot on Steve's heels. "Not a chance in hell. Petty cash? That petty cash is my back rent money, which is, oh, three months overdue."

"I hate to burst your bubble, Gary, but have you seen the petty cash lately?" Mark is referring to the cigar box kept under the driver's seat where all the money made from and to support themselves on tour was kept. They started out with a few hundred bucks with the aim of making that back and more. They were coming home with under fifty.

"N-n-no. Why?"

"Because all the rent it's going to pay is for one night." He jerks his thumb again over his shoulder like a superstitious person with a shaker of salt. "Anyway"—he forgets the idea and motions to Gary's menu still in his hand—"what are you having?"

"A heart attack," he replies.

"Me," Steve pipes up, still not listening to their conversation but examining his choices, "I think I'll stick with my cheeseburger. With chili on top."

The waitress comes and they give their orders: two burgers, and a turkey sandwich for Mark, odd man out. Steve and Mark both order root beer floats when Gary gets one for himself.

A few minutes later Gary breaks off a chunk of the sub-
merged vanilla ice cream floating in the root beer with his long-
necked spoon and says, "I know why Mark doesn't want to go
home yet, why he wants to spend another night away from
home."

"Why?" Steve asks anxiously. "Why?"

Mark would also like to know, but he figures Gary will explain
even if no one shows interest.

"It's because he has Laura waiting at home for him *and* he has
a guilty conscience."

"Guilty conscience?" Steve is shaken out of examining the dessert menu. "Why? Oh, because of the one-night stand?"

"It wasn't a one-night stand," Mark whispers, leaning across
the table and then looking nervously around.

"Oh, really?" Gary takes a sip of his float, the two ingredients
now melting into a creamy, frothy mixture. "So you're saying
that you're going to have a deep, meaningful relationship with
that whatever her name was. Hell, I bet *you* can't even remember
her name!"

"That's not what I'm saying." Mark tries to stall, hoping Gary
doesn't bet him because Mark can't remember her name, either.
"I'm just saying that it wasn't as crass as all that. You know, a
one-night stand, like I fucked her in the back of the van using
my cymbal case as a pillow so she wouldn't keep ramming her
head into the wheel well."

"Hey, don't bring me into this," Steve says, catching the obvious reference to one of his own exploits that happened outside
the 40 Watt Club in Athens, Georgia, with a junior editor of
Flagpole magazine. "Besides, that was different. I don't have
some girl I've been dating for, like, what's it been now, three
years?"

"Uh, four, actually," Mark reluctantly acknowledges.

"Four?" Gary gasps. "Jesus, don't you get any time off for
good behavior?"

Gary and Steve laugh and punch each in the shoulders in the
same way they've been doing all tour, and that's really starting
to annoy Mark.

The three meals arrive, and Steve and Gary dig into them
instead of Mark.

4

" 'I'm not your mother,' " Ashley says, popping a garlic puff into her mouth.

"It figures that'd be your first choice." Craig tries to cross his legs underneath the small table but can't. He takes the last bite of his Caesar salad, trying to choose from all of the song titles racing around his head.

" 'Feed Me,' " he finally says.

"Aha!" Ashley is quick to respond. "You said favorite Blake Babies song, and 'Feed Me' is a Juliana Hatfield song! Disqualified! Try again, buster."

"But"—Craig tries to defend, but Ashley is tossing her blond hair back and forth, not even listening—"she based that on an early song that was a bonus track on the *Earwig* CD, remember?"

"No go." She laughs, poking at her pasta. "Pick again."

"Um . . . how about 'Out There.' "

"Jesus!" she shouts, draining the last swig of her second glass of red wine and motioning toward the waiter for another. "How *obvious*! I mean, that was a single not to mention a video which got played all the time. Craig, you know I love you, but try to be a bit more original."

"You know, there's a reason they always pick certain songs to be singles. It's because they're the best! Why do you think they're the singles?" Craig playfully slaps the table top. "Duh."

"Yeah, but, that's what's so great about album tracks. You have to tread through a morass of substandard—"

"Okay, okay," he cuts his girlfriend off. "It's almost ten. They'll be opening the doors at The Scene soon."

"Big deal. We're going to be the only ones there, and then we'll have to just sit there and stare at Jack wash beer glasses for forty-five minutes. Oh, I forgot, you like to get the good bar stools."

"Fine, you make a joke, but when we get there late and have

to sit near that brass rail thing where everyone claws their way in to shout out their orders in your ear"—he quickly checks his watch—"you'll thank me."

"Back to the task at hand. Please?"

"Okay. 'Girl in a Box.' Happy?"

"A John song? Why would you pick a John song? That's like saying your favorite R.E.M. song is 'Near Wild Heaven.' Why did you choose that?"

"Look, I like 'Girl in a Box.' It has good guitars, and it pre-dates that whole *Boxing Helena* thing by a couple of years. And" —he plays his trump card—"it's an album track."

"Yeah . . . but . . . it doesn't even have drums."

"Okay, okay. How about 'Temptation Eyes'?"

"That's a cover!"

"All right, all right." He searches his mind and, in memory, his record collection. "I've got it!" He snaps his fingers. " 'Lament!' It's off that obscure import EP I've got called *Slow Learner,* and it's not a single . . . I don't think."

Ashley is silent, mulling over Craig's choice.

"Okay," she decides, nodding her head slowly, "I'll accept that."

"This reminds me of the time we saw them in Richmond, with the Lemonheads. Remember?"

"Yeah." She thinks back three years ago to her undergraduate days when she and Craig were just starting to get serious. That night he had driven the entire way from the University of Virginia campus in Charlottesville to Richmond and back. When they finally got to his dorm, he wouldn't let her go home, saying it was too dangerous to walk across the well-lit campus at three in the morning even though she lived only two buildings away. He was being half-honest. That was the first night they spent together. In the morning they slept late, skipped classes, and she made him breakfast. "That was fun."

He takes another bite of his dinner, trying to swallow and laugh at the same time.

"I remember you kept calling them The Blakes all night." He clears his throat and speaks in a falsetto: "Oh, The Blakes sound good live, don't they? Isn't Juliana the perfect lead singer for The Blakes? Wow, I *really* like The Blakes." He chuckles and has to force down a mouthful of water so he doesn't choke.

"I kept thinking, 'Wow, she's cute and smart, but jeez, how pretentious.'"

She kicks him under the table but then keeps her slender leg there, sliding it up to his thigh.

"Hey, I never complain when you call The Velvet Underground The Velvets, or why don't you just call Yo La Tengo, The Tengos? Or how about calling Some Velvet Sidewalk, The Sidewalks? Or maybe The Fastbacks. Well, okay, that last one was a bad example, but you do it, too!"

"Yeah, yeah," he mumbles, adding under his breath, "The Blakes. Jesus."

They both turn again to their meals and alternate small talk between bites. Ashley tells Craig a few stories about her classes that day and how her counselor thinks getting into a good graduate school should be no problem. For his turn, Craig tosses forth a few workplace anecdotes culled from his Round the Watercooler file. Then out of nowhere:

"Craig, would you cheat on me if you could?"

"What?" he asks nervously, his eyes darting around the small Italian restaurant.

"I asked," Ashley says again, "would you cheat on me if you could?"

"Would I?" He stabs at a ravioli, swabbing the plate with it to soak it with sauce. "Or have I?"

"I don't know." She straightens up, pushing her back into her chair and her chin high into the air. "Have you?"

Craig examines her through the dim half-light of the restaurant, their sole light source a candle firmly ensconced in a wine bottle overflowing with the wax trails of many candles past. This makes her eyes flicker, her nose waver, and her eyebrows seem comically high. *What exactly is she looking for? What has she found already?*

"Now, Ashley, you'd better get working on your angel hair pasta, angel, if we're going to make it in time to catch the opening band, and—"

"Oh, fuck the opening band." She drains her third glass of wine in under half an hour. "You hate that band, Flat Duodenum Splits, or whatever the hell they're called. I asked you a question."

"But why? Why are you asking me this now? All of a sudden?"

"Well, it's just . . . I got to thinking of that line from that song by The Blakes, 'Cesspool,' where she sings, *They'd do almost anything if the price was right enough,*' and, I don't know, it just made me nervous. Like, you might if you had the chance."

"No," he says, exhausted. "I haven't cheated on you."

"That's not what I asked. I mean, do you even want to?"

"What's the difference? I love you and I'm not going to. I'm not going to mess up our relationship like that."

"But you shouldn't even want to. Don't you see? You might as well already have done it."

"Well then, if my wanting to cheat is the same as my actually committing the act, maybe I should then. Since, as you said, it's all the same."

"Stop kidding around, Craig. This means a lot to me. What if you could and I'd never find out? What if that Victoria's Secret model you like so much came up to you and said she thought your growing paunch was *très* attractive. And what if I was away visiting my parents or something? What would you do?"

Craig makes the mistake of actually forming an answer.

"What's taking you so long? You shouldn't even have to think about it." She reaches across the table and whacks him with a breadstick.

"Ashley, stop this, it's ridiculous. Where is this coming from?"

"You know"—her tone grows softer—"we've been living together for a couple of years now, and . . . I don't know . . . it's just sort of cooled off lately. It makes a girl wonder."

"Ash, we're older now. It's not such a big deal. Back when we were in college it was like we were getting away with something. I'd bribe my roommates to get lost or else we'd do it in the bathroom at your parents' house while your father was mowing the lawn, but now . . ."

"What? You're saying that once the challenge goes out of it that it's no good? That it's not even worth pursuing?"

"Of course not, Ash, it's just . . . I don't know. You do realize that you're putting me on the spot like this, don't you? It's just . . . we're more mature now."

"Come on, Craig, don't. Every time we have some crisis lately you say it's just that we're becoming more mature. Like when I commented on how we never talk in the morning over breakfast, never just sit and hug and kiss like we used to. I mean, I've never been this ailing Victorian romantic, but I'd just hate to admit all this atrophy in our relationship is due to maturation. It sounds more to me like decomposition." She shakes her head, trying to get the subject out of her mind. She grabs hold of her slight buzz and tries to hang on to it. In a sober state the real world is too scary a place to return to. Stay here awhile. Craig looks nicer from here. Like he used to be. *Like how I remember. Like when I first met him. The way he did that made me fall in love with him. But now* . . . "It's just . . . I need to know that we still mean something to each other."

"Of course you mean something to me," he says, grabbing her knee under the table.

Ashley spots a couple sitting across from them who are most likely on their first date. She's feeding him a spoonful of cheese-cake while he's making choo-choo-train noises. It makes Ashley want to go over and say, *Don't get used to it. It ain't going to last.*

"Look, Ashley, it's ridiculous to discuss this right now. Just let me pay the check so we can get out of here and hit the club, grab a couple of drinks, and then go home, okay? It's not even eleven, and already I'm not having a good time."

"Fine." She juts her chin out and crosses her arms over her chest. "If you want to go listen to some stupid rock band while our relationship is *on* the rocks, go right ahead."

Craig ignores her, pulls out his wallet, and places a twenty and a five on the table.

"By the way, Ashley," he says, getting up and slipping his wallet back into his jeans, "you do know that 'Cesspool' was a single, don't you?"

5

"Where you headed?"

Eileen hears the voice only slightly and at first doesn't even think it's real. She attributes it to some old country-and-western song playing on the jukebox with a middle-eight break like *"Girl, since you left me, ain't nothin' seems to be workin' out right."* But when the question is repeated, "Where you headed?", after the song has died out and the jukebox is mute until another sucker/customer plops in a quarter, Eileen realizes someone is trying to talk to her.

"What?" she asks again, broken out of her nebulous thoughts.

"I said," remarks a slimy-looking guy to her left, "where you headed?"

Before answering, Eileen surveys the situation: While gassing up at some godforsaken Chevron station just outside the Virginia state line she spotted the little honky-tonk dive where she's presently nursing a Long Island Iced Tea, giving serious thought to driving to Long Island instead of home. Unable to sit for another hour in the driving position she'd been in since leaving Florida almost ten hours ago, she decided to get off the freeway for a drink and some rest. She's supposed to be heading back from her grandparents' house in Jacksonville to her own hometown, Baltimore, where her apartment, parents, friends, and job are waiting obediently for her.

"Where you headed?" he finally asks again, his determination at least admirable.

Eileen glances at her recently purchased Mickey Mouse watch. 10:39. *Better hurry if I want to hit Maryland tonight. But do I?*

"Um, New York." Unable to judge the mental capacity of the strange man due to the dim lighting in the bar, Eileen lies. Safer just to lead him astray than have him following her down the interstate.

"New York, eh? Wow, the big city. Where you comin' from?"

Just go, go away, is what all her friends advised. *Take some time for yourself. Take some time to forget about Don. Forget about the breakup. Go. Go find yourself.* And yet three weeks of somnambulating at her grandparents' condo in Florida had only left her pissed-off, edgy, filled with even more dread. And now, halfway home, with just a few more hours to go, Eileen keeps thinking: *What home?*

From across the room a sound is heard like a marble falling down a pachinko chute as a cowboy in the corner drops a quarter into the jukebox. *"All my exes live in Texas, that's why I reside in Tennessee."*

"Oh." Eileen stumbles again, speaking up over the music as she delivers yet another lie. They were right; they did come easier over time. "I was coming from Texas."

"Really?" he drawls, moving over a bar stool.

Now that the guy has moved in even closer Eileen can see that he's an inch or two below her own meager five feet five and so may not be as much of a threat as she had first thought, but she's still not taking chances. She feels the back of her head, her long black hair up in (she hopes) an unattractive ponytail. In the large Rolling Rock mirror behind the bar she notices that her brown eyes are sagging. She pats down the pockets of her faded Levi's for the little tin Sucrets box with the assorted pills inside, but it's nowhere to be found. *Damn. Left it in the car.*

"Texas?" The man laughs. "Well, then, what in hell are you doing here? You could have taken Route Sixty six all the way across and gone straight through!"

"Yeah, well." Eileen gets nervous and takes a quick sip of her drink; instead of galvanizing her, it only makes her more jittery. "I was visiting friends in, er . . ." Her mind races. She remembers watching the news last night to get a weather report, to make sure no tropical storms were going to attack the East Coast, even though she was sort of hoping they would because it would mean putting off her drive home yet again. She's trying to remember the shapes of the states in the little southeastern part of the country, and perhaps from there a familiar name. "Atlanta?" she says, unsure of her answer.

"Oh, yeah, I guess I see that," he says, figuring out the route in his head. The man, satisfied with her answer, leans on the bar and orders another beer. He motions to order another for Eileen as well, but she politely declines.

"So what you got waiting for you up in New York? A job or a man?" He takes a deep drag off his beer and then spits on the floor.

"A . . . job," she stammers. "In . . . advertising."

"Oooh," he draws out the word. He reaches one hand inside his forest green flannel shirt and scratches before adding, "Big bucks."

"Yeah, well." Eileen tugs at her black T-shirt that is frayed around the collar. Inside she's laughing. *Advertising, ha! Back in*

Baltimore I was a waitress and lucky to get that clerical job at the shelter.

"You see, I used to drive a truck to Chicago, so I know what that part of the country is like, and you listen to me, little girl. You'd better watch your head around them Yankees up there. 'Specially a pretty little girl like yourself."

The truck driver launches into some Carveresque monologue consisting of interstate anecdotes of unloading at The Wharf, the dream diner meal and that one waitress years ago, and he wished he had ridden her curves rather than the road's one more time. Eileen catches lines or words every few minutes, like, "You ever had ribtip?" and "Take it from me, never take Greyhound cross-country," but for the most part she just swivels on her stool, unable to respond. She remains silent mostly because the man's conversation is like gridlocked traffic with no space to cut into, but also because she can't even muster up enough strength to be rude. The moves just aren't coming to her, and so she lets the man continue his incessant talk of Peterbilts, exit books, Illinois State Troopers, the best damn coffee from Mississippi to Michigan.

"Listen, honey." The man stops for a second, patting down his blue down vest. "I can't stand to watch you suck on those ice cubes anymore. Let me buy you another."

"You know what, Buck?" Eileen says, rising off the bar stool and heading for the door.

"My name's not Buck, but what?"

"I can't stand it, either."

None of the exits have names, only numbers. She is looking for Piney Grove Avenue, and three exits back the sign announced that the role of Piney Grove Avenue would be played tonight by Exit B12, as if it were a vitamin for her aching, an elixir for her discomfort, a panacea for her traveling woes. Five minutes later she is staring at the blue-and-white reflecting letters, Exit B12, and it doesn't mean anything until her brain clicks—three seconds too late, of course. *Don't worry about it,* she decides. *It's not worth swerving over three lanes like a maniac to make the ramp. I'm sure there's another Waffle House down the road.*

The towns keep flashing by: Emporia, Jarrat, Stony Creek.

The road signs appear in the headlights and then disappear just as quickly: Gas, Food, Lodging. Welcome. Thanks for Visiting. Good-bye. I95 winds into the night like a chain of Christmas lights, lit up and tangled, twisting and turning.

The highway is filled with truckers and empty space, and she keeps running into both. The truckers flash their brights as she goes by, which always makes her paranoid and mad. She resents being told what to do, as if she should take their advice as to when to cut back into the fast lane. They're bored, doped up on pills, so she cuts them some slack, thinking, *So am I.*

Eileen fishes the old tin Sucrets box out of the glove compartment of her yellow VW Bug. She places it on her lap, alternately keeping her eyes on the road and glancing down at her midsection, trying to pry open the pillbox with one hand. Finally it opens with a pop. She picks out two black capsules, places them at the back of her throat, closes her mouth, and expertly musters up enough spit to swallow them.

"Ahhh," she sighs, forcing the pills into her empty stomach with a few birdlike jerks of her head.

A white Mazda drives by with a Matador Records sticker cluttering the small rear window. It passes her and she blinks her lights like a seasoned pro, guiding her four-wheeler through the crisp night: *It's okay to pass now, honey, the coast is clear. Let me ride inside your slipstream for a little bit while you take the lead.*

Her limbs have practically frozen in their position—her arms clutching the wheel at ten and two o'clock as Mr. O'Brien taught her seven years ago in driver's ed. The ankle of her left foot, feeling as if it were cast in stone, rests lightly on the clutch just in case she needs to downshift unexpectedly, yet looking out at the limitless horizon makes her think there could be worse things than resting her foot on the dash for a couple of miles. Her eyes keep watering, keep wanting to be closed, keep feeling as though they're going to rise up in revolution and close the gates for good. She had planned to drive straight through, but now, at two o'clock in the morning, even with the pills popping to life in her stomach, it doesn't look as if that will happen.

She pulls off at exit C15 and cruises into the parking lot of another Waffle House. The engine dies in a fit of knocking, like a smoker with a hacking cough.

"Table for one, sweetie?" The host is an oldish man with about twelve teeth and just as many strands of hair. His tie is untied, simply looped around his neck like the strap of a saxophone. "If you need any company, I'll be in the back." His wink is a silent insult.

"Don't let him bother you none. He's like an old toothless dog," an old waitress is talking gaily, waving around her order pad like a baton. "He's like a dog with no teeth—all bite, no bark or, well, you know the saying."

"Heh, heh," Eileen squeaks out, her voice cracking. It isn't until she speaks that she realizes her ears haven't fully popped after coming down a steep grade fifty miles ago. For a few minutes it's like being in a badly dubbed Japanese horror film: Her words trail along two seconds after her lips say them, hopelessly out of synch.

"I said," the waitress is repeating, "what can I get cha?"

"Oh, just a tuna salad on wheat . . . and coffee."

"On the double."

As the waitress is posting the order on the empty steel wheel hanging from the kitchen window, the host pinches her ass, laughing as she turns around to slap him. He slinks to the front of the restaurant, laughing madly, as if he's gotten away with something, which, Eileen figures, he has. The waitress looks over at Eileen, then away, into the salad bar, the rack of dirty silverware, anywhere to avoid looking into Eileen's eyes.

Eileen tries to crack her back, stretching her tense muscles; her jeans make farting noises as she shimmies against the orange plastic booth. She grabs the small silver box offering white paper napkins on two sides. She looks at the mirrorlike surface, measuring her own reflection in the slightly curved image; her face appears much wider and taller than usual. Her brunette hair is still up, but now a dozen strands have come loose from the bone pin. She brings the napkin holder closer, getting a look at her dark brown eyes, which are circled in pools of dull black skin. Her face is all around sort of worn out, her usually slightly pale complexion now ghoulishly white. Depressed, she puts the napkin holder down and fishes through her pocket for the Sucrets box, but she left it in the car, again.

As Eileen is getting up, the waitress brings her a pot of coffee along with a caddy of cream and sugar. "You need anything, you just holler, ya hear?"

Eileen sits back down, empties two packets of sugar into the beige cup, and adds a large dollop of cream until the coffee turns to the color of the mug. While waiting for the coffee to cool, she examines the plastic tent display listing the "Waffle House's Homemade Desserts."

"Scrumptious old fashioned cheesecake," she reads; the slice looks withered underneath the studio lights. It's a bad sign when the food doesn't even look good in the photos. The pitch continues: "Just like Mom used to make."

Mom never did. She laughs.

Eileen looks out the dirty restaurant window and into the darkness, seeing more of her own reflection than any of the landscape. From her seat in the diner she can see the highway, raised about two stories, taillights passing by every few seconds.

"There you go," the waitress says brightly, putting the food down in front of her.

It looks unappetizing. The lettuce is brown, the tomato badly bruised, lacerated, third-degree burn. Eileen pushes the plate away as soon as the waitress retreats. Instead she grabs the seat, trying to hold on to something. She braces herself, grabs each shoulder tight, just trying to get a grip. It suddenly strikes her that she's really not going anywhere. There is nothing left for her in Maryland. The vacation to calm her nerves instead only set them on a low boil, and she was going back now as bad as she had been before, if not worse. She sings to herself a line from her favorite Tom Waits song: *"And it's true there's nothing left for him down here."* It's how she feels right now. The pills on her tongue at the back of her mouth are a sweeter memory than her last relationship, and all she can do is look forward to the next black beauty and not a man.

She reconsiders the meal and takes a few bites of the sandwich, gets a few refills of coffee. After another half-hour she's feeling a little bit better, although she realizes she'll have to stop in about fifteen minutes to go to the bathroom. The waitress skips by, dropping off the check: $4.28. Eileen drops a five and a one on the table and waves to the waitress as she leaves.

As Eileen gets into the car, her bones instantly assume the position. She tries to start the car, but nothing happens. "Oh, fuck." She tries again. It won't turn over, won't anything. In desperation she turns on the radio, which works. She tries the headlights. They work, too. "Maybe I've flooded it," she hopes, saying the words out loud so the engine will hear her. She waits a few tense minutes, cursing under her breath, then tries again. Nothing. She gets out of the car, kicks the fender, jumps in, and tries again. Nothing. Just as she's beginning to pound on the steering wheel, she hears a knocking on the windshield.

" 'Scuse me, miss? Car trouble?"

It's the waitress, standing in the parking lot, a burgundy windbreaker pulled over her yellow waitress outfit.

"Huh? Oh, yeah. I was driving from Florida to Maryland, and I don't know. I stopped earlier, and it started then, so . . . I don't know what could be wrong."

"Hmm, pop the hood. Let me take a look."

A few minutes later the waitress is touching various tubes, checking the oil, tapping her finger against the fan belt.

"I really appreciate this," Eileen says, "but don't you need to get back in there?"

"Huh? Aw, heck no. You're the first table I've had in over an hour. Besides, if anyone goes in, I'll see 'em. I just thought you might need a hand."

Poor old lady, Eileen thinks, glancing up at the interstate where every car except hers runs perfectly. *Nothing better to do than help stranded motorists after she's served them dinner. Talk about service.*

"Look, darling, we'd better push this into the gas station next door. I think Hal's on duty till six A.M. You steer, I'll push."

At first the car just heaves one way, then lurches back in the opposite direction. *This is never going to work,* Eileen thinks, until slowly, inch by inch, the VW starts crawling toward the Happy Face Gas 'n' Go. They steer it around the back, and Eileen can see through the window a small office with a light on.

"Wow, thanks a lot!" Eileen jumps out of the car. "I don't know what I would have done without—"

"It's nothing. In fact, take this." The woman shoves a ten-dollar bill into Eileen's surprised hands and then embraces her in a bear hug. Before Eileen even has a chance to turn down the offer, the waitress continues. "Whatever you're going through, honey, whatever's wrong, things will get better." She lets go, stands a few feet away, and looks dramatically into Eileen's eyes.

"It will, trust me." She then skips across the parking lot back to the restaurant.

"Well, well, what do we have here?"

A tall lanky guy, about ten years older than Eileen's own twenty-three, is standing beside the car in greasy overalls, looking over both the car and her.

"I'm not sure. I was driving to Maryland, uh, from Texas . . . I mean, Florida. It just . . . stopped."

"Let's take a look." He props open the hood the way the waitress did minutes before. He fiddles with a few things, goes *aahhh* and *hmm* like a doctor does when he asks you to take a deep breath and stick out your tongue, and then tells you with a smile you have six months to live.

"The prognosis?"

"Afraid I can't tell right now. Not allowed to use tools during the night. 'Course, once morning comes . . ."

"Can't use tools? Why the hell not?"

"Insurance reasons, so the boss tells me." The mechanic smiles, showing off a row of teeth with more than a few missing. "Besides, I'm the only one here. What happens if I was under a car and the jack gave out? Can't have some kids going through the cash register while I'm pinned underneath a Buick, now can we?" He leans in close, his odor of human sweat and gasoline overpowering her.

"No, I guess not." She rushes through the small talk. "So, what do I do?"

"Well . . ." He pushes back an STP cap and scratches his head, the grease leaving black trails in his dirty blond hair as if his roots were showing. "Best thing would be to get some place to sleep tonight and come back tomorrow—I mean, later today." He laughs gruffly. "By that time the day crew will be in. They should be able to tell you what the problem is. If it's nothing major, you should have your car back and all set to go by noon, I'd say." He turns and flashes some of his remaining teeth. "Of course, if you need a place to stay, I live just down the road."

Asshole This Left. Jerkoff Turn Right. Slimebag This Exit. These men are like road signs. They shouldn't have names, only numbers.

"No, thanks."

He turns, the grease in his joints squeaking as he slithers back

to the garage to, Eileen guesses, apply more dark grime underneath his fingernails.

"Hey, where am I anyway?"

He smiles slyly and spits out a wad of chew that misses the
curb and splats against the hood ornament of her car, turning
the metal insignia into a web of sinewy slime.

"Welcome to Kitty, Virginia."

6

The city rolls into view like a pop-up book, first the tall banks
downtown and then the church spire in the east end, which
slowly gives way to the new arts center on the community college
campus and the cafe on the hill at the foot of the old abandoned
department store just beyond the poorest section of town. Mark
takes all this in with barely open eyes, half-awake, his numb
hands clutching the wheel.

Steve and Gary both lie huddled and snoring in the back;
Gary's prostrate body is propped up against the black bass drum
case, which is inaccurately stenciled PINK FLOYD in white paint,
while Steve crouches with his back against the door that is only
half-closed, rattling as if it could fly open at any minute. One leg
lies sandwiched between the floor of the van and his bass case;
the other, shoeless, above.

Mark wipes away a yawned tear from his left eye and tries
to shake the three-month tour off his bones. His twists up his
shoulders, takes a hand to his chest, and lifts his gray T-shirt off
his chest and then lets it fall back, sending a gust of body odor
into his face. Mark coughs. He is wearing the smell of a dozen
cities, a victim of too many nights in the damn van, stale beer
in dried trails almost everywhere, and the sweaty and musty
remembrance of a fan three towns back that he's been trying to
forget about more than anything, especially since Laura is now
just a few minutes away. The guys were right; he does have a
guilty conscience.

Mark glances down at the fuel gauge that has been flashing EMPTY since he got off the interstate fifteen minutes ago, and decides to risk it. The city is just waking up, but for a small city like Kitty, it looks as if it has overslept a little. While in places like New York, Los Angeles, Chicago, or Boston, shopkeepers wake with the sun, wipe off their front stoops, and make conversation with the man who drops off the bushel of tied newspapers just after dawn, in Kitty it is now almost nine o'clock and stores are just beginning to creak open, and mostly by the hands of the minimum-wage-paid employees. The managers will show up later, and the newspapers won't come until the grade school boys whose job it is to deliver them get bored with their Sega and Nintendo and get out their bikes, roll up the thin paper, and aim for your head, tossing the rolled-up news against the sky like the ape's bone in *2001.*

Jesus, what was that girl's fucking name? Mark is trying to remember, not noticing the knocking of the engine, the large puffs of black smoke choking out of the tail pipe. *Name?* He reconsiders. *Hell, I'll settle for a face.*

The images are coming back to him, but they're fuzzy.

He was already a little drunk, even before the show. The three of them had been fighting, as usual. The crowd was thin, and that always set him a little on edge, made him defensive and reckless, like if they didn't care, why should he? He remembers that she approached him, and somehow that made it okay for him, as if he were not the progenitor of the betrayal. That if somehow he was hauled into some sort of tribal, communal court where boyfriends and girlfriends go as a practice for the messy divorce proceeding, which in this day and age was most likely to follow years down the road, that this fact would get him off whatever hook they hoped to dangle him from: *She approached me.*

Bits and pieces are coming back to him now, such as: long, very straight brown hair. *Mary? No. Magda? Marilyn?* She was wearing a pair of very old Adidas, like something the Beastie Boys now parade around in and sell new to kids who are too young to have bought them the first time around. Only hers looked old and authentic, as if she had gotten them at one of the many thrift stores in the area. She was wearing a tight dark blue T-shirt that read PAVEMENT POWERED in a style of writing that mocked the Peavey logo.

"You've touched me," Mark remembers her high voice saying as she interrupted a conversation he was having with a few guys from the local college radio station, "and now I want to touch you."

"Wha'?" Mark hears a groan from the back of the van. "Huh?"

He reaches up and angles the rearview mirror and sees that Gary is beginning to come to. He's yawning, running a hand through his filthy hair that is standing up wildly in all directions, and trying to get his legs out from underneath his instrument. Finally he yanks it hard and knocks over Steve's high hat, which crashes against a space of bare floor with a liquidy, metallic crunch.

"Hey, asshole, watch it!" Steve shouts, springing to life. He wipes his eyes and kicks at his bandmate with a socked foot, the toe of which is comically elongated and drooping.

"Why don't you shove your click-track up your ass," Gary retorts, grabbing at the cotton bath towel that has served as his blanket for the past twelve weeks.

"Don't go back to sleep, boys, we're here."

"Home?"

"Check it out."

Steve springs up and peers out the dirty back window of the van and sees Kitty ambling by.

"Thank fucking God." Steve exhales, causing a circle of fog to appear on the glass. "Home sweet home."

"Yeah, that is if all your appliances haven't been turned off and if Phil, your damned brother, actually remembered to water your plants," Gary says, his voice drenched in sarcasm.

"Well, at least all of my stuff won't be scattered all over the lawn because my roommate never liked me in the first place," Steve combats.

"Now, now, you two, we're almost there," Mark calls out from the driver's seat, just as his father used to do to him as a child, swatting him with a free hand as he sat in the backseat, for humming "Rhinestone Cowboy" or "Taking Care of Business" too loudly.

Mark turns a couple of corners, just a few minutes away from

Gary's place now with Steve's on the way. In anticipation, Gary has risen off his ass and is beginning to rustle up a few things, mostly scattered clothes from all corners of the van, his tooth-brush stuck between Mark's *American Metal* distortion box and a clutch of Steve's broken drumsticks that no one knew why he was keeping. While Gary is looking for the house keys he hasn't needed in three months, Mark continues to search for clues.

He can't remember where they were, whether it was her house or some friend of hers, but he does remember that the sex was mediocre and quick. From the beginning of foreplay to sleeping soundly with a wet spot under his belly was a matter of perhaps twenty minutes. But if the screwing did not last long, the night certainly did, and that's what made it seem more of an affair than just sex. It was the way she dawdled over him, the way she tucked him in, gave him an old boyfriend's The The T-shirt to sleep in (with a picture of a bullet going through a man's head), the way she let him sleep late in the morning while she escaped briefly to the Piggly Wiggly for eggs, bacon, orange juice, milk, and bread. How she gave him a ride back to the club where Gary and Steve were pissed off to have to spend the cold night alone in the van, jealous that Mark had escaped while they had struck out the night before. Since the sex had been so spectacularly mediocre (even Laura on her worst night moved Mark's cock more than this stranger), it was all the accoutre ments of the event that make him feel like shit. Thinking back he realizes he was half-drunk, half-hard, and came very quickly. He sincerely doubts she even came anywhere close to reaching an orgasm, yet that never seemed her goal. She seemed to draw out another kind of climax over the ten-hour period he was there, tending to him, serving him, offering to do his laundry and drive to the next city to give it to him, washed, clean, folded. It was just too fucking weird.

"Here we are," Mark announces, pulling up in front of Steve's yellow duplex apartment building. Even from the sidewalk you can see the mail and circulars overflowing the mailbox, littering the doormat where years ago Steve had added a large NOT just above the WELCOME. The lights that are supposed to be left on all the time, to give the illusion that somebody is home, are off. It looks as if Phil has indeed forgotten.

"Fuck." Steve sighs, hopping out of the van.

"Hey." Mark stops him halfway up the walk. "Aren't you taking your drums?"

"Nah, I'm too tired. Just let them stay in the van for a while," he shouts back, noticing a letter, tucked in one of the bushes, that is bloated and streaked from water, marked DATED MATERIAL PLEASE OPEN IMMEDIATELY.

"Okay," Mark shouts, "but remember, you're coming over to help me clean out the van so I can get this thing back to my father, who's already having a heart attack that it's been gone so long."

Steve sort of mumbles, "Yeah, yeah," and heads for the front door.

Mark and Gary wave a quick good-bye before peeling away.

"Hey, aren't you going to run out of gas?" Gary asks, crawling up into the front passenger seat.

"Shut up, I'm almost there."

Gary lets a few blocks of familiar territory roll by before broaching the subject again.

"Boy, Mr. Grouchy, you really aren't looking forward to going back to Laura, are you?"

Mark is silent for a moment before answering.

"There's more than Laura waiting for me in Kitty. It's just, she's the first in line."

"I guess so, but . . . how's this any different from that time at my friend's house in Tuscaloosa? Remember that blond chick with the tits?"

"It gets easier." Mark sighs, catching the sight of the needle-like fuel gauge dipping into the red. Running out of gas. "But that doesn't make it right."

Gary formulates a rebuttal, but it disappears the moment Mark pulls up in front of his courtyard, where he shares a corner apartment with a roommate named James.

"Look, pal"—he places one hand on Mark's shoulder while the other flings open the van door—"don't sweat it, okay? Let's all just recharge our batteries and take it from there."

"Yeah, Gary, whatever you say. See you later."

"Yeah," his friend says, half out the door. "See you, Mark."

Mark waits until he's sure Gary is safe inside, then lingers for a few minutes, trying to find excuses to stay, not wanting to go home. He starts up the van, puts it in drive, and reluctantly pulls away from the curb, merging with traffic like a small boy being dragged through a mall by his mother.

The van begins shaking as Mark turns onto his street. Pulling up to the driveway he spots Laura in the window, peeking out from the sheath of venetian blinds, which now trail along her back as her head is smashed up against the glass.

Like a fucking puppy, Mark thinks with a sigh. He didn't know this was a coincidence, that she had been looking out for the paper boy.

The van finally sputters and dies just as Mark maneuvers onto the spotty yellow lawn of the beige two-bedroom house he rents for $350 a month.

He sees Laura move from the window. She is now waiting at the door, wearing a forced smile. He wonders why he asked her to be there, why he couldn't just have gone over to her place later. How could he think this would be some joyous home-coming instead of the mutually awkward event it was destined to be?

"Just wake up?" Mark calls out, approaching the porch.

"Yeah," she says through a grin. "You been up all night?"

"Yeah. I look like shit, too." He passes her, entering the house that already feels like a worn glove on his hand. "And don't try to tell me I don't, 'cause I do."

She laughs a little, pulling a strand of light brown hair out of her eye, tucking it back into the bun on top of her head. She nervously shifts her weight back and forth on her light frame, her thin bones looking for some sort of distinction in the company of so many of his possessions.

Mark glances at the worn jeans and T-shirt she's wearing as he heads back out to the van to bring in a load of stuff.

Like a skirt would have killed you? He grumbles as he sees her yawn. She sees him noticing her and tries to stifle it, mustering a weak smile in the ensuing wash of post-yawn tears.

"Why don't you do that tomorrow, Mark." She places a hand on his back as he shuffles through the door with a hard-shell guitar case in each hand, another bag tucked under an elbow, and a fourth looped around his left wrist.

"Yeah, you're right," he answers, dumping his load in a corner of the living room.

He turns and faces Laura who's still standing at the open door, the mid-morning sun streaming in, casting a shadow over her face. *She could be anyone.* He tries to smile.

"Miss me?" he asks, dropping to the ground a blue duffel bag filled exclusively with dirty socks, underwear, and soiled T-shirts.

"Oh, yeah, yeah," Laura honestly replies, blushing and moving toward him. While Mark was gone she did miss him, but she also got used to the idea of his not being around.

"Well then, come here." He pulls her into his arms.

At first she startles at the touch of his embrace. She feels more like a mold in his arms than a person, the same way she had been feeling more like a groupie than a girlfriend in the weeks before he left.

As he holds her, burying his face in the stringy top of her head, her various scents assault him, and not just the expensive perfume, with the French name he can't pronounce, that she receives every Christmas from her parents. It smells of crushed rose petals and powder, but she seemed to be wearing less of it; she also smells of the free-flowing odors of her body. After all these years he has finally gotten used to her light body odor, hardly apparent at all but cropping up around the base of her back and in thin coats on her arms; then there's the musty female scent between her legs, which she also used to cover up during courtship but dispensed with a long time ago; lastly, there's her breath. He has not only grown accustomed to her bad breath but sometimes welcomes it, the shrill sourness a sort of stamp.

Her hands reach up and find the thick muscles at the tip of his back and the base of his neck that stretch out like a plane's wings. His own hands are looped through her arms and are clutching her ass while his mind fuzzily compares it to the girl he slept with on the road, but without enough information to go on, he gives up and kisses her.

He leans in, welcomed by her acrid breath that's part garlic and day-old clam sauce, and spots a few yellow flakes of crud on her two front teeth. She feels slightly damp and, he guesses, probably hasn't shaved her legs in a while.

That's okay, he reasons, imagining the stench he is currently wearing like a second skin. *I'm sure I don't smell very good, either.*

"Easy, easy," she says as he overcompensates with his lips, his mouth open too wide, enveloping both her bottom and lower lips, his tongue bashing repeatedly into her clenched teeth. "You're slobbering on the floor."

"Sorry. . . . It's just . . ."

"It's just"—she pulls back for a second, looking deeply into his eyes—"what?"

Her stare is like the scrutinizing glare of a microscope. He tries to avoid her, glancing into the various corners in the room, trying to get a handle on exactly how many inches of dust all of his things are now shrouded in—anything to get his mind off the stare of the girl in his arms.

"It's just that . . . what?"

He breathes in deeply. "It's just . . ."

"What?"

"It's just . . . nothing."

No Unrest for the Wicked

1

Craig is waking up.

Ashley is sleeping silently next to him. He glances over at her slumbering frame, her hair flowing over the pillow like a frozen stream. The glasses she forgot to take off the night before lie diagonally across her face. Craig shrugs and contemplates hitting the snooze button yet again but, deciding he is late enough as it is, he pulls himself out of bed and tries to shake off his encroaching hangover.

Once in the shower it takes five minutes of hot water rushing over his face for his eyes to separate fully. At first it stings; his eyes are not adjusted to the harsh, glinting light of the bathroom, so they close like a turtle jerking back into its shell. He fills his mouth with water, spurts it out like a fountain, and opens his eyes again. This time they stay open. He grabs for the soap and haphazardly washes himself, slathering his body with the stubby end of the white bar the way an Ab Ex artist randomly takes brush to canvas.

Craig picks up a Buf-Puf pad floating in the inch-deep puddle surrounding the hair-and-grime-clogged drain, rubs it against the soap, then scrubs the top of his hand, trying to get rid of the OVER 21 stamp from the club the night before. After a few minutes the back of his hand is red and raw and the black ink is now purple, the words still visible, soaked into his skin like a faded tattoo.

Craig glances down at his cheap digital watch. 7:43.

"Shit."

He reluctantly turns off the shower, grabs a towel, and then pats himself down. Leaving a trail of watery footprints he walks into the spare room which is filled with clothes, boxes of books, magazines, records, and an old Austin flying V electric guitar he bought at a garage sale for twenty dollars before noticing it was a lefty.

"*Aaaawwww,*" he yawns, fishing the least-wrinkled white dress shirt from a pile in the corner. After tugging on a pair of Home of the Whopper novelty boxers which he surprised Ashley by actually wearing, he places the shirt on a drafting table, tossing aside two copies each of *Yummy Fur* and *American Splendor* comic books. He begins smoothing it out with his hands, trying to fold down the collar that is obstinately sticking up. Next he puts on a pair of beige socks with holes in the toe on one foot and in the ankle on the other, then slides on some khaki chinos, walks over to the closet, and nudges his feet into a pair of beat-up brown leather Doc Martens Crazyhorses.

"Undershirt," he mumbles, wiping the crusts of sleep from the corners of his eyes. He examines the slightly amber waxy substance for a second before balling it up and flinging it against the wall, where to his amazement it sticks. He can't find an undershirt, so instead he reaches for a white cotton T-shirt that reads KILL ROCK STARS in gold-and-black lettering. He puts the dress shirt on over it, buttons it up, and examines it in the mirror. The words from the T-shirt are plainly visible. "Oh, well," he mutters.

Craig goes back to the closet and retrieves a tie from a hanger where half a dozen are hanging already tied. Another two are lying on the ground, also tied. He picks a Nicole Miller knockoff that is imitation silk and has musical notes, records, and a drum set floating against a jet black background. He lifts up his collar until it is hugging his cheeks and slides the already doubly Windsored tie over his head. He clutches the oval ball hanging at the center of his chest and begins tightening, pausing to let out a gargantuan yawn.

Craig can't imagine being awake for a day job. He hates any form of employment that requires a tie, a name tag, or, even worse, a uniform. He likes strong coffee, loud music, and sleeping in but isn't much for bosses, time clocks, and minimum wage. Kafka once said, "Employees always know more than their employers." Craig and his friends pretty much agree with that, but they're not too sure who Kafka is. Craig is a lot like Bobby Fischer was at his age, only Craig doesn't play chess.

He slides the knot snugly to his neck, then hooks his finger into it and pulls, releasing it about half an inch so he'll be able to swallow. He then tries to fold down his collar. As happens every morning, about an inch and a half of the nether region at the back of his head refuses to lay down flat but instead rides up and sits on his neck when it should be lying down in a straight line at the base of his shoulder along with the rest of his collar. This wouldn't happen if Craig had his shirts professionally laundered, but he can't afford it. He reaches his hands around, arches his back, twists his wrist, anything to get a good angle. After three more attempts, he still can't get it; there's just not enough fabric to allow him a good grip.

If Ashley were up, she could do it for him, no problem. He glances toward the bedroom door, imagines he hears her snoring; she won't be up for hours. He thinks back to the previous night, getting into a fight with Ashley at The Scene, where he then forgot about her, drifted into the crowd, and concentrated instead on the band and the liquor. Lately it seems as if something is always coming between them, ruining meals, wasting nights out or in. Then there were those fights in the morning that left a bad taste in their mouths for the rest of the day. But he can never figure out whose fault it is, until he deems it no one's fault and that maybe he's just falling out of whatever it is with Ashley that he'd tripped into.

Craig struggles with his collar for a few more minutes before glancing again at his watch. 8:11. "I'm already late," he says with a sigh. "Fuck it, I'm leaving."

Craig walks quickly into the kitchen, scoops up his wallet and keys from the table, and grabs a silver foil packet containing two chocolate Pop-Tarts from the cupboard and a small carton of pink lemonade Hi-C from the fridge, which together will form the nucleus of his lunch for the day. He'll add perhaps a supplemental packet of Cheez-Its or a Slim Jim from the vending machine in the break room.

On the way to the door he heads to an end table in the living room for a five-dollar bill he needs for gas on the way in. He stuffs it in his pocket and, turning heavily on his clunky Air Wair soles, catches sight of something. His bachelor's degree from the University of Virginia is, he thinks, staring at him. Winking. A smug grin in an otherwise frowning room.

He goes to the couch, leans over, and plucks the degree off the wall with one hand, moves back a few steps, raises one of the couch cushions, and begins to shove it under. It stops with a loud crack halfway in. Craig picks up the cushion to see what the problem is. It bumped into Ashley's diploma, framed just as elaborately, covered in dust.

2

The dirt and bird shit covering Mark's car is gathered in little clumps every few inches instead of forming an entire dirty sheen over the whole auto. The beige Nissan Sentra looks like the scoop of a cowboy boot made out of plucked ostrich hide.

"Jesus Christ," Mark exclaims, walking out of the house and examining the car closely for the first time. "This looks like some sort of shit leopard. How'd it get so fucking dirty?"

Laura yawns and ambles out of the house as well, to hear what all the fuss is about. She sees Mark standing at the curb, his jaw agape, running a finger over the hood of his less-than-beloved car and not liking what he sees.

"Look at this!" He rushes her from the sidewalk leading up to his door.

Mark pokes the thin index finger of his right hand into her face. Laura yawns again before examining it, completely bored.

"Yeah, it's dirty, so what?"

"So what?" Mark's voice cracks as he says this, rushing back to the car's side. He points over and over at the various mysterious splotches on the car, white, black, dusty brown, and a few strange colors whose genesis Mark doesn't even want to guess at.

"Look, Mark, you were on tour for three months. You had to expect it to be a little dirty."

"Sure, but what's with this weird pattern?" He stands over the hood and bends in close to examine the strange swirling of grime. He notices what looks like half the carcass of a mutilated bumblebee, its thick spiral torso stuck underneath one of the windshield wipers, legs like black twigs cracked in the center, the head missing.

"It rained, you know, once or twice, but not hard enough to wash it all off." Laura retreats back into the house for a second to retrieve a gray Navy blanket, which she twists heavily around her waist like a sarong. "So it just sort of, well, you can see, *smeared* it. Anyway, I don't see what you're making such a big deal about. It's not like you can't just wash it off."

Mark runs a hand through his hair, coming back with sweat at the tips of his fingers even though it's not hot out. She's right. He takes his hand from his head and puts it to his chest where he can feel his heart beating rapidly, and is he crazy or can he really see it push forward the cotton of his T-shirt every couple of seconds?

"Jeez, Mark, you're acting so weird about this, Mark."

Mark. Mark.

He hates it when she does this, says his name over and over again as if to drive home the point of what an asshole he's being. She of course knows how much this bothers him, and that's the main reason she does it. After four years she knows what gets results.

"I mean, come on, Mark, get over it."

He glares over his shoulder at her.

Mark. Mark. Mark.

He hears his name in his head, but not just Laura's voice in a tone that's sort of whiny, definitely tired, still happy to see him but wearing off already. He hears his name spoken by others, by Gary and Steve barking out directions from the back of the van: "Left, Mark, left!" or "A bar, right *there*, Mark, on the right, a *fucking* bar!" He hears his name spoken by fans, asking him for his autograph. And then there was her, that fan who gave

more than most, seductively whispering his name into his ear as
he wriggled on top of her.

"I mean"—Laura scrutinizes his perplexed, scrunched-up
face—"you sure you're not upset about something else?"

"What? Oh, no," he says lamely, not even convincing himself.
"Not at all. In fact"—he pushes his luck by continuing with the
subject, something making him feel cocky—"what makes you
say that?"

"I don't know." Laura shrugs, not really wanting to get into it
herself. The clues were there, all the little things she had noticed
in the short span of just a few hours, but she was too tired to
drag them out onto the lawn like an emotional garage sale. She
can see them now: the guarded way Mark is standing, one hand
fidgeting with a worn belt loop, the other scratching his left
cheek while he shakes his head. "It's just . . . forget it."

The truth is, it was nice for Laura to have him away. She
hadn't relaxed or spent that much time alone since her brothers
first went away to college. Sure, she missed Mark occasionally,
but even when he deigned to call her on the phone (and it was
usually right after a gig when he was still sort of high from the
show and that was all he wanted to talk about), he never asked
her how she was doing, but she always accepted that. She realized that this was a big time for Mark, that he was out there on
the road and, most of the time, didn't enjoy it, but it was all
working toward something greater—at least that was the plan.

But there were also times—and they usually hit late at night,
right when Laura was going to sleep and her defenses were
down—when she asked herself how much longer she was going
to put up with being just another roadie in Mark's rock-and-roll
fantasy. How much longer would she put up with him talking
about *his* music all the time, *his* songs, *his* new guitars, never
asking about what was important in *her* life.

Mark fishes out the lone car key that he'd hung on a nail near
the stove just over three months ago, slips it into the lock, and
twists the silver object delicately to the right. The door sticks for
a second and a whoosh of stale air rushes by his face. He gets in
and surveys the interior of the auto that seems a stranger to him
after only a short while. The quirky smell hits him immediately
and brings back many memories. It makes him feel seventeen

again, reminds him of when his father gave it to him, tossed the keys to him from across the lawn, and Mark had sprinted from the grass to the curving blacktop driveway where the car, a graduation surprise, was sitting.

Mark runs a hand over the dashboard but finds his finger still dirty from before, and he's not sure which dirt belongs to which, so he skips it. He positions the rearview mirror, and Laura, standing on the curb with a scowl, comes into view.

"Uh oh," Mark says to himself in a sing-songy voice.

Something had happened while he was away, and it wasn't just the obvious. Something had cooled, something had been lost or maybe just forgotten, but in any event, it wasn't there. And he could tell she was feeling the same way. Her semi-joyous reception had seemed strained, like a performance, and trooper that she is, she played the part with gusto and verve, but already, hours later, cracks were appearing in her smile and Mark got a good look at what was underneath—an expression he recognized from looking in the mirror. He thinks back to fitting into her earlier, and now fitting into his old car. At the sensation of both he was flooded with memories, sights, smells, an obdurate feeling of physical presence—and with both the feeling was like a quick buzz that was sure to wear off.

Mark puts the key in the ignition, but it just won't start.

Around the fourth or fifth week of Mark's decampment, Laura found herself alone on a weeknight. She fixed a Caesar salad in her kitchen that never looked so clean, without Mark's stream of beer bottles, frozen-pizza-smeared paper plates, and assorted fast-food takeout trash, and she had rented *Slacker* to watch, a film that she had missed when it came back on a double bill with *Dazed and Confused* a few months ago. Just as Richard Linklater was being picked up at the bus station and was absentmindedly ruminating about the girl he could have met, she was crossing her clean living room with her salad on a plate in one hand and an almost overflowing glass of sweet tea in the other, and the thought hit her. It happened as she was settling into the couch with the silence of the room almost rising above the slang-filled dialogue of the actors on the screen. The thought came to her: *I could do this.*

Within minutes she lost track of the already thin thread of the film's plot, characters passing the camera's focus to one another in a cinematic baton handoff. Instead of focusing on the TV screen, densely populated with various hipsters, conspiracy freaks and out-of-work musicians, she looked around the room empty except for herself on this night she had planned for her alone. She felt incredibly warm and right. She felt happy. And it shocked her.

Mark tries again and again. He tries to start the car with the clutch out, the clutch in, laying heavily on the gas, pumping it rhythmically in four-four time. Other times he places both feet squarely on the threadbare dark brown mats. But the car just won't start.

A chugga chugga chugga chugga. A chugga chugga chugga chugga. Mark keeps turning the key and pumping the gas pedal, but it just won't turn over.

"I *said*"—Mark is now repeating for the third time—"my car won't start."

"Well, what do you expect?" Laura shouts over the stale repeating of the faltering engine. "It hasn't been driven in three months."

"Yeah, but haven't you been starting it every couple of days?" Mark shouts back, Laura a blurry vision through the filthy windows. "Like I asked?"

"Well, sure, a couple of . . . I mean, yeah." Now it's her turn to stammer as she tries to hide the truth that she started the car only once, just a few days after he had left. She had attempted to a second time two days ago, but it would not start for her, either.

A chugga chugga chugga chugga.

"Fuck." Mark slams his hand against the black rubber steering wheel.

"I don't see why you're getting all mad over something you can't do anything about," Laura says snidely as she sees Steve turn into the crowded driveway. "I mean, what a fucking childish thing to do!"

"Jeez, what's her problem?" Steve asks as he walks up, rattling his knuckles against the dusty white van and noticing Laura stomping into his house as her words still vibrate through the air.

"Ah, who says they need a reason?" Mark says as he gets out
of the car and slams the door as hard as he can. This is punctu-
ated a second later as Laura slams the door of the house, rattling
the four windows on the front face of the building and sending
two potted plants crashing to the sidewalk.

"Great, just great," Mark mumbles.

"So," Steve says lightly, rubbing his hands together in a hopefully innocuous gesture, not wanting to give Mark another reason to blow up. "We still cleaning out the van for Pops?"

"Yeah, Pops, yeah, another asshole, *sheesh*, the world's fucking
full of 'em," Mark grumbles, and he crosses the lawn and un-
latches the two back doors of the van.

"Whew!" Steve says as stagnant air billows from the inside of
the van and slaps him in the face. "Did this thing smell that bad
while we were on the road, or is this something that fermented
in the past couple of hours?"

Mark is also wincing at the residual smell of shit, body odor,
rotten food, and a sort of gasolinish haze.

"Hell, yes; in fact, then it was worse. Remember right outside
of Spartanburg when you made another one of your forest runs
and, Jesus, we all about fainted? Man, I was hoping we'd run
across a skunk or something for a little bit of relief."

"Hell of a way to spend three months." Steve crawls wearily
into the small space that he can't believe was his home for a
quarter of a year. He picks up a few handfuls of trash, mostly
Ding Dongs and Twinkies wrappers, the only food he ate during
the trip, before turning to Mark and saying, "You know, I don't
think I could do this again."

Mark is entering through the passenger side, tossing spent
McDonald's soft-drink cartons and red french-fry holders into a
blue Gap bag.

"I know what you mean," he says, filling the plastic bag quickly
with garbage. "Next time it's going to be a lot different. First
off, you're going to take some Pepto-Bismol, and we're getting
a map that we can actually follow, and—"

"No, Mark, that's not what I mean."

"Huh?"

"I mean"—Steve stops before delivering the conclusion he
came to last night as he felt the layered sweat of three months

on his skin like sedimentary rock and added it up to nothing in his mind—"there probably won't be a next time."

"But Steve. Easy, pal. We talked about this and decided to try to get our shit together. You know, the demo tape. Remember the demo tape idea?"

"Yeah, sure." Steve laughs and pauses for a second to itch a scratch emanating in the folds of his grumbling belly. "I remember. I also remember our having that idea when we were seniors in high school. I remember our passing back and forth an issue of *The Big Takeover* in which you had highlighted a bunch of record labels in the reviews section where we were going to send our stuff. I also remember that, Mark."

"Oh, come on." Mark tries to laugh, and substitutes the already overflowing Gap bag for one that reads PUBLIX, which they had picked up at a grocery store in Florida. "You can't expect everything to turn out exactly the way we planned. I mean, where's your sense of adventure?"

Steve picks out from between Gary's half-stack and Mark's amp a red-and-white kitchen towel that is now dried hard and stained brown.

"Some adventure," he says.

"Jesus Christ, man, when did you get so cynical?"

"Cynical?" Steve laughs and jumps out of the van and onto the lawn. "I think cynical could be described as putting a distrustful spin on assumed fact, but look"—he points to the interior of the van that looks like a freshman dorm room turned upside down—"I'm not putting the spin on anything here. The facts are the facts, and the facts are . . . this is no way to live."

"I'm not asking you to camp out here on my front lawn forever, dumb shit. I'm just saying I don't want the band to break up completely."

"Hey, don't waste the sermon on me. There's someone else in this band who's thinking of quitting, and you'd better start convincing him, too."

"Gary?"

"Who else?" Steve says incredulously.

"Gary?" The bag in Mark's now limp hand drops to the lawn, where it rolls down the subtle angle of the ground, emptying its contents over the grass. "But what's wrong with Gary?"

. . .

On his first morning back Gary neither sleeps in nor wakes up too early, somehow avoiding that feeling of not knowing where he is which seemed to plague him for the entire tour. Instead he wakes up promptly at nine, lingers in bed until nine-thirty, and then goes to the door where he finds the previous day's edition of the *Kitty Courier* among a pyramid of yellowed, soaked, uncollected issues from the weeks before.

After clomping his feet on the soiled bath towels outside his door, he drags both the paper and himself back inside and takes a seat behind the round wooden table in the kitchen. In a workmanlike fashion he dissects the newspaper. He quickly discards the ridiculous Styles section (always just a human-interest story like the old woman on the edge of the county who collects hubcaps and has been profiled twice already this year), the Opinions section (a meager foldout, even on Sundays, of moribund Letters to the Editor about topics ranging from putting in a new stop light at the corner of Main and Sycamore to the debate on whether or not the Board of Education should ban Beavis & Butthead T-shirts from the junior high), and the News and Food section, dropping the papers to the floor until he comes to what he's looking for, the Classifieds.

He spread-eagles the thin, cheap paper over the table and munches on a granola bar, the only thing left in his cupboards that has not gone stale or odorously rotted during his absence.

Gary keeps yawning as he goes over and over the Help Wanted section. He twirls a pencil in his right hand, then tosses it to his left and back again. He passes it from finger to finger, one after the other like a rotating baton, each of his digits rhythmically synchronized. He taps the tabletop, then gnaws on the sour eraser, spitting out flecks of the hard bologna-colored rubber. After scanning for ten minutes, nothing looks good.

"Jesus, Gary," he says to himself, "you're being too picky. You *have* to be."

He turns to the beginning and starts again, this time trying not to be too choosy.

"Hmm, receptionist . . . light typing . . . and it's close to here.

Salary's not bad, either." He's about to circle it when he sees a few words at the bottom of the ad in fine print. "Lotus? What in the fuck's Lotus? Isn't that where you sit with your feet in your lap? And what do they mean by Windows? Is that like, uh, washing them?" He takes a nibble of his rock-hard granola bar, wondering if it, too, hasn't gone stale, but how would he know? "I'd better forget that one."

He focuses on an ad for a legal aide until he notices something written next to the large salary.

"Eighty words per minute? Who in the fuck are they kidding? I took a typing test a few years ago when I got some jobs as a temp and scored a thirty-five, and they said that was good. So I don't even want to think about what kind of sideshow freaks they're looking for who can type— Hey!" An idea pops into his head. "Maybe I'll check out a few temp agencies."

After scouring the ads again, he finds a few temp agencies that seem to be recruiting and have even listed jobs that pay decent salaries. Gary's hand is halfway to the phone before he reads, "Word processing experience A MUST."

"Word processing?" He takes another bite of his breakfast, grinding coarse oats, barley, and honey beneath teeth that are almost too used to softer foods to accommodate. He washes down the pasty mixture with a mouthful of saliva, but only barely. "Is that like typing? Oh, well, better not risk it."

After another few minutes of searching, and even then lowering his standards further than he had originally planned, he is left with just a few prospects.

"Fucking busboy . . . sell magazines over the phone . . . AAA Escort Service, and I don't even want to know what that entails. Fuck!" He slams his hand down on the spread-out newspaper with a crackle. "I told Mark finding a job was going to be a bitch, but no, he's always got his dad taking care of him. So what does he care about us? What does he care if my life is screwed up every time he wants to go on the road and fuck some groupies?"

James, his roommate, walks into the room wearing a pair of boxers and an old frat shirt from Duke.

"You talking to anyone in particular, Gary, or just the walls?"

"Fuck you," he snarls, reaching for the phone.

"Yeah, yeah," mumbles James as he reaches into the fridge, grabs his pint of milk (labeled, of course), swigs, and shuffles out of the kitchen, calling afterward, "I hope you're not eating my new cinnamon and honey granola bars."

Gary almost chokes on another mouthful of trail mix and wheat germ when he examines the green wrapper and sees James's telltale smiley face territorial sticker.

"Shit." He sighs as he finds the number of the only job that looked halfway within his reach: a waiter position at the Whales Fin Restaurant. *Dave works there, so who knows? Maybe the connection will help. I hope so.*

Before heading into the bathroom for a shower, Gary crumples the green foil granola bar wrapper and tosses it the length of kitchen, hoping to swish it into the faux basket made from a paper shopping bag with the edges curled under to give the rim some support. Instead of a no-rim basket, it caroms off the counter and rolls into the living room, where James has started watching cartoons, slurping at his milk.

A second later Gary hears him shout, "Thanks, asshole."

"No problem."

The shower is his first real shower since they splurged and all three slept in a fifteen-dollar hotel room outside of Harrisburg. Standing underneath the nozzle Gary can't believe the amount of grit and grime that's flaking off him. He lathers up his bare hands and swabs at his neck, feeling the sheath of dirt come off underneath his fingers like the layers of glue-skin he used to apply in elementary school. He stares down at the drain in amazement as a black ring appears around the lime-stained grille.

Rinsing out his hair for the second time, digging into his scalp with his short, stubby fingernails, he still finds grains of sand from a side trip they took to Hilton Head in South Carolina almost ten weeks before. He digs into his ear with the tip of his pinky, returning with a crown of yellow, orange, and brown wax, along with more sand.

He dries himself off with one of James's towels (he can't find any of his own) and then weighs himself on the scale. He suspects he's lost some weight on the tour, as he always does on a tour, but he can't remember how much he weighed before so has nothing to compare his current 157 pounds to, though it seems thin for being six feet tall.

Gary takes his bootleg Young Marble Giants T-shirt from the floor and wipes down the fogged-up medicine chest mirror. He examines his tired eyes, worn-out reflection, and slightly pissed-off expression. Instead of musing further on his current condition, he opens the cabinet and takes a cheap white Bic disposable razor that he is pretty sure is his. He takes off the orange slip of plastic covering the blade and tosses it into the toilet. He examines the thin strips of metal set into the plastic and can see trails of bluish soap scum on each of the two blades. He takes out a few other razors, but they all seem to be in the same state of ill-repair. Instead of using one razor three or four times and then tossing it, Gary always uses every razor once or twice and then keeps it around. "Fuck," he says, slamming down the razor, and the hollow plastic core of the handle sings for a second in the steamy room.

He decides on his first choice, the least decrepit of the bunch, tosses the rest, and tries to remind himself to stop at the drugstore on the way back from his job interview. He lathers up with a soapy white lotion that has an acrid, alcoholic smell which supposedly makes it good for his skin but instead makes his eyes water and nose twitch. After rinsing the blades in scalding water for a few minutes, he takes the first sweep of his face, up from the jawbone to the tip of his left sideburn, which ends around mid-ear. The razor cuts this section easily because it's a straight line, no challenge there. He always leaves the chin and underside of his face for later, letting the lotion completely soften the wire-brush stubble that grows there.

He shaves down a few strokes to get a whisker he missed on the way up, before repeating the same procedure to the opposite side of his face. Once that's been tackled he tucks his upper lip into his mouth so as to make the region below his nose as straight and narrow as a billboard covered with prickly stubs. He jerks his wrist back and forth, making quick, short cuts with the razor. At the corner of his mouth, where a few errant whiskers always seem to pop up, he takes the razor sideways and brings it toward his lips, only it catches on a few long hairs, so he presses harder until he feels a slight pinching sensation.

"Shit." He glances in the mirror, which has fogged up yet again due to the constant stream of hot water running from the tap.

At the end of his lip a trickle of red is mixing with the shaving cream on his chin, turning an appetizing pink and reminding him of the dark fruit juices that always mix with the frosting in a strawberry shortcake.

Finishing up, he shaves upward from the base of his neck to the rim of his chin, where the hairs grow at odd angles, not in order as on the surface of his face. He cuts himself again on a mole just to the right of his Adam's apple (as he has done a million times) and again just below his bottom lip.

After wiping off the excess shaving cream with James's towel, he notices he has traded some of his blood to the beige cotton cloth while it has clung to his cuts with little bits of fuzz, clotting his injuries.

He drapes the towel over the shower curtain rod, making sure to tuck under the sides with the now purple bloodstains.

He wanders into his bedroom and picks from his closet a blue dress shirt, slightly pressed, ironed once six months ago but never worn. Gary shrugs, figuring it was bound to get wrinkled somehow. He matches this with a pair of khaki trousers and dusty brown penny loafers he hasn't worn since his high school graduation. The tight shoes pinch his toes and bind his ankle in a snug triangle. He limps to the full-length mirror in the hallway (where James laughs out loud, passing him on his way to the kitchen) and examines himself. The shoes are indeed too tight, with little tufts of sock bulging out at the leather tongue and over the stretch of black stitching at the ankle. His pants, left-overs from formal wear not worn in five years, are floods, their hemmed cuffs exposing about two inches of once-white Target socks, now gray.

He tucks the shirt in and notices that the top half of his outfit makes up for the bottom. The worn Perry Ellis shirt looks nice but is still comfortable, the soft chambray cool against his skin, unlike those stiff white shirts he had to wear to the dances at the country club when he still lived at home, where the hot southern nights would make him sweat and the stiffly starched front of his shirts would often rub his nipples raw.

James walks through the hallway again, with a bowl of Quaker Oats instant oatmeal in his hand, on top of which he's poured a healthy dose of milk, a few raisins, and some brown sugar. He watches as Gary finishes up his grooming with a dash of Polo cologne behind each ear and wrist.

"What are you, a girl?" James says, laughing until he is well into the other room.

"Fuck you."

Gary sniffs and, glancing down at his scented hands, is positive he's applied too much. He rushes to the bathroom to rinse them off. He again tries to gauge the amount of cologne on his body, but it is now impossible since the scent is in the air, still wafting out of the bottle and also slathered somewhere on him.

"I'm sure it'll be okay once I get into the air," he reasons, taking a last look in the mirror before heading out.

"Peee-yooooo," James squeaks out in a high voice, pinching his nose as Gary crosses the living room.

"Born of frustration," Gary mutters to himself as he puts his key in the ignition, the green Volvo starting to his total amazement.

The blue-and-red neon sign that hangs above the entrance to the Whales Fin hums and buzzes on a cool afternoon. The sky blue outline of a whale pulses with light, the charged air running through the tube like runners around a track, while the blood-red lettering flickers until the W and I fizz out completely and the sign reads: HALES F N.

Gary shrugs as he gets out of the car, again trying to measure the amount of Polo on his hands and neck. He sniffs around his cuffs and collar but can't smell a thing.

"I just can't win, can I?" he mumbles as he walks up to the double doors that are decorated with a plastic swordfish bolted against a background of various seashells and dried-up puke-green netting.

"Table for one?" A too-happy hostess accosts him before he's even through the door.

The small crowd of diners waiting for tables look up at him as if he is a leper, unable to find anyone willing to share a meal with him.

"Actually, I'm here for a job . . . interview. I called earlier and spoke with the manager. I have an appointment."

The girl looks slightly disappointed. She rips an application from a gummed pad beneath the counter and hands it to Gary, pointing to the bar.

"Fill this out. The manager will be with you in just a second."

He sits down at the bar and looks over the application. In a split second all the old dread comes washing over him again. *References?* "Shit." He reaches for the pen in his back pocket. *Why do they need to know the address of the last three schools I attended? And phone numbers? Who are they going to call and talk to, my home-room teacher?*

"Uh, can I have a drink?" Gary says to the bartender, wiping sweat from his forehead. "Vodka and tonic."

The bartender delivers the drink and picks up three of the four dollars Gary has laid out for him. With one hand Gary is filling out the application, while the other fiddles with the trident swizzle stick, twirling it in the glass that's already half-empty.

He keeps biting his tongue, trying to recall all of the required information, but most of it is outside of his reach. Thinking back, he remembers there were a few fours in the phone number of that chicken-rendering plant he worked in two summers ago, and puts down seven numbers that look good together.

Gary comes to the question that reads, "Have you ever been convicted of a crime?" He pauses for a second, debating whether to write in "Never convicted." He laughs and is about to put that down on the page when he stops, thinking, *Man, this isn't funny. I need this job.* He self-consciously looks around and sits up straight on the bar stool.

"All done?"

Gary looks up and sees a large man only a few years older than himself standing in front of him with a clipboard and a lit cigarette in his hand.

"My name's Dan, I'm the manager. We spoke earlier." He looks over Gary and is pleased until he spots the rocks glass, now completely empty except for a twist of lime and a few ice cubes. "Ready for the interview?"

"Uh, sure." Gary turns to the application, sort of winks at it, and signs his name before handing it to Dan, who adds it to the pile on his clipboard.

"Great. Come with me."

Gary follows Dan behind the bar and into the alley where half a dozen waiters dealing with the lunch rush are all running around frantically. Gary nods to Stoner, a drummer in one of Dave's bands, as he follows the manager through a set of swinging double doors into the back of the restaurant. At the end of a long hallway overstuffed with various supplies, such as barrel-sized cans of Homemade Clam Chowder and tablecloths and napkins bound in shiny plastic, there is a small employee lounge with a door at the opposite side.

"Jesus, Rowland, get back to work," Dan growls when he spots Dave talking on a pay phone and sipping soda from a paper snow-cone wrapper.

"I'll call you back," Dave whispers before hanging up and turning around. "Oh, hey, Dan, what's up?"

"Probably your lunch orders."

Dave laughs nervously before noticing Gary.

"Hey, Gary, what're you doing here?"

"Just looking for a job, as a, uh, waiter." Gary tries to speak conscientiously, his chest forward and his voice steady.

"Well, good luck. And have Mark call me!"

"Now get back out there, Rowland. By the way, I just cut Carlos, Stacy, and Eric . . . so as soon as they turn over their tables, you and Bill will have the entire restaurant until the dinner shift shows up. Have a nice day."

Dave's face turns white as he jumps up and heads for the kitchen where, as Dan had guessed, his food is growing cold in the window.

Dan opens the door to a small office that reeks of cigarette smoke and fish. Gary sits in a red plastic seat across from Dan's cluttered desk. Dan also sits, crosses his legs, and begins looking over Gary's application.

"So you're a good friend of David Rowland, huh?"

"Yes, sir," Gary says confidently.

"Great. Rowland is one of our best employees." Dan's eyes are still scanning Gary's application like a printer carriage, back and forth, back and forth. "At least he used to be. These days . . . I just don't know."

"Well, um"—Gary coughs into his sweating hands—"the truth of the matter is, we've never been *that* close."

"In any event, Gary, here at the Whales Fin you're not just a worker, you're part of a team. Now, why don't you tell me what you think are the ingredients of a good team."

"Um, well . . . of course, uniforms," Gary says half as a joke, half serious. "Which you, you know, have, what with the whale bow ties and the aprons, but, I think, more important is the spirit of the workers, to feel proud about what they—"

"Hang on for a second," Dan interrupts, waving his hand in the air. "What's that smell?"

Gary sniffs in unison with Dan's own nostrils comically flaring and then retracting like a heartbeat in slow motion until he, too, picks up the scent. Quickly Gary dabs a finger behind his ear and finds a wet spot of shaving cream, stinking up the tiny office like a barbershop. Gary swats at it, stealthily cups his hand on the way from his ear to his waist, and smears it on the underside of the plastic seat.

"Oh, well." Dan gives up, unable to pinpoint the odor. "Anyway, you were saying?"

"Um, yes, as I was, er, saying . . ."

As Gary unbelievably hears himself begin to spew forth some middle-management mumbo-jumbo, he feels like taking the silver ballpoint pen in Dan's hand and sticking it deep into his own throat.

What in the fuck am I doing? Why am I practically begging this guy for a shit job I don't even want? Since when did I get so desperate? Jesus, this is so humiliating.

"So, you see, sir, that a team is only as, uh, strong as its, uh, strongest—no, no, make that, its weakest, link. Yeah, that's it."

"Hmm. Interesting ideas. But to be honest with you, Gary, without previous experience I just don't think we have room for you at this time. I mean"—he taps at the clipboard in his hand —"I've been turning down applicants with one, two, and three years' experience in the service industry, so I just don't think that we can . . . Wait a second." Dan stops the interview yet again.

"What?" Gary asks nervously, his underarms cold and wet against his biceps. For fear of stains he keeps his arms close to his side, moving his upper body in one stiff piece.

"It's something else." His nose twitches like a rabbit's. "What's *that* smell?"

Gary keeps quiet as the blood rushes to his face, his lower body still trembling.

3

"I have an idea." Randy bursts into the apartment.

Chipp, saddled with a hangover, doesn't respond.

"Hey, asshole, I have an idea," Randy repeats, slapping his roommate on the shoulder. "Don't you want to hear it?"

Chipp wearily raises his head from the bowl of Trix that he's been trying to get down for the past half-hour. After thirty minutes the hard-as-plastic balls of cereal have merged into a gelatinous muck, the Day-Glo colors streaking the milk like— well, Chipp really doesn't want to think about it.

"You're going to hear it anyway." Randy pulls out a chair and sits down. "We are going to start a fanzine."

Chipp's stomach turns over like a car engine, rumbling, trying to kick into gear. He tries to remain calm, holding it down.

"Yeah, you know, like *Flipside* but local." Randy is jumping all over the room, a nervous ball of energy. "Shit, there are enough bands in Kitty that would want to be interviewed and get us into their shows for free, and we could review records and books, and shows, whatever we wanted to, and, you know, give it away free all over town, and it'd be great. See what I'm saying?"

Years ago at his grandmother's house Chipp remembers seeing a picture of some religious figure sitting on top of the manhole cover to hell, all of the demons trying desperately to crawl their way out, but some chick is just sitting on them,

blocking their way with a smile. That's what he's trying to do
right now.

"And then record labels would send us all kinds of promo
stuff for free. We don't even have to listen to it, really, just
say we like it so they'll send us more stuff next month. Man,
everybody's doing something like this."

"That's the problem." Chipp gurgles the words. His usually
tan skin has turned a whiter shade of brown, his eyes are wide
and bloodshot. His lips are dry and chapped, and he keeps
puckering his cheeks as if he were going to spit but never actually does.

"Jesus, what happened to you last night?" Randy asks, finally
noticing Chipp's condition.

"Heather and I . . . sat around . . . and drank," he manages to
get out.

"Okay, there's explanation number one. Now, for the grand
prize, what in the hell did you drink?"

Chipp gets up slowly and waddles to the couch, where he
collapses in a spread-eagle position over all three cushions.

"What didn't we?" Chipp cups his swollen head in his numb
hands. "Oh, fuck, why didn't I stop? You know how you get to
that point when you've got a really good buzz? You've had
maybe six or seven drinks, you can still walk and talk, but you're
drunk enough so that everything is kind of hazy and easy to
take. It's kind of like, you know, cruising altitude?"

"Sure, I guess." Randy takes a bite of Chipp's bowl of Trix,
but finding them too soggy, spits them back into the dish.

"I reached that point. Then kept going."

"Then what happened?"

"Oh, the usual. We played some records and talked a lot. I
think I passed out a couple times. A few hours later we were
doing shots, and then she started throwing up all over the place
and I blacked out, I think. Or else I wanted to."

"Jeez, sounds like a romantic evening."

"What'd you do?"

"I went with Sarita, K.K., and Jason to some party in Tiger
Bay."

"How was it?" Chipp keeps asking Randy questions because it
means that he doesn't have to talk, he can just sit there, listen,
and recover.

"God, it was a nightmare." Randy leans back in his chair, staring out the window. "All these snobby little high school kids drinking too much beer and thinking they are cool. I guess some kid's parents were away on vacation or something."

"Well, of course, you dumbshit." Chipp turns over, but the couch cushion smells like moldy beer, so he turns the other way, facing the floor, but there's a cloudy stain on the carpet and he remembers what it's from, so he stares at the ceiling, which is relatively clean. "Like a kid could afford to live out there?"

"Anyway, that's where I got this idea for the magazine."

"Sounds great: 'In This Issue: How to Throw a Really Lame Party.' "

"No, you shithead. Afterward we went to The Scene, and The Deer Park was playing, as usual, but they've upped the cover on local bands to four bucks! Can you believe that shit? And all because Violent Revolution put out a goddamn seven-inch single which you can't even buy at DISContent anymore, so I don't see what the big deal is."

"No, you can get mail order. I saw an ad in *Fiz*."

"Would you let me finish? Anyway, that's where I got the idea for the mag."

"Magazine? I thought it was going to be a fanzine."

"Same difference."

"No, a magazine has to look good, a fanzine just has to, well, be looked at. And anyway, I thought we already went through this six months ago when you convinced me to do it, and we came within a good week's worth of work to finish it, and you disappeared to Chapel Hill with Jen for a weekend."

"I was different then, Chipp. Come on, I'm serious now. Dedicated. And you just said so yourself, most of the work's already done. Hell, all those bands whose records we reviewed just came out with new albums. All we have to do is change the titles and a few of the song references—like instead of saying '*Hey Babe* is a classic pop album, and "I See You" is the best song,' we say, '*Become What You Are* is a classic pop album and "Supermodel" is the best song.' See how easy that is?"

"Ha!" Chipp shouts. "See how dishonest it is, is more like it."

"Oh, come on." Randy nudges his roommate with the toe of his black boot. "It's not like either of us is in school or presently employed. What else are we going to do?"

Chipp's head is swimming. His brain, still shaking off the alcohol from the night before, repeatedly swan-dives into the back of his aching eyes. Remembering the old cure, he takes a sip from an Evian bottle lying at his side. He bought the bottle six months ago at a Circle K, ferociously chugged the contents after slamming at a Firehose show, and since then has just filled it up from the tap. Randy is always amazed at how Chipp finds the money to buy imported water all the time. Last month Randy took a swig and told him, "You're wasting your money, man. It doesn't taste any different than the water that comes from our faucet."

While Chipp is mulling over the idea, Randy gets bored and turns on the TV. He flips around for a few minutes before settling on an old Bugs Bunny cartoon.

It's not the idea that's stopping Chipp, but rather his proposed partner. In the past Randy has been less than reliable, and Chipp is reluctant to plunge into yet another project with him only to find Randy becoming bored after the first few days. When they were still in high school, Randy wanted to be a film director. He had just seen *Breathless* in a French film festival at the Capital Cinema, and for the next few weeks he had his sister cart him around town in his uncle's wheelchair while he cradled an ancient Super 8 movie camera, all because he read that was how the DP shot *Breathless*. (DP stands for Director of Photography, an annoying term Randy still uses today. For example: "Robby Mueller was the DP of *Paris, Texas*. He was also the DP for *Repo Man* and *Barfly*. Man, what a great DP!") Randy was then set on the idea of making his own film, a Godardesque mixture of jump cuts, wheelchair dolly shots, and a sparse, existential screenplay, written by himself, of course. The whole project lasted less than a month and is still a sore subject for Randy.

As Yosemite Sam's voice fills the room, all Chipp can hear is Randy's voice replaying in his head. Chipp splices in an extra word. "What else are we *ever* going to do?"

"Let's do it," Chipp says quickly.

"Huh?" Randy asks, annoyed. "Do what?"

"The fanzine. Come on. Let's get started."

"Not now." Randy waves him off, scratching his chin and turning toward the brightly colored screen. "Cartoons are still on."

· · ·

"So what do we call it?"

Randy is now playing with the Amoco patch that is hanging onto his blue cotton jacket by a few loose threads. He fidgets for a few more seconds, as if it were a loose tooth he wants to handle but doesn't want to pull out yet.

After sitting around the apartment all day trying to iron out the details of their zine, Randy's become more and more edgy, the surprise that Chipp actually agreed to his idea slowly being replaced with a fidgety uneasiness. Every time Randy wants to take a break, Chipp silences him with "Hey, look, this was your idea," a remark for which Randy has yet to come up with a clever comeback.

"Huh?"

"The name? For the zine? We've been trying to think of one for three hours. Can you forget about your damn jacket for two seconds?"

"Yeah, but . . ." Randy doesn't look up. He's still picking at the patch. "I don't want this to fall off and lose it."

"So what if you did? You've never even worked at Amoco. In fact, your cousin gave you that jacket, and it had a Sears patch on it at the time. You ripped it off and put that one on."

"Well, sure. Sears isn't cool."

Chipp shrugs.

"And Amoco, a fucking gas station, is?"

"Yeah, it's like . . . industrial. Grungy. You know, like the Beastie Boys are wearing stuff like that now. Like in that video —one of 'em's wearing a post office uniform."

"You idiot." Chipp's eyes are blurry, and his ass hurts from sitting in a wooden chair all day. "That's House of Pain, not the Beastie Boys."

Randy looks stunned.

"Really?"

"Yes."

He rips off the patch completely and tosses it across the room where it lands squarely in the trash.

"So what have we got?" he asks with renewed enthusiasm.

"Okay, that's more like it."

Chipp takes a swig of beer and looks at the yellow legal

pad that they've been brainstorming over for names to their fanzine.

"Um, the first is *Reservoir Kittens*."

"Lame."

"Why?"

"Why? Why not?"

"It's because of that movie, you know." Chipp is using his hands like two little guns to get his point across, then a slicing movement across one ear. Randy is staring at him through his dirty glasses, his volleyball-sized head slightly tilted.

Silence.

It's been two years now. They've lived in this apartment ever since they were thrown out of college for setting a small fire in their dorm room. To this day Randy and Chipp cannot agree who started it. The fights usually go something like this:

Randy: It was your fucking hotplate.

Chipp: No, it wasn't. It was your goddamn lamp you bought at that slimy garage sale in Richmond for a buck. You know, the one with the frayed cord.

Randy: Chipp, quit kidding yourself. If it wasn't your hotplate, then it was that piece of junk microwave your brother *gave* you.

Chipp: He did give it to me. It's just, at the time he needed some money, so it may have looked as if he made me pay for it, but that's really not the— Look, it was probably those damn clove cigarettes you were so into, remember? You would sit around and listen to The Cure and smoke your cloves?

Randy: Stop it! I did not! You tell anybody and I'll—

Chipp: You'll what?

At this point they start wrestling violently, and whoever is around has to pull them apart. If they're alone, they just start pushing each other around, and knowing they're both too lazy to do anything about it, stop by themselves.

"I know the movie, dickwipe. I was with you when you saw— Hey!" Randy sits up in his chair as if he's just sat on a tack.

"What? What is it?"

"Dickwipe!" He's looking at an imaginary marquee. *"Dickwipe Fanzine.* It's perfect!"

"Are you kidding?"

"No." Randy is offended. He shoots out of his chair and gets another beer. "It's brash and punk. Straight edge, man. It shows we're serious."

"All it would show is that we're stupid. Besides, how are you going to explain a title like that to your mom?"

Randy is standing in the kitchen, making the third side of a triangle that includes the right angle formed by the refrigerator door and his body. He tightly clutches his beer, moistened with dew. "Yeah, maybe you're right." The sudden silence in the background grabs his attention. "Hey, put on another record."

"You put on another record."

Chipp can see his lips about to form the witty rebuttal, "No, *you* put on another record," but he backs down and instead stomps across the room. Talking to Randy is sometimes like playing tennis, only no one ever wins.

"Just don't play that damn Archers of Loaf record again. If I hear 'Web in Front' one more time, I think I'll puke."

"Hey, if you're too lazy to get off your ass and put on another record, then I get to choose. Actually, I'm sick of Archers of Loaf, too. How about Pavement?"

"*Perfect Sound Forever* or the *Watery, Domestic* EP?"

"I was thinking *Slanted and Enchanted.*"

"Even better."

Randy sits down just as "Summer Babe" begins. For a few seconds they drink in the gorgeous tune, the fuzzy guitars, the sinewy bass, Steve Malkmus's deadpan vocals that always make them feel as though they can do anything. By the second verse, with far too much work to do, they snap out of it and get to it.

"Okay, next," Randy says.

"Um, *Distortion Vox*. Get it? Like distortion box, only instead of box we put—"

"I get it, I get it. Anyway, isn't there a British music magazine called *Vox*? It's like a supplement to the *NME*?"

"Yeah, so?" Chipp defends, rising up in his chair.

"Well, what happens when this thing gets super huge, and we start putting out foreign editions? We'll get sued and have to change our name to *Distortion Vox USA* like the *UK Subs*. Or else *Distortion Vox Jr*. That's lame."

"All right, all right, I'm not married to it. Next: *The Imploding Tie-dyed Toupee*. Uh, that one was yours, I'm pretty sure."

"What do you think?" Randy's eyes are wide, his face full and innocent like a child immune to the horror and cruelty of the real world.

"Too sentimental."

"All right, go on."

On the stereo, Pavement is tearing into "Conduit for Sale." Randy, by now totally bored, is singing along.

"I'm tryin', I'm tryin', I'm tryin' . . ."

Chipp clears his throat loudly.

"Youth Body Expression Explosion," he says proudly. This one was his suggestion.

"Is that all one damn title?"

"Yeah, so?"

"Kind of long, don't you think? I mean, there won't be any room left on the cover. Besides, wasn't that a song off the last Mudhoney album that you paid through the nose to get on vinyl because now they're major label sellouts?"

"All right, all right, fuck you." Chipp gets up from the table, his chair skidding loudly across the floor. "I just don't care anymore." He paces around the apartment, restless energy suddenly flowing through his body. "All we've done since we decided to put out this magazine is argue over what to call it, what to write about, and who to put on the goddamn cover. I mean, Jesus, it's about time to start making decisions, don't you think?"

"Hey, I'm perfectly ready and willing to make a decision. It's just that you're being a total stick in the mud about everything." Randy is pointing a bony finger in his roommate's face. Chipp slaps it away and continues pacing. "How about that idea I had of you posing for the cover, with you singing into a microphone and the cord going into your ass?"

"That was the stupidest, sickest thing I've ever heard of in my life!" Chipp screams. "You seriously thought I would go for that?"

"Why not? It's artistic. Kind of a Mapplethorpe meets the Butthole Surfers sort of thing."

"That's the problem with all of that crap. A legitimate guy like Duchamp turns a toilet into a piece of art, and now every chump in the world thinks he can frame whatever comes out of his nose and call it art. You can't just take a piss onstage and call it—" Chipp stops for a moment, getting off the subject. "If your plan is so brilliant, then why don't you stick the cables up *your* butt, and I'll take the picture?"

Randy curls up into a little ball, nervously picking at the shredding label on his beer bottle.

"Er, it's my camera, and the lens is kind of screwed so I've got to take the picture. Yeah, that's it . . ." His words trail off.

"And another thing is that I seem to be doing all the work. I've been calling printers and copying places getting quotes, pricing covers and typesetting and stuff. What have you been doing?"

"I've been out on the street making important business contacts!"

"Like who?" Chipp sits back down. Heather called him earlier, and he never called her back. Right now he's wondering what she's doing and why he isn't doing whatever it is she's doing. Randy is squirming in his chair trying to come up with some great important name to appease him. Tim Yohannan? Joe Banks? Ahmet Ertegun?

"Like who?" he asks again.

"Uh, Jess . . . yeah, that's it."

"Jess?"

"Yeah," Randy says, trying to sound sure even though he's not.

"The guys who schleps sludge down at the coffeehouse?"

"He also stocks books. Yeah, uh, Jess said we could put copies in his window, you know, along with the other zines."

"Well that's not so bad, especially if—other zines? What other zines?"

"Oh, didn't I show you?"

A picture appears in Chipp's mind: his strong hands around Randy's dirty neck, squeezing, Randy's voice box collapses in a snap, his eyes bug out, his pale flesh turning purple.

Chipp hands Randy a publication entitled *Piss Poor*, subtitled "Kitty's Awesome Alternative." The cover is a drawing of a stick figure with a mohawk and a smiley face, thin fingers in a fuck-you gesture. Chipp flips through it quickly. It doesn't look too bad, sixteen pages, more than a few photos, all printed on a web press, the cheapest there is.

"Jesus Christ, now we've got competition!" Chipp shouts.

"Relax, Chipper. These guys aren't really serious. Look here. It says the next issue will come out—" he takes it out of Chipp's hands and reads the fine print at the bottom—" 'Whenever the hell we feel like it.' See? It's a one off. Don't worry."

The competitive fire begins to die down inside Chipp. *Piss Poor.* Chipp laughs. *Jeez, what a stupid title.*

"If nothing else it proves that a zine is a good idea in this town." Randy tosses it aside. "So what do we call our magazine then?"

"I don't care." Chipp wearily runs his hands through his hair. "I really don't."

"How about we just take the next name on the list and, no matter what it is, we use it?" Randy's eyes are wild, his brain sizzling with his anarchistic suggestion.

"Gee, Randy, I don't know."

"What's the matter? Chicken?"

"No, it's just that—"

Randy cuts Chipp off and starts gobbling like a chicken. He gets up and starts waddling around the room, really getting into it. Chipp hasn't seen this tactic used since the fourth grade. Now Randy is gobbling even louder, practically shouting.

Chipp bites his nail, trying to stay calm in the face of ridicule.

Randy must be getting really desperate to think I'll decide to call our fanzine any old dumb name just because he keeps making that ridiculous sound, trying to convince me I'm a coward.

"Okay! Just stop it!" The words blurt out of Chipp's mouth before he can stop them.

Randy jumps across the room, landing at the base of the table. He picks up the yellow pad, glowering, slobbering a drum roll between his thin lips.

"And the winner is . . . your favorite fanzine and mine . . . Kitty's newest entertainment guide . . ."

"Will you just say it!"

"Peesh!" He spits, trying to emulate a cymbal. Before telling Chipp the name, he breaks out laughing, drops the legal pad to the ground, and dances around the room.

"It can't be that bad, it can't be that bad." Chipp is mumbling to himself as he picks up the pad from the floor.

"*Godfuck?*" he says softly.

"Yeah, ain't it great? That was one of mine! Woo hoo!"

"Now look, Randy. I don't think we should—"

"Oh, no. A deal's a deal. And the deal was we'd pick the next name, no matter what it was. And remember, you promised to wake up bright and early tomorrow to go solicit advertising. Remember?"

"Yeah, I suppose."

"And I'm going to see about getting a P.O. box and check out the postal rates."

"But Randy, wait a minute. This name could offend a lot of people. Why don't we—"

"Bock, bock, bock!" He raises his arms and starts in on some enthusiastic gobbling.

"Okay!"

"Well, better turn in." Randy dances into the hall, chuckling.

Chipp stands in the middle of the room, the song "Here" floating up to the ceiling.

"*Your jokes are always bad,*" Pavement is crooning on the stereo.

Chipp softly sings the next line: "*But they're not as bad as this.*"

4

"Who is it?" Eileen wearily shouts out.

"Housekeeping! Are you checking out today? Do you want me to turn down the bed? Do you need more towels?"

Her bloodshot eyes focus on the doorknob as it wiggles back and forth slightly, just inches to either side but not all the way.

"Um . . ." Eileen shouts back, not exactly sure of her plans yet. "Come back later."

The doorknob stops jiggling and through the window she sees a large woman's shadow pushing what looks like a shopping cart filled with groceries down the sidewalk to the next room. Eileen can hear her mumbling something in Spanish as she starts all over again on the room next door.

As the maid pounds on the door down the hall, Eileen realizes that any hope for more sleep is completely lost. She glances at the clock. 9:47. It's the earliest she's woken up in the past two months.

She sits up in bed and looks out the window again. She can spot the shadowy figure of her car in the parking lot of the garage across the street. She raises a fist to her mouth and begins absentmindedly gnawing on a knuckle. She glances down at the phone, about to call the garage to tell them to begin work on the car so she can resume her trip. Then she changes her mind and decides to call her mother to tell her she won't be home for a while. She picks up the black receiver, but there's no dial tone. She tries dialing 0, then 411, even 911, but there's just dead air. Reluctantly Eileen crawls out of bed, brushes her hair back, puts on a skirt and green T-shirt, and heads out of the room to the hotel office.

The door to the office creaks horribly, which she guesses is cheaper than one of the those light sensors that goes off every time someone enters, and even cheaper than a set of bells wrapped around the handle. The room is barely standing space, consisting of a few chairs and a counter, atop which lies a tarnished bell with a little sign next to it that reads RING FOR SERVICE. Just beyond the counter is an apartment where the owner lives.

"Ahem," Eileen fakes a cough.

Through the open door she can see the right half of a TV screen, black-and-white, flickering hopelessly, continually scrolling as if the entire program were made up of credits rolling over and over. She can also see the left corner of a recliner, brown and stained, set to the upright position, jeans rolled over dark cowboy boots propped up on the footrest.

" 'Scuse me!" she chirps out in a song. A few seconds later there's a faint grunt, then a large furry arm reaches down near the boots and pulls back a lever that collapses the footrest, delivering the clunky shoes swiftly to the floor.

"What?"

He's wearing just an undershirt and jeans, his auburn beard is scraggly, and he has rose-colored aviator sunglasses over his eyes so Eileen can't tell what color they are. His voice is thick, rugged, but devoid of any accent. His words are pure and his locution straight, not curved like the locals who seem to have mush in their mouth, a strange combination of syrupy southern and tightassedly eastern seaboard.

Eileen looks at the stranger and laughs to herself, figuring that he must have ended up in Kitty the same way she did: by mistake. It scares her to think the two of them could have so much in common.

"Hi, room number one-oh-nine. Um, my phone won't work."

"Need a deposit," he says slowly. "Ten dollars."

"Oh, I didn't know . . ."

"Ten dollars," he says again.

Eileen takes a twenty out of the T-shirt's pocket and waits as he ambles into the other room for change. The room smells musty and dry. In the corners the wallpaper, which couldn't have been fashionable even when first purchased, is peeling badly. The events of the past few months are jumbled in her head. Rather than sort them out, sort anything out, she just lets them sit there, knowing that every day she ignores the situation it becomes more and more hopeless.

Jesus, Eileen, get out of this place and don't look back.

"Here you go." The man comes back with a mouthful of something and hands Eileen a ten-dollar bill.

Back in her room Eileen dials the familiar number.

"Hello?" Her mom sounds chipper, as usual.

"Mom? Hey, it's me."

"Eileen? Why, I'm so glad you called! I've been so worried! Where are you? Grammy said you left early yesterday and should have been home by now. I've been worried sick! What's happening? Where are you?"

"One question at a time," Eileen says, picking at a toenail.

"Well, where are you?"

"In Virginia. Some small town called Kitty, which is next to— Actually, I'm not sure what it's next to, but it's not all that bad. I mean . . . Anyway, I still don't know when I'm coming back." She pauses for a second. "If ever."

"What?" her mother's voice says in shock. "Why?"

"Well, my car broke down, which is why I had to stop last night, and the . . . the garage said the car will be ready in a few more days," Eileen lies. Spotting the Sucrets box hiding underneath a thick black sock, she pokes the tin with the big toe of her left foot and drags it toward her body. While her mother is rambling on about their mechanic, Sam, back home, Eileen rests the phone against her head and shoulder, pries open the pillbox, and extracts a small white tablet. She places it far back on her tongue, musters a small pool of saliva, and quickly jerks her head back, sending the drug careening down her throat. "Look, Mom, slow down. I'm not going to have my car towed all the way to Maryland just because Sam has been working on our cars for the last twenty years."

"But I'm just trying to help, and—"

"Look, uh, I've got to go, okay?" The pill lands in her empty stomach like a clumsy high jumper. "Call you in a couple days."

"All right, but remember, we're thinking of you."

Eileen hangs up and closes her eyes, fighting back tears. She wonders why it's so easy to lie to her mom when in the past they had been so close. But in the past five years everything has changed, mostly because Eileen needed to change but her mother wanted her to stay the same, to dress her up and show her off at parties, drag her down to Hilton Head in the summers and Orlando in the winters when all Eileen wanted to be was Eileen, and she wasn't even sure who that was anymore.

She curls up on the bed into a little ball, the sound of the maid leaking through the walls as she vacuums the room next door. Sometimes Eileen thinks of Don, her old boyfriend of two years, but most of the time she doesn't or else stops herself when she thinks of it too much. Surely he's been wondering. Surely he's like her parents, wondering when she's coming back.

If ever . . .

A cold breeze brushes across her rosy cheeks. It's a slightly overcast day, and Eileen searches for the sun behind the gray clouds, but rather than a blanket of light, there is a waterfall of rays streaking out of the sky.

She steps outside her cluttered hotel room, locks the door, and heads into town.

She hikes perpendicular to the freeway for a few blocks, passing some closed factories and assorted businesses. She passes the Kline Steel Mill, which looks like a giant skeleton, most of its windows broken, abandoned machinery everywhere. A giant crane with a small glass bubble at the stem where a worker once sat is now overgrown with weeds.

Lining a side street is a row of dilapidated houses that look more like storage sheds than anything else; houses, maybe, for lawn mowers and tools but not for humans. As Eileen passes them, each one more broken down and dirty than the next, she creeps onto the lawn, heading toward the door. She does this only to explore, thinking the houses are empty, that surely nothing inside could be alive except perhaps mildew and spiders. But every time she is more sure than she was the last time that the shack is empty or condemned or just plain deserted, she spots a candle in the corner shining meekly through a dirty, broken screen door, or else a row of white teeth set deep in a black head, smiling from a rocker on the stoop.

As she turns another corner she stumbles upon the Sacred Faith Baptist Church of Kitty. Standing on the front lawn is one of those portable displays that has removable letters and looks like part of a movie marquee. It reads CAN ONE BE CURED OF HOMSEXUALNESS? The church is a small, white clapboard building. The paint is chipping, and the two simple black wooden crosses that flank the tall, thin doors are just coarse, knobby, ordinary pieces of wood nailed together.

She walks farther down the road, turning right on another street, away from the freeway and toward town. The houses are improving in condition but are still old. They would be amazing today if they had been kept up, but even these nicer, Victorian and southern Gothic homes look practically haunted with rusting hinges holding up ramshackle shutters that hang at weird angles. A few older women and men, here mostly Caucasian, sit on porches, talking to neighbors, conversing with the mailman, trading recipes and gossip. So this is Kitty.

The downtown section is sparsely populated although it seems to have been overcrowded with businesses at one point. For

every two stores open there is one closed, and a parking struc-
ture built in some optimistic growth spurt of the '60s now holds
nothing but dust and empty space, the sleek cars it was supposed
to hold being driven around other cities in the Southeast.

There are a few small clothing stores, a record store, a thrift
store, a few furniture shops, and what looks like an old department store, except that black streaks of charcoal swirl out of
shattered windows, revealing a burnt-out core. A smattering of
nice restaurants and a flood of not so nice ones plug in the
spaces between the various mom-and-pop video, drug, and grocery stores, while the side roads lead off to even more lanes
overstuffed with fifty-year-old tract houses.

On the corner, at the top of a steep hill, is a place called The
Novel Idea Cafe and Bookstore. Over the double doors is a large
sign, a Tennielesque illustration of a few stacked books atop
which is a steaming teacup. From the sidewalk Eileen can see
a large room, walls overflowing with books. In the center are
couches and chairs, none matching the decor and most of them
occupied. So far, Eileen decides, this is obviously the only cool
place in this little town to hang out.

As soon as she walks in, the strong odor of coffee beans and
old books (never a palatable combination) envelops her. She
circles the bookshelves before sitting down, finding a decent
collection of first-edition hardbacks and the usual assortment of
remainders mixed with an eclectic array of well-worn paperbacks.

"What can I get for you?" a guy behind the counter asks.

"Um, an iced mocha."

As he's fixing her drink, Eileen looks over the crowd. There
are a few couples, a few small groups of friends, two guys playing chess in the corner, and more than a few individuals sitting
alone, some reading books or writing feverishly in journals. Eileen takes a seat at the large oak counter.

"Is . . . something wrong?" the guy says, sliding Eileen her
drink as she passes him a five-dollar bill.

"Why? Does it look like something's wrong?" It comes out
sounding incredibly snide.

"No, you're not in disarray or anything." He puts her change
on the counter. "But you seem, well, preoccupied."

"Yeah, it's a . . ." The weight begins to lift with only the slightest prospect of telling her problems to someone. But Eileen quickly decides against sharing too much too soon, a combination that has proved ruinous in the past. "A long story, that's what it is."

"Just trying to help."

Eileen takes a sip of the mocha, which is thick, sweet, delicious.

"I thought it was bartenders who listened to people's problems, not the guys who ran the espresso machine. I mean, people don't cry into their café au lait, they just sit there beside it and write bad poetry or pretend to be reading *Gravity's Rainbow*."

"Actually," he whispers, smiling, "I'm Thomas Pynchon."

She smiles.

"Well, to be honest, the name's Jessup." He offers his hand. "But you can call me Jess."

"Nice to meet you, uh, Jess." She stifles the temptation to laugh at the name Jessup. "My name's Eileen."

"So, Eileen, what else can I get you?"

"Actually, I need a place to live. And a job. And a new car." The list could have gone on, but she spares him.

Jess runs out from the bar, dashes across the room, and returns with a sign from the window that Eileen hadn't seen when she walked in. He sets it on the bar in front of her. PART TIME HELP WANTED.

"Well—" she bashfully smiles—"one out of three ain't bad."

5

Even though the rush of a few hours ago has thinned out and the restaurant's not crowded, Dave is still trapped in the weeds. Dan's decision to cut everyone except Dave and Bill may look good on paper and certainly keeps costs down, but it does nothing for the sweat dripping off Dave's forehead and onto the menus of the customers whose orders he's taking.

"Well, I hope you're hungry!" Dave expertly balances his large tray filled with food and drinks with one hand while the other flips open a tray caddy with the jerk of his wrist. At least that's what's supposed to happen. "Heh, heh." He tries to lighten the moment even though it's sinking fast. He jerks again with his wrist, giving it a slight twist, shaking it, anything. Finally he just tosses the trayjack aside and sets the overflowing tray onto a table filled with dirty dishes. The uneven surface sets the dishes at a slant; a tide of tartar sauce rises to the lip of the soufflé cup, melted butter drips from the plates onto the cork surface of the tray.

"Okay, sir, you had the blackened catfish." Dave puts the dish before the frowning man. "And you, ma'am, had the broiled swordfish."

"No, I had the broiled catfish," the man announces.

"And I . . ." But before she finishes her sentence Dave knows what's going to follow.

"The blackened swordfish? Yeah, um, okay . . ." Short of shoving the food into their mouths, Dave realizes his choices are decidedly limited. "Give me ten minutes, okay?"

The older couple scrutinizes Dave for a few seconds before accepting the offer.

"Great." Dave whisks away their plates and heads for the kitchen. Once inside he dumps the food in the garbage and then examines his order ticket, now impaled on an aluminum spike along with all of Bill's, and sees that he had written down the order correctly. But like a rumor that gets twisted as it passes from lips to lips, from his ticket to the line cook, something had changed.

"Uh, 'scuse me, Stoner?"

Stoner, wearing headphones, is rustling something up in a pan, his hips swaying to the radio beat.

"Stoner!" Dave yells, pounding on the metal counter.

"What!" Stoner shrieks, annoyed.

"Will you look at this order? You just gave me a broiled sword and a blackened cat." Dave tosses the ticket toward the window where, instead of being intercepted by Stoner, it falls into a vat of sour cream. "I need the opposite, on the fly. Now I'm dragging a whole goddamn table!"

"Sorry, man. Didn't you read the board?" The headphones lie

around his neck like a choker, his body still vibrating to the tune.
"Eighty-six sword."

"What?"

"Yeah, man. Just ran out. In fact, I gave *you* the last piece."

Dave stands there, gravely looking toward the large tub of
half-eaten food and scraps, atop which sits the order he dumped
just a few seconds ago. *Just a few seconds* . . . the words are rever-
berating through his head like a mantra. *A few seconds* . . . This
is quickly replaced by *Who would know?*

Dave goes over to the trash and begins skimming one of the
fillets off the top of the heap when a busboy barges through the
double doors and empties his tub of water and bits of food into
the can.

"Thanks, Jose," Dave mutters on his way out of the alley.

"There he is!" the woman exclaims as Dave reenters the room.

"Uh, sir, ma'am, I have a bit of bad news . . ."

The couple looks as if they're receiving the diagnosis of their
only child who has been the victim of some macabre accident.
Their mouths are open, their gazes are motionless, stupefied
with the notion, just the mere possibility: *Dinner is not on the way?*

"Dave?" a voice asks from a booth behind and to the left.

Dave turns around.

"Is that you?"

"Tim?"

"Yeah, how ya doing?" His old college buddy is sitting alone
save for the seafood platter and three empty beer bottles.

"Excuse me, sir!" the old man interrupts. "What about our
meal?"

"Look"—Tim leans forward and whispers—"I'm in town for
a few days. Let's have a drink later. Talk."

"Sounds perfect. Meet me at the, uh, old hangout. Around
midnight?"

Tim nods and turns back to his food, and Dave turns to his
predicament.

"Um." Dave gets on his knees and puts his arms around the
couple's shoulders, who wince in his grasp. "You see, it's like
this . . ."

6

Craig blares the stereo. Vomit Launch's "Hence the Box" tears out of the speaker like a convict hellbent on escaping. Seconds later Ashley storms into the room with a pencil behind her left ear and an unhappy look on her face.

"Just what in the fuck do you think you're doing?"

Craig undoes the top button of his shirt, slips a finger inside the knot of his tie, and yanks it down a couple of notches.

"Writing to the Bridget Cross fan club, what's it look like?"

Ashley plants her hands on her hips, her bottom lip sticking out, her feet perpendicular to her shoulders: attack mode.

"It looks to me like you're being wildly insensitive. You know I have finals all week, three papers due, and—"

Craig plants his arms on Ashley's forearms and pulls her in close.

"Look, I've had a long day and I'm just trying to relax. I want to hear a few songs, maybe smoke a few cigarettes, watch a few episodes of 'The Young Ones,' and then go to sleep. Does that sound okay to you?"

As the song ends and there are a few seconds of silence before the next one begins, the moment seems frozen in time. Ashley stares into Craig's raccoon eyes, and Craig sees a weary image of himself in Ashley's scuffed-up cat's-eye glasses. Sometimes when she has her glasses on and her hair is up she looks like a completely different person. Craig loves this and has encouraged her to wear the glasses and to try new hairstyles, always with some bullshit excuse like "You need a new look" or "With all that studying, you'd better wear your glasses more." The truth is that Craig likes to play the game that he is living with a new and exciting woman, not Ashley, whom he has known for almost four years. Now her body, mind, and tempers are as familiar to him as a favorite song that he used to hum all the time but now slowly wonders why he liked in the first place.

Sometimes Craig seduces Ashley when she is studying, when he's sure she'll be wearing her glasses and her hair will be up in a utilitarian fashion. He'll begin by kissing her quickly, overtaking her with emotion until the last thing on her mind is her glasses and she won't want to stop everything to let her hair down and put her glasses on the end table.

Craig stares at Ashley and silently whispers names to himself: Amanda, Judy, Shade, Paula, Yvonne—any name that this mystery woman might be. Craig dreams of all the places this mystery woman might take him.

The CD begins playing the next song, and Craig loses his thoughts in the shimmering guitar and frenetic drum playing. The female's vocals come oozing through the speakers, and Craig wonders what Trish is like, wonders where she would take him.

"This is just so fucking typical of you. You come home complaining about your job and how hard you work." Ashley wrestles herself free and stomps toward the couch where Craig has just sat down. "Like you're the only one who has a job? What do you think I do all day? I've been working my ass off for the past month trying to get these term papers in order, and all you can do is complain about your own damn job. Like selling that shit to people on the phone was brain surgery."

"Well, maybe if I was going back to school for even more bullshit, I wouldn't have to have such a menial fucking job." Craig pulls off his tie as if it were a rip cord, as if he were falling and needed to be caught.

"Oh, now we're going to start that again, huh? About how I just think I'm so much smarter than you. How I should date someone who's my—let me see, what was your word? Equal?"

"Yeah, someone like Andrew," Craig spits out the name like it was a piece of moldy food.

Ashley throws her hands toward the exposed wooden beams of the apartment. "He's just a friend. Why can't you get that through your head? We study together. There's nothing there. I love you, don't you know that?"

The music ends again, leaving the room cocooned in an uneasy silence. Craig gets up and begins scouring his CD rack.

"Where's the Unrest CD?"

"Craig, I love you. Aren't you listening to me?"

"Yeah, yeah. Now where's the goddamn Unrest CD?"

Ashley backs into a corner and bites what's left of her right thumbnail.

"Which one?"

"What do you mean, which one? My favorite, the one I've been playing all week." His girlfriend stands there, motionless. "Ashley?"

"I hid it."

"What?"

"Well, you were up till three last night swigging from that bottle of zinfandel and listening to that damn CD, so I just . . . hid it."

Craig can't believe his ears. He's already burned out one import LP version of *Imperial f.f.r.r.,* has lent out the seven-inch singles of "Yes, She Is My Skinhead Girl" and "Bavarian Mods" to a friend, who hasn't returned them. And now this.

"Where?"

Ashley continues backing up but runs out of space.

"That's just it, you see. I don't know. I mean, I did it this morning when you were pulling out of the driveway shouting *Suki, Suki* over and over. But then later I knew it was a stupid thing to do and tried to get it back but forgot where I put it. I swear I looked for it for an hour but gave up. But . . . it's got to be here somewhere."

Craig walks over to the fridge, slowly, and takes out the bottle of wine which now has about four good swigs left, maybe enough for two or three songs if he nurses it.

"I'm really sorry," Ashley whispers.

"Yeah," Craig says as he puts the bottle back, grabs his jacket and heads for the door. "Me, too."

Craig's been to all the decent record stores in Kitty looking for the Unrest CD, but none have it in stock, and a few don't even know who the hell he is talking about. There's only one store left, the Record Rack, the hairy chain in the mall that charges sixteen dollars for Pearl Jam's *Ten* and still keeps it in the New Releases bin even though it came out ages ago, as if some sailor is going to wander in after being out to sea for two years and be all, "Whoa! When did *this* come out?" and plunk down a twenty and not even wait for the change.

Craig pulls into the mall, the garish lights of the parking garage causing his pupils to dilate. He locks the door, knowing it is hopeless, knowing there's no chance in hell, but he feels he must somehow see the day to its logical and disappointing conclusion.

"Hi, um, do you have . . ." Craig begins the little speech he has delivered at the previous record stores. The girl behind the counter looks young, cute; her hair is up in a sort of forties fashion with a number of long burgundy strands flowing down around her ears. "Unrest's *Imperial f.f.r.r.* on CD?" He feels stupid saying the title because he's not really sure what it means. Usually he left out the '*f.f.r.r.*' part, thinking it was some sort of odd in-joke Mark Robinson had put there to confuse everyone, but this time he throws in the whole title in case the girl has to look it up on the computer that's off to her right. Craig's biggest fear (and this pertains not only to the Unrest CD) is that pretty much everything has a real and special significance but that he can't figure out what it is and so is missing out on quite a lot.

"No, we don't."

Direct hit.

"But I wish we did. It's a great record. My old boyfriend had it. In fact, he knew a girl whose sister was dating the drummer, I think. She goes to school in South Carolina now, don't ask me why."

"Really?" Craig's interest is piqued. He moves in, leaning one elbow on the red plastic counter. Michael Bolton is blaring out of the speakers.

"How can we be lovers if we can't be friends?"

"Yeah," she continues. "Pissed me off when we broke up and he took the CD, even though I think it was his anyway. I saw Unrest once, with Tsunami and Kicking Giant up in New York."

"You know that they're from Arlington, don't you?"

"I thought D.C."

"Oh, whatever. By the way, my name's Craig."

"Charmed. My name's Brook." She twists a long strand of hair around a finger and begins curling it, staring at the ceiling.

Craig stands there, unable to think of anything to say.

"Listen, I get off in a few minutes and I live right around the corner if you want to come over and"—another twist—"listen to some records."

"I'll wait for you outside," Craig blurts out.

Once outside he begins pacing up and down the sidewalk. People passing by give him queer glances, wondering what he's doing milling around in front of the mall. He feels the need to explain it to people, but explain what? *"Hi, My name's Craig, and I'm waiting for a beautiful young girl to get off work so we can go to her apartment, even though I already live with someone."* Just thinking about it all makes him realize how crazy it is, how he should just go home, apologize to Ashley, and climb into bed beside her. As he's turning to leave, Brook approaches him and slides her arm inside his.

"No, it's this way." She turns him around on the sidewalk and leads him away from the parking lot.

Brook's apartment is nothing more than a futon, hot plate, and record player stacked on a broken old mini-fridge with a bunch of records kept inside. A few assorted knickknacks pull the room mercifully back from the edge of depressing, like a strange black sculpture in one corner, a cheap lamp with a Mondrian ripoff shade in another. On one wall is a large collage of photos. Craig spots a wedding, a prom, and many smiling faces but no Brook.

"These your friends?"

"No, it was here when I moved in. It keeps me from feeling lonely."

Her record collection is large and pretty impressive. She's a member of the Sub Pop Singles of the Month Club and has a healthy amount of new seven-inch singles, including one by Polvo he didn't even know had come out.

"If you're this into cool music," Craig says as he scoots next to her on the futon, "how come you work at that gross chain store?"

"I know, it's a drag"—Brook kicks off her blue eight-eyelet Doc Martens—"but it pays more. The manager's a real asshole, always coming on to me and saying how eccentric he thinks I am, but I know he thinks I'm a nut."

"When you're rich you're eccentric, when you're poor you're just crazy."

"Yeah." Brook laughs, puts on a record, and then swings her legs onto Craig's lap. The music finds all corners of the small room, occupying the space almost like another person, turning their almost embarrassing encounter into a ménage à trois.

"You can never give the finger to the blind . . ."

Craig leans back, feeling the soft underside of Brook's thighs atop his lap. He begins thinking of her face, her body, her body with no clothes on, her body with no face.

"Do you like me?" Brook asks, staring into a dark corner of the room.

"Uh, sure," Craig fumbles, trying hard not to blow it even though he's thinking, *Hell, kid, if you've gotten this far . . .* "Of course I like you. Why do you ask?"

Brook contemplates the question for a second, shifting her weight on Craig's bony lap.

"I just want to make sure you like me, is all," Brook says, almost pouting. She gets up, grinding her hipbone into Craig's. Crossing the room to the window, with her back to Craig, she kicks one of her boots out of the way.

The large pane of glass is drawn and quartered by painted black wood that matches the trim around the door, closet, and crown molding. Two feet outside Brook's window is another, more elaborate apartment building. Her window directly faces another, like two eyes locked in a staring match. In the apartment across the way a family is getting ready for bed. A dark, slightly ethnic-looking woman pats two small children on the head and escorts them out of the room while a tall man in an undershirt yawns and scratches his belly before extinguishing the lights.

"You live alone?" Brook asks in a queer tone.

"N-n-no," Craig stutters, shaken out of the song he is concentrating on.

"You know I try to please ya, you're under anesthesia . . ."

"Roommate," he adds.

"Lucky." Brook's finger makes lines in a patch of fog left on the glass by her warm breath. "You know, living alone—" she

stops for a second—"in a small place like this—" She leans into
the glass, peering into the house next to hers, trying to soak up
something of their lives. "Sometimes I come home to this little
apartment and I . . . want to scream, I get so lonely." She begins
to tell him about the late-night phone calls to strangers, of cor-
nering people in the middle of the night into conversations, no
matter how short or inane, just to hear someone's voice. But she
suddenly stops, not wanting to scare him off.

She moves from the window back into Craig's arms. After
kissing for a few minutes, Brook pulls away and whispers in his
ear: "Why don't you give me a hand with this?" They both get
up and fold down the mattress of the futon, turning the couch
into a bed. "That's better."

They lie down and resume kissing. Little bursts of excitement
race through Craig's body like electric shocks. Her lips are thin
and soft, different from Ashley's. He is trying to gauge Brook's
kissing style. Ashley uses her tongue a lot, whereas Brook keeps
opening her lips in small gasps with short visits from the tip of
her tongue in between. Craig, having grown complacent, is trying to relearn this old behavior.

Brook's breath is bad, reeking of a taco she must have eaten
earlier at the mall's food court. Craig remembers Ashley earlier
in the night with her glasses on and hair up, how she looked like
someone else. He opens his eyes a little and sees Brook's nostrils
flaring, the edge of her tongue darting into his mouth. He can
see her burgundy hair still up, soft strands of it lightly whipping
his cheeks as they rock back and forth.

"Something tells me we're going to need this." Brook stops
kissing long enough to produce a condom, from Craig doesn't
know where.

Afterward, Craig drives back to his apartment numb, worried,
and still a little pissed off that he doesn't have his CD. As he's
fishing around in his pockets for a breath mint, he comes across
a Record Rack receipt with Brook's phone number on it. He
crumples it into a ball and tosses it out the window.

His apartment is covered in shadows. At first he thinks Ashley
has gone out, until he hears a rumbling in the bedroom.

"Oh, it's you." She stumbles out of the room. She tucks in a
corner of her shirt and puts on her glasses. "Andrew is here and
we're, uh, studying."

"Good for you," Craig replies.

Ashley stands there waiting for Craig to say something while Craig waits for Ashley to give up and go back in the room.

"You're such an asshole," Ashley mutters as she reteats.

As Craig tries to slip between the couch and the end table, he knocks over a huge pile of magazines and bills. "Aw, shit." After picking up the pile and throwing it on the couch he notices a silver glare coming from the corner of a jewel box half-shoved under the couch. He pulls it out. It's the Unrest CD.

He slips it in and presses PLAY.

7

Dave pulls up to the bar with mixed feelings of dread and nostalgia. He's been avoiding his old high school hangout ever since he came back to Kitty; not that it was easy to steer clear of anything in a town this small, but Dave would raise a flat palm to the side of his head every time he drove by, narrowing his vision like a horse wearing blinders. Seeing it now brings back memories of fake IDs, puking in the parking lot, drawing straws to see what girls he and his friends would try to lay that night, usually without success.

Years later Tim, who seemed so funny to Dave in high school, seemed dim under the illumination of college. Not that this was necessarily Tim's fault. At a time when Dave's concept of what was interesting was expanding beyond the realm of fart impersonations via armpits and the ability to burp on cue, he found himself spending less and less time with his old high school chum. And yet, as much as Dave ridiculed Tim for being simple if not, at times, downright stupid, somewhere in Tim's cluttered bachelor pad, amid the neon Budweiser sign, Playboy pinups, and framed Nagel prints, was a college diploma—while Dave, for all his supposed erudition, had run away from UVA.

As Dave pries himself out of his blue '79 Honda Civic he stops for a moment, his legs sore, his back aching from pulling yet another split shift. His pockets, usually bulging, especially after working both lunch and dinner, are as light and airy as birds' nests, jingling with a coin foundation.

"There he is! There he is," Tim shouts as Dave enters.

"Yeah, sorry I'm late, but I had extra side work tonight." Dave props himself up on a stool. "Rolling my silverware took forever."

"What?" Tim is laughing at Dave's pedestrian occupational tasks. "I thought they hired some retards to roll the silverware. Wasn't it set up by the mayor's office or something?" He takes the last swig of a beer, orders another.

"Uh, they did for a while. Then something happened, I don't know. I never got a straight answer. Last thing I heard was spoons began disappearing. Anyway, now it's back on our shoulders."

"So when the retards can't cut the mustard, they call on you?" Tim slaps Dave's back. "That's some corporate ladder you're on, Davy boy. I'd say in the pyramidal scheme of things you're, well, those things had basements, didn't they?"

Dave glumly orders a beer. This isn't what he needed tonight. If he had wanted to feel bad, he would have gone over to Stacy's house and watched *What About Bob?* for the umpteenth time and listened to her drone on about the injustice of giving Richard Dreyfuss just as much screen time as "Bill."

"Man, can you believe this place?" Tim is looking around the room, which is empty save for the bartender, Dave, Tim, and a couple slow-dancing to the jukebox. "They haven't recovered a bar stool or added a lick of paint in seven years. It looks exactly the same."

"What? You haven't been here lately?"

"Are you kidding? Who has the time? I've been interning with Senator Johnson for the past couple of summers. Before that I had that job up in New York, remember?"

"Yeah, I guess." Dave is rummaging through his memory the way one pulls everything out of a closet looking for a matching sneaker. "Now that you mention it, sure I do," he lies.

"I don't get back to Kitty much. I'm here now only to visit my mom who's not feeling well." He shoves a handful of peanuts into his mouth.

Tim stops for a second, sipping his beer. The song on the jukebox ends, and the couple stands around awkwardly for a few seconds, waiting for another to begin. Dave looks around the room: the half-dozen barstools, a few tables with laminated menus, a dart board in one corner, a few video poker machines in the other and an Are You a Good Lover? video game.

"Dave, whatever happened to you?" Tim asks out of the blue.

"What?" Dave chokes on a gulp of beer.

"Aw, come on, you know what I'm talking about. In school it was you who was getting the good grades, not me. You had all the chicks, the friends, knew what to say at a party. When we'd go to a kegger, I'd just sit back and watch you from across the room."

"Tim, it's too late for this shit."

"No, listen to me. I'd just watch people, guys and girls. You'd wink and be clever to the girls, maybe get a phone number or a place to spend the night. For the guys you'd pull some obscure reference out of your hat, like you knew exactly what they wanted to hear. You were going to be a journalist, a writer, and now . . . well, fuck, I don't even know what you're doing."

"Well, you know . . . I've got this record label."

"How much money do you make off that shit you sell?"

"Not much. But that's not the point. If it weren't for the independent record labels, music in this country would—"

"Oh, please. Save that shit for your Greenpeace friends. So if you're not making any money off that, that means you're a waiter. And the Whales Fin? Jesus Christ." Tim smacks the bar. "Do you remember when we'd go there after football games and make fun of the assholes they had working there? Huh? We left their tips at the bottom of a water glass or stuffed a buck in a crab claw and made them pry it out."

"Yeah, yeah, Tim, that's great. And do you want to know something? We were fucking assholes." Dave's voice is rising. "We were seventeen then. We thought that kind of crap was funny. Now we know better."

"You knew better then, too, Rowland. Like you know better now." Tim points at the spots of cocktail sauce on Dave's shirt, the worn cuffs. "Better than that."

"This is fine, it's honest, it's—"

"Yeah, but what I'm saying is, don't you want anything better?"

"I'm working on a few things. These things take time, and I know that I'm—"

"Please, Dave. Knock off the excuses." Tim gets in close. "I want to know because you used to be my friend. What in the world happened to you? Why'd you leave school like that? I asked your old roommate Pete, and he was as clueless as I was. He said he came home from spring break and all your shit was gone and there was this note, if that's what you'd call it, that said, 'Had to go. Sorry.' Like you were out taking a piss or something."

Dave is trying to block the words out of his head, concentrating instead on "Free Bird" as it lumbers out of the tinny jukebox speaker and the couple try to slow-dance to the epic Van Sandt guitar solo.

"Dave? Hello?"

Free bird.

Two girls enter the bar and take stools a few feet away from Dave and Tim.

Are you a good lover?

"Well, looky here." Tim relents for a moment. "Maybe this evening won't be a total bust." He raises his voice. "Uh, girls, care to join us?"

"No, Tim, don't," Dave pleads, but it's too late. The girls separate like a cell in mitosis, one drifting to each of their sides.

They look like they're probably still in high school. Dave thinks how sad this is, remembering when he used to see older kids in this hole in the wall, wondering why they didn't drive up to Charlottesville where the action is. What were they doing in Kitty? Why were they settling? Five years later, instead of knowing why, he shrugs it off as a stupid question.

"My name's Cherry," says the one Tim already has his arm around. "That's Cindy."

"Cherry and Cindy, huh? C and C?" Tim jokes. "Like C + C Music Factory?"

The three of them break into laughter, but Dave wants to puke.

"What do you say," Tim, on a roll, continues, "we all go somewhere and make some music? If you know what I mean."

"Sounds good to me," Cherry says, chewing on a piece of hair. Cindy nods in approval.

The four of them pile in Tim's car and head off into the night.

Are you a free bird?

Cindy and Dave are walking through a field on the outskirts of town. The whole area is an abandoned farm that has been deserted for years. Dave remembers coming here in high school, making doughnuts with a friend's Bronco at five o'clock in the morning, whipping fertile soil high into the air. This is where Tim, battling a near fatal bout of nostalgia, has taken them, promptly disappearing into a barn with Cherry, leaving Cindy and Dave alone.

"Nice night," Cindy says. "Don't you think?"

Dave, wrapped up in his own problems, doesn't answer.

Cindy ignores him, keeps on walking, Dave sheepish by her side.

God, this guy is creepy, she is thinking. *But cute.*

The night is clear, and the almost full moon illuminates the plain before them sharply, the outline of an old tractor looming fifty yards ahead. Cindy is hugging herself to keep warm, running her hands over her exposed shoulders. Long fingers twist her brown hair into a bun, which stays in place for a few strides before falling apart.

"So what do you do?" she asks.

"Oh, I run a record label. I mean, I'm a waiter."

"Really? Where?"

"The, er, Whales Fin."

"Yeah!" She snaps her fingers. "I've been there before. My friends and I go there after games sometimes. I think I've seen you."

"Do you remember when we'd go there after football games and make fun of the assholes they had working there?" Dave hears Tim's words in his head.

"You don't say," he replies meekly, kicking at the ground.

Why do I feel so old? Why does a few years into my twenties already seem too late? This girl, who's a junior at most, is the future while I'm just in the way. No, that's not true. I'm the one they make fun of. At this point I'm essential fodder for their transformations. Am I just unwilling to play the part that others have played for me? Does that mean a few years from now Cindy will get a job at the Whales Fin and will be laughed at by a new breed of Kitty High snots? I'd like to think there is more to all of this than me just being a bad sport. Are the kids all better looking than when I was in high school? Why is it no one ever addresses that? Why isn't that on the front page of the Courier? *Are they getting away with more than we ever did? And if so, and at this rate of progression, when my kids attend school, what will be left? Everything up to your twenties is like a plane climbing through the air, taking off at birth and steadily climbing. From there you level off and cruise for the next few decades until you begin your descent. A number of scenes appear in my mind: faulty equipment, air pockets, someone shooting me out of the sky. The truth is, I just don't want to level off. I'm just jealous of this girl—what she has ahead of her and what I have only behind me. God, could I be that big an asshole? Cindy reaches out and grabs my hand, clutching it tightly, like I was her prom date or something. Sorry, Cindy, I don't think so.*

"Let's stop for a second," she says, pulling Dave aside.

"Look, we can't—"

"Shhh." She wraps her arms around him and leans against a tree. A cool breeze rushes between them. "Keep me warm."

"Hey, how old are you?"

"Old enough." She buries her head in his chest.

Give me a fucking break.

"Cindy, I shouldn't be doing this for a myriad of reasons."

She unbuckles his belt and slips a hand inside his pants.

"Cindy, I mean it." Dave pulls on her hand, now caught in the various flaps of his briefs. "I mean, you don't even know me."

"Yes, I do. You're Dale."

"Dave!"

She snakes her hand over his chest.

"Dale." She kisses his neck. "Don." Nibbling an earlobe. "Dan." Biting his lower lip. "What's the difference?"

"The difference is . . ." He pulls her off him. Faces are flashing from high school. Girls Tim and Dave brought here and made out with on nights much like this one. What exactly were their names? What's the difference? "I don't know what the difference is, it's just I'm not good at this anymore."

"How do you know? We haven't even started."

She stretches her hand out to caress Dave's cheek, but he pushes it away.

"Look, why in the hell are you attracted to me anyway?"

"Who says I was attracted?" Cindy says matter-of-factly. "It's more of a boredom-type thing."

" 'Boredom-type thing?' Wasn't that a fucking song by the Stone Temple Jerkoffs? I mean, that's real flattering." He laughs. "You really know how to make a guy feel good. You know, I saw a crazed drifter on the highway a few miles back. I'll bet he's free for the next few hours."

"Oh, stop being such a kidder."

She grabs Dave again, but for some reason the machinery's not working. What used to be an often-run subroutine is getting jammed with a syntax error only a few steps into the command. RUN, Dave is typing. RUN. LIST, SAVE, LOAD, ANYTHING! God, this is so BASIC, but he cannot get into it. *This is a kid*, he's thinking. *Barely sixteen, seventeen at most. This isn't sexy, it's sad.*

"Why won't it get hard?"

"Cindy, stop. Come on, let's go back to the car."

She rotates her shoulders in a why-not motion, and they start heading back to Tim's Iroc.

"Hey." She stops in her tracks. "If I give you some money this weekend, will you buy beer for me?"

Don't You Fugazaboutme

1

"Lick my legs of desire, lick my legs I'm on fire, lick my legs of desire!" Breathy, slightly raspy, as if he's gasping for air. His cheeks suck in as if in a bad fish impression, dancing around the room, wheezing out a song: *"Lick my legs I'm on fire! Lick my legs of desire! Lick my legs . . ."*

Life can play tricks. Unfortunately they were rarely of the "hey, how'd you do that?" variety.

This is what Chipp is thinking as he lies on the couch watching his roommate dance around the room belting out PJ Harvey lyrics. The look on Randy's face as he goes from the fridge to the cabinet, pours cereal in a bowl, and then searches for a clean spoon (there isn't one, so he uses a fork) is pure elation. He keeps singing these two lines of a song from his current favorite record of all time, skipping around the apartment delirious in victory.

For the past couple of days it's been nothing but *Godfuck* this, *Godfuck* that, his plans for their zine growing wildly beyond anything they'd ever discussed: T-shirts, flexis, sponsoring local shows, Jane's Addiction re-forming for one time only as a fundraiser for *Godfuck*. Randy was planning on world domination by the third issue.

"And once our distribution in Europe is finalized, we'll look into the Third World countries. And, hey, thank God the Iron Curtain came down, eh?"

"Randy, will you hold it for a second?" Chipp finally blurts out.

"What?" Randy's already large eyes are magnified from the thick lenses in his horn-rimmed glasses, his nearly white blond hair is shorter than usual. He tugs at the fraying collar of his Le Tigré polo shirt. "Hold what?"

"This crap you're talking about. I mean, we haven't even put out the first issue, and you're planning the next ten."

Randy ignores him and continues singing, *"Lick my legs of desire! Lick my legs I'm on fire!"*

"Will you shut up for a second and answer me?"

"Yeah, well," Randy finally says, "it helps to plan ahead. That way we won't be, uh, under the gun for ideas."

"Ideas?" Chipp says slowly. He points to an ottoman (a stolen upside-down orange crate) that is covered with scraps of paper, legal pads, candy wrappers, club flyers, fast-food receipts, all covered in Randy's unintelligible scrawl and each one an *idea*. "Don't you think it's time to pick a few of these stellar ideas and put them in an issue?"

Randy looks at Chipp as an epiphany slowly spreads through his body. He reaches for the pile of torn paper like an alcoholic reaching for help.

For the next few hours they hammer out the rough contents of the first issue of *Godfuck*, which will consist of a few band interviews, record reviews, a rant here and there, and whatever classified ads they get. Chipp fights tooth and nail against Randy's insipid Open Poetry Forum idea, wherein any slob in town could send in what resembles a poem and have it printed, free of "objective editorial opinion and hassle," as Randy had grandiosely stated on the flyers he posted all over town. After they received the first submission, which Chipp stopped reading after the first line ("Were you really having fun that night or just trying to convince yourself?"), he put down his Converse All Star and said, "No more." Randy sheepishly concurred, although the fact that they received nary another submission proved Chipp's case an easy one to uphold.

The more *Godfuck* begins to take shape, the more apparent it becomes to Chipp that Randy is awash with the joy of creation, even if it is just their measly little zine. Da Vinci, Van Gogh, Michelangelo, like it or not, he is now joined irreparably with them. In Randy's mind, they were watching; it was his move.

He has this idiotic grin on his face, mumbling through a smile, *"Lick my legs . . ."* After drifting from job to job, girl to girl, and especially from ideology to ideology and band to band (which sort of seemed like the same thing these days), Randy felt more and more disconnected—from Chipp, from his other friends, from what he was told to think he was. Whenever Chipp and Randy got drunk, Randy would open up and talk about his family history, which was a tad less convoluted than Poe's. He told Chipp once about this uncle that, two years after Randy had been kicked out of the University of Virginia, still asked, "How's school?" His parents always grinned and urged him to play along, no sense in making trouble.

"Now," Chipp announces, going down the to-do list, "it says here 'Distribution: Randy.' Well?"

"Uh, yeah, er . . ."

"Well, what? Did you take the dummy copy around?" Chipp picks up the rough draft cover of *Godfuck,* its splashy logo comprised of the title made up of bits of bone, trash, spit, and recognizable body parts.

"Yes, yes, I did," Randy says quickly, as if on trial.

"And what did they say?"

"Let's see. The restaurants I took it to said it was going to make the customers sick, and most of the record stores said it would . . . scare children."

"That's ridiculous! When's the last time you saw an eight-year-old reading *Profane Existence?*"

"Even Jess at the cafe told me it would give him nightmares."
Chipp shrugs.

"So what does this mean?"

"It means no one wants to touch the goddamn thing!"

It finally hits Chipp that Randy's been close-mouthed all day about the reaction he was getting at stores. Chipp suspected it was because he was hoping to be spared another one of Chipp's I-told-you-so speeches that he seemed to run as often as the Capitol Cinema showed *Taxi Driver.*

"Look, fuck the restaurants. That's not a big deal. When you and I conceived of the project, we both decided that there were really only a few essential places that needed to be hit, right? Like The Scene, The Novel Idea, DISContent, and the junior college campus. I mean, Jesus, those are the only places the cool kids hang out." Chipp's tone turns somber. "But if we can't put it anywhere, then we're seriously screwed."

"Maybe we shouldn't have named the thing *Godfuck*," Randy says under his breath.

"Oh, no you don't!" Chipp shouts. "You don't start that shit now! The time to think about how stupid this name is was back when you wrote the fucking thing down on the potential names list, not after I went to the post office and stood in a gigantic line to get a P.O. box. And then that old lady called at me from across the room 'What was that name again?' And I had to pipe up in front of thirty-five old people, '*Godfuck*, ma'am!' Shit, they looked at me like I was Satan. Remember when the mailman wouldn't even deliver *Maximum Rock and Roll* last month because the word *Fistfucker* was printed on the cover?" He starts laughing. "Jesus Christ, I hate small towns. It's a good thing we're Xeroxing this thing ourselves because I doubt there's a printer in town who would touch it without thinking his fingers would fall off. So it's too late now, bub. For better or worse, it is *Godfuck*."

"Okay, okay," Randy says, pouting.

Chipp doesn't care, Chipp figures, let him pout. After all, it was Randy's idea to have this brash, punk rock name, and now he's receding from the idea like the tide of pudding from the rim of the bowl left in the fridge for a month.

"What's next?" Randy heaves an epic sigh that Chipp barrels past.

"Um, 'Band Interviews: Chipp.' Oh, that's me."

"Come on, cough 'em up. Where are they? I want to see one. 'Stephanie Seargent Speaks!' Or maybe, 'The Last Words of Charlie Ondras!' Let's go, come on!"

"I haven't gotten to them yet, but I did borrow a tape recorder from that kid who hangs out at the junior college bookstore."

"Aha!" Randy pounces on Chipp's Achilles heel. "Jann Wenner seems to have fallen behind on his own task list. It's nice to see I'm not the only slacker living at Eight Hundred Prosperity Street, apartment number four."

"Apartment number *three*, you dumbass. No wonder you're always giving me mail for that guy across the hall. Remind me to ask him how he liked the cookies my mom sent but I never received. Anyway, I'm working on a few things. I talked to Jim at DISContent, and he told me that The Disappointed are looking for yet another rhythm guitarist but that The Deer Park are in town and could be a possible interview. He also said that Bottlecap just got back from their tour and may be breaking up. Jeez, he's such a gossip. But both The Deer Park and Bottlecap are opening up for Superchunk on Friday." He pulls out the monthly calendar for The Scene from underneath a stack of Randy's ideas. "I'll make some calls and see what I can set up."

As Randy starts in again on where to put the classified ads and how to slant the banner, Chipp's mind starts wandering.

Interview? What in the hell do I know about interviewing anyone?

2

Dave guides his Honda into a parking space in the corner of the mall, carefully, as if a bomb were aboard that might go off at any minute. He slides out the keys (his fourth set this year) with care, then lays them in his lap. He sits there silently for another moment before picking up the key ring again, selecting the small golden key, and holding it up to the rearview mirror and saying the prayer, as he does every time.

"I believe in the key. The key is all that is good. The power of the key is all knowing. The key *is* good."

After this phase of the ritual has been dutifully staged, he gets out of the car and begins walking to his box. His post office box isn't in the post office at all but in a store called National Mail Services, which is in a garish strip mall located across from the court building.

Sometimes Dave thinks it's a drag to come all the way across town to check his mail every day when the post office down the street would be more convenient, but at the time they were all full, so Dave has no other choice. But since then he's cultivated his daily trip into something more: a ritual. He had even questioned why the box was necessary at all. Surely the twenty-dollar rental fee every three months could have been better spent (well, at least spent), but in forming his record label he was initially wary of having his home address stamped on one thousand copies of anything, let alone records with songs like "You Fuckin' Suck." He had visions of irate customers not liking what they heard and searching him out for some sort of ghoulish *Cape Fear* retribution. So he rented the box, even though he met a girl at a bar one night and when he began to tell her his address she floored him with "Dave, *everyone* knows where you live. You're the record guy." Besides, at this point he likes the idea that his mailing address has a street and suite number, as if he had a high-tech office, a bevy of employees, and a beautiful blond receptionist with an unrequited crush on him who would answer the phone as if blowing into his ear: *"Violent Revolution Records. How may I help you?"*

Dave also likes to park far away from his box so the walk to it will give him time for more prayer and reflection, and the walk back gives him the chance to rip open all the envelopes to see if he's gotten anything good. Whenever he receives a long letter or an order, Dave never waits until he gets home to read it. He either sits in the car or else stops like a statue in the middle of the lot and won't move until he's finished reading the letter or is repeatedly honked at.

Sometimes the mail flow rains, sometimes it pours. Lately, clear skies and not a cloud in sight. Every time Dave slips the key in, there is a rising tide of hope; this is the day he would get that check from his distributor; this might be the day he would get a letter from some kid telling him how much he liked the work he was doing, was thankful for the music Dave introduced, or something, anything.

Dave hops up onto the sidewalk from the tar-covered lot, begins walking faster, then, out of superstition, slows down. *Don't want to jinx it,* he mumbles to himself, before adding, *Jinx what? Like mail that was there when I was walking slowly isn't going to be there now that I'm walking fast?* Dave makes a mental note to slap himself. *Duh.*

He walks into the store and, seeing it's crowded, is relieved. He always hates it when the employees watch as he comes in and idiotically takes out his little gold key and checks his box, because they know whether or not he has any mail. But then he always assures himself that these employees have better things to do with their time than keep track of Dave's correspondence. He's positive he's being paranoid, as he's prone to be, and that they barely notice him and probably don't even know his name. He is wrong. They do.

Dave holds his breath, looks through the small window, the yellow wall visible behind it. For a second it feels as though he's been punched in the gut. Tears, a stupid knee-jerk reaction, appear for a second in Dave's eyes before he relentlessly pushes them away. *Why the fuck hasn't anyone written to me? What's going on out there? Doesn't anyone care about what I do? Jesus, I feel like I'm living my life in a black hole.*

Dave figures he might as well continue with the routine, playing out his hand even though he knows he should fold and quit while he's ahead. Without passion or hope he puts in the key and quickly twists, pulling open the door. The long rectangular shaft is dark and bare, almost cold, a few shadows from the opening on the other side letting slight streams of light in.

Just as he's turning to leave, he notices a wafer-thin envelope lying flat on the box floor. He quickly pulls it out and rushes out of the store. It is an off-white envelope with a metered stamp and a return address that reads Wells Fargo Bank, with a California address. Over this is a black stamp that reads BLACKLIST MAILORDER. Dave makes it halfway through the parking lot before ripping open the envelope and tearing out the contents. It's a check along with a letter printed on beige paper with the letterhead in stencil computer font and a black bar on the bottom, which says in reverse lettering, "Recycle This" surrounded by two hearts.

Please find enclosed payment for merchandise received 2–14–93. Thanks. Take care, Claudine.

He quickly examines the check. It's made out to David Rowland for forty-eight dollars. In the corner, along with the Blacklist address in San Francisco, is a small graphic of a woman showing off a television. Dave rereads the check, making sure it's signed, that it's for real.

"Forty-eight bucks!" Dave shouts, jumping like Rocky in the parking lot, cars swerving to avoid him. He bolts to his Honda but then, struck with an idea, dashes to a pay phone outside Marshall's department store. He shovels in a quarter after two dimes are rejected, thinking, *When in the fuck did this become twenty-five cents?*

"Hello?" Stacy answers.

"Stacy, this is Dave. Put on some clothes. We're going out."

"I am putting on clothes, Dave, except it's my uniform. I've got to work the dinner shift."

"But . . ." His shoulders slide down like an avalanche. "I just got a check in the mail. I wanted to celebrate. Dinner and a movie. A Bill Murray movie."

"Ah!" Stacy screams.

"Haven't you checked the Weekend section of the paper? *Groundhog Day* is back and is playing at the dollar theater. I thought you wouldn't mind seeing it again, my treat."

"Oh, Dave, that's really sweet, and, well, you know I would." She pauses for a second; rustling is heard in the background. "But seriously, I've got to work tonight, and I couldn't get out of it if I wanted to, which I don't since I really need the money."

"No shit," he says, watching the traffic cruise down the road. "How'd you get a dinner shift? After my screw-up the other night, I've only got three lunches this week and that's it."

"I don't know." She giggles. "Dan likes me, I guess."

"Tell me about it," he mumbles.

"So will you wait for me? Tomorrow night? Same Bat time?"

"Not tomorrow. I'm seeing Superchunk at The Scene. A few of my bands are opening, and I have to make sure that Todd doesn't try to rip us off. I still haven't even talked to any of the guys in Bottlecap except for Gary, and even he's probably pissed off at me because I couldn't get him a job at the Whales Fin. How about Sunday night?"

"Sure," she says brightly. "It'll be a nice break after working all weekend."

"Yeah, yeah," he says with a sigh.

"So what are you going to do now?"

"Cash it and go shopping, I guess. There's nothing to eat in the house except stale Cap'n Crunch cereal and powdered milk, and I'm not that desperate. Not yet, at least. I guess I'll stock up on supplies and maybe rent a video. Anyway, see you on Sunday night? Movie starts at eight. Drinks after?"

"Sure, sure. Come over to my place at seven-thirty, and we'll go from here."

"Okay, bye."

"Bye, and congratulations on the check."

"Thanks," he says and hangs up the receiver.

Five minutes later Dave briskly walks into the bank holding the check proudly, as if it's the Olympic torch. He spots the teller who, days before, tore his check in two and then only hesitantly taped it back together the next day. He races through the velvet ropes leading up to the teller's window, making screeching noises as he rounds each curve.

"I'll be cashing this today, if you don't mind," Dave says with a smile.

She takes it and examines the chicken-scratch signature Dave scrawled while at a stop light.

"I.D., please," she says through a yawn.

Dave panics, pats down his back pockets, front pockets, shirt pocket, even his socks. He hasn't been carrying around his wallet lately because it's been empty for the last couple of weeks.

"I'm sorry, sir, but I can't." The teller is winding up for her speech, her toes sliding toward the silent alarm button set into the floor.

"But you've got to remember me," Dave pleads. "David Rowland? I was here last week and we went through *Dog Day Midmorning*, remember? Violent Revolution Records? Aw, you're not going to pull this again, are you?"

"Rules"—now she's smiling—"are rules."

"Aha!" Dave pulls his license out from the stretchy band of a pair of patterned cotton boxers.

The teller grudgingly snatches the mangled and somewhat moist license out of Dave's hand, runs the check through a computer, stamps it, and then puts it to the side. She pulls out a sheaf of twenties from a steel drawer and smarmily counts off two as if teasing Dave with the entire pile. She takes a five, dabs her thumb in a small dish of green goop, and fishes out three ones.

"ThanksandhaveanicedayNEXT!" she says in a single breath, trying to get rid of him.

"No, *you* have a nice day."

Dave gingerly folds the bills and puts them in his back pocket. He gets into his car and starts it up, ignoring the blinking white EMPTY sign, the glowing orange thermometer, and the blinking red battery icon. He also notices the oil gauge is pointing straight down, and even though the car is idling, the speedometer is registering 78 mph. The car backfires twice as Dave pulls away from the curb, heading for the market.

He pulls into the Piggly Wiggly across the street from the mall. He takes a shopping cart from the outside and heads, as always, directly for the frozen food aisle, noticing a song playing over the sound system with the vocals actually left in.

"Hey, I know this!" Dave says, beginning to croon, "*Connnn . . . stant . . . cra . . . ving . . .*" He parallel parks next to the frozen pizzas and begins to decide what next week's worth of meals will be.

For a few minutes he just stands there with the door to the freezer open, weighing his options as the cool air rapidly escaping causes fog to pour into the aisle, looking like the stage for a heavy-metal rock band.

"Now Stouffer's French bread pizzas are great, and both of them make a good meal, but at around three bucks, that's expensive." He puts the red rectangular box back into the freezer. "With Totino's you get a bargain at around a buck fifty, and they're pretty tasty. But they have those mutant square pepperoni pellets, and that's always a bad sign. Besides, one pizza is not enough to fill you up completely, and with two the extra will only go to waste. But it's a good snack." He pulls out a square package from the bottom row. "These Jeno's mini-pizzas are okay but again, they're good for a snack unless you're going to eat all five pizzas at once. Jeno's pizza rolls are a classic, so I don't know how they can be so good at one thing and so mediocre at another." He replaces the box, and looks over a few of the new boys in town: "Red Baron and Tombstone . . . I don't know.

Looks like a classic case of the emperor's new clothes. What are they offering we haven't seen before? That reminds me, where's the Hot Pockets?" He stands up straight, examines the top shelf. "Celeste is an old favorite but they come in only huge and small, and neither is suited for a single meal. And, man, if you don't eat these babies while they're hot"—he fingers two boxes that have a photo of an old woman on them—"forget it. Besides, their pepperoni looks and tastes like a silver dollar, and that crust is pasty and hard. Still, if I had a dime for every one of these I ate as a kid . . ." He inches his cart down the aisle, making sure to keep out of the flow of traffic. "These gourmet pizzas" —he picks up two or three boxes that are printed in pastels and feature toppings like chicken and shrimp—"are okay, but for five bucks I might as well spend a few more and order a Domino's. It's like those Chicago Brothers' deep-dish pizzas. Yeah, they tasted great, but for five bucks one of those Windy City siblings ought to come to your house and slice it for you." He tosses both of them like Frisbees back into the freezer. He finally decides on a Stouffer's, two Totinos, a box of Pizza Rolls, and a Celeste Pepperoni Personal Pan Pizza for nostalgia, mouthing the word *abbondanza!*

He pushes his cart around the corner, one wheel spinning wildly, independent of the other three. He fights with the cart, trying to keep it straight, heading for the meat and dairy section. While looking over the bologna, he sees Carlos.

"Hey, what's up?" asks Carlos.

"You off today, too, huh?"

"Yeah," he replies, examining a no-name brand of chicken hot dogs for sixty cents. "I've got, like, eight hours this week."

"Tell me about it," groans Dave.

"That's because Dan makes out the schedules, and he gives all the good shifts to Amy or Natasha, or whatever that chick's name is."

"Sasha," Dave corrects. "But, yeah, I know what you mean. He gives all his little girlfriends the choice shifts while you and I get thrown a lunch now and again as a bone. And lunches are good for what? Fifteen bucks if we're lucky? And that's horseshit about the recession hurting business. He says that to cut two waiters early on a dinner shift so the other two have to handle the whole restaurant and run around like maniacs all night trapped in the weeds."

Carlos laughs.

"Yeah, lunches suck. Hey, does this sound familiar? 'We'll both have the special and two cups of water. Do you charge for ice?' "

They both crack up.

"Meanwhile, how are we supposed to eat?" Carlos says. "If I have another one of those fucking Helper meals, I'll fucking throw up."

"And it's so sad when you can't even afford the hamburger part. I mean, talk about needing help."

Dave glances down at Carlos's cart, which is filled with a box of chocolate Cookie Crisp cereal, hotdog buns, Fritos, a six-pack of beer, and a Chef Boyardee Two Cheese Pizzas Mix.

"Watch out for this stuff." Dave reaches in and pulls out the yellow box as if reaching into a cradle for a baby. "They say *cheese* on the box, but it's only a little packet of fucking Parmesan cheese."

"Yeah, I know." Carlos sighs. "I learned the hard way that if you follow the directions on the box, you'll be eating prison food. So what I do is buy this for the crust and sauce since I hate the Ragú and Progresso sauces. I augment the recipe with a pack of mozzarella cheese and then buy a package of pepperoni, and instead of making two pizzas like the box says, I make one big one on a cookie sheet, eat about half, and save the rest for breakfast the next day."

"Not bad." Dave runs a hand over his stubble. "But this mix alone is about two fifty, right? Cheese is at least a buck fifty unless you buy the cheap stuff—which, if you do, why even bother? That shit doesn't even melt and comes out looking yellow, not white. Pepperoni is another buck and a half unless you pay a buck for the kind that comes like a sausage, and then you have to stand there and cut it up, and if you're going to go through that kind of trouble, you might as well just cook something. So after all this you've spent almost seven bucks and I don't know how many man-hours."

Carlos is nodding intently, making notes in his head.

"I mean, that whole Boboli and Contadina prebaked crust

scam is the exact same thing. For that kind of money go to Little Caesar's and get two pepperoni pizzas for about seven fifty. Stick one immediately in the fridge and eat the other. Just heat it up the next night, and it'll be as good as new." Dave wipes imaginary dust off his hands. *"Voilà."*

"You are the master, I must admit." Carlos bows mockingly.

"Well, what else are we supposed to do? Look at this shit." Dave turns to the rack of cold cuts, trying to find the cheapest bologna. "Look at all this Oscar Mayer crap. This stuff's too expensive, and it's bad for you to boot. I'd like to get this Healthy Choice brand"—he points to a row of packages outlined in green with yellow writing, slogans like LOW FAT and SODIUM FREE printed on the see-through plastic covering—"but this stuff costs three times as much. It's like this whole system is devilishly set up to weed out poor people by forcing us to stuff ourselves full of garbage. It all comes down to the fact that I can't afford to eat right. Stacy's always getting on me for eating macaroni and cheese mix for dinner, but what the fuck else can I afford for fifty cents? Hell, one bell pepper costs more than that."

"That reminds me. Did you get the new Smashing Pumpkins CD?"

"Yeah! It's really fucking amazing. I bought a new pair of headphones, too, because I read where they used, like, twenty tracks for the guitars alone. It's really great."

"Cool, cool," Carlos says, tossing the pack of hotdogs into his basket. "I picked up that Godstar record as a limited-edition double ten-inch and also got that Nothing Painted Blue LP that has this cool picture of Encyclopedia Brown on the cover and— oh, that reminds me. That redheaded guy at DISContent, the manager . . ." Carlos is trying to remember the name.

"Big curl, likes Prince, used to be cool, is now a corporate geek," Dave says, still pissed-off at Jim. "So?"

"He mentioned something about the used CD thing, that the big labels had backed down and so DISContent would still sell used CDs. I was looking for *Evol*, and he said Geffen was going to reissue the whole Sonic Youth catalog so I should just wait and—"

Dave cuts him off.

"So it's back to normal at DISContent?"

"I guess."

An old lady pulls up with her cart filled with cat food, paper towels, and Lysol. She's coughing politely, trying to get access to a package of sliced ham.

"That's great!" Dave ignores her. "Jim had taken my stuff off the shelves along with some other labels because he was losing major label advertising and was tight on cash for a while. But if he's got it back, he'll continue making easy money off Madonna and all that crap and can afford to help out a small guy like me. Hell"—he leans into the air-conditioned recess in the wall—"it's his moral obligation."

"I don't know about that." Carlos winces, noticing that the old lady is mumbling something under her breath as she stomps away. *What the hell is her problem?*

"Why do you say that?" asks Dave.

"I mean—" Carlos hesitates—"I mean that Jim's so drunk on the idea of being a big business in this town. He loves the big fish, small pond scenario, and I don't think he likes the idea of your telling him how to run his store."

"Aw, I don't buy that. After all, today is my lucky day. I'm just going to sit back"—he takes down a packet of Healthy Choice Lean Honey Roasted Baked Turkey—"and enjoy it."

3

"Um, what's that noise?"

Eileen crinkles up her nose as she blurts out the obvious question, her buttonlike proboscis shaking back and forth like Elizabeth Montgomery's.

"Noise?" the landlady innocently asks, shuffling her feet, clearing her throat, crumpling up the lease in her hand, trying anything to create a distraction.

In the past few days Eileen had made the round of half a dozen potential living spaces in Kitty, trying to find a place other than the motel. In only twenty-four hours Eileen was shown more places she is sure she doesn't want to live in than she knew existed. It got to the point where, after only a day of looking, she had developed a sixth sense for this thing, a sort of apartment radar. Usually, within five seconds of stepping inside, she could tell if the place was perfect, just okay, or like an ugly guy with a heart of gold, something she could grow to love over time.

The feeling manifests itself first in the form of a twitch in the nose or maybe the perking up of an eyelash on spotting either a glimpse of hardwood floor (very good) or a swatch of bright yellow-and-orange wallpaper (bad). Unfortunately for Eileen she has the keen ability to make snap decisions in under a minute but is devoid of the cruelty to hurt a landlord's feelings overtly (especially the cute, cuddly, old ones) by rejecting their wares in milliseconds and often lets herself be shown around, accept an application, and swallow a slice or two of carrot cake before scramming for her next appointment.

"Yes, that noise," Eileen repeats, walking around the otherwise charming apartment.

It's a two-story house split into four apartments. Thick carpeting, plaster walls, those glass door handles she always envied when she saw them at a friend's apartment back in Baltimore. But that sound. She walks into the spacious bedroom. "Nice," she coos, the incessant dripping slightly less audible than it was in the living room but still annoyingly present. She tiptoes through what the landlord calls the "spacious breakfast nook," imagining lazy Sunday mornings before heading into work for what Jess jokingly called the "antichurch crowd," further explaining, "Look, this is a cafe. These people don't believe in God. Those people are all having brunch somewhere, politely declining the complimentary champagne." But just as she notices the four-by-two-foot recess in the wall for a phone, the noise rises up again, a steady trickling, as if there were a leak in the ceiling, though no water is visible. Eileen wanders back into the front room where the landlady is rapping her high heel against the floor.

"So do you like it?" she nervously asks.

"Yeah, it's great, and cheap, too." Eileen stops a second before she continues, making sure it's still there, confirming her sanity. "But what *is* that?"

"What?"

"Oh, come on." Eileen rushes for the drapes and pulls them open. "It sounds like someone is taking a huge piss, only no one could drink that much."

Standing in the center of the courtyard (something she hadn't even noticed before since the landlady had rushed her up the back stairs) is a large, circular, cement fountain meekly spitting out a thin stream of gray water.

"Is that thing on all the time?"

"Well—" the landlady hesitates—"they turned it off for a week last year to clean it, but otherwise . . . yes."

"Thanks, but, uh, no thanks," Eileen mumbles, glancing at her watch. "Sorry, I've got to go. I'm late for work."

She quickly exits the apartment, trying to remember the way to the cafe. After turning down a few streets that look familiar at first but end up dead-ending in a set of rusted railroad tracks, Eileen spots the hill atop of which is the cafe.

"You're late," Jess says when she finally arrives, more as a joke than a serious reprimand.

"I'm sorry," Eileen says, hurrying under the counter, trying to tie her apron on with one hand and clock in with the other. "I was out looking for an apartment again."

"Oh?" His eyebrows perk up. "So you've decided to stay in Kitty?"

"Yeah, I guess so." Eileen empties out a bus tub into the sink. "I mean, I've got a job, I might as well get a place to live."

"Where are you staying now?" Jess asks, fishing out a box of cone filters from a cupboard above the bar.

"That old Sleep and Save motel down near the freeway."

His face curls up in a grimace.

"Tell me about it," Eileen agrees. "It's quite an interesting walk, but I'm afraid I'm going to have to give it up. I'll have to use every penny I make here to use to pay the hotel bill. I guess it's an okay room, and it is sort of fun to have someone clean up after me, but if I'm going to stay, I need to find something else."

"How did you ever choose Kitty, anyway?"

"It was sort of by default." Eileen laughs, not able to believe the story herself. "It just sort of happened, and, well, I've got nowhere else to go."

"Why does that strike me as something Richard Gere once said?" He laughs gently. "I'm sorry, but you don't seem that tragic a figure to me, at the end of your rope like that."

"Well then, let's put it this way." She slides under the counter and turns back to Jess. "Let's say I've got nowhere to go that I actually want to go to. So Kitty will be a nice change for a while."

"I don't know about that," groans Jess.

Eileen spots a couple entering the cafe and sitting down near the window. The man instantly begins looking over the bright red menu sandwiched between an ashtray and a cream dispenser.

"Why? This town seems perfectly fine to me. Quaint, even. Quite a nice change from that big city bullshit in Baltimore— you know, fighting for parking spaces, smog, high prices, et cetera."

"Sure." Jess shrugs. "It's true that the only time you see a traffic jam in Kitty is when some old guy is selling his *Playboy* collection at a garage sale, but it's just . . . this town is so small."

"So? I like that."

"Sure you do because you didn't grow up here. It's just that, wait!" Jess stops in mid-sentence. "I have got an idea."

"What is it?"

"Brenda lives above the cafe. You know that, right?"

"Yes."

"Well, there's another apartment up there—*furnished,* even. A few years ago it was rented out pretty regularly, but then the fire marshal said something about Brenda's lease being for only a single family dwelling or— Anyway, I'm sure you could stay there a little while."

"Is it nice?" Eileen looks up at the dark ceiling, imagining what could be above.

"Yeah. We were using some of the space as extra storage a few months ago and I thought it looked really cool."

Eileen stands, rolling her bottom lip between two rows of teeth, weighing the decision in her head.

"Want me to run up and ask her?" Jess offers.

"Yes," says Eileen quickly before heading toward the couple near the window. The man is starting to look annoyed, and the woman is trying not to notice the man who's noticing that Eileen is finally coming to take their order.

Hours later she can't believe she's doing this. For the first few seconds it felt exhilarating, spontaneous, wild. Now, alone in a strange room, all of those emotions are being replaced by loneliness, doubt, fear.

When Jess told her about the apartment, that it was there if she wanted it, it was like a new lease on life, a ticket to somewhere else. Before, the job was temporary, paying for her motel room and not much else. It was as if she was that Ping-Pong ball floating steadily over the pipe, wafted up by a solid current of air, not falling or rising, just sort of suspended. But when Jess offered her the apartment and Brenda surprisingly agreed, it was time to put up or shut up.

Now it feels as if she's closing her eyes in the scariest part of the movie, as if she can't bear to see what comes next—and yet all she's ever wanted is to see this film.

The floor above the cafe is actually three apartments, the largest occupied by Brenda, whose sole question during the brief job interview the other day was "You sure?" Another of the apartments is used as storage, filled to the ceiling with boxes of books and an old rusting espresso machine tattooed with a large eagle, the copper long turned green. The other apartment is Eileen's.

It's a furnished studio apartment with hardwood floors, a high ceiling, and a built-in bookcase. In one corner is a small kitchenette, sink, and a bathroom door, to the left of which is a water heater surrounded by a small pool of liquid at the bottom. In the other corner a twin bed is cradled in an old wrought-iron frame. In another corner is a vanity and chair, and in the center of the room sits a velour couch. The furniture is very old and rickety, squeaking every time Eileen sits down. She excitedly moves from bed to couch, couch to chair, even jumps up on the dresser and stretches out, soaking up her new living quarters. She quickly discovers that every time she sits on the bed it creaks violently. First comes a major squeak, then minor shock waves of noise. The thick plaster walls are painted a subtle off-white and decorated with reproductions of Victorian paintings in dark-brown oval frames.

The large window in the corner beside the bed looks out on

the street below. Eileen cranes her head through the shutters and glances down at the Novel Idea cafe sign sticking out from the side of the building like a bud. Farther on, the city is spread out in a gentle slope, an open book lying on its spine. Hovering over the scene is the glimmering moon, almost full, a thin slice hiding a shy eye deep in space. As Eileen loses her thoughts in the image of the suspended moon, she realizes that this is the same moon her mom might be staring at, wondering where she is, wondering when she's coming home. *If ever.* The Virginia moon. The Maryland moon. The Florida moon. The moon they have just seen in London and are waiting for in Japan.

4

Mark is home for a full three days before he gets around to returning the van to his parents' house just a few blocks away. While driving the short trip, he curses to himself, slaps his palm against his forehead as in those V-8 commercials, and considers turning around and doing it the next day.

"Aw, fuck," he says out loud, surveying the dusk falling over the town, "they're going to think I planned to have dinner, too." He plants his hands squarely on the wheel and looks out for a side street to turn into so he can turn around, but then decides against it. "I'll just make up some excuse," he tells himself. "Yeah, that's it." He would pat himself on the back if he weren't using both hands to take a curve. "A real quicklike getaway."

He makes a right and heads into an exclusive section of Kitty called Tiger Bay, where his parents now live but not where he grew up. He spent most of his preteen years across town in a nice but modest subdevelopment that, by the early seventies, contractors were making by rote: plain houses neatly laid out in a rigid geometrical design that looked like a circuit board from the air and some sort of suburban hedge maze from the ground. Just after Mark left to attend college, his parents moved into the swanky section of Tiger Bay. But because Mark did not grow up in his parents' new house—spending only a few Christmases and a Thanksgiving here and there, along with assorted family quarrels—he doesn't really feel at home there. During his extended stays after college when he was, as his father euphemistically put it, "getting back on his feet" (Mark preferred the term "hitting rock bottom"), even then he never felt comfortable inside the expensive, decorous walls.

"Moving on up, son," his father said as he sucked on a pipe and watched a team of mostly black movers sweat in the August heat the day they moved in four years ago. "If you play your cards right"—he poked his only child in the ribs with the stem of his pipe—"you'll be in a house like this someday, too."

Mark felt then as he does now: *Who gives a shit?*

Every time he enters the gilded gates of Tiger Bay he feels as though the air is being sucked out of him, or else the air in this area is thinner or pumped full of drugs, and that's the reason the inhabitants are groggy, small-minded, and stupid, his own parents included.

His mother, who never had a job, now takes golf and tennis lessons three times a week, and his father has cut down his workdays at the office to only three or four a week, leaving him ample time for fishing, hunting, and perfecting his bridge game.

It seems funny to Mark that he lives such a short distance away and yet rarely sees them. In a town the size of Kitty, this takes some doing, and Mark often takes alternate routes to such everyday locations as the supermarket, drugstore, and gas station, even going so far as to shop for food in the next county lest he run into his mother in the produce section and then have to hear her lecture him about the GWAR MUST DIE T-shirt he is wearing.

He pulls the van past the fence surrounding the house and then through another white gate to the side of the dwelling. (Tiger Bay is sort of a set of Chinese boxes, doors inside doors and rooms inside rooms, and this continues until you can go no farther and you are trapped in a basement that is nicer than Mark's entire block.) He parks the van next to a twenty-five-foot boat, another of his father's playthings. He kills the engine and moves to place the keys underneath the black floor mats when he notices that he missed a spot and there's an off-white stain running the length of the mat in the shape of a comet, bulbous at one end and thinning as it goes. He groans when he remembers what it's from. He digs the heel of his shoes into the mat and tries to ground it in and then wipes the longer hairs of the carpet over the stain. Despite his efforts it's still visible, and he's sure he'll be wakened the next morning with a phone call from his father, who will have noticed it as well.

Walking through the overgrown backyard, he spots his parents sitting in the Florida room, having a drink. In his father's hands he recognizes the telltale scotch and can smell the sweet cherry odor of his pipe as it escapes through the plate glass doors of the added-on room. His mother, still dressed in her tennis outfit, is comforting herself with a white wine spritzer. Mark tries to stomp his feet on the red-brick walkway that he helped his father put in three years ago, so as not to scare them as he approaches, but they still jump a foot when he knocks on the window.

"You scared me half to death, son." His mother rushes to greet him.

"Sorry, sorry," he says, entering the warm room from the cooler night air.

"Are you feeling okay, dear?" his mother remarks as she steps back to examine him. "You look thin . . . and pale."

"No, no, no, Martha," his father finally acknowledges him, rising out of his deep leather chair. "He's not thin, just lean."

"Well, in any event, you're staying for dinner." His mother turns to leave the room.

"But I've got to be at—"

"Nonsense," she calls back to him. "It's too late. I'm setting an extra plate."

Mark awkwardly crosses the room and sits down on a hunter green couch with oak claws for legs.

"So, uh, how's it been going around here?"

"Fine, Mark, just fine."

"Good, that's . . . good."

"Son?" His father walks toward him and puts his face close to Mark's. "Remember our deal?" His voice is deeper than his son's and could be used as the voice of God for a cartoon.

"Deal?" Mark's voice cracks.

From the kitchen Mark can hear the rattling of pans, his mother putting dinner on the table. He hopes she'll return quickly because his father never lays into him when she's around. After all, you always have to keep up appearances.

"The deal." His words cruise on a slight scent of scotch.

"Oh, yeah, the deal. Sure, about how if I borrowed the van again that I'd have to wash it out and clean it, especially after Gary got sick that one time and threw up all over the—"

"No, not that. The job."

"Hmm?"

Mark plainly remembers the deal he had made with his father almost four months ago when he had approached him about using the van yet again, and this time for the longest stretch of use ever. His father was cool to the idea, as he had expected, and at first flat-out refused. It took a few weeks of protocol and careful negotiation on Mark's part to finagle a deal. The final terms were that this would be the last tour his father underwrote. Mark agreed, saying that next time it would be different. "We have some big things happening for us, Pop," he had said in this very room fourteen weeks ago, in the throes of trying to convince him.

"Big?" his father had said gruffly. "Like what?"

"Like . . . getting a record deal. A *real* record deal, not like the one we have now where we have to stay up all night folding the covers. You'll see. One day I'll make a living off my music, and then you'll be proud."

Mark let the words sink into the blue pipe-smoke air and waited for the reply he had waited all his life to hear: *"Son, it doesn't matter to me what you do as long as you're happy."*

Instead of this he was treated to the usual patronizing barrage of fatherly double-talk, cheap words of familial loyalty and supposedly "grown-up" responsibility.

"You're becoming a man now, Mark, and it's time to get a real job, to quit playing and get serious."

At the time Mark had wanted simultaneously to cry and to strike his father. How could he be so blind? So hurtful? Over the years he had never ventured into any of the clubs to see his son play his music, never even tried to think of what it meant to him, and yet he was constantly asking him to give it up for some mundane but stable job that would pay the bills, as if that's all that mattered in life.

"I'll make you a deal, son," is the way the pact began. "You can have the van one last time, and if you come back a success, with enough money to live on, with enough resources to support yourself and not have to come to the back door begging for scraps like a goddamn dog, and don't think I don't know about the loans Mother has been shoveling your way"—he pointed at him with the nibbled stem of his pipe—"if you come back from this trip a man, I'll forget all about ever trying to make a difference in your life."

"And if I don't?" Mark's voice creaked again. He felt ten years younger than his twenty-three.

"And if you don't"—the old man's voice was inscrutable, as if he wanted his son to fail to prove his prognostication correct—"Then you'll do as I say."

At that point most of the tour had been booked, and Gary, Steve, and he had already quit their jobs, the bridges of their former lives still smoldering. There wasn't enough in their strained budget for renting a van, and without one, there was no possible way to go on tour. So Mark rose out of the leather chair, crossed the room, and shook hands with his father only because he didn't know what else to do. Looking back it seems foolish, but at the time he was sure that this tour was going to make a difference in his life, that it was going to be a success.

On the road a few days ago, drifting back into town, he knew that his father had been right. He had failed, and maybe his father had been right all along. Gary and Steve kept prodding him in the back as he drove, slump-shouldered, wanting to know what was wrong with him as they slouched over the Virginia state line. They laughed and made jokes, thinking it was just his guilt over his sexual indiscretion that was gnawing at him when in fact it was something else entirely. He had never told them about the conversation he had had with his father a week before the tour.

"The deal," his father now repeats, moving behind the bar to refresh his drink.

"Yes, sir, the deal," Mark says like a zombie. "Okay . . . you win."

"Good." His father marinates the trio of ice cubes in a small pool of Glenlivet. "Why don't you stop by the human resources department at the college first thing Monday morning. Ask for Mr. Harrison." His father breaks into a devilish grin. "He'll be expecting you."

"Oh, Randall." His mother finally breezes back into the room and lays a hand on her son's sunken chest. "You haven't been laying into him again, have you?"

The three of them walk through the kitchen and into the dining room.

"Of course not, dear."

The cool night air slams against his still burning ears, and he imagines steam is coming off him as his anger dissipates.

He rams his fist over and over again into the open palm of his hand, where it lands with a leaden thud and not the wet-slap *smack* of flesh on flesh as it did in the movies.

"Why do I always let him get to me like that?" he asks as he rounds a corner. A pair of headlights approach him, and he feels like an escaping fugitive wandering in the middle of the street, so he heads for the shoulder. "Why?"

The streets are eerily dark as the tall pines sprouting up from the expansive trees block out any traces of moonlight and the absence of streetlamps only cocoon the air further in a black shroud. Mark keeps stumbling over the exposed roots that wrangle their way out of the ground.

Once outside the gates of Tiger Bay, as if the place itself had a spell on him (which he always suspected), he begins to cool down. His anger and frustration drain away, and he begins to enjoy his walk. He speeds up, and it feels good to begin to hollow out his now full and solid stomach. His beat-up thrift-store boots do not provide the best walking shoe in the world, especially as the exposed leather heel digs mercilessly into his ankle and wears quickly through the shell of the bleach-weakened sock, slowly slicing each of the seven layers of skin. But still Mark's steps perk up. He begins whistling and marveling at the clear night sky.

Over the past few months he had always volunteered for the

night shifts of driving. He told Gary and Steve he did this because he wanted to be a nice guy, that he would unselfishly take
the night shift so they could rest and keep normal human hours
while he would have to hibernate, sleeping during the day like a
damn bear with a guitar. But the truth was that he liked to drive
at night because it was less complicated; there wasn't any traffic,
and it was usually all interstates and large main roads. It wasn't
until around midday that a map had to be pulled out and routes
from the highway to the small club they were playing that night
had to be found. Mark wished that usually troublesome task on
Gary or Steve, anybody but himself.

A pleasant side effect of his late-night shift was that he could
use the quiet to think, dream, and wait for the ringing in his
ears to subside. He would stare blankly at the night sky that was
almost always crystal clear thanks to the icy autumn wind.

It's strange for him now to look up and notice stars and con-
stellations he was watching hundreds of miles away just a few
weeks ago from the inside of the smelly, dirty van. How he
wished to be home then, and now that he was, how he wished to
be someplace else. He kicks at some loose rocks collecting near
a drainage ditch, stones too big to fit through the steel grating,
and he agrees with Steve that he never wants to tour like that
again. He knocks one of the bits of gravel into the street where
it bounces once and then hits the side of a car with a metallic
crash. As he looks back to see if anyone has noticed the sound,
he catches a glimpse of Kitty in the background and knows that
staying here is no solution, either.

He starts fishing for his keys when he gets two blocks away
from his house, thinking it will give him something to do since
both the clear night sky and his own thoughts only depress him.
He clutches his keys now that he's four houses away, and he has
his arm outstretched, ready to find the keyhole with still a full
hundred yards to go.

As Mark enters the living room, the red blinking light on his
answering machine catches his eye.

"It's probably Laura." He groans, crosses the room, and
presses the small gray PLAY button. "Great, now what?"

He kicks off his shoes and tosses his wallet on the kitchen table
as he waits for the machine to rewind and then play his message.

"Uh, hello, I'm looking for a Mark Pellion?" an older, confused voice says, a voice that Mark doesn't recognize.

The confused tone in the caller's voice is due to the fact that instead of having the standard "I'm not home right now, please leave a message and I'll get back to you as soon as I can" message, Mark has a full minute and a half section of dialogue from one of his favorite cheesy movies, *Pandemonium*.

"Uh, anyway," the male voice, which sounds close to middle age, continues, "my name is Henry James, and I'm an A and R man for Subterfuge Records here in Los Angeles. I read about you in *Alternative Press* magazine, and I've heard your single of the month on Sub Pop, and, well, I wanted you to know I'm going to stop in and see your show Friday night at a club called, I think, The Scene. I'll talk to you more then, okay? Bye."

The message ends, and an excited Mark is standing in a pool of silence. His heart is beating rapidly. Sweat is beginning to form on his forehead and underneath his arms. He glances down at the phone machine on the end table, marveling at the message he has just heard, as if it had been left by a Martian.

Wait a second. Did I just hear what I think I heard? Is my desperate mind playing tricks on me? Is this the break I've been waiting for or a sign that I'm breaking up? To confirm his sanity he presses the gray button again.

"Uh, hello, I'm looking for a Mark Pellion?"

Yes.

5

"Jesus Christ, has it been that long?"

Craig stares at Ashley, and Ashley, drunk, is trying to stare back.

What had begun as a discussion of the night's previous events (including subjects such as Where Did Craig Go for Five Hours? followed by What In the Hell Was Andrew Doing Here at Midnight?) was quickly obliterated as the wine they cracked open to unwind ended up unwinding them like yarn from solid spools. Somehow the conversation turned from infidelity, love, and morality to a popular song of the mid-80s.

"Yes." Ashley slurs her speech, fumbling for the wine bottle as she counts the years silently in her head: four, five . . . six!"

"Shut up!"

Well, she thought she was counting silently.

"I was in high school, a freshman, I think—yeah, when *The Breakfast Club* came out. 1985. Yeah." She takes a sip of the cool white wine. It slides slowly down her throat, tingling its way to its destination. The river of booze in her stomach is swirling, her lucidity caught in the undertow, her motor functions drowned in the tide, her inhibitions lost at sea.

"*The Breakfast Club!*" Craig scoffs. "Ha! My friends and I went to see *The Breakfast Club,* and we threw shit at the screen. For chrissakes. Judd Nelson, right? You probably had a crush on him."

For an answer Ashley reveals a toothy grin.

"Have you ever seen his nose? My God, it's got its own area code. There are movies where his whole role gets left on the cutting-room floor, but there's just no way to cut out his nose."

Ashley bursts out laughing.

"So there's like this huge unattached nose floating around, like something out of Gogol."

Now Ashley is rolling all over the floor, belting out laughs, holding her side, her face flushed.

Ashley's laughter makes Craig laugh until he realizes that Ashley is nearing sloppy drunk territory, and he could as well have gone to the cupboard, taken out a box of cookies, and read the ingredients in a deadpan voice, and Ashley would have laughed at that, too.

"Yeah, anyway, now I know why you're always so hot to rent *From the Hip.* Jeez." Craig picks Ashley off the floor where she was lying on her back. "I can't believe you ate up that crap. All that John Hughes adolescent angst bullshit. Instead of Sturm und Drang it's Shopping und Dry Cleaning."

"Hey! John Hughes knows what he's talking about!" She tries to defend.

"Are you kidding me? John Hughes is a capitalist swine making a fast buck off a bunch of stupid kids. His insights are about as deep as any puddle in downtown Kitty. What's one of his immortal lines? Wait, I think it goes something like, 'My parents shit all over me.' I mean, he's desperately trying to—"

"Wait a second!"

Craig is shocked. "What?"

"If John Hughes sucks so bad, how come you can quote lines from his movies? That's *Weird Science*, if I remember correctly."

"Er, um . . ."

"You're just as bad as those senators on those antipornography committees who sit around and watch skin flicks all day, saying how horrible it all is; meanwhile, pass the popcorn and the hand lotion."

"That's not true! Sure, I've seen a few John Hughes movies, but just enough to form an educated opinion about the man. After all"—Craig leans back into the sofa slowly—"I don't want to go off half-cocked."

"No, Craig. Not you."

"It's like," he starts again, "he's trying so hard. I mean, if he ever just relaxed a little and tried to think about what it's like to be a kid rather than what kids like, he might make better films. You know?"

Ashley is not really listening. She is running her tongue against the front of her teeth, which she is convinced have become fuzzy.

"The guy is not a fool. He's definitely smart, but conniving."

"Yes, fuzzy, like a little rabbit's tail," Ashley is mumbling with a lisp, her tongue now sliding across her molars.

Ignoring her, Craig marches on with his speech. "And then what's with this Ferrari bullshit in *Ferris Bueller's Day Off*? That was so lame. Like that kid doesn't get along with his father, so the way he reaches out to him is to destroy his sixty-thousand-dollar car? Well, what if I don't get along with *my* father but he doesn't happen to have an exotic foreign car that I can trash in order to get his attention? What do I do then? Get an extra job and start saving?"

Ashley snaps out of her trance for a moment and jumps off the couch.

"You're so full of shit!" she yells.

"Easy, Mario, easy . . ."

"That was the only way he could get his father's attention. He tried talking to him a bunch of times, but that car meant more to him than the kid, so . . . he . . . um . . . I think I'm going to be sick . . . had to . . . trash the . . . Ferrara . . . rari . . . " She mangles the last word.

Ashley makes her way toward the bathroom, stopping for a second as the tidal wave in her stomach subsides and gentler waters prevail.

"Oh, please! The whole idea is so elitist. And if that's one guy's story, how is that going to have relevance to some fifteen-year-old kid in Kansas City whose dad is a coal miner? Do you see what I'm saying? It's like that insipid remake of *Father of the Bride* where all the supposed comedy comes out of the fact that Steve Martin is shelling out like a hundred thousand dollars for this wedding that goes haywire, wokka, wokka, wokka! That guy is fucking lucky he's got money to go haywire with! It's like in Henry Miller's *Tropic of Cancer,* the only thing that starving guy can think about is breakfast. That's all he's thinking about. He doesn't have the luxury to be neurotic." Craig pauses for a second, running low on steam. Ashley, sitting next to him with her arms crossed over her chest and her eyes closed, is mumbling. Craig drains the last few swigs of the bottle and thinks, *Fuck. . . . Another goddamn night.*

"Ferris Bueller, *sheesh.*"

Ashley jumps up and begins screaming, " 'Twist and shout! Come on, come on, come on *bay-bee* now!' " She yells out a few more lines before clutching her stomach and rushing to the bathroom.

Craig is lying on his back, staring at the ceiling fan.

"Simple Minds—man, what a shitty group. I bet you even bought that sound track, right?"

"What?" Ashley is in the bathroom, brushing her teeth for the third time, trying desperately to get that post-throw-up acid residue out of her mouth.

"*The Breakfast Club.* I'm sure you bought the sound track!" Craig shouts out, yawning. "All those lightweight new wave bands. God, it's enough to make *me* puke."

Ashley spits, exits the bathroom, and finds one of Craig's Hang Ten thrift-store shirts on the floor, and pulls it over her head.

"Yeah, well," Ashley says sarcastically, "we all couldn't be the prototypical punk rocker like you."

"Damn straight. When you were fawning all over that jerkoff from the Psychedelic Furs, I was driving up to D.C. to see Fugazi!"

"What?" She climbs into bed. "Fugazi wasn't even around then!"

"Well, it was Minor Threat then. Yeah, at the 9:30 Club."

"No, I think that was still too late."

"Rites of Passage?"

"Those were the other two guys, I think."

"Embrace, okay? I saw Embrace, and Ian was there and he talked about something political—yeah, that's it. And he wouldn't sell me a T-shirt, and it was really cheap to get in. Now do you believe me?"

Ashley is rearranging the pillows.

"All right, all right, I believe you." She curls up against his body. "So do I call you Craig Vicious now? Huh, Mr. Punk Rocker?"

"I don't know." Craig grins. "I kind of like Craig Rotten better."

He turns his head and kisses Ashley lightly, then turns over and begins to drift off to sleep.

Within a few minutes Ashley can sense that Craig has fallen asleep by his deep breathing. Still feeling a little queasy, she tries to ease out of bed, but as soon as her feet hit the floor, her stomach begins churning, turning over and over. Ashley freezes, thinking, *Stomachs can sense fear. They're really as afraid as I am.* She's afraid to move, afraid to get up, as if an inch in either direction would mean staring into the toilet again for half an hour. Trapped like a prisoner without a ball to bounce off the walls, Ashley's mind wanders:

I saw The Breakfast Club *at the Capitol Cinema, which was back before the Goo-Goo Plex Theatres came and relegated the Capitol to showing films in confusing languages about even more confusing subjects. This was even before the mini-malls and Wal-Mart; there was only one McDonald's and no Hardees. Back then Kitty seemed more like a town than a commercial opportunity. I was just a freshman. Yes, Craig was right. I had a crush on Judd Nelson, but who didn't? Actually, Andrea didn't, and even back then I couldn't understand why not. Of course Andrea, always a sucker for jocks, fell instantly for Emilio Estevez. Me, I couldn't get past the name. I mean, can you imagine screaming, "Oh, Emilio! Emilio!" I'd think I was in bed with some migrant orange picker. No can do. Andrea called me recently to tell me that Emilio and Paula Abdul were getting married. I couldn't believe that after all these years Andrea, a mature and intelligent woman currently weighing three offers from large corporations who want to hire her, still felt pangs of passion for an old crush. "She's not right for him," she said as I tried not to laugh. "It'll never last." It's amazing the way those things stay with you. The weakest tether is often the only one that holds. Of course it's easy to like people like that for so long if you never have to meet them, see them on a bad hair day, or smell their breath in the morning. Anything is possible in the realm of the unfamiliar. Craig was also right about the sound track. Sure I owned and loved it, and what's wrong with that? Will somebody show me the crime I've committed? That Simple Minds song ruled then (if that phrase hasn't expired), and, to be honest, it rules now. If Craig wasn't so worried about being on the cutting edge all the time, racing home with his brand-new CDs like they were the cure for cancer and steps toward making the world a better place, maybe he'd realize, or at least acknowledge, that some of that stuff from our youth wasn't so bad. To this day every time I hear "Don't You Forget About Me," I think of my freshman year in high school: passing notes in class, going to football games, and sitting in front of MTV for hours. Back then at the top of every hour they showed the little astronaut guy landing on the moon, planting a Day-Glo MTV flag, and Nina, Mark, J.J., Martha, or Alan, would tell you what was coming up in the next hour. Would it be Steve Miller's "Abracadabra" or J. Geils's "Centerfold" or Fleetwood Mac's "Hold Me" or that new band Def Leppard's "Bringing on the Heartache" or Michael Jackson's "Beat It" or that unknown out of New York everyone was talking about, Madonna's "Borderline"? And the hours would roll by, with that little man landing on the moon every couple of minutes, it seemed. Outside the sun had been replaced by the moon in the span of what felt like a handful of videos. Things have changed so much since I was younger. I remember being over at a guy's house, and while he was sucking on my neck, I was still watching MTV, my eyes glued to the screen while some stranger's*

lips were glued to my earlobe, then shoulders, and then, depending on
how distracted I was, my breasts. That was all before I was even thinking
of sex or was on the pill, before I knew how to give oral sex or, more
important, receive it. Back when I seemed more like a person than a
commercial opportunity. When I was fourteen, I thought Molly Ring-
wald was the luckiest person in the world to get to work with Judd Nelson
for all those months and be his girlfriend, even if it was fictional and for
a limited time only. It's more than I've ever spent with Judd. Instead I
ended up with Craig. A good catch? More like a bad throw.

Ashley drifts off to sleep, a pillow burying half her face, one
leg sticking out from underneath the covers. Unconsciously she
kicks Craig, her knee snapping out of reflex, a muscle retracting
for no reason. The blow shakes Craig awake, and he curses at
the glowing L.E.D. display: 3:24 AM.

I saw The Breakfast Club *at the Capitol Cinema. I loved it then,*
and, I'm ashamed to say, I love it now. I couldn't admit it to Ashley, but
the truth is, The Breakfast Club *spoke to me more than any film I'd*
ever seen before (except maybe Valley Girl*) and with the exception of*
sex, lies and videotape, *more than any film has since. Not that it was*
all that spectacular a movie, but it had the benefit of hitting me at a time
in my life when I was just forming an idea of who I wanted to be, and
in that dusty theater I was presented with five suggestions. And yet all
that did was anger me. Like, if it's so easy to know what I'm thinking, I
must not be thinking much. If my thoughts are so close to the surface that
you can see them just by kneeling down on the pier, I'd better swim
deeper. The Breakfast Club *seemed so real to me, like these were people*
I knew or else desperately wanted to know. That film was so real to me
and to so many others that, back then, it was the closest thing we had to
Virtual Reality. And I was envious of every one of them: the Rebel, of
course, because he's a rebel. The Jock because he had the body, the
prowess, the power. The Geek because he was smart and, when it was all
said and done, would end up a fabulously rich lawyer. Ally Sheedy was
like the weird side of me, except that I lacked the courage to wear, on a
twenty-four-hour basis, the mask she wore as a uniform, opting instead
to keep it at the bottom of my closet to pull out whenever I needed it.
Molly Ringwald looked so hot in that movie. That scene where she was
doing her new wave dance, I elbowed my friend and said something like,
"What a fucking joke." But in my heart I wanted her, to be in the
stairwell doing that lame dance with her—I couldn't have cared if it

was the watusi or the shag—just to have gone home with her and her Calvins. And that scene where Judd Nelson falls through the ceiling and lands between her legs, only to be looking up at her muff. I jacked off so many times to the mental image of the view from underneath her skirt, her thighs and panties resplendent in cinematic Technicolor. I remember being sad in the theater because the movie was like this great party no one had invited me to. There was no way to get in. No one I could schmooze who would say, "Yeah, you're okay. Come with me, I'll get you in." God, it sounds so stupid to think this little film affected me so much, especially since that's just what Hughes was after. I guess I'm just mad I was co-opted so well. I'd hate to think John Hughes went around humming "The Reflex" knowing I'd be stupid enough to fall for it; whispering to his wife at the premiere, "That oughta hold the little SOBs!" As cartoonish and lame as it sounds, those people still seem like my friends, acquaintances who never call or write, and I spent only a short time with them. Ashley thinks I'm always trying to paint a picture of myself when I was young as this moshing punker, my hair sculpted into a two-foot-gelatin reinforced mohawk while my leather jacket sported SSD and Blitz patches. Sure, some of it is true, like I went to hardcore shows and slammed, but it was mostly because no one in Kitty could understand why I'd want to drive up to D.C. just to get tossed around. Like if all I had wanted was to get my ass kicked, I could have put on a shirt that read I LIKE BLACKS *and gone into any honky-tonk in town. But they missed the point. It wasn't the slamming or even the music, it was the feeling, the experience, the whole evening turned on its side, and you were never quite sure what was going to happen next. I was finally part of something. There was a party out there I could get into even if they were charging me cover. Yeah. Fuck Simple Minds and all their friends.*

Craig has got a smile on his face; he is crushing the pillow under his head and scratching his belly with a ragged nail.

Bizarre Love Rectangle

1

The tips of her nipples never felt the same after he started playing guitar. Where once he was totally in control of her pleasure, able to judge when to hold back or give in completely, he now fumbled around with his nerve-deadened hands, calluses on the ends of his fingers like a leathery hide.

Mark rubs the blunt stub of his left index finger over Laura's rosy areola, unable to feel the pimply pleasure rising out of her breast. He frowns, leans in close, examines his abnormally flat fingertip, his fingernails unavoidably chopped off as far as they will allow. He thinks of his hands landing notes on the fret board, whizzing up and down the dark rosewood neck while the sparkling steel strings sing out underneath. Hitting that difficult chord felt like acing a triple axel jump in ice skating. The waves of sound blare out from his amplifier behind him like a wind machine, slapping him in the back of the legs, almost pushing him over with force. The rest of the band pummels barely an inch away from sloppy insanity and maybe another encore. And now Laura stares at him, wondering what in hell he thinks he's doing, making the form of a Bmaj7 chord on her chest.

"Sorry."

Mark took up playing guitar to get close to Laura's heart, and now that he was, he almost can't feel it.

"What do you want to do?" she asks, crumpling up a pillow and sticking it behind her head. Her shoulder-length brown hair is frazzled, some in her face, some sticking up, some splayed out on the pillow. She rubs her tired green eyes, trying to lift her head up enough to read the clock sitting on Mark's milk-crate nightstand, but his shirt is hanging over it. Her postcoital glow is slowly wearing off, the feeling returning to her midsection, the low sexual hum being replaced with the nagging feeling that she has to urinate.

"Hungry," he mumbles, his head lying on her soft stomach.

"I can try to be domestic," she says, pushing him off her and reaching for her black panties. "Do you have anything to eat?"

For a second Mark doesn't reply. He just stares at her as she fumbles around for a second, trying to find her bra. Finally, unable to track it down, she skips it and pulls over her head a large blue denim shirt of Mark's, leaving her tank top and crumpled-up jeans lying in the corner where they were casually thrown an hour and a half ago. She shivers at the ice-cold touch of the back of a pin piercing the front of the shirt that reads I LIKE HATE AND I HATE EVERYTHING ELSE. She looks back at him and grins before heading into the kitchen.

As he wipes himself off on one of his paisley-patterned sheets and then pulls up his boxer shorts, he can hear Laura going through his various cupboards, opening and closing the refrigerator, double-checking the pantry, searching for something edible.

"Is this all you have?" She appears in the doorway holding a six-pack of Maruchan's Chicken Flavored Instant Lunch.

"Yeah. So?" He runs a hand through his messy straight hair.

"So?" she asks back, disdainfully looking at the dried food. "This soup-in-a-cup stuff is like the poor man's Top Ramen. I mean, *please*."

"Hey." Finally rising off the bed, he glances over at the clock, no longer obstructed: 1:41. He sighs. Long morning. Long night ahead. "You leave my soup-in-a-cup stuff alone. I think it's just fine." He snatches the packages out of her hand and heads to the kitchen.

"Well," she says slowly, watching as Mark pulls out a kettle and begins filling it with water, "considering the alternatives."

He places the kettle on the stove and fires up one of the gas burners in the front.

"The trick is not to get it too hot." Mark is whispering, peering into the kettle. "If the water is really boiling, you're likely to melt right through the Styrofoam. Just a minute more. We're getting closer."

He pulls out two cups from the six-pack and sets them side by side on the counter.

"Can't we at least put them in bowls?" Laura asks.

"That's defeating the purpose," Mark replies, carefully peeling back the aluminum lids only halfway. "If I wanted to dirty up a few dishes, I'd cook a real meal."

He peers into the lunches. The dried noodles are like wavy coral sprinkled with a golden powder and green specks, on top of both are half a dozen dried peas, niblets of corn, and carrots.

"This should be about right." He grabs a rag and places it around the handle of the kettle before picking it up. He brings it to the counter and expertly pours the steaming water into the first cup.

"Remember, fill it up to the line. See the line? Right there?" He is pointing to a small indentation on the inside of the cup.

"Yeah, yeah. Mark, I'm hungry. Will you hurry it up?"

"But I like mine a little more brothy"—he ignores her—"so I'm filling mine up all the way."

He drains the last of the water into his own cup, places the kettle back on the stove, and turns off the burner. He takes two mismatching spoons out of a drawer, folds back the covers of the cups, and places a spoon on top of each one. Small trails of steam escape from the gaps at the edges of the aluminum foil, curling from the heat of the water, barely held down by the skinny tongue of the silverware.

"In three minutes we'll have a meal. Well, almost a meal."

Laura smiles as Mark runs back and forth from the kitchen to the dining room, clearing off the table, finally throwing away magazines and three-month-old pizza boxes.

"You know," she calls out to him, "if we'd gotten married years ago we'd be doing this all the time." He reenters the kitchen with another armful of trash. "Wake up late, make love in the daylight, fix each other lunch, and then just . . . hang out together."

"First of all, thank God we couldn't find the map to Vegas, and"—he frowns—"we just did all that."

She slaps him on his bare back as he leans over, tossing a mound of stuck-together paper plates into the trash.

"Laura, remember you're looking at the guy who actually drove all the way to Charlottesville to buy the book *Too Cool to Get Married*. Do you remember that?"

"Yeah, yeah." Laura bobs her head up and down, closing her eyes and distinctly remembering every time he has told that story. Told it to his friends. Told it to her friends. Told it to crowds while on stage. Mentioned it in interviews and even to her parents. Everyone seemed to laugh except her. "Yeah," she says softly, "real funny." She looks at him and remembers how she felt when he was away—more confident, more sure of herself. Back barely a week, and already he was eating away at her, trying to keep her in her place, eroding any kind of future together.

"Hey . . . I'm sorry." He scoots off the counter and takes her in his arms. As he leans in for a hug, he notices he can smell himself on her, the dried sperm he'd rubbed over her chest ten minutes ago and her own natural scent smeared all over his thighs. He wants to tell her what he's done, about what happened on the trip, so they can get on with whatever would be left of their relationship. He looks into Laura's blank face, and checks his hair in the glare of her eyes.

"So"—he pushes back, resisting—"What would you like to drink?"

"What have you got?"

"Um, water, water, or, I think, maybe, some water."

"How about water?"

"Good choice." He fishes out two extra-large plastic cups from the cupboard, each with a scene from the movie *Batman* on them along with a faded Taco Bell logo. He tosses in a few ice cubes and holds them under the tap for a few seconds, filling them to the brim. He places them on the table, then the lunches as well. He pulls out Laura's chair for her, and she slaps his hand away when he keeps it in her seat as she is sitting down. He unfolds a paper "Somethin' for Nothin'" Domino's Pizza napkin and places it in her lap with large, comical gestures. Then he scurries around to the other side of the table, sits down, and pronounces, "Peel away."

"You sure this is going to be enough for you?" Laura asks as she blows on her spoon, cooling the steaming broth. "After all, you do have a show tonight."

"I know, I know. I hate going on stage with an empty stomach, but at this point I'm nervous enough."

"Why?" She daintily takes a sip, the liquid burning the tip of her tongue. "Because of that guy?"

"Jesus!" He gulps down a large mouthful of noodles, biting off the excess, which splashes back into the cup. "That *guy*, as you so calmly refer to him, is only the biggest A&R guy for Subterfuge Records, which is only one of the biggest major labels around."

"Mark," she says quietly, reaching across the table for his hands, only they're too busy clutching at his cup-of-soup and spoon. "Do you really think this guy's going to sign your band?"

"Why else would he come to this little fucking town? I mean, don't you think we're good enough?" He stops, wipes off the splatter marks around his mouth, and swallows. "Don't you think I'm good enough?"

"Yes, of course, honey, it's just . . ."

"What?"

"I don't want you to get your hopes up. That's all."

The phone rings in the living room and Mark stares into Laura's eyes for a full thirty seconds before getting up to answer it. *Maybe she's right. Maybe it's nothing.*

"Hello?"

"Hey, Mark?" He recognizes Gary's voice. "What's up?"

"Nothing, Laura and I are sitting around, and we're just having lunch. So can I call you back?"

"Uh, sure. Well . . . look, let me ask you one thing first. I just got off the phone with Dave, and he didn't mention anything about tonight. Didn't you tell him?"

"What do you mean, the gig?" Mark arches his head into the hallway and can see Laura's bare legs, crossed underneath the card table covered with a red-and-white-checkered tablecloth. "No, I didn't tell him, but he knows."

"Not about the gig, the *guy*."

"Oh, you mean Henry."

"Henry!" Gary shouts. "Since when are you on a first-name basis with this bozo? Two days ago he was Mr. James."

"Well"—Mark twiddles the phone cord around his rough finger—"I figure if we're going to be doing business with this guy, we ought to call him by his first name."

"But who says we're going to do business with him? All he's going to do is come and hear us play, right?"

"Yeah, but that's just the beginning."

"Look, Mark, I'll be honest with you. I don't like the fact that you didn't tell Dave. How could you not? He's like our manager, we're on his record label and . . . we owe him."

"Dave's a fucking loser, Gary. Wise up, okay? Haven't you noticed that our stuff's not even selling here in Kitty anymore? Not to mention every other record store we passed through in the past three months. Remember?"

Laura leans her head in the room and shoots him a "You're being too rough with him" glance. Mark turns the other way, avoiding her.

"Gary," he says with a sigh, "do you or don't you want to get out of this town?"

"Well, sure, but . . ."

"But nothing," he snaps. "You don't tell Dave. Got it?"

Silence.

"Got it?"

"Yeah, yeah, I got it. See you at soundcheck."

Mark hangs up the phone. Laura's stern disapproval is evident even though he hasn't turned around to see her crossing her arms and tapping her toe.

Long night ahead.

2

"Mail call!"

Brenda barges into Eileen's room as she's getting out of the shower, a blue towel wrapped around her body and a green one around her head like a turban.

"What?" she asks, shaking the water out of her ears. "What did you say?"

Instead of answering, Brenda flaps an envelope back and forth in a pudgy hand.

"What is that?" Eileen says again, still confused. "Is that for me or something?"

Brenda vigorously shakes her head, proud that Eileen is actually receiving correspondence from someone, as if she were a wallflower who has finally been asked out on a date.

"It's from Baltimore," Brenda whispers for no apparent reason.

"Great," Eileen says sarcastically, dipping back into the bathroom to slip on a pair of sweatpants and a T-shirt. "It's probably from my mother"—she twists the word. "For some dumb reason I actually called her and gave her my address after she bugged me about it for half an hour. 'For an emergency,' she said." Eileen takes the letter and sits down on the couch. "Yeah, right. Like if I slip in the tub here my mom's going to send our family doctor from Baltimore? It'll take him half a day to get here. But, well, that's my mom."

Eileen puts her feet up on the coffee table, then looks at her name on the envelope, written in a script not immediately recognizable but certainly not, she's sure, her mother's.

"Wait, this isn't from my mom after all," she says in a semi-whisper, more to herself than Brenda.

"Oh, really?" Brenda gasps, intrigued. She sits alongside Eileen even though there's really not enough room.

Eileen rips open the envelope with her good hand (her other arm trapped underneath Brenda) and pulls out the letter.

> *Dear Eileen,*
>
> *Hi. I'm sorry it's taken me so long to write to you, but your mother gave me your address only today. I've wanted to write to you for a long time saying how sorry I was about everything, and how I wished we could just go back to the way we were a few months ago. I really miss you and wonder when you're coming home. Things aren't the same here without you and . . .*

Eileen stops reading, throws the letter on the ground.

"What? What!" Brenda asks excitedly. "Who's it from?"

"Don," Eileen says meekly.

"Don? Who's that? Your boyfriend?"

Eileen gets up wearily.

"Well, he was."

"So? What happened?"

"Let's just say he was more boy and less friend."

"What?"

"Oh . . ." She shakes her head, confused by it all herself. Even though it happened only a few months ago, the images seem shaky, hard to recall. The last few shouted conversations between her and Don are hard to remember. The words that once rang in her ears for days afterward had faded like an echo that becomes less penetrating until it finally dissolves into nothing. "I don't know what happened. We just weren't right for each other. You know?"

"Trust me"—Brenda looks down at the ground, trying to read a few sentences of the letter, only her eyesight is not good enough—"I know."

"But now he knows where I am and . . ." Eileen begins nervously pacing around the apartment.

"So what? Is he like a *Sleeping with the Enemy* type?"

"No, he's more like a *"sleep with your best friend"* type, but that doesn't mean he won't come here and try to convince me to return. Only this time I don't want to go."

"You're starting to like it here, eh?" Brenda asks in a curious tone of voice, as if there's more behind her question than what's readily apparent.

"Sure, Kitty's fine. Why?"

Brenda keeps jerking her head toward the floor, as if it is being drawn by a magnet, released, then attracted again.

"What? Why are you suddenly smirking?"

"Is it that you like Kitty or someone *in* Kitty?" Brenda can't help erupting into spasms of laughter between each word.

"What?" Eileen finally asks, not catching on. "Who?"

"Jess!" Brenda exclaims, as if it had been apparent the entire time.

"Jess?" Eileen pronounces the name as if she had something sour in her mouth.

"Yeah, what's wrong with Jess? He's a nice kid! He's been

working downstairs for almost a year, and he's never been late, not once!" Brenda slams her hand down on a nearby tabletop before continuing. "Besides, I know he likes you."

"How?"

"A woman knows—except for you, since he's been giving you the eyes for almost a week now, and you've been too dumb to notice. Are you not interested because of this guy?" Brenda motions to the letter on the ground.

"No, not really. He's sort of the reason I'm here, but trust me, there's no love lost where he's concerned. It's just . . ." Eileen breaks into a wide grin.

"What? What is it?"

"I don't know. It's just . . . I never thought of that." Eileen looks out over the city, thinking of Jess.

"I'll have a decaf Al Pacino," a young man in a black turtleneck says, turning away from a virginal copy of Ginsberg's *Kaddish* for a moment.

Eileen brushes a strand of dark hair out of her eyes, wipes down the counter, and then looks up.

"A what?"

The young man smiles; his friends are now watching. He places an expired lottery ticket in the book as a bookmark and closes it. The black-and-white volume rests on a chess board.

"I said"—he fights a grin—"I'll have a decaf Al Pacino."

His friends break up in laughter as Eileen continues to stare at them blankly.

"Decaf Al Pacino? Decaffeinated cappuccino? Get it?" the young man says, now somewhat embarrassed. "It's a joke."

"A joke?" she says curtly, one arm still wiping the counter. "Sorry, that's not on the menu."

Eileen walks away as the young man's friends start giving him a hard time. She's sporting a self-satisfied grin as she ducks under the counter to deliver the order to Jess.

"What are you so happy about?" he asks, mixing up a hot chocolate.

"Oh, nothing," she replies nonchalantly even though she's still a little high from the victory. She pulls out a slim piece of cheesecake from the fridge under the counter and places it on a dish. "You see that group of neo-beatniks over there?"

Jess looks over the cafe. Half the crowd matches the description, all clutching beat-up copies of *On the Road* or *Naked Lunch*. The others are wearing plaid thrift-store clothes with ripped jeans and haphazardly pass joints under the table, some not even under. Finally he spots the group in the corner, all clutching volumes of City Lights' *Pocket Poetry Series*.

"The hardcores? What about them?"

"Well, I just put one in his place."

"What'd you tell them? That 10,000 Maniacs wrote a song about Kerouac and that he was actually *for* the Vietnam War?"

"It was nothing like that. Just a put-down." A piece of the chocolate topping breaks off, and Eileen quickly places it in her mouth. The candy melts almost instantly, its sultry taste stinging her palate. As she gulps in pleasure, another piece somehow breaks off, and she eats it, too.

"You'd better think of some more witty rejoinders," Jess says, pointing to the table with a shaker filled with cocoa. "They're waving you back."

"Great," she says with a sarcasm-filled sigh. "It reminds me of what that critic said at the premiere of *Howl* at that art gallery in San Francisco? Wasn't it something like, 'You're all in for a bumpy ride'?"

"No." Jess is laughing. "That was a Bette Davis movie. What you're thinking of is 'Ladies and gentlemen, prepare to go through hell,' or something like that."

Eileen grabs a tray of mugs and desserts, and heads off toward the mélange of tables, casting back what hopefully is an alluring glance. "Same difference."

After a few days of working and living above the cafe, it is safe to say that Eileen likes one and not the other. She's been a waitress before, so the job certainly is no great challenge, although the mores of a cafe are in deep contradiction with the fast-paced diner she used to work for in Baltimore. In the diner atmosphere the patrons were as eager to leave the establishment as she was. They wanted their food hot and fast, and with the check following close behind. In a cafe the customers are languid to the point of lethargy, nursing mugs of thick coffee over supposedly deep conversations or chess games that end in stale-mate or frustration as often as they do in victory or defeat. Someone in a cafe will slowly work on a *caffè latte* for an hour and will dismiss you with utter contempt if you suggest another cup or a slice of dessert in any of those sixty minutes, but at the precise moment there is not another drop of caffeine, they get pissed, and you'll be severely chastised for not attending to them sooner.

The living arrangement poses just as many challenges, but none are as easily solved by a few tips from Jess and a split shift or two to get her feet wet. It was as if Brenda, because she had provided Eileen with a space to live and work, felt she could barge in on her at any time. Often it was to say hi or to ask advice or for a cup of sugar (or, like that morning, to bring her the mail that she'd already held up to a lightbulb) and just as often it was when Eileen was sleeping, soaking in the tub, or lying around the apartment in a nightshirt and nothing else. A lot of girls feel comfortable around one another, but Eileen is not one of them. Movies and TV shows (especially in sweeps week) are constantly portraying women, much to the delight of men, frolicking at near-lesbianic slumber parties, running around in satin jammies, doing each other's hair and nails, and so on. Eileen was never one of them and likes her privacy, to the point of rudeness, perhaps, and it is hard for her to explain that to Brenda. She always feels compelled to say, "I'm glad you feel close enough to share this with me, but don't."

The supermarket, which was just a few blocks away, had been providing Eileen's only respite from the cafe. She walked to the market slowly, enjoying the trip as if she were some asthmatic who had been forced to stay indoors under doctor's orders. A few people had tried to befriend her—assorted patrons from the cafe, and even Jess had suggested going out for a drink after work—but she turned them all down. She was trying to remain strong in her self-imposed isolation, but the loneliness was get-ting to her.

Still, after a couple of days in Kitty, she found herself happier than she'd been in a long time. Every once in a while the names would pop up: Mom, Dad, Don, but she pushed them down, fought back a tear, pressed on.

"What are you doing later?" Jess asks, his blond ponytail bobbing back and forth.

"What? Sorry?" The din of the crowd nearly drowns them
out. "I couldn't hear you."

"I said"—Jess talks in an exaggerated manner, using his arms
in a grotesque sign language—"what are you doing later." He
turns normal. "You know, it's Friday night."

"Nothing, I guess."

"You can't be doing nothing. Everybody's doing something."

Tongue in cheek, she replies, "Well then, count my nothing
as a something."

"What do you say we do nothing together? Listen to a few
records. Maybe have something to drink that doesn't involve
boiled lactose."

Eileen weighs the decision, wondering if it's connected to the
conversation she and Brenda had earlier in the day. Probably,
but thinking it's cute, she grins. Jess looks practically comical
with his long hair, like an unkempt island boy, but very cute.

"Sure, why not."

"Great. Just stop by after the shift." He grins, spins around,
and grabs two mugs from the counter. "What's the order?"

"Oh, I nearly forgot." She fishes her pad out from the kanga-
roo pouch in her apron. "One café au lait and two decaf Al
Pacinos."

Jess stops in his tracks and stares.

"Wait a second. What in the hell is a . . ."

3

The glass whizzes through the air like a missile, narrowly missing Craig's face. Ashley picks up another, this time a mug, and
drops back like a quarterback, fading, faking to the left, while
Craig, her unwilling receiver, runs for the door. Ashley lets
loose a Hail Mary pass, its high arc cut short by the ceiling.

"Ah hu huh ha huh huh ha ha!" Craig blurts out the Woody
Woodpecker laugh.

The mug drops to the floor, bouncing off the thick area rug, and is retrieved by Ashley. Craig is caught up in the locks of the door, nervously turning keys and latches. Ashley hurls the mug again at Craig. It hits him squarely in the gut, then falls to the ground, shattering like an exploding firework.

"Now look, Ashley. Just calm down!" Craig is trying not to laugh. Fear is replaced by farce as the scene becomes surreal, his girlfriend hurling crockery from across the room, him caroming off the walls trying to avoid the falling debris. *Just exactly what were we fighting about?*

Hot tears are streaming from Ashley's squinting eyes as she firmly grips a vase, trying to judge the distance.

"Ashley, no!" He laughs again.

"You called me a cunt!" she screams.

The humor drains out of Craig on hearing the fierce rancor in Ashley's voice and seeing the desperate, hollow look in her bloodshot eyes, her stooped-over stance supported by spindly, trembling legs. His grin melts into a frown, and he approaches her.

"Ash, I'm sorry," he says slowly. The vase is still aimed at his sandy blond hair matted onto his forehead with sweat. "I didn't mean that. I mean, calling you a . . . you know, the C word and all. I'm really sorry."

The porcelain object begins to descend a few inches.

"It's just . . . you get me so crazy sometimes. You act all high and mighty, always butting into my business . . ."

The hand raises again like a drawbridge.

"And that's . . . good. Yeah, that's it, because then I, uh, know how you feel. Yeah, and as long as I know you still love me, well, then, as far as I'm concerned, I'm the luckiest guy in the, um, world."

She sets the vase back down on the table, and begins to head into his arms but instead collapses onto the couch.

"Well, why did you say those things in the first place?" Her voice is now filled with frustration instead of anger.

"I don't know, I get crazy."

Sensing the moment of real danger has slipped away, Craig goes into the kitchen and gets out a wine cooler, rolling the chilly bottle across his flushed face.

"You know how I am. I start out getting a little jealous, suspect a few things here and there, and the next thing I know, I think you're sleeping with half the town."

"Don't you know how unfair that is to me?" Ashley clutches a pillow, playing with a loose tassel.

"I know, I know." Craig takes a deep drag on the cooler, the sweet berry taste lightly streaked with alcohol. "But I can't help it. I told you about my last girlfriend. She was a tramp, and I never found out about any of it until afterward. I mean, this girl made Madonna look like Sandra Dee."

"So now *I'm* suffering?"

"That's what it looks like," Craig says matter-of-factly, switching on the TV.

A few seconds later Craig can feel Ashley's glare, like an unsuspecting ant feels the agonizing stream of heat from a magnifying glass on its back.

"I mean," he repents, "it's wrong, and I'm going to work on it."

"Damn straight you're going to work on it. And, my God, how could you suspect me of cheating with Andrew? I mean, that's sick!" She slaps the satin pillow instead of Craig.

"Well," he says with a shrug, "I get paranoid. I mean, you're always out studying with him or you two are working on a paper. Or like the time I came home and found you two in the bedroom together, and you came out tucking in your shirt. Or the time you were housesitting, and I found out later Andrew never really went anywhere. Just little things like that, I guess."

"Yeah, that's all, er, crazy." Her voice cracks. "We're just friends. You've got to believe me."

Ashley reaches out for Craig who embraces her in a long, steady hug. Craig likes to give these conch-shell hugs, but Ashley can't stand receiving them. She always smiles, mildly hugs back, looking for a way out and thinking, *Let go of me, you big ape. I may love you, but I don't want to morph into you.*

"You know what we should do?" Craig breaks the seal.

"What's that?"

"We should have Andrew over for dinner tonight. You know, as sort of a goodwill measure. I mean, I'm always kind of blunt with him every time he calls or picks you up for one of your all-night study sessions."

"I'm not sure." She's biting her lip.

"Why not? I think it'd be a good first step toward you and I reestablishing some modicum of trust between us. I need to face my fears. Besides, it'll be nice to have some company over for a change. Have him bring a date. It'll be like a dinner party."

"Yeah, but Andrew?"

"Who else?"

"It's just, I see him every day on campus, and that's enough for me. And he's so picky about what he eats. You've never seen him in line at the cafeteria and watched as he changes his order for the tenth time."

"We're not doing this for Andrew, remember? We're doing this for us. For this relationship. So I can prove that there's no hard feelings between us. That I completely trust you."

"I don't know." She sighs.

He cradles her. She lies in his lap and puts her feet on the armrest, thinking about painting her toenails.

"Come on, Ash." Craig kneads the back of her neck. "You'll be glad you did."

4

After a handful of phone calls, Chipp is sitting in The Scene, nursing a beer and looking over his questions. He's waiting for The Deer Park to arrive and set up their gear for a soundcheck. It's a little after seven, and the club, which won't open for another three hours, is empty except for Chipp, Todd (the owner), and Jack (the day bartender) who's waiting anxiously to get off his shift. Jack is staring at Chipp, waiting for him to finish his beer and leave, or else sip faster and order another. Chipp keeps his eyes trained on the carved surface of the bar. Nervously he checks his questions again. He feels for his pen, wallet, watch, and tape recorder. As he eases the recorder back onto the stool next to him, his hand brushes the spare console and it starts blaring, "Testing, one, two, three, testing . . ." seguing into a not-so-on-key rendition of "Rid of Me" by Randy until he's silenced by Chipp in the background shouting, "Shut up, asshole!" Chipp quickly shuts it off, but not before Jack is glaring at him again, this time harder than before.

At the back of the bar, to the right of the stage, a large door opens, the last rays of sunlight suddenly streaming into the dank, cavernous room. Chipp spots a medium-sized guy with black hair who lugs in two guitar cases and drops them unceremoniously on the raised stage. He's followed by a short blond guy who drops his load of a bass drum, returning in a few seconds with a handful of cymbals and two pedals. The two of them continue like this for about half an hour, bringing in tomtoms, a snare, a small seat, amps, two more guitars, as well as a backpack full of accessories: distortion pedals, strings, three straps, tuning keys, electronic tuner, and half a dozen cords.

Chipp finally recognizes the guys as Stoner and Johnny, the rhythm section for The Deer Park. They mill around for a second and Chipp keeps quiet, waiting for the rest of the band to arrive. They don't. Chipp is just about to say something when another guy comes through the back door, but he's not in the band, either.

"What took you so long, Dave?" Stoner calls out as he's setting one of the amps on a folding chair and positioning a microphone against the glittery fabric facade. "We have half the stage set up already."

"Don't start with me, Stoner. I'm not having a good week. Uh, Jack, is Todd around?" the guy calls out to the bartender. "I want to talk to him about the guarantee."

"Guarantee?" The bartender laughs. "Since when does Todd give guarantees to local acts? Hell, if the Beatles re-formed and played a reunion show here on a Friday night, Todd wouldn't guarantee them anything, and that's *including* John."

"I know, I know," Dave says, pulling up a stool a few spaces away from Chipp. "He's a slimeball, but that's why he's a promoter. So is he around or what?"

"He's in the back." Jack puts down the mug he's been rinsing. "Let me go get him."

Dave suddenly turns to Chipp, who's been staring at him, trying to remember where he's seen him before.

"What do you want, kid?"

"Oh, I'm here to interview The Deer Park."

Dave looks him over.

"The fanzine, right? What was the name of that thing? *'God-damn?'* "

Chipp clears his throat. "No, that's, uh, *Godfuck.*"

"Ooh, that's great." Dave laughs. "Send me extras for my sister. I'm Dave. We spoke on the phone."

"Yeah." Chipp smiles. The stranger's face finally falls into place. "You run the label. I thought I'd seen you here before. So how's it going?"

"Don't ask, sport." Dave sighs and pats down his pockets for something that isn't there. "You ever have one of those days?"

"Sure, I guess."

"Well"—Dave pauses, flashing a pair of bloodshot eyes—"I'm having one of those lives." He moves on. "The band is in the van. They're waiting for you."

"They are?" Chipp swallows nervously.

"Who else walks around with a tape recorder?"

Chipp nods sheepishly and starts to gather up his stuff when Todd comes through the side door that leads out to the alley. He's eating a huge orange and streams of juice are caught in his thick goatee.

"What's this I hear about a guarantee?" he says with his mouth full, spitting out the words along with little bits of pulp and seeds; a white fleshy vein sticks in his beard.

"Todd, you promised me. Now don't even try to . . ."

As Chipp heads for the back door, he can still hear the conversation, both voices starting to rise, filling with anger.

"I told you," Todd continues with his mouth full, "I'd split with you what I got at the door. If you don't trust me, then why don't you—"

Once outside Chipp spots The Deer Park's van parked in the corner of the empty lot. The back doors are open, and he can see two pairs of legs hanging out. Puffs of smoke appear every few seconds. He approaches the van slowly.

"Hey, I'm Chipp." He pokes his head around one of the rusting doors. "Uh, I'm from *Godfuck.* Didn't Dave tell you?"

They both nod, one of them taking a deep drag from a dovetailed joint.

"Let's see, you're Johnny." Chipp points to the one who is not smoking. "And you're Stoner, right?" He points to the other. They both look at Chipp dumbly. "Just, you know, making sure."

Just as Chipp sits down, Johnny says, "There are two questions we refuse up front to answer, and they are 'What are your influences?' and 'How has the success of Nirvana affected you?' *Capisci?*"

"Sure, sure." Chipp fake-laughs, getting out his list of questions and scratching off the first two. He places the recorder on the floor of the van between them. He tries to press PLAY and RECORD together, but when he presses the buttons of the recorder, it slips into the steel grooves of the floor and only one of the buttons catches.

" 'LICK MY LEGS OF DESIRE! LICK MY—' " Chipp stabs the thing with a clenched fist as Randy's voice hangs in the air for a few seconds.

"Sorry."

Chipp straddles the recorder over the grooves, presses PLAY and RECORD, and begins the interview.

"So how long has The Deer Park been around?"

"Um"—Johnny fields the first question since Stoner is preoccupied with picking at a WE'RE THE MEAT PUPPETS AND YOU SUCK! sticker on the door handle—"since about '90. Neither of us came aboard until about six months ago. I'm not really sure how Ben and the first couple of guitarists got together. You'd really have to ask them."

"Okay," Chipp says, checking the question off his list and moving on to the next. "Where'd you get the name from?"

"From a book," Johnny says, wiping a long greasy strand of jet black hair out of his sallow face. "But the guy who wrote the book got it from somewhere. Ben explained it to me once, what it was, just in case somebody asked. It was something like the Deer Park was this big place in France where the aristocra . . . arista . . ." He struggles with the word for a few seconds before giving up. "Where the rich people brought all the virginal girls from the small villages, and guys just did whatever they wanted to them."

"The loss," Stoner deeply intones, "of innocence."

"Yeah," Johnny agrees. "That, and it also sounded good."

"Next question," Chipp mumbles, trying desperately to read his list in the dank half-dark of the van. "If you were trapped on a desert island and could bring only ten records, what would they be?"

Chipp tosses the question, and it lands on the other side of the van, sitting there for a moment as Stoner releases another lethal blast of smoke from his recently lighted skull bong, and Johnny rolls his eyes a couple of times, formulating his answer. In the downtime between yelling into the canyon and waiting for the echo, Chipp's eyes scan the van.

Filling the steel grooves on the floor of the van is a clear, sticky goo that most likely is some hybrid of assorted liquors and sweat, the snail trail of slime starting toward the driver seat and emptying out onto the bumper. Stickers and *Hustler* pinups line the inside of the van, which, as Chipp is beginning to notice, smells like a trash can with moldy food at the bottom. He checks the barely lit corners of the vehicle for perhaps a carton of month-old Subway sandwiches or a green pizza with growing fuzz anchored on a guitar stand. Johnny is sitting on a case of beer, and Stoner is leaning against the door with a curled-up and stained *Star Wars* blanket.

"*Raw Power*," Stoner begins his desert island disc list, adding, "*Raw Power, Raw Power, Raw Power, Raw Power, Raw Power, Raw Power, Raw Power, Raw Power . . .*"

"Well," Chipp says with a sigh, "that's only nine, but, whatever. Johnny? How about yours?"

"Stupid question." He shifts his weight. "Ask something else."

"Okaaaayyyy," Chipp draws out the word as he scrambles for the next question on his increasingly short list. "How do you guys come up with the lyrics?"

"We don't," Johnny burps, ripping off a leg of his chair and drinking it. "Ben does."

"How about the music? Where does *it* come from?"

"You'd have to ask Ben," Stoner says, trying to act out of it.

You'd have to ask Ben. You'd have to ask Ben. How many times have I heard that in the past half-hour? Jesus, what do these guys know? So when you're alone with a girl, how do you know she cares for you as much as you care for her? Chipp imagines Stoner doing his best Syd Barret impersonation: *You'd like, wow, have to ask Ben.*

"What are your goals for The Deer Park?"

"To keep making good music, plain and simple," Johnny answers.

The more frustrated Chipp gets with the rote answers, the angrier he gets at himself for asking such lame questions.

"Well, that's all the questions I have," Chipp says, leaning forward to turn off the recorder. Johnny says thanks and politely shakes his hand, while Stoner just sits there taking hit after hit off his bong.

Back on the sidewalk, Chipp exits the parking lot and heads for the street. It's nearly dark, the sky colored like a bruise, dark blue, purple, black. Walking is difficult. The few bong hits he took (not to mention being cooped up with Stoner for almost a half hour) slowly take hold, and he finds it hard to resist a grin and begins laughing out loud.

The streets of Kitty are nearly empty. Chipp walks quickly along the uneven sidewalks, kicking at cans and debris in his path. He thinks of Stoner and Johnny back at the van, preparing for later in the evening when they'll spend an hour pounding on their drum skins and bass. *Why do they do it? What possesses them? Why bother?*

He stumbles loudly up the stairs to his apartment and finds Randy lying on the couch. Randy is listening to Chipp's records, using Chipp's headphones, with an empty bag of Chipp's Cheetos by his side. Chipp sits down at the kitchen table, pulls out the recorder along with a pad of paper, and a pencil, and gets ready to transcribe the conversation. He giggles again and Randy twitches, as if he is being electrocuted. Chipp rewinds the tape, presses PLAY.

"So, how long has The Deer Park been around?"

To his own ears his voice sounds strange, tinny, not at all how he thinks it sounds. He laughs again, tries to concentrate, and begins writing down their answers.

It's a quiet night, and Chipp can hear the music seeping from the seal between the headphones and Randy's ears. He figures he'll transcribe the interview, order a pizza, and then see if Randy and Sarita want to go to The Scene with him and Heather. Why not?

5

Craig is chopping basil and anxiously watching the clock, waiting for their guests to arrive.

"Who did you say his date was?" Craig calls out to Ashley from the kitchen.

"What?" she shouts back.

Craig chops some red potatoes into quarters and drops them into a pan with butter and parsley, adds a dash of salt, and mixes it all together. He turns down the flame and walks into the bedroom.

"I asked you who Andrew was bringing."

Ashley is pulling on a pair of white tights, pulling at the excess slack gathered around the knees and thighs in small handfuls and bringing the elastic band just over her belly button.

"I don't know. He didn't say." She grabs a dress from the closet and pulls it over her head.

There's a knock at the door.

"I'll get it," Ashley says, flipping her head to each side as she puts on a pair of earrings. As she heads for the door, Craig returns to the kitchen, stirs the potatoes, and then covers them. He hears the door open, and a few pairs of footsteps enter the hallway as Ashley feigns interest. "Really? Traffic? Wow!" He hears Ashley being introduced to Andrew's date but doesn't catch the name, just the muffled scuttling of high heels and pleasantries being passed around. "No, *you* look nice."

"Craig?" He can feel a presence behind him. "They're here."

He sets down a steaming wooden spoon and turns around.

"This is Brook." Ashley points to an attractive young girl with burgundy hair wearing a summer dress, leather sandals, and a sly smile. Craig is in shock. "And Andrew, well, you know Andrew."

Everyone laughs except Craig until everyone notices he's not laughing, and then he jumps into the fray with a mild-mannered guffaw that's obviously forced.

"Well," Ashley ventures into the ensuing silence, "how about a drink?"

"That'd be great," says Andrew, nervously tugging at his chambray shirt.

"I'm game," replies Brook, staring directly into Craig's green eyes and red face.

The four of them enter the living room and crowd around a table on which sit four glasses, two bottles of wine, and a small platter of cheese and crackers. While Ashley is serving the guests their drinks, pouring the pink Chablis to the brim of juice glasses (the wineglasses were broken earlier in the day), Craig is numb, biting his lip.

Craig's mind is racing. *Is she going to give me away? Why would she?* He remembers her giving him her number, leaving him with the scrap of paper and a kiss: "Call me." But he never did.

As the other three engage in some moribund conversation concerning recent news events, Craig twists in his chair like Alex from *A Clockwork Orange* sat in the lair of his former victim who hadn't yet recognized him. Or so Alex thought. *We had a fling. A one-night stand. Surely she wasn't expecting anything else. She probably gave me her number out of habit, not because she was hoping to get me into her life, wondering what kind of person I was, did I like kids, what my favorite movie is. Please. Brook is smart enough not only not to want that but not to expect that, either.* Craig grins, slightly smug, as if he has just pulled off a flawless robbery. Or so he thinks.

"Don't I know you?" Brook asks.

The conversation between Ashley and Andrew halts abruptly, all passengers sent careening into the seats in front of them.

"Uh, me?" He can feel sweat forming on his upper lip. *Easy. Cool. Take it easy.* "N-n-not that I know of."

"Really? Because I could have sworn." She is waving her index finger in an I-told-you-so fashion. "I'm usually quite good at these things."

Why is she doing this to me? Besides fucking her and then never talking to her again, what have I done?

Noticing the perplexed look on the faces of Andrew and Ashley, Craig tries to proffer some sort of explanation. "I, you

know, just sort of have one of those, uh, recognizable faces . . . I
guess."

"Well," Brook says with mock disappointment, "I guess I was
wrong."

Craig shoots out of his chair and rushes into the kitchen.
He absentmindedly begins stirring, whipping, chopping, adding
spices to the open sink. Anything.

"Can I get an ice cube?"

He turns and faces Brook, who is twirling a long strand of
straight hair around a pencil-thin finger.

"What are you doing to me out there?" he whispers as forcibly
as possible while pulling her into the kitchen.

"Why, whatever do you mean?" she says innocently.

"Oh, come on. Is this a joke? Is Andrew in on this? How did
you know I lived here?"

"Don't flatter yourself, *Craig*." She says his name as if it had
been a filled-in blank on a preprinted form: THIS SPACE FOR
SALE. "I had no idea you'd be here tonight. Andrew just wanted
me to come along and meet a few of his friends. How did I
know I had already met one of them? I mean, after all, Kitty's a
small town."

"No shit. Too small. So you like sleeping with Andrew?" A
quick look at the competition in the room.

"Please, he's not exactly the most adventurous person in bed.
For instance, one time I said, 'I want to tie you up,' and he
thought I meant with commitment."

As she leans in and nibbles on his ear, Craig spies the slit in
Brook's dress exposing her thigh. "Now you, on the other hand,
were a *tiger*."

Craig smiles for a moment before being struck with a ques
tion.

"Hey, wait a second. Was Andrew the guy who ran off with
your Unrest CD?"

"No, but I'm impressed you remembered. I met Andrew at
the Novel Idea cafe. We both reached for a hardback copy of
White Noise, and we've been sort of dating ever since. But I get
the feeling he's involved with someone else or at least in love
with someone else. But she's dating some jerk who has no idea
what's going on. Can you imagine being that stupid?"

"Gee, I'll try," Craig says as he reaches for the steel spoon that has been lying in the pan of sizzling potatoes.

A few minutes after Brook disappears into the kitchen, Andrew scoots two inches closer to Ashley. He looks around the room once, then twice, as if he were crossing a busy street, making sure the coast is clear.

"Why have you been avoiding me?" he says in a hurt, hushed tone.

"Look, Andrew, drop it. I never would have invited you tonight if I thought you were going to start in on all that again. We had some fun, maybe they were mistakes, I don't know."

"Mistakes?" he says, astonished. "I love you, Ashley."

"Oh, please." She dismisses him, turning to her drink which she downs with a jerk of the neck.

"Why haven't you answered my letters? I must have written you half a dozen. Didn't you like the poems?"

Ashley's indifference turns to anger.

"Speaking of the letters, just what in the hell did you think you were doing, mailing them to the apartment? Suppose Craig had seen them? Thank God he has a day job. And as for your poetry . . ." The cross hairs circle about the room before zeroing in on the center of Andrew's already slightly caved-in chest. "The only thing worse than your syntax is your sorry excuse for meter. Onomatopoeia? Sorry, Andrew, but Iammagoingtabesicka."

Andrew begins quietly weeping as Ashley rises from the couch, again pulls up her slouching stockings, and refills her drink.

Back in the kitchen:

"Do you expect me to act like nothing's happened?" Brook says sarcastically. "What about our special night together?"

"Oh, cut the crap, Brook. You couldn't have given a shit about me, and I feel the same way about you. Maybe if I had stolen your VCR or something, you'd have come looking for me."

"So? Does that mean I can't have a little fun?"

"Fun? Watching my life go down the tubes is fun?"

"No." She kisses him lightly on the lips and grabs his crotch. "*Causing* your life to go down the tubes is fun."

. . .

During dinner the scene underneath the table is a freeway of feet: Brook's slender foot angling its way up Craig's hairy calf as he tries to shake her off. Andrew, who has kicked off a loafer and is afraid his sock smells, tries to lift the edge of Ashley's skirt with his toe. At one point Andrew is feeling up Craig while Ashley has relented for a moment and lets Brook caress her inner thigh.

"More chicken anybody?" Craig announces as he jumps out of his seat after finding Andrew's hairy paw in his lap.

Ashley and the guests all agree they've had enough, and the small dinner party moves back into the living room. After a large meal and two bottles of wine among the four of them, the scene is nice and hazy, the music pouring easily into the senses. The light in the room seems diffused, like a shot of Ingrid Bergman in *Casablanca*, every sharp corner rounded off, every glitch in real life somehow smoothed out.

Craig goes to the kitchen to retrieve another bottle of wine. There is nothing left but a jug of Burgundy a friend had given them as a housewarming present nearly six months ago. Craig shrugs, screws off the cap, and pours four generous glasses.

"There you are." Brook appears from around the corner.

"Brook, please, stop it." He can hear Andrew and Ashley discussing the latest Updike novel in the next room, and Ashley is complaining it has too much sex, while Andrew thinks there isn't enough.

"Look, normally I go for this kind of thing in a big way," Craig says, "but not right now. I can't."

"Why can't you? It's not like you're married or anything." Noticing his hands are full and he is thus open to an attack, Brook plants a wet kiss on his neck.

"Oh, I know that. That's not what I mean. I mean, she'll see . . ."

Before leaving, Brook slides her tongue from his ear to the base of his neck, leaving a wet trail. Craig revolves his shoulder, bringing his head against his chest, trying to hide the mark.

"We're out of white wine, so . . ." As Craig hands the glasses around, Ashley catches a trace of lipstick on his neck.

"But what I was saying—" Andrew shoots Craig a nasty look for interrupting his conversation, thoughts, and life—"is that compared to any of the Rabbit books, *Memories of the Ford Administration* is a minor work."

"Well, get over it, Andrew." Ashley takes a sip of the red wine, shuddering instantly at the harsh taste that seems like vinegar after the smooth pallor of Chablis. "Because Rabbit's dead. Harry ain't coming back."

"I had a rabbit once," Brook says. "But he died. His name was Stimpy."

"No," Andrew says harshly. "We're not talking about an animal." His voice rises well out of the range of polite conversation. "We're talking about a literary character. If you weren't so fucking stupid, maybe you'd understand . . ." His speech peters out in frustration, his head buried deep in his hands.

The room falls silent as Andrew's hostile comment takes a few seconds to evaporate. If there were a vinyl record playing in the background, it would have skitted off in Hollywood fashion, a brief scratching, then silence, leaving an open hole for drama. Instead the CD continues to play "Under the Surface" by Bettie Serveert.

"Look, why don't we . . ." Ashley, ever the diplomat, tries to change the subject.

Brook's lower lip is trembling as she holds back tears. She knows these people are smarter than she is or at least is positive they all think they are. Andrew and Ashley both have degrees, while Brook is still three years into junior college and that's only because she had a crush on one of her teachers. She's not sure about Craig, but he talks a good game, and Brook figured he could fake his way through most intellectual discussions, which really seems the point anyway. The word Updike meant as little to her as the other words they had been using that evening: allegorical, pedantic, epistemological.

Brook knows that Andrew thinks she's stupid. She knows that she's his pathetic walk on the stupid side: a girl who will give him blow jobs, not a challenge; will lend him her body, not books; stimulate his groin, not his mind. Brook knows this and yet keeps seeing him. Mostly it's because the crush at junior college fizzled out and she was lonely. From the first instance at the cafe she knew Andrew was acting condescendingly toward her. Ever since, he's left his brain at his place whenever he came over to hers. She'd been snubbed by the town's small assemblage of literati for so long that to have one be attracted to her, even if it was under suspicious terms, still counted. It was like when she was in elementary school and all the rage was K-Swiss sneakers, the ones with two leather strips perpendicular to the legs that striped the area just above the toe. They cost around eighty bucks, and Brook's divorced mom couldn't afford them. Her older brother had a pair left over from his days on the junior high tennis team and gave them to his sister. Brook wore them proudly. The beat-up pair was hopelessly too big and a style or two away from the currently popular model, but Brook still grinned, her braces like the grille of a car. They were still K-Swiss.

Brook starts crying.

"I'm sorry." Andrew heaves forward and attempts to rub Brook's back, but she brushes his pink hand aside.

"Get away from me."

"I think . . . I'm drunk . . . " he says slowly, as if to exonerate himself from his thoughtless outburst. "And now I'm . . . going to be . . ." His cheeks bulge suddenly like the theater doors in *The Blob,* holding back an avalanche of warm ooze.

"Come on," Ashley says wearily, dragging her recalcitrant lover into the bedroom to lie down.

"Yeah, go let him rest, and I'll, uh, comfort Brook," Craig mumbles.

"I'll bet," Ashley says as a parting shot, disappearing around the corner.

"He's such an asshole," Brook mutters, her face slightly streaked with mascara.

"Then why are you with him?" Craig slides off the couch and sits across from Brook on the floor. "I mean, Andrew's the type of guy who just sort of has *geek* written on his forehead. I'd think most of the guesswork was taken care of for you."

"It's just, I don't know . . . when you never called . . ." Her hand slides again to his thigh.

"Brook, stop that. That's bullshit." He pushes her hand away and vacates the floor for the couch.

"Is it?" she says as she gets up slowly.

Craig grabs his wineglass and gulps down the warm liquid that, after four glasses, is beginning to taste like Kool-Aid. The more he drinks, the better it gets. He takes another big swig, then rests the glass in the center of his chest. He watches Brook rise slowly, like a killer in a horror film getting up for the third time as the poor victim watches in fearful amazement. The candles in the room cast dancing shadows over the wall; the entire apartment is shaded in a flickering spider web. Brook pulls her dress around her waist, exposing white cotton panties, and sets a bare knee on either side of him.

In the bedroom, Andrew is fumbling with the sheets, trying to crawl inside, peeling back layer after layer of linen until he finally slips between the bare mattress and its foam covering.

"No, Andrew, you're not going to—oh, hell . . ."

Even from this distance Andrew can smell the residue of Ashley's rosy perfume joined with the musky natural scent of her body. It reminds him of the aftermath of his own bed on a few occasions. Often he would sit and just smell the place where Ashley had been, every act of her female ritual a mystery to him: the way she did her hair, the application of makeup, why she hurried to the bathroom after they completed sex. After she had gone, Andrew would proudly wrap himself up in his sheets that had been layered with Ashley's delicate odor, as if he had been granted admittance to a strange and secret tomb. He felt like Indiana Jones.

"I love you," he blurts out.

"Not so loud, you fool." Ashley lightly raps him.

"I love you," he says again, his arms grabbing, but their drunken state lend them a rubbery quality. Andrew cannot connect with Ashley. He begins absentmindedly reciting one of the many poems he has written her over the past few weeks: "Were you really having fun that night, or just trying to convince yourself . . ." He stops, unable to remember the rest.

"Andrew, I mean it!" Anger fills her voice. "Don't make a scene."

He buries himself deep in the covers and begins weeping. His head pushes defiantly against the rough diamond pattern of the mattress in a burrowing motion, as if to disappear.

On the couch Brook's arms brace the back of the frame while the top half of her body, pivoting at the hips, descends slow and exact, the distance between her and Craig's lips a straight line. Brook's chest pushes up against Craig's stout juice glass, still half-filled with red wine, but it proves a meager obstacle. Brook pushes the small cup forward, until it overturns and the tepid liquid runs down Craig's numb chest. He barely notices it. *"I want you."* Their faces meet and lock. Brook's tongue thrusts into Craig's dazed mouth, which responds more out of habit than anything else. Brook begins grinding her pelvis in Craig's too-drunk-to-fuck midsection when suddenly there's another pair of heels scraping against the hardwood floor.

Brook dismounts like an Olympic gymnast.

"How's what's-his-name?" Craig asks nervously.

"I guess Andrew will be okay." Ashley sits in a chair, noticing the wet spot on Craig's chest out of the corner of her eye. "He just needs to sleep it off."

"I'd better go check on him," Brook says quickly, darting out of the room.

Ashley waits a moment before casting her accusation into the still water.

"Craig, do you know Brook? I mean, did you know her before tonight?"

He gulps. "No, how could I?"

"I don't know." She bites a fingernail and spits out a flake of bitter polish. "It seems as if you've gone out with her before. Maybe I'm just crazy."

"Look, I've no more gone out with Brook than you've gone out with Andrew." Craig tosses the bomb, which Ashley catches and quickly buries it. "Is that clear?"

She gets up from the chair and joins him on the couch.

"Clear as an azure sky," she quotes one of their favorite movies. Ashley bends her head down so she can put her arm around him. He smells like chicken and wine. "Clear as an unmuddied lake."

They sit for a moment as the candles, at their wicks' end, begin to flicker out.

Craig plants a smelly kiss on his girlfriend's cheek.

"Now aren't you glad we had them over?"

6

"The problem with you," Sarita keeps saying, lunging at Randy, who's so tired of trying to avoid her that he's stopped. She runs into him again, her outstretched finger curling up against his chest, her jade green eyes dazed with alcohol, and her brown hair covering half her face.

"The problem with you," she starts over, "is that you're all a lost generation." She burps as a period.

"Will you shut up?" Randy, who's been quiet most of the night, finally says. "You've been saying that all night, and you're not even saying it right!"

"What?" Sarita burps again, covering her mouth with a small hand whose stubby, slightly chewed nails are covered in glittery purple polish.

"That line—you know, your little Hemingway quote—you're saying it wrong. It's not 'The problem with you is that you're all a lost generation,' it's just, 'You're a lost generation.' I mean, where do you get 'The problem with you is' part?"

"Aha!" Sarita laughs and lunges again, stopping in mid-hurl for another burp that Randy does not find attractive. He zigzags out of her way and crosses the street. Sarita follows. "It's not a Hemingway quote, you moron, it's a Gertrude Stein quote that was only prefaced in a Hemingway novel! So there!"

"Yeah, yeah," Randy mumbles, thinking he should have received points for even making the Hemingway connection.

"Hey, at least I do a Gertrude Stein impression! How many other girls—or, well, guys, too, I guess—do a Gertrude Stein impression?"

Randy sighs. "Just no more Picasso stories, okay? Better yet, why don't you do an Alice B. Toklas impression. At least then we could all eat hashish brownies and get stoned."

Sarita joins Randy. He forgets for a moment that he is mad at her and opens his arms, pulling her warm body alongside his.

He pulls her in close; this is only their fourth date, and already he's getting to know her body, how to slide his arm under hers for a perfect fit, slowing down his own lanky gait and allowing her to catch up.

Sarita wrecks the moment by breaking into laughter.

"Again with the laughing?" Randy asks, pulling his arm away. "God, I can't believe you actually laughed during *Wings of Desire*. Jeez, that's so classless."

"It was funny!" Sarita defends. Down the street behind them, Heather is nibbling on Chipp's ear, and he's too numb to notice. "That guy Baretta, or whoever he was, I mean, was he supposed to be acting that way?"

"Colombo, not Baretta. Didn't you ever watch any good TV? And, yes, he was supposed to act that way. I mean, I guess so."

Sarita runs in front of Randy, her thick heels clattering against the wet sidewalk, sending echoes down the deserted street. Lights go on in a few of the windows, unhappy homeowners wondering what in the hell all the racket is. Half a block away Chipp and Heather have stopped walking and are now sitting on a bus-stop bench, necking. Sarita brushes her long bangs out of her eyes, readjusts her thick red glasses, stoops over, and says in a slow, scratchy, New York accent tinged with a hint of senility behind a tough exterior: "Am I as good an actor now as I was twenty years ago?"

Randy keeps on walking, muttering, "We're going to be late," and trying to hold back a laugh that Sarita deserves. A rickety-blue-and-white bus rounds the corner, stopping for Heather and Chipp, who jump off the seat, startled, and run down the sidewalk toward Sarita and Randy.

"Hey, wait up!" Chipp calls out with his arm around Heather. Heather's orange hair and bright blue skull tattoo are visible even through the murkily lit night, while Chipp, in a black T-shirt and black jeans, fades into the shadows.

Sarita stumbles on a crack in the street, regains her proper footing, and sprints a few feet to catch up before saying it again. "You know what your problem is? You're all a lost generation. You're . . . you're . . ." She can't remember the next line even though she has been repeating it all night. "You're just damn lost, that's what you are."

Randy stops in his tracks, surveys the street that doesn't look familiar. He retraces their steps from the Capitol Cinema, trying to lead them to The Scene.

"You know, you may be right?"

The A&R man slithers against the back wall of the club. He's thinking, *Where did I put my damn earplugs?* He pats down his blue blazer. Nothing. He winces at the four guys on stage jumping around, smashing their fists into their instruments, sending waves of cacophonous noise barreling down the thin club, hurtling like a tsunami toward the A&R man. The moment of impact nearly knocks him down. *Great! I'm going to go deaf thanks to these monkeys.*

After a few more songs, the lead singer, hair draped over his face, belches into the microphone and announces, "Thank you. Good night. We love you, Kitty!" The A&R man breathes a sigh of relief and heads for the bar as the crowd begins to retreat from the front of the stage.

"White wine spritzer," the A&R man calls out to the bartender.

Jack shoots him a look and grudgingly gets his drink.

"What'd you think of the band?" the bartender asks, throwing down a cocktail napkin covered with jokes.

"Are you kidding?" The A&R man throws down a five, laughs, takes a sip of the drink, and leans in close. "Between me and you, my grandmother could sing better, and she's senile!"

The A&R man laughs. Jack does not.

"My brother's the singer," Jack replies, tossing the change onto the bar. The coins bounce onto the floor, and the current from the air conditioner directly above the A&R man carries the two bills away into the crowd.

"Look, I don't want any trouble." The A&R man picks up his napkin and the drink, and tries to disappear into the group of kids.

Whew! That was a close one, he thinks to himself. *Probably some junkie hopped up on dope. And when is this damn band going to go on?* He takes tiny sips from his weak drink, hoping the trip wasn't a mistake.

Back on the street, Randy, Chipp, Heather, and Sarita are still trying to get their bearings. After stopping off at a convenience store for directions and guzzling down two beers, the four of them finally amble up to The Scene. Since the show's been on for an hour already, there's no line, although raggedy kids can be seen hanging around within a two-block area, hanging out in parking lots and smoking joints in the bushes. Chipp pulls Heather close to him as they approach the door. Todd is sitting behind a large podiumlike stand, underneath which is a stack of money and two stamps, one marked OVER 21, the other UNDER 21, alongside a rectangular ink pad.

"Guest list, *Godfuck* fanzine," Chipp calls out from three feet away; he sticks out his hand and it's stamped UNDER, barely breaking his stride, "plus one."

After they are waved in with a mumbled "Yeah, yeah, guest list, my ass. More money out of *my* pocket" from Todd, Chipp leans over and kisses Heather's ear.

"My cute little plus one!"

Behind them, Randy and Sarita are getting out their wallets in anticipation of paying the cover charge. Sarita readies her fake I.D. while Randy pats down his pockets, suspecting for a moment that he has left even his real I.D. at home, not to mention his fake one.

Once inside, Sarita gravitates toward the bar and buys Randy a beer. As Heather predicted earlier, they missed The Deer Park, which was all part of Chipp's plan, despite the fact that that's the band Heather wanted to see. Stoner and Johnny are just finishing loading their equipment into the van while Ben and their current rhythm guitarist sip free drinks and talk to a small group of underage girls. Chipp dissolves into the large crowd, heading for the edge of the bar, trying to avoid Stoner and Johnny even though it's no use: They had spotted him the moment he arrived.

The Scene is a large rectangle, the bar on the left, a small deck to the right with three or four tables, and some video games and pinball machines lining the wall. At the far corner of the deck is where the bands usually sell T-shirts, records, and other assorted trinkets that help them pay for gas and meals on the road.

"Hey!" Chipp sidles up to Randy, who is leaning on the tarnished brass rail, watching the bassist from Bottlecap plug in his guitar while the guitarist tapes a set list on his microphone stand. "Jack just told me that some A and R guy from a major label is here to check out Mark tonight."

"Mark"—Randy points to the stage with his long neck—"the guy in Bottlecap?"

A couple knock into Chipp as they make their way to the end of the bar.

"Yeah," Chipp continues, "Jack said he's been here all night."

"But what in the fuck does A and R mean?" Randy asks, spotting a good-looking girl playing pinball on the deck. "Isn't that a record label?".

"That's A and M, you dumbshit. A and R means Artists and, uh, Representing Artists or . . . I don't know for sure, but it's like a talent scout."

Randy spots the guy in the crowd; wearing a suit, he's hugging the wall, looking half-scared.

"So Bottlecap is going to be rich and famous?" Randy says as a joke just as Bottlecap takes to the stage and bursts into their first song of the evening.

"Looks like it!" Chipp shouts over the blaring noise, then kisses Heather on the cheek and rushes into the crowd.

Randy polishes off the rest of his beer, winks at Sarita, and bends to kiss her the way Chipp kissed Heather a moment before. She grabs onto his shirt and whispers in his ear, "I want to fuck you." She pushes him away just enough to be able to look deeply into his eyes before pulling back and adding, "As soon as we get back to your place, I want to fuck you."

With the slight stirrings of a hard-on Randy heads into the sea of bodies after Chipp. *I want to fuck you.* The words keep going through Randy's head over the waves of distorted guitars and shouted vocals.

"I've been talking . . . to-ooh-ooh . . . Stephen Hawking," Mark screams out while feverishly strumming his dark green Fender Jaguar, *"and he said it's not in the stars for us."*

Randy begins to pogo with the crowd, jumping up and down, tossing his head to the music, jostling against the throbbing bodies.

"Look into his twitching face . . . as he points a spindly finger out toward space and says, 'It's not meant to be,' " Mark sings just before going into a guitar solo while the bassist and drummer pound out a frenzied rhythm.

It's a trio, thinks the A&R man, *just like Nirvana.* He looks over the twentysomething crowd, all bobbing their stringy heads in unison to the beat. A few youths near the front of the stage are jumping up and down, knocking into one another. "Slam dancing," says the A&R man to himself. "I know what that is."

"It's a clear sky tonight, and I hope you're somewhere being held tight . . . because I have got to get light-years away from you." Mark is now jumping up and down, slashing his right arm up and down over the strings in a seesaw fashion. *"Yes, I have got to get light-years away from you-ooh. . . ."*

One of the kids makes his way up to the front of the stage, crawls up on the speakers, stands up, faces the cheering audience, and then leaps out, landing on the heads and arms of the other kids. *Doesn't that hurt?* thinks the A&R man. *Why don't they all just let him fall?*

After a few more songs, Randy can't concentrate on either the music or the scene around him. The sensations and images of Sarita naked above him keep revolving through his head. He begins to fight his way out of the crowd, maniacally tossing kids aside on his way to the exit.

"Randy." Chipp stops him, pointing at Randy's third T-shirt of the week, which reads ATARI GENERATION. The charcoal is streaking down his soaked chest like mascara trails on a crying woman. "Randy!" he shouts again, finally stopping Randy, who's bounding against his grasp. "You're running!" He points to the shirt.

"I know." Randy breaks his grasp and leaps past him and out of the club.

Forty minutes of thrashing, writhing punk-pop later, it's over. The A&R man is relieved. He spots the lead singer hustling to get their instruments off the stage before the headlining band goes on.

"Excuse me, young man?"

Mark doesn't notice him.

"I said excuse me."

The singer finally spots this strange sight resting against one of the monitors.

"Yeah?"

"Loved your set. I'm from A & R at Subterfuge Records. I believe we spoke earlier in the week? Here's my card." He offers both his hand and the slip of paper to the singer, who takes both. The card reads HENRY JAMES, ARTISTS AND REPRESENTATION, SUBTERFUGE RECORDS. The address is on Sunset Boulevard in Los Angeles. "Uh, what's your name again?"

"Mark, Mark Pellion. And this is Steve." Mark pulls the drummer aside as he's trying to shove his bass drum into its large black case. "And over there is Gary." He points across the club to where Gary is standing against a wall smoking a cigarette, talking to a young-looking girl with long straight black hair and acne.

"Well, Mark, it's nice to meet you. Um, is there someplace we could go and talk?"

Music bursts out of the bar's P.A. system to entertain the crowd between bands, but the clinking of beer bottles, general chatter, and shuffling anticipation quickly drown it out.

Chipp rotates back to the bar where Heather is sitting, nursing a beer. Wiping the sweat off his forehead, he asks, "What happened to Randy?"

"I don't know," she replies, bored. "I saw them leave almost a half-hour ago. So guess who I've been talking to all night?"

"Who?" Chipp raises his hands to motion for a drink, only Jack doesn't see him, and Chipp tries to play it like he's just stretching.

"Nobody, that's who."

Instead of listening to Heather, Chipp notices that there are two different designs of Superchunk T-shirts stuck to the wall with black tape, along with a few singles and The Deer Park's and Bottlecap's releases on Violent Revolutions Records. Sitting next to the stock, alongside a table on which sit an ashtray holding a lit cigarette and a cigar box with a few dollar bills sticking out of it, is a guy who Chipp swears was in his English class in high school.

Turning back to the crowd he sees that the audience is divided into two sections, the old and the young. Most of the young (late teens) are huddled near the stage, interested in hearing the music, jostling one another for a better position, crowding near the front, being crushed against amps and monitors, but wanting to be as close to the band as possible. Most of the older members of the audience (mid-twenties to early thirties) are sitting around the bar, smoking, drinking, content to watch the show from bar stools or chairs, any place that's close enough so they won't have to be pried out of the crowd with a can opener if they want another drink.

While Heather is buying two beers with her fake I.D., Superchunk unceremoniously takes the stage. They look exactly like the crowd, dressed in cut-off shorts, tank-tops, T-shirts, and sneakers. Jim (the rhythm guitarist) is wearing jeans with holes in the knees. Laura (the bassist) is already jumping up and down to the music that hasn't even started. Jon (the drummer) is making sure all his cymbals are in place and positions an extra pair of drumsticks in the silver tuning keys of the bass drum. Mac (the lead singer and guitar player) straps on his Les Paul Jr. guitar over a faded My Bloody Valentine *Loveless* T-shirt, turns up the volume, and yells out "one, two, three, four" as the band rips into the first song of the evening.

"I put a stick in your spokes, and you'd better laugh at my jokes . . ."

The crowd starts to pogo slightly, jumping up and down. There's a handpainted sign to the left of the stage that reads NO STAGE DIVING, but no one pays any attention to it.

Chipp is singing along to "Seed Toss," and Heather is bobbing her head to the music, as if she wants to seem *into* it. She's afraid she'll look dumb if she just stands there. To the left of Chipp is a short guy with a Ween T-shirt who is slamming wildly even though there's no pit yet. He's just bumping into people left and right; they push him away, annoyed, as if they're swatting at a fly. This is the one guy you find in every crowd whose behavior is a polar opposite to everyone's else. If the crowd is just standing there, this guy will be jumping around like a fish out of water, as though he has the music running through his veins and just can't control himself. If the whole floor is moving like a wave, up and down, this guy is like a buoy propelled by the current, trying to sit there and enjoy the music. Chipp laughs as he watches a big guy with a leather jacket send him to the floor.

"Thank you, thank you," Mac perfunctorily says after the first song. The band members wipe off their heads the sweat that has already formed and take drags off the assorted beer bottles that have been placed for them throughout the stage.

Superchunk plunges into another fast song; both guitars wail, sending a wash of noise down the cavern of the club. The bass is making Chipp's jeans flap against his thighs. He can feel the drums pulsating through the floor. The vocals slap him in the face. His ears burn at first and then go numb.

Chipp shoves his way through the crowd to the circular opening of the mosh pit. Kids revolve in circles, crashing into each other and then caroming off and setting a new course, aimed for somebody else. Chipp waits, looks for an opening. Seconds later he tosses himself into the chaos and is instantly struck from the back, shot like a bullet toward the stage. He bangs up against the back of some guy about two layers away from the stage. The person in front of him pushes out his ass, juts out his elbow (the only defense), peeling Chipp off him like a sweaty sock.

Chipp always feels sorry for the guys in the pit with their girlfriends. Kids are moshing left and right, slamming into the girl, smacking her in the head, the back, and the poor boyfriend has his arm around her, trying to fend them off, but the crowd is always too much. She just wants to hear the band play her favorite song, a slow tearjerker that the couple plays whenever they make love, but instead she's getting black and blue marks, and the boyfriend can't stop it from happening.

Chipp pogos back into the pit, grabs a guy by the shirt, throws him into the crowd, and then has the same thing happen to him. Somebody crashes into him, and for a moment he and the stranger make eye contact. The stranger's bloodshot eyes open widely, excited. He frees a hand from his chest and sticks it in Chipp's face, pointing toward the ceiling. "You want up?" Chipp screams, but with no chance of being heard over the band's three-chord din. It doesn't matter anyway; the message is clear, and Chipp knows the routine. He and the guy make their way toward the stage. The stranger faces Chipp, his back to the band, and raises a foot. Chipp bends down and clasps his hands together under the kid's foot. The kid, hoisted up by Chipp, crawls on top of the crowd. The crowd, who meet another stage diver's presence like old people meet mosquitoes, begins the club equivalent of swatting him; they push him toward the stage and out of their collective hair.

The bouncer is late to catch the action, and there's no way he'll catch the kid in time. The kid gets dropped on stage, stands up quickly, faces the crowd, and jumps out, landing on assorted heads and shoulders. A space is quickly made, and he's dropped down on the ground again where, pumped up by adrenaline, he screams and begins pogoing higher than before. The bouncer eyes him in the audience and screams out a warning, though no one can hear. The kid finds Chipp in the crowd and, as an act of appreciation, slaps his shoulder, crashes into him, throws him against the undulating wall of bodies.

The next song, "Mower," is a slow one, and rather than slam, the crowd just sways back and forth like a wave. Troublemakers in the back of the audience push forward until the bodies shift quickly in one direction, then roll back in the other. Those at the very front of the stage, pinned against the monitors, hold their breath when the waves come, then push out with asses and elbows, releasing their pent-up air and frustration when it recedes. Chipp, in the middle and surrounded on all sides by smelly kids in ripped T-shirts, is caught in the motion and sways backward, frontward, sideways, whichever way the forces propel him. For an instant, while being shuttled to the left, he lifts his feet off the floor and is held upright and in place by the compactness of the crowd. He is carried a full ten feet before he rests his now unlaced Docs back on the cigarette butt-strewn floor of The Scene.

The song ends and the band pauses for a moment before beginning another, again wiping their faces and taking swigs of beer. Mac says something to Jim and laughs, but it can't be made out over the P.A. system. Laura switches her bass for another, and the drummer wipes his face with a white towel from the ground.

The crowd is still for a second, and Chipp tries to stuff the long-undone laces of his shoes into his socks so he doesn't lose them. He takes off his watch and puts it in his front pocket along with his wallet. He wipes his sweaty hair out of his face and quickly catches his breath. Mac drains his beer, throws the bottle to the crowd, then places his hand over the fret in a barre chord. *This is going to be good,* Chipp thinks quickly.

The band ferociously rips into Chipp's favorite, "Skip Steps 1 & 3." The guitars slice, the drums pound, the bass pummels, and the vocals screech. It takes the crowd only a second to react. By the second bar of splendid noise the pit is formed again, and kids are flying left and right, off the stage, against one another, sweat and a trail of blood here and there. Chipp bumps into the kid from before, and this time it is Chipp who gives the signal.

"You've been sucking wind so long it makes you feel full," Mac screams out. He skips around the stage, pounding his guitar, the music bursting the seams of the tiny club. The room is alive with energy equal to a neutron bomb.

The guy from before nods quickly and moves into position. Chipp turns his back on the band and leans up against the row of kids trying to watch the show. The stranger lifts him up, and Chipp wiggles his shoulders against the crowd, inching his way on top. Once there he feels multitudes of hands against his body, as if he were a centipede, a squiggling line of sensation from his head down to his feet.

He lurches slowly toward the band, which is jumping around the stage and sawing their respective instruments with lightning quick gestures of their fists, oblivious to Chipp and the pulsating crowd. Hands finally toss Chipp onto a monitor shaped like a Lite-Brite console. Chipp rolls down it and finds himself face-down on the surface of the stage, which is covered with scraps of tape and cords and beer. He scrambles to his feet, catching sight of the bouncer running to grab him. He turns quickly to the crowd, sees arms wave, one face here, one there, mouths opening and closing but the sound lost amid the grueling beat of the band. Chipp is about to jump when he feels two hands on his shoulders. The bouncer tries to drag him off the stage, but Chipp zigzags out of his grasp and hops to the far side of the stage. Before the bouncer can counter this maneuver, Chipp leaps over the crowd, twisting in the air, and lands with his back on the hands, heads, and shoulders of the crowd. For a few seconds he faces the stage, then various hands push him toward the back of the club and he is turned over and over until he is facing the back of The Scene. He can see people drinking, the EXIT sign flashing. All the while hands caress, grab, and propel him in all directions. After a full minute on top of the crowd he feels himself falling, his shoulders plummeting to the ground. Someone is still hanging on to his legs and his shoes are slowly slipping off, but he reaches out his hands to break his fall. Finally he is dumped completely on the ground, the view of legs like tree trunks in a forest. People are slamming all around him, and the music is muffled. Suddenly he feels more hands on his dazed body, people pulling him up, out of the way of the stampeding crowd. Realizing the moment of danger has passed (if it ever existed), Chipp joins the pit for another song of slamming, madly pogoing, pulsing with the music, feeling the sweat roll off his body, celebrating his victory.

The next song is another slower song, and the crowd thins out. A half-dozen kids head to the bar for another beer. Chipp takes the advantage of the path cut in the dense crowd by a guy in a leather jacket almost a foot taller than Chipp himself.

"Did you see that!" he screams to Heather, who is leaning against the bar, sipping on a Bacardi and Coke. "Did you see me stage-dive?"

"Yeah!" she screams. "Cool!"

"Fuck, I wish I had a picture! For the magazine!"

"What?"

"PICTURE!" He leans in close, cupping his hand to her ear. "FOR *GODFUCK!*"

She pulls back at both the shrill of his voice and the rancidness of his breath. Still, she smiles, not fully hearing what he said.

"Yeah! You bet!" She gives a stock answer.

After ordering a beer and quickly draining it, and soaking up the sweat on his forehead with half a dozen gag bar napkins, Chipp heads for the bathroom near the entrance. Once inside the restroom most of his senses are immediately attacked: His nostrils wither at the combined odor of pot, cigarette smoke, and urine; his eyes are jarred by the layers of graffiti, bumper stickers, and horrible jokes written in front of the urinals ("What are you reading this for? The joke is in your hands.").

After relieving his beer-filled bladder, he spots a figure hunched over the toilet in the corner. Neither of the stalls has doors, so Chipp can't help but notice the poor guy on all fours, throwing up into the bowl so hard that little flecks of water are splattering back in his face.

"Dave?" Chipp asks loudly enough to be heard over the music, which is again fully rocking.

The figure doesn't answer, burps instead, and spits against the wall several times, but Chipp recognizes the figure from earlier in the day. He moves in and grabs him by the shirt, carefully, as if his hangover could be transferred by mere touch. Dave rises off the ground a few inches, falling only when Chipp loses his grip on the T-shirt, which snaps back and clings to Dave's sweating body like a yanked bra strap. Dave knocks his head against the dirty gray toilet handle, one hand falls into the water, and his body drops to the ground.

"Shit," Chipp mutters.

Chipp looks both ways and quickly exits the toilet. He sees Heather at the bar, who spots him and waves. *It's not like he's going to remember me or anything.* He makes it halfway to the bar before raising a hand to Heather and heading back in the other direction.

"Okay, Dave, come on," Chipp says as he forcefully lifts Dave from the floor. Chipp drags him to the sink and broken mirror, wets a towel, and cleans off the spittle forming a crusty ring around Dave's mouth. Then he runs the cold water and splashes it against Dave's face.

"Dave!" Chipp is shouting and lightly slapping him.

After a minute or two Dave finally comes out of it.

"What! Who! . . . Why I oughtta . . ." His words trail off into a slur. His eyes open for a second, then close just as quickly. Chipp continues jostling him, splashing cold water on his face, slapping him lightly. A few minutes later, Dave has fully come around. He looks around the dingy bathroom and spits out the acrid aftertaste in his mouth. "I feel like"—he pauses for a second, picking out little bits of half-digested food from his teeth—"shit."

"Well, at least you're conscious," Chipp says. "I thought you were going to die."

"Like John—" Dave burps, fights down the rising tide in his stomach, and continues—"Bonham?"

"Who?" Chipp asks.

Dave ruefully shakes his head, wipes his face, and smooths his hair with a wave of his hand. They both exit the bathroom, and Chipp drags Dave to where Heather is still sitting at the bar.

"Where in the fuck have you been?" she yells. "Two-thirds of the opening band has tried to hit on me, and I think in another few minutes the drummer's going to give it a shot."

"Who's that hanging out with the musicians?" Dave says to no one special, burping. "That's the drummer!" he says, laughing uproariously, bumping into a few people before climbing onto a bar stool.

"What's *his* problem?" Heather asks, eyeing Dave.

"He—" Chipp begins, only to be interrupted by Dave.

"—had a real baaaaad day," he says, doing his best Bill Murray. Stacy would be proud.

"Dave, can someone give you a lift home?" Chipp shouts.

Dave doesn't answer.

"Who are you here with?" he tries again.

"No one," Dave finally answers. "I drove mysef," he says, leaving out the *l*.

"Look, Heather, I'm sorry," Chipp shouts in her ear. "I think you're going to have to go home without me. I'd better drive Dave's car home and make sure he's okay."

She pulls back as a cloud of bad breath descends on her. The idea of going home alone begins to appeal to her. She'd rather face denouncement from Jen than Chipp's odious mouth for a kiss.

"That's fine with me, but how will *you* get home?"

"I'll just crash with Dave. I'm sure he won't mind. Besides, I've seen him in the neighborhood. I'll just walk home in the morning."

The band delivers one more power chord before screaming, "Thank you! Good night!" They begin to unplug their instruments and load their equipment onto the van in anticipation of heading to the next town.

"Okay," Heather says, hopping off the bar stool. "See you later."

"Thanks for understanding. You're a doll," Chipp says, moving in to kiss her good-bye. She ducks out of the way and joins the crowd slowly moving toward the exit.

"A doll . . ." Dave mumbles before sliding off the stool and tumbling to the ground.

7

It's a clear night as Eileen walks to Jess's apartment, which is just a few blocks away from the cafe. He skipped out early so he could go home and "tidy up," he said, and she's hoping he's not setting up the place instead—like when a guy knows a girl is coming over, and he leaves the track medals and half-open books lying around so she'll be impressed. "Oh, wow, *Swann's Way*. You read Proust?" And then they brush their nails across their chest and say, "Actually, I'm *re*reading." Jess always seemed harmless enough in the cafe, cute, funny, easy to be around, but Eileen is wondering if he'll turn out like all the others and if going to his apartment is a mistake.

She turns the corner onto Prosperity Street, fighting the impulse to turn back. The street is practically empty save for the sound of a couple fighting in a second-story apartment and the low rumbling of a television set somewhere. A breeze brushes her cheek, instantly drying the tear that had formed a second earlier. Somewhere a dog barks. She can hear a scooter two streets away. That couple is laughing now, and they put on a record. A phone rings, feet scrape on the sidewalk behind her, and again she sniffles and fights back tears.

What little she knows about Proust is that his thesis was: There's no such thing as the present. Things happen much too quickly to analyze. The moment is gone before you can even begin to reflect on it. She listens for the dog to bark again, but it doesn't. The scooter is now parked or headed toward the suburbs, and the stranger, once behind her, brushes past her, keeps on walking. The stars, even if she can't see them, have shifted a million miles to the left since she stopped in her tracks. The second she was trying to contemplate is now gone. So is this one. And the next.

She plunges her hands deep into her faded jeans and keeps walking.

"Hey, glad you could make it!" Jess greets her eagerly at the door. In the background she can hear music playing. Maybe it is a bad sign, maybe not. She decides that if she discovers champagne chilling in a silver bucket, she's going to leave.

Jess shows her around the small, cluttered apartment: movie posters on the wall for *Who's That Knocking on My Door?* and *Billy Liar*, a Macintosh on a wood desk in the corner surrounded by a modem, printer and a few Xeroxed software manuals, an old couch that looks comfortable and has no visible scale of notches.

"Nice place you have here," she says, sitting on a huge wicker chair that looks like a bowl propped up on an ottoman. It's comfortable but kind of like a cage, and she sinks into it.

"Thanks," he says politely, handing her a beer she hasn't asked for. She takes it anyway. Jess pulls out a cigarette and lights it. It's funny; He's never smoked at the cafe, and whether or not that was one of Brenda's weird restrictions or just Jess's choice, Eileen isn't sure, but it seems like another part of the act. She watches carefully to make sure he's inhaling and not just using it as a prop. He takes a deep puff, holds it for a second, heaves his chest, and then blows the smoke out in a quick puff. He's either inhaling or else has been practicing. "It's a little messy right now, but you know how that is."

"Yeah, I guess," she says awkwardly. More and more Eileen is getting bad feelings—not from Jess, because he seems okay, but from herself. A few nights ago she really could have used the break from Brenda's neurotic worries, but tonight she just needs to be left alone.

"It's not much"—Jess points to his bohemian surroundings—"but at this point it's all I need."

"Uh, yeah," she says lamely. "Whatever."

"You like Morrissey?" he asks, kneeling at his stereo in the corner.

"What? Oh, yeah, he's all right, I guess."

" 'All right?' The Smiths were the best band of the eighties."
Jess defends, sliding out a thin black record from its almost
blank white sleeve. "Granted, most of Morrissey's solo work
hasn't been up to par. But The Smiths? They were *awe*some."

"I don't know." Eileen sits up uncomfortably in her chair.
"They always seemed really whiny to me."

"Whiny?" He places the single onto the player and rests the
needle in its groove.

"A child with a curious face, a man with sullen ways"—a voice
comes on, thick as honey, dreamy and spare, strummed guitar
in the background.

"What you're listening to is this super-rare, limited-edition
Factory single called 'I Know Very Well How I Got My Note
Wrong.' "

Jess hands Eileen the cover, and she fingers it carefully.

"Rare, huh? Says who?"

Jess snatches it back.

"Says anyone! And anyway, The Smiths were *not* whiny," Jess
continues, "just emotional. I think you're afraid of emotions."

"Why do you say that?" She crosses her arms on her chest and
sits up straight.

"Look at you." He points to her hands firmly gripping her
shoulders. "You're like this castle that won't let its drawbridge
down."

"Th-that's bullshit," she stutters, thinking of Don and trying
to get her mind off the subject.

"Look, Jess, I just don't think—"

"I'm sorry," Jess cuts her off, sensing her anger. "Change the
subject? How's that?"

Eileen nods quickly and leans back.

On the stereo the song is cruising along beautifully until the
guitarist obviously plucks the wrong note, and both guitarist and
vocalist break out into laughter. Jess picks up the needle and
pops *Hatful of Hollow* into the CD player.

"So, uh, how are you doing living above the cafe? Things
working out?" He takes a seat on the couch.

"Oh, okay, I guess. Brenda's a little hard to take. It's weird.
It's like she means well, but she just has a way of getting on my
nerves."

"I think I know what you mean. She sort of ran the last girl who worked there out of the job. She couldn't stand Brenda hanging around all the time. And that apartment's been vacant for a while. I guess she's just lonely is all . . ."

Eileen is not really listening to Jess but instead is taking note of the items he has in his house: Far Side desk calendar, The Smiths posters, a few Vonnegut paperbacks, copies of the *Utne Reader* as well as a biography of Michel Foucault. *Foucault, Proust.* She laughs. *Same difference.*

"Well, actually"—Eileen jumps back into the conversation—"I don't mind it sometimes. It's just that she stops by all the time, and it's getting to be a drag. Still, it's nice to have a friend. I guess she's really the only friend I have in Kitty."

"What about me?" Jess says in a mock-dejected voice.

"Yeah, you, too," she concedes

"Well then, why don't you come a little closer?" He pats his hand on the well-worn cushion.

Eileen extricates herself from the cocoon chair and joins Jess on the couch. The scene is familiar, not necessarily with Jess sitting beside her, but a man. All the old feelings come back— the longing, the fear, wanting him to touch her, wanting to touch him back. The curiosity followed by the dread that she may actually find out.

She and Jess talk for about an hour, drink a few more beers, play the music louder, and then start kissing. His hands caress her cheeks, the back of her neck, then run softly through her hair, not missing a trick. He nibbles lightly on her earlobe, the sensation burning all the way down her curved spine.

Eileen and Jess remain standing as they slowly undress each other, their progress halted only when Jess is caught up in the buttons of her jeans and, inevitably, the clasp of her bra. "No, no, it's in the front," she tells him. He pauses for a second and takes a condom out of a night-table drawer.

They slide under the sheets, his hands still caressing, lips still kissing. The scene is oddly familiar yet markedly different. For a moment she stops and wonders why she's doing this. Instead of coming up with an answer, she pushes the question aside and climbs on top of him. Neither of them speaks. It is dark. It feels nice.

Forty-five minutes later he's fast asleep, his face like a child's, lips mumbling the lines to some far-off dream. Eileen slips out from underneath his arm, slips on her clothes, and heads out into the early morning air.

8

Dave wakes up as Chipp is making a sharp right turn onto Prosperity Street. Overcompensating, he jerks the wheel back harshly, sending Dave's head crashing into the side of the door.

"Ah!" Dave screams, then shakes his head and sits up in his seat. "Where are we?"

"We're in the general vicinity of where you live, I know that much." Chipp tries to concentrate on the road as Eileen walks quickly down the sidewalk, her jet black hair up, her face confused, her cheeks red from the night air. "I've been circling around waiting for you to come to."

"Take a left here. No, not *here*, at Euclid," Dave says weakly.

Dave's stomach, still unsteady, is heaving back and forth thanks to Chipp's erratic driving. He slips back into his seat and begins hiccuping, which is not a good sign. His mouth keeps filling with spit in anticipation, but his throat never delivers the load his mouth is waiting for, so instead he keeps spitting on the side of the door.

"Ppfft!"

"Aw, Jesus, Dave. This isn't even my car. I wish you wouldn't do that."

"Take a right," Dave says between spits. The door is now streaked with half a dozen shots of spit, slowly drying on the fuzzy paneling. "The white apartment building. Number nine."

Chipp parks the car, jumps out, and pulls Dave out.

"Number nine, number nine," Dave mumbles in a vaguely British voice.

"What in the hell is that?" Chipp asks.

"We become naked," he says shrilly before answering: "What? Jesus, you're kidding, right?"

Dave sits on the curb for a moment, contemplating the throbbing sensation in his head before he lurches to his feet and stumbles to the door.

"Keys . . . keys . . ." Dave mumbles.

Chipp hands them to him.

"Been having more and more trouble with these little fuckers lately," Dave says, opening the door.

Dave leads the way in. Chipp follows tentatively behind him. The smell of rancid garbage meets them both as they enter the messy living room. Flies buzz about a knocked-over trash can and various types of debris scattered across the floor.

"Jesus," Chipp says, eyes scanning the mess. "Do you have a dog or something?"

"No," Dave says plainly.

Chipp sits on the couch, making room by tossing two pizza boxes into the corner.

Dave kicks off his shoes, turns on a few lights, and begins skulking around the living room.

"Can I help you?" Chipp asks. "Looking for something?"

"Aha," Dave chirps, picking up an old Coke can from the floor. "Found it."

Dave exits the living room for the kitchen where he begins to wash out the can, then dries it by shaking it up and down.

"Can I turn on the stereo?" Chipp calls out.

"Yeah," Dave calls back, pulling a large sewing needle out of a drawer.

Chipp flips through Dave's records and finally settles on the Jesus Lizard album, *Liar*.

The first song sounds as if the first two seconds were cut off, throwing you right into the middle of the song, like walking into a movie after it has already begun.

"I'm calm now," David Yow is screaming, his voice distorted, the drums pounding, the guitar ferocious. *"I've calmed down, but I'm shaking. . . . Make me another boilermaker . . ."*

Dave runs out from the kitchen, a bulging plastic bag and the Coke can in his hand.

"No, no, no, no." He grabs the needle and the music disappears from the air like a plane dropping out of the sky. "That's the last sort of thing I want to hear right now. Remember me on all fours a half hour ago? Good. Now put on a Spacemen 3 record or something."

Chipp just sort of shrugs, gets down on his knees, and puts on the Spectrum CD, offering his apologies; "This is the closest thing I could find."

As the ambient soundscapes fill the room, Dave sits in a tattered orange chair, resting the Coke can and the plastic bag on the coffee table.

"Is that ganja?" Chipp asks loudly.

"First of all, it's *pot*, not ganja. If you were Bob Marley, it'd be ganja. And do you think you could talk a little louder? I think one of the neighbors didn't hear you," Dave whispers.

"Sorry." Chipp picks up the plastic bag, opens it, and breathes in. "Wow, good stuff."

"Oh, really?" Dave says, laughing.

"Ye-ye-yeah," Chipp says nervously. "You think I don't know good weed when I smell it?

"Jesus Christ, I'm going to smoke pot with Cypress Hill all of a sudden. Weed, *sheesh,*" Dave says, then turns to Chipp. "Listen, Scarface. Take out all the seeds and stems while I get the pipe ready."

Dave picks up the Coke can and, holding it with both hands, carefully pushes in with both thumbs, making a small dent. Then he takes the needle and begins making a series of holes in the center of the dent.

"Nice pipe," Chipp says snidely.

"Oh, sorry, Slash, but I lent my Confederate flag bong to a friend, along with all my Black Sabbath records." Dave laughs, feeling better. "You know"—he stops for a moment—"I remember back when the Record Rack sold bongs."

"No way. That place in the mall?" Chipps puts a few seeds on an end table.

"Yeah, it's true. Only it wasn't in the mall then, it was at the outdoor shopping center near the Capitol Cinema where the

Target is now and where the old Sears used to be. Across from Moore's Mall. In the late seventies when I was like ten or eleven, it was like this heavy-metal head shop. You know, bongs, those black posters of skeletons and roses that had the raised graphics." He pokes hole after hole, remembering things he hadn't thought of in years. "I remember picking up a copy of the *Fabulous Furry Freak Brothers* and reading it cover to cover in one sitting, laughing my ass off."

"The Fabulous who?" Chipp sets down two more seeds.

"Jesus, you don't know the Beatles, you don't know Zeppelin. I mean, I'll admit I don't know everything, but you know even less."

"Ah, who cares about all those moldy old rockers. Didn't Jimmy Page just make an album with that pretty boy from Whitesnake? You know, that guy who was married to that chick from the new WKRP?"

"Yeah, I know they're losers *now*, but then . . ." Dave takes the plastic bag from Chipp's hand and places it on the table. "In their heyday they were a great rock-and-roll band. In fact, so much of the stuff out there today is just a rehash of Zeppelin, Sabbath, even Blue Cheer, the Stooges. Everything." He takes a small handful of the dark green and slightly yellow substance and places it in the groove of the Coke can. He puts the regular opening in the can to his lips, careful to keep the can horizontal. He pulls out a Zippo lighter from his back pocket and shoves the flame into the marijuana while he sucks through the hole. He breathes in a chestful of smoke and holds it there, then passes both the can and the lighter to Chipp. "What I'm saying is"—his voice is raspy, breathless; the smoke is still seeping into his lungs, and the longer he holds it in, the better—"you have no point of reference."

Chipp watches as the flames disappear into the marijuana while he inhales and moves his hand in circles over the weed. The marijuana burns brightly for a few seconds as Chipp takes a last gasp; the weed glows orange for a second before going out.

Dave exhales and leans back. "But do you know what's really sad?"

"What?" Chipp replies in a squeaky voice, holding the smoke in his chest and passing back the can and lighter.

"What's sad is that I feel old."

"How old are you?" Chipp finally releases the smoke, unable to hold it in any longer. He begins to feel lightheaded and smiles for no reason.

"Twenty-four," Dave says, taking a long toke, the air burning the back of his throat.

"That's not so"—Chipp searches for the right word, but it just doesn't come, so he goes with his inevitable first choice—"old."

"Fuck, I *am* old. Who am I kidding?" Dave looks around the room, and his eyes finally set on his guest.

"How old are you? Nineteen?"

"Twenty," Chipp says defiantly, insulted.

"Shit." Dave burps as he inhales. The smoke escapes from his mouth before it has a chance to make it to his lungs. "I bet you used a fake I.D. to get a beer or two tonight, no? Maybe an older brother's or some friend who looks just like you?"

"That shows how little you know. It wasn't my fake I.D., it was Heather's. Boy, you think you're so smart."

"Yeah, yeah." Dave is smiling. The pot is starting to take effect. His already numb head becomes heavy, his neck feels rubbery. He moves his head in crazy directions, back and forth, up and down. "Po*ta*to, pota*to*. Your dad probably still pays your rent for you, right?"

"He, uh, helps." Chipp takes another drag.

Dave shakes his head, his sweaty bangs falling into his pale face. For some reason he finds something funny and begins laughing. He controls himself and returns to the conversation.

"And tomorrow you'll go home and sleep in, maybe listen to a few records and do some work on your zine if you feel like it, right?"

"Hey, lay off the zine, I don't see you trying to—"

Dave cuts him off. "While I go to work hung over, lug around plates of frozen-fresh seafood to old people, having their grandkids point and say, 'Grampy, he *smells*.' I'll be pouring a glass of water, and my hand will be shaking so bad I'll spill it all over my shoes." Something else in the room attracts Dave's attention. His speech peters out. "Be lucky if I don't drop a tray . . ."

"So what? I'm supposed to be ashamed because I still have my youth and you don't? I owe you something?"

"Yeah, a little respect, maybe. For your elders."

"Elder?" Chipp laughs like a hyena. "You're four fucking years older than I am!"

"But things are different now." Dave leans forward quickly and falls out of the chair. He scrambles to his feet and gets back in before Chipp, staring at his fingernails, notices. "Technologies come and go in less than six months. It takes half a second—no, less—for information to travel around the world. Airlines have gone out of business in the time that we've been talking. Governments have fallen. Computers move faster. Cars move faster. *Life* moves faster. Four years now is a lifetime. I don't know who you are, *what* you are."

"What I *am*, is hungry," Chipp says, suddenly besieged by the munchies.

"Listen to me, Kip—"

"Chipp!"

"Whatever. I'm serious. I go to a club, and there's real animosity there."

"So what are you saying? That even though you're just a few years older, you can't understand me? That there's a, like, generation gap?"

"What I'm saying is the rules have already changed somewhat. I mean, how do you feel when you see a carful of good-looking sixteen-year-olds?"

"I feel, I don't know, pissed off."

"And?"

"And . . . I don't know. I move on. I just don't think about it."

"Aha!" Dave screams. "You have no conception of why I'm so depressed, and I just can't believe why you're *not* depressed."

"But I've got . . . the zine." Chipp says the words as if *Godfuck* were a life raft, which maybe it is.

"The zine!" Dave shouts. "Jesus, that's all we need. Another one of those. Haven't you seen *Factsheet Five*? That thing reviews, like, a thousand zines! No, more! What's going to make yours different?"

The question bores a hole into Chipp's soul. He is befuddled, lost for an answer.

"It's just," Dave continues, "I remember, when I was sixteen, seeing people my age and laughing. I couldn't believe they had a job, an apartment, rent. I thought that if they weren't millionaires or didn't at least have a nice car and a cool apartment, they were losers. And now . . ." Dave is staring into space, dissolving into the tune, disappearing into the music.

"What?" Chipp asks. Dave's inaction is giving him the creeps. "What are you doing?"

"I'm just waiting to get paranoid."

"Oh," Chipp says, motioning toward the Coke can. "Because of the pot, you mean?"

"No." Dave sighs. *"Not* because of the pot."

Apocryphal Now

1

Around 7:30 in the morning is when the night really ends.

It's a little after six on Saturday morning, and Craig is some-how yanked out of sleep. All of a sudden he finds himself lying on his back, staring at the ceiling, incredibly alert. He looks over at Ashley. She's lightly snoring, her tongue between her teeth as if in a perpetual lisp, hands in a praying position under her blond head. *That bitch,* Craig thinks. For about fifteen minutes he tries to fall back asleep, trying all his favorite positions: flat on his stomach with his arms back, palms facing the ceiling; fetal, with his legs interlocked like a pretzel and hands shoved underneath the pillow; one leg thrown over the bed, his toes dangling above the floor, with one arm curled underneath his body and the other cradling his face. None of them works.

Instead of being mildly tired or even refreshed, he's wired. He stares at the ceiling again. It is way too early for him to even think about getting up, so he moves to plan B. He closes his eyes and tries to imagine he's very tired, as though he's just come home from a hard day's work or has eaten a huge turkey dinner or . . . fuck it, that's not working, either.

He slips his right hand into his shorts and plays with his limp penis, trying to decide if he should masturbate or not. Usually it relaxes him, and in typical male egocentric fashion, once he has come, he's ready for sleep. But sometimes the opposite effect

occurs, and it makes him more wired. Besides, he would probably wake Ashley, and she would be pissed. And there is also the
smell and the cleanup . . . so fuck that, too.

Craig slips quietly out of bed. He tiptoes (the hardwood floor
silent in some spots, creaking in others) and curses the door that
always sticks. It pops open, and Craig freezes for a moment,
examining Ashley. She stirs slightly, yawns, and turns over, facing the wall and the alarm clock that reads 6:18. Craig shuts the
door behind him, tiptoes to the living room, and lies down on
the couch. He switches on the TV, and an immediate blast of
sound fills the room—what didn't seem loud last night while
waiting for a decent video on MTV seems wildly inappropriate
for an early Saturday morning. Craig lays into the volume control, hitting MUTE first and working his way up from there.

He surfs through the channels quickly. On channel 64 is some
religious sermon being beamed in from this unbelievably pala-
tial church that looks more like the inside of a convention center
than a sacred dwelling. All the glass and metal—whatever happened to rococo and frescoes? The program cuts from shots of
the preacher in a neon suit earnestly reading the Bible to close-
ups of the parishioners, who whisper "Amen" and shed tears at
the right time. Now the preacher has gotten up and is singing a
song with some incredibly lame lyrics, like "He's the father, he's
the creator," and Craig still can't believe they're clinging to this
whole creationism scam.

The program is getting to the part Craig really loves, the
healing segments where the preacher asks people who have
problems ranging from deafness to bad backs to come to the
edge of the stage, and with the wave of his hand (and a rather
theatrical fainting from the sick subject), the people are healed
by the "miracles of God!"

"Yeah, right," Craig mumbles to himself, trying to remember
if there is any pizza left from two nights before. "Like God could
give a shit about Aunt Bertha's corns? Fuck. If God is wasting
time on shit like this, he's a real asshole. Why isn't he doing
something about the rape camps in Bosnia or political prisoners
being tortured all over the world? Ooops, I forgot. It's not their
God, so he doesn't bother. It's like the whole thing with Super-
man that I never understood as a kid. What happened if you
were in trouble but didn't live in Metropolis?"

Craig switches the channel, watches Popeye for a second, switches again, stops at Headline News, but it looks like just another boring story, so he keeps going. He keeps his finger on the UP arrow button and watches as the channels change every half-second, the numbers flashing at the bottom of his TV in red L.E.D. Sometimes, when he's scanning for channel 42 but overshoots it, rather than go back he starts from 2 and goes around again. Sometimes he'll just flip for a few seconds and then stop, committing himself to watch for at least a few minutes whatever he lands on. Now he flips onto one of the Conan movies. He watches for a second before switching to "Webster" (whatever happened to that poor kid?). Then his eyes stop on a grotesque figure on the Mexican channel.

On the screen is a poor guy who looks about Craig's age, mid-twenties, except that he has *gigantism,* a disease that causes his head, hands, and feet to become enormously huge while the rest of his body remains pretty much the same size. The kid is waiting awkwardly in some sort of store, his mother or keeper by his side. His face isn't exactly big in size, not like his hands which are perhaps five times normal size (each knuckle like a baseball and each finger a fleshy hotdog bun), but his features are excessively accentuated. His brow extends almost like a visor, casting a shadow over his otherwise delicate, boyish, almost handsome face. His ears look like a pair of rubber novelties. His lips are wide and full, nothing extreme, but his jaw juts out ferociously; if he pushed his head against a wall, only his forehead and jaw would touch while the rest of his face remained a few inches away. His head is crowned with a heap of healthy brown hair combed obediently to the side. The commentator is rambling on in Spanish so quickly that Craig can barely catch the few cognates thrown his way, such as *deforma* and *misfito.* Craig's attention is diverted for a moment by footsteps in the outside hall.

He gets up quietly, goes to the door, and looks through the peephole. He sees a girl leave the apartment opposite his. She closes the door and then starts down the steps, wiping sleep from her eyes. Bill, the guy who lives there, didn't even have the decency to walk her to the door. Craig figures he could still be sleeping soundly, and she just slipped out of bed and into her ripped white Babes in Toyland dress and conveniently let herself out. Craig shuffles discreetly to the window overlooking the road to see her walk quickly down the street, hop into a black Jeep, and drive away. Craig sighs.

On TV the kid's now seated while his helper and a woman from the store try to fit a sock over his enormous foot. Close up, the foot is disgusting, bigger at the ankle than anyplace else and square more than round. The bricklike foot branches off to a mishmash of toes pointing in all directions, not one of them touching the floor. They get a close-up of his grinning face, and he doesn't seem to be embarrassed at all, not by the cameras or the lights shining in his eyes or the gawking customers or the frustrated attempt to get the fabric over his behemoth of a foot. After pulling, tugging, rolling, and yanking the sock, it mostly covers the bottom of his foot. The worker, grinning the whole time for the camera, retrieves a bowl of milky-looking liquid from off camera and a bunch of cloth torn into strips. She begins to slather the boy's foot with what Craig has determined is some sort of paste, and plasters the cloth around the base of the foot. Craig grins, satisfied, as if figuring out the "Wheel of Fortune" board before anybody.

"They're making him shoes," he whispers to himself.

Craig wonders if the boy's sexual organs are dramatically affected by the disease, but then figures, what if they are? Even if he is hung like a horse, Craig reasons, no girl would want to get close enough to find out. Craig ponders the irony of the boy trapped inside the beautiful temple, or, rather, the ugly temple with the one cozy room inside that no one will ever see.

Suddenly other footsteps sound in the hall, but this time they come from one of the upper floors. The floor creaks loudly as Craig lumbers to the peephole of the door. The girl in the hallway stops for a moment. Craig freezes, still managing to peek out the hole. The girl, who looks as though she's under a microscope thanks to the fish-eye glass in the peephole, stares at Craig's door. His heart starts beating fast; he clutches the wall to maintain his balance. She flashes what seems to be a brown eye at his door, then continues down the hall and down the staircase.

Breathing a sigh of relief and catching a quick glance of Gigantic Boy laughing as they present him with a cast of his foot, Craig peers out the window. He recognizes all the cars on the street except for a few; most belong to the tenants in the building.

The girl tiptoes out onto the sidewalk and begins walking. Craig notices her unclasped sandals and her frenetic shoving of a pair of black tights into her slinglike purse. She gets into her car, a Karmann Ghia with the top down, throwing her bag onto the passenger seat. Craig can spy her fishing out her keys and putting them into the ignition, but she doesn't start the car. She just sits there.

Craig leans into the glass, pushing his nose into the chilly pane while a balloon of fog grows from his mouth.

The girl reaches a hand up to the rearview mirror and pulls it toward her. Craig can see the tiny reflection of her eyes as the girl rubs a hand over her face and hunches over slightly, resting on the wheel. For a full five minutes she sits there before wiping her eyes, which Craig swears look redder than they did a few minutes ago. The car starts, lurches away from the curb, then meekly rolls down the street.

Craig steps away from the window, but not before swabbing at the four-inch wet spot with the cuff of his long-sleeved Gap T-shirt. He sits back down on the couch, hoping to see another glimpse of Gigantic Boy, but it's too late. Some horrible Mexican sitcom is on, showing an old man dressed up as a young boy with red circles on his wrinkled cheeks. He switches the channel.

He leans back and half-smiles, not at anything funny but at the feeling of not being able to find anything funny to laugh at. He thinks of the two girls making their early escapes. He grins because of the remembrance of both escaping and being escaped from. He tries to think of their names, the one-night stands from a few years ago, and Brook, that mistake from just a few nights ago. Names pop to the surface—Ann, Christine, Jacklyn—and then odd things, like the inside of them or their showers, their beds or their hands. He misses it all for a second, but then reconsiders.

In all his one-night stands, either alcohol or anxiety had consumed him, and each had its own insidious way of clouding the performance. After so many girls and so many nights, and also the betrayals thrown back and forth between him and Ashley like a tennis ball, it all seems like something so sad rather than sexy.

Craig remembers being fourteen when all he could think

about was having money, a car, and a girl who would sleep with him. And now, barely ten years later, everything he'd hoped for has caught up and captured him with a vengeance: The last time he dared open his American Express bill, he was informed that a collection agency was after him and that a hitman would be the next step. Three years after he got his dream car (1969 Mustang), he ran a red light, too busy to notice it had changed because he was singing along to Courtney Love's "Don't Mix the Colors" and swerved to miss a school bus and instead smacked into a Camaro head-on. And women. All he ever wanted was to hold one, and yet now that he had one, all he seemed to be doing was letting go of her.

Whenever he found himself in either the early-morning or late-night well of self-pity, looking up, he blamed his various schools for not educating him better in all three areas. Driver education was a joke because the teacher just hoped you weren't on drugs and wouldn't injure him while you were at the wheel. Craig slept through math classes, and toward the end they let you bring in calculators, so what finally was the point? And sex education (the week allocated for it, sandwiched between education films, "The Importance of Being Fluoride," and the stimulating lecture on hemoglobin) was woefully insufficient. *So why didn't they tell us?* Craig always wonders, with his hands full of another dying relationship. *Right after they unrolled the condom down the sawed-off end of a broomstick, why didn't they explain what it meant to stick the real thing inside someone or have it stuck inside you? Why didn't they explain that something like that cost more than the six-pack of beer it took to get you there and that there are invisible costs everywhere, only you never find out the price until it is too late.* At this point Craig always sighs and figures out that the reason his teachers never told him was simply that they never knew.

And still he was tangibly excited by strangers. He still yearned to have a strange girl leave by the back steps while his juices were dried on her stomach, or hunt for socks under an ottoman on the awkward Morning After. Losing a girl like Ashley, who could truly love him despite his flaws, seemed to be something he would risk. A risk he was willing to take, maybe, but one he never saw himself taking. The months that dragged by featured both fights and good times, and sometimes a rerun of both, while others were just weeks and weeks of stares across the dinner table, of coming home late with no questions asked because the correct answers were already guessed. Craig feels stuck in mud that he's telling himself is cement.

Shaking himself out of thought, Craig gets up quickly and bumps into the coffee table. Pens slide off, and a small picture frame falls loudly to the floor. He curses, picks up the frame. It's a photo of him and Ashley taken last New Year's Eve at a friend's party. She, drunk, is smiling largely, and he, also drunk, looks blurry even though the rest of the photo is not. A deep crack now runs across the glass, splitting the couple in two.

"Honey, what is it?" Ashley asks sleepily, poking her head through the bedroom doorway.

Craig tosses the object onto the couch and scampers to the bedroom.

"Nothing," he says in a whisper, tucking her back in. "I broke a glass, that's all." He brings the blankets up to her chin and then folds them over. "Go back to sleep." But almost before he can finish the sentence, a low, almost inaudible snore rises from her mouth and her nose twitches ever so slightly.

He sits back down on the couch and picks up the photo. Examining it, he starts to laugh, stuffing a fist into his mouth to control the volume. After he's calmed down he goes into the kitchen to put on some coffee and, still chuckling, says quietly, "The fissure king."

2

Proust was certainly right about there being no such thing as the present; emotions such as guilt and regret had an eerie way of reminding one of past deeds with amazing clarity. If the moment of analysis was now far off, if it ever could have been harnessed, then there was an entire lifetime left for regret, sorrow, and shame.

This is what Eileen is thinking as she wakes up and can hear

Jess already in the cafe. She remembers the night before, and hindsight slaps her hard as she gets out of bed and thinks of facing Jess in a few minutes. She washes her face with cold water and pulls on a dark blue skirt and gray T-shirt, puts her hair in a ponytail, and heads downstairs.

"Hey," she calls out as Jess sweeps up the stoop.

"Well, hi," he says suavely.

Eileen brushes past him and into the cafe. She takes a German chocolate cake out of the freezer and places it on the counter, readying it for the display case. She takes the little pieces of wax paper from between the slices as Jess approaches her.

"Well?"

"Well what, Jess?"

"Don't you have anything to say?"

It's hard to read anything into his voice. *What's he looking for?*

"About what?" Eileen asks, still searching for clues.

"About last night, maybe."

"What is this, 'Mamet Movie Adaptations' for one hundred dollars? If you have something to say, Jess, I wish you'd say it instead of playing these games." She drops a slice of cake on the floor. Rather than cut around the dirty part and save it for lunch, as she usually does, she tosses the whole thing in the trash, cursing under her breath.

"I just thought you might have something to say about what happened, that's all."

"Like what?" she says, incredulous. "Like thanks? Is that what you're looking for?"

"No!" he says, offended. "Maybe that . . . I don't know," he fumbles his words. "Maybe that it was special for you or that you've been thinking about me. I just want to make sure you're feeling the same thing I am."

"I am." She shrugs. "I am. I mean, it was nice."

"Nice?"

"Yes, Jess, nice! What am I supposed to say? Life-shattering? I'm sorry. You'd better call Federal Express, I didn't get the script this morning."

"It's not like that, it's just—I want to make sure no one gets hurt here. I mean, I want to make sure we treat each other fairly."

"Jesus Christ!" she shouts, her voice echoing in the empty, cavernous cafe. "What's with all you sensitive males these days? I can't turn over a rock without finding one!"

Jess turns to her. His face is scarlet.

"What's that supposed to mean?"

"I mean for years all you guys wanted was to get into my pants, and now all you want is to get into my brain."

"What do you mean, 'all you guys'?" He goes from embarrassed to jealous in a flash. "Just how many guys have there been?"

"Look, Jess," Eileen says with a heavy sigh. "I really don't think that's any of your business, okay? So just tuck your bruised little ego into bed, and I'll check on it later and tell you you were great, marvelous, stupendous in the sack. Is that what you want to hear?"

"I want to hear"— now he starts shouting as well—"that you feel the same way I do!"

"Which is what?" Eileen rushes him like Steffi Graf playing close to the net. "Come on, say it. Love? *Please.* Like? Sure, maybe. How about we're friends who maybe did something we shouldn't have done?"

"How can you say that?" He staggers to a bar stool, as if shocked, and hoists himself up.

Jess is beginning to feel—dare Eileen say it?—used. She feels like giving him a laminated card and saying, "Welcome to the club."

"I th-th-thought we shared something"—Jess curls up on the stool—"special."

A few years ago it was easier. Eileen knew where she stood with men, which was across the bed. Certain things were a given. He would rather take her to bed than to *Wild Strawberries,* and he prayed she wasn't a virgin, but not a slut either, just experienced enough to please him. Sleeping with 2.3 males ought to have done the trick.

"What do you want from me?" she screams, moving across the room.

"I want you!"

"You've *had* me!"

"No!" Jess runs his hands through his hair and pulls at his

long blond strands as though he's being driven crazy. "I need your body and your thoughts. I don't even really know who you are."

"When in the fuck did this occur? For years all anyone ever wanted was my body, and now you're after my mind, too?"

"Yes," Jess whines.

Eileen quickly grabs an upside-down chair from one of the tables, slams it to the floor, and sits down.

"Well, I'm sorry, Jess. I'm not used to coming as a package deal. It's usually one or the other. I haven't felt that, uh, the other way in a long time."

Eileen is starting to feel bad for Jess. It's not that the concept was insane, because it wasn't; it was just that the circumstances weren't right for it at this point. With Don it had been that way, but she had given him everything: her body, her mind, favorite records, the list goes on. And when the dust of the breakup settled, it was heart-wrenching to go through and count the inventory. She still had her body and the vinyl import of *Psychocandy,* but Don had escaped with something she didn't even know she had until then: the ability to care for someone without limits, as if her emotional credit card had no ceiling. And now Jess is staring at her. Perhaps she had given him too much too soon, but asking for it back is not only impossible but impolite.

Jess covers his head with his hands, wondering what to say next.

It is always so odd to see someone the day after a casual affair. Little things keep coming to Eileen's mind: his knobby knees that she had never seen before last night, the look on his face when he had his orgasm. Where are they to go from here? Eileen searches the emotional landscape for road signs offering advice. All of the familiar landmarks are there—the uneasy familiarity, the postcoital embarrassment—and yet it's also awkwardly comfortable, as if all the bad news had been done away with, and they are now down to their essential parts. All the bullshit had been strewn to the side of the road. Sure, they both have secrets from each other, but their shared truth is more immediate than that. Eileen feels she can really get down to knowing this person and decide whether or not she wants to become seriously involved with him. It was a hell of an entrance exam, but at this stage nothing else seems right.

Am I crazy? She holds herself tightly, a pair of arms this sensitive male is afraid to offer her. *Is everything I've done up to now completely wrong?*

"There, there." Eileen gets up and crosses the room to rub his back with an outstretched palm. "It's going to be okay. You can stop crying."

"I-I-I'm not crying," he sniffles. "I just have something in my eye."

"I know," she says, rubbing her hand in circles in much the same manner as she wipes off the counters. "I know."

3

"Where in the fuck have you been?"

This is how Randy greets Chipp.

"At first I thought you had gotten lucky and had gone home with Heather, but she called here looking for you this morning. She said you went home with some guy." Randy clutches his arms to his wiry chest; the cuffs of his long-sleeve shirt cover his hands. "I mean, if you wanted to experiment, why didn't you—"

"Oh, please." Chipp silences him with a wave of his hand and heads for the kitchen. "I went home with that guy Dave from Violent Revolution Records. He was way fucked up and couldn't drive himself home. Man, that's one sorry guy." Chipp, his stomach about to stage a riot, pulls back the refrigerator door like a bank robber clutching a vault. "Oh, I see you were so worried that you ate all my peanut butter. You probably hoped I wasn't coming back."

"Look, you know that when I get upset I eat. Remember when The Pixies broke up, and I ate two large Domino's pizzas a day for three days straight?"

"Yeah, the delivery boy knew you by name, and toward the end you didn't have to call him. He just read your mind or smelled it in the air. Big fucking deal."

Chipp pulls out a chicken leg that was too old to eat a week ago when he had the munchies but figures what the hell. He grabs an open beer he doesn't remember seeing before and sits down on the couch.

"So what'd Dave say? I hope you were buttering him up for an ad because we need at least—"

"Jesus," Chipp says, reacting both to Randy's insensitivity and to the leatherlike hide of the chicken leg. The entire blanket of skin falls off, exposing naked purple flesh. "The guy's going through a rough time right now. You know, he can't sell his records at DISContent, and he's slowly going broke. So I think he has more to worry about."

"Did he find out about the A & R guy who was there last night to see Bottlecap? I mean, Mark told him, right?"

"He didn't mention it, so I doubt it. He was in the bathroom puking his guts out most of the night." Chipp sits back and puts his feet up. "But he's really in bad shape. I guess he dropped out of UVA last year."

"Ha!" Randy cackles. "What a puss." He sits down and taps his feet on the floor. "The cool thing is to get *kicked* out."

"And now he's reliving that 'just drifting here in the pool, Dad' scene from *The Graduate* over and over again. It's like he keeps getting fucked over at The Scene, and now his bands are starting to jump ship and he's asking why."

Randy stops tapping for a moment. "Why what?"

Chipp rolls his eyes. "Why do the label, idiot. You know, why stay in this town? Why bother? Why keep losing money every week? I mean, DISContent stopped stocking his stuff, and his landlord is hassling him, and bills are piling up. Bottlecap's probably going to ditch Kitty for California without telling anyone, and who can blame them for not wanting to come back? It's starting to get hairy for Dave. If things don't pick up soon, he'll be selling insurance door to door."

"Well, you know what they say," Randy says without compassion, examining the fingernails on his left hand. "If you can't stand the heat . . ."

"Have your dad pay the rent?" Chipp finishes the sentence.

"That was for a few goddamn months!" Randy screams. "Jeez, you just don't let a guy forget anything, do you?"

Chipp laughs and waves Randy off with two hands in front of his chest and his fingers wagging like ten tails, begging for a confrontation. Randy rises out of his seat, gets halfway up, and sinks back down. After a few minutes of silence, save for the grumbling of Chipp's stomach, Randy speaks.

"I keep asking myself the same things, though."

"What?" Chipp asks, not paying attention. Instead he thinks of Heather or, more directly, Heather's refrigerator.

"Dave, I mean. I keep asking myself that question."

"What question?"

"Why. The question of why. Why live in this fucking town? Why not move to D.C. or even Charlottesville? Maybe New York, like we said." He slumps even lower in his chair, saying as if out of breath, "Oh, I don't know."

"Well, that's why we finally got off our asses and are finishing the zine. Right?"

"I guess." Randy shrugs. "But maybe that's coincidental. Like, what else do we have to do? Spin our Sleepyhead seven inches a few more times and wait for *that* to change the world?"

"Ha!" Chipp screams. "Yeah, that sure as hell ain't gonna change anything, but *Godfuck* will?"

"No," Randy begins, standing up, "but it'll change me."

"So did you get much work done?" Chipp asks.

"Yeah, actually." Randy moves across the room to the kitchen table, which is now, along with a crowded ottoman and coffee table, *Godfuck* headquarters. "The record reviews are completely done, even the ones I didn't have time to listen to."

"What?" Chipp asks, getting off the couch and joining Randy at the table. He pulls up a wooden squareback chair. "But how did you—"

"Simple," Randy says, beaming with pride. "I judged them either by the look of the record cover, what label they're on, or the name of the band. Although"—he grins slyly—"nothing got too bad a review because we want the record companies to send us more free stuff."

Despite Randy's cherubic explanation, Chipp still can't get past the facts.

"But I don't see how you could actually write a review when you didn't listen to a note of the music. I mean, how?"

"Chipp," Randy says dumbly, "how many reviews does a magazine like *Alternative Press* run in every issue?"

"I don't know for sure, but I'd say around seventy-five."

"And how many reviewers do they have?" His voice is calm, like Mr. Rogers's.

"Let's see: Tim Segall, Jason Pettigrew, Dave Thompson, that bitch JoAnne Greene, and a few more, I guess. Maybe a dozen."

"And you really think they actually listen to all the records they write about?"

"Yes!"

"Seriously, Chipp," Randy says, "now who's being naive?"

"Anyway, they all have your name on them so if"—he glances down at a review in the *Godfuck* Singles column—"Slant 6 wants to come and kick your ass because you don't know what you're talking about, that's your problem."

"Ahh." Randy shrugs. "Big deal. A couple of girls. I could whip them in a minute."

"That's just great, Randy. What else?"

"Well." He shuffles the sheets, pulling out some from the bottom. "Your interview's almost done, right?"

"Yeah, yeah." Chipp stifles a yawn. "I'll finish it today."

"Cool. Since that's done, all we have to do is finish our columns."

"Really?" Chipp says, not expecting it to be so painless.

"Well, yeah. At least with the writing part. But then we have to do layout and actually print the fuckers."

"Ooh." Chipp feels the pain in his chest he has every time there is work to be done. "I forgot about that."

"And I want it to look as good as possible, too. Remember how most zines—and even that other local one, *Piss Poor*—are just taped together in one of those do-it-yourself ways? I want *Godfuck* to look as good as it can."

"Well, given the budget that we're working with, which is your friend's borrowed typewriter and whatever kind of scissors and glue they have at Kinko's, good luck."

"Speaking of!" Randy's eyes light up. He runs from the room, dips into his bedroom, and returns seconds later.

"Close your eyes," he demands.

"Randy, no. I'm much too tired for any—"

"Close 'em."

Chipp relents, letting out a sigh and shutting his eyes for

a moment. He stretches out his hand and suddenly feels something cold thrust into it. It is square, made of plastic, slightly heavy. Even after Chipp opens his eyes, he's not sure what it is.

"Yeah, so? It's a blue plastic brick?"

"No, you prick. It's a copy meter from Kinko's!" Randy is shouting, obviously proud of himself.

Chipp is unimpressed.

"I still don't get it."

Randy rips the thing from Chipp's hand and holds it in front of his face. "See these?" He points to a small window in one of the shorter sides of the rectangle, behind which is a five-digit number counter, currently set at 4,738.

"Yeah? So?"

"So?" Randy frustratingly runs around in a circle. "So this is the thing you plug into the copier to make it work. " He turns it around to show off the six silver prongs at the opposite end that fit into a matching receptacle on the machine. "You see? Right here? And this thing keeps count of how many copies you've made." He is walking in place, pantomiming for Chipp. "When you walk up to the counter and hand this to the disgruntled Kinko's employee who is pissed off that he or she is not only making minimum wage but has been working since five in the morning"—he holds the meter out in midair—"then he or she looks at it. It says, say, thirty, then you are charged—shit, I don't even know what it is, like a nickel or ten cents per copy. They put it in a machine, which resets it to zero, and put it back in circulation."

"Randy, yeah, that's great. Thanks for the helpful demonstration, but it's still too early for me to understand any of this."

"What we do is grab a meter when we go in. Make like, I don't know, fifteen or twenty token copies, then slide in this decoy"—he waves it proudly—"and do the real copying. You know, the hundred or however many we need for the first printing. When we're done, we slide the decoy back into a backpack or pocket, take up the other one, pay our buck fifty or whatever, and go home. Simple as that."

"Yeah, but what happens when they see you carrying out three stacks of paper?"

"Jesus, Chipp, who's going to care? Like when you worked at that restaurant, did you ever give a shit when some kid stole an ashtray?"

While Chipp is formulating an answer, Randy picks up the ashtray from the table and shoves it toward his face.

"Yeah, but what if Kinko's employees aren't as disgustingly immoral as we are?"

"Trust me," he says confidently, "they are. I mean, what is that, some sort of career move they're making? They want to go into—oh, I don't even know what they'd call it." Randy racks his brains for half a second before continuing: "Advanced Photocopying Technician Consultant? Get real. It's just another shit job for those short-timers, Hell, do I even have to sing 'Slack Motherfucker' for you? I mean, that song says it all."

"I know, I know." Chipp sings a line: "'I'm working, but I'm not working for you.' Big deal. I just don't know if it's a good plan."

"Listen, Chipparoo. Let me put it another way: If we don't go through with my little scheme, the copies will end up costing us over two hundred dollars. Do you have that kind of money handy?"

Chipp remembers bumming a fiver off Heather the night before so he could buy a beer.

"Okay. I guess it'll work. By the way, what name did you finally come up with for your column?"

"Indie Kids," he says proudly.

"Jesus." Chipp laughs. "That's got to be the worst title I've heard in my life."

"Oh yeah? What's yours called?"

"Kitty's Kats."

"That's the second worst."

"Ha"—*yawn*—"ha." Chipp yawns again uncontrollably, a battle fatigue-level lack of sleep finally catching up to him.

"Man, I'm tired. I'm going to bed."

"Yeah." Randy laughs. "You need some rest after your *big* night. So what about Dave? Since he was so wasted, is he going to be okay?"

"Aww, don't worry about him," Chipp says, pausing for another tremendous yawn. "He'll be okay."

4

The room is upside down.

Dave wearily begins to raise himself as if doing a sit-up in slow motion: his arms outstretched in front of him in zombie-walking fashion, his midsection curling slightly, his toes pointing up, waiting for the rendezvous. He makes it almost halfway before a headache kicks in, his temples throbbing, his forehead undulating, the back of his head bubbling like one of the more painful-to-watch scenes of the transformation sequence in *An American Werewolf in London*.

"Ahh, shit," he says, lying back down.

He lies on his back, staring at the ceiling, breathing heavily. His headache dissipates as he becomes motionless. He turns on his side; his plan is to inch his way to the bathroom, and then take an entire bottle of aspirin and maybe a hot shower.

Once all his weight is on his left shoulder, the headache returns but is not as bad as before. The blood rushes to his head, sort of sloshing side to side like the blue water in one of those Plexiglas conversation pieces where a wave is perennially tossed back and forth for absolutely no reason.

The pieces are slowly coming back to him: *I got very drunk, smoked way too many cigarettes, and the last thing I remember was sitting on a bar stool arguing with Todd about the take at the door, and then . . .* He draws a blank. Crunching up his face, he reaches far back in his brain to retrieve the information, but he just can't find it. It's as if he has hit a dead end on a road he is positive leads somewhere.

Holy shit! Then what happened? This had happened to him only once before, two years ago at UVA after a Halloween party. All of a sudden he regained consciousness on the floor of his apartment with Pete, his roommate, and two girls, all four of them partially naked. They woke up to the absurd sight of their landlord, who had let himself in, wearing a hilariously bad skeleton outfit. On finding the four of them on the floor naked, partially covered with a life-size Elvira beer display Pete had swiped, he became embarrassed and left. Dave thought it was a hallucination until he was evicted the next week.

Rolling over, he lands on his face, his one arm caught underneath his body, the other flailing away at his side. Half his face lies against the chilly hardwood floor and slowly becomes numb. After five minutes of fitful sleep, Dave wakes up again. He slowly retracts all limbs and tries to lift himself in the form of a push-up. Half an inch off the ground his headache kicks him in the temple, fades, then slams him right behind the forehead. Bull's-eye.

The tide in his stomach is turning, the alcohol shifting, and his already overtaxed stomach acids lose the battle they have been fighting all night. Like an out-of-control subway, a stream of vomit races up his throat so quickly that Dave snaps his mouth shut barely in time to catch it. Thin, custardlike streams shoot out, spraying the floor and dribbling down his chin. His eyes become soaked with water and his cheeks bulge out like Dizzy Gillespie's, barely containing the warm spew.

He scrambles to his feet and rushes to the bathroom. His jaw unclenches the moment he enters bathroom air space. Throwup coasts through the air in an arc, hitting the rim of the toilet bowl, some sliding into the water, the rest onto the floor.

Dave falls on his knees and feels the grooves of the black and white ceramic tiles sectioning off his skin, exposed through rips in his jeans. He clutches the toilet bowl seat and spits out the chunky remains, runs a tongue on the back of his teeth, hacks to get the acidy taste out of his mouth. He remembers the half-bag of Ruffles and peanut butter and grape jelly sandwich dinner he ate the night before while stoned. The toilet bowl, now cloudy with a pale substance, is yellowish, swimming with purple chunks.

He feels it coming up again but holds a hand over his mouth; his eyes tear up again. He tries to hold it back, hold it steady, but it doesn't work and instead shoots up his throat. He tries to block the back of his throat, blows the air out of his mouth. He chokes for a second; thin streams of vomit trickle down his nose, over the fingers of his clenched hands, around his dry, flaky lips.

He flings his hand away and, helpless, lets the throw-up exit his mouth. At one point the stream is so powerful it shoots straight up and, hitting the concave roof of his mouth, splatters in all directions, like a spoon held underneath the tap of a sink.

He coughs, spits, and dribbles into the toilet bowl. Every few seconds his stomach heaves with aftershocks. He feels the sensation again, but nothing comes out. His throat constricts, his stomach rumbles, but there's nothing else to send up.

"Ug, blu, shren . . ." He mumbles incomplete words, a sentence of blabberspeak, just sound to let himself know he's still alive.

After ten minutes of silence from his stomach, with his headache still pounding, he pulls himself off the floor, careful not to slip on the puddle at the base of the toilet. He goes to the sink, splashes cold water on his face, and then gargles three or four times to get the stinging aftertaste out of his mouth. He opens up the medicine cabinet, grabs a bottle of Advil that Stacy left one night, and swallows six of the sweet clay-colored pills. He slams the medicine cabinet shut and is forced to stare at himself in the mirror.

There is a crack in the lower left corner, a section of shattered glass that creeps up and over like a growth of ivy, each section beveled, uneven. He runs a hand over his four-day-old stubble. Feeling it over and over again reminds him of the touch of his father's kiss, being a child, having his dad reach down and throw him up to the sky, nudging his stern face, full of semi-pride and years, pockmocks and discipline, against his own that was, as recently as last year, soft to the touch. Dave closes his eyes, still thinking of his father, and the smell comes back of his father's aftershave, his body odor, the musky smell that engulfed Dave whenever he wore one of his father's shirts to a formal dinner because he owned none of his own. Even though he was roughly his father's size, he still felt small in those clothes. The feel of them, well worn, against his skin, not worn at all, seemed like some absurd dress-up game, make-believe, pretend.

Dave glances back at his room, the unpaid bills piling up, his old waiter's uniform not needed in the past couple of days, the trash and the dishes strewn everywhere. He laughs and considers the wreckage not seen by the eye but just as important—all those friends now gone, both girls and guys. Girls you had to fuck to get them out of your life, while guys never needed a reason, just a way. He thinks of Bottlecap and remembers the rumors he heard the night before, that someone from a major label was on hand to check out one of *his* bands. Dave runs an aching hand through his hair, returning with a palmful of dandruff, and he thinks, *If they hit the big time, they'll have to take me along for the ride.* He laughs, glad to see he still can. *They'll have to.*

Turning his head to the left he catches a glimpse of his long jawbone, nearly identical to his father's, and again it makes him think of him. When was his father's birthday? It had been weeks since his dad had called him. He remembers something about a trip to D.C. "Will call you from there, maybe catch a commuter flight down. We'll have lunch." But Dave never got the call. He thinks about his friends, most of whom don't even know their parents' middle names, let alone their fears or desires. He thinks about going to the living room to call his dad, to say hi, to ask him something about his childhood, to get him pissed—only nothing is coming to mind.

He heads for the phone anyway, picks up the black handpiece but draws a blank.

"Shit," he says, his headache slowly becoming a memory. "I can't remember his number."

Still holding the receiver, he dials Mark's familiar number. It rings three times before being picked up by his cryptic answering machine.

"Hey, Sandy, want some candy?"
"Some candy'd be dandy."
"Hey, Candy, want some candy?"
"No candy for me, Randy."

There are four different voices shooting the lines back and forth and Dave is almost positive he can hear Mark in the background, chuckling as he was recording it even though he must have watched this scene ten times already.

"I'll have some candy, Randy."
"Okay, Andy, I'll give you Candy's candy."
"Can I also have Mandy's candy?"

"What in the fuck is this?" Dave says to his living room.

"No, Randy, don't give Andy Mandy's candy, give him the
candy that's handy."
  "All right, Sandy. So, Andy, what's your favorite candy?"

There is a second of grainy silence before the voice spurts out
in a deadpan:

"Mints."

BEEP!
"Uh, yeah, Mark. It's Dave. Give me a call. I heard some
things, and I just . . . well, wanted to talk to you. *Please* call me.
Bye."
Dave hangs up the phone but has the slightly paranoid feeling
that Mark was standing over the machine, screening his calls
and letting out a cool sigh of relief when he discovered that
Dave had been tricked by the machine and seemed, by the innocent tone in his voice, to fall for the charade. Though Dave has
the gnawing feeling that his message will never be returned, it
doesn't dampen his somewhat optimistic spirits. He keeps thinking of Bottlecap as his ticket out of here, this stale room, this
confining town, his own darkest fears.
"Success may be just around the corner," he says, his voice still
scratchy as his stomach rumbles uneasily, needing more fuel to
burn. "The only problem is, it's a blind corner, and you never
know what's going to hit you."

5

Nothing is ever where they say it is.
  Ashley blows a tuft of hair out of her eyes, pushes her glasses
down on her thin nose, and examines the rack of books. *It doesn't
matter what kind of fucking computer system they have,* she muses,

stabbing a pencil behind her ear. *If the damn students don't put the books back where they found them, the books ain't there. I don't care what the computer screen says.*

She crouches on the floor, examining the entire rack for the title, and now she is on tiptoes, craning to spy the faint binding on the uppermost row.

"How long can you keep this up?"

Startled, she jumps back before spotting Andrew standing at the entrance of the small submarinelike passageway with room enough for only one person to stand while another carefully scoots by. He is wearing an Apple sweatshirt, long-since-faded Birkenstock sandals, khaki shorts.

"Andrew?" she whispers, annoyed. "Not now."

"Not now?" he says in a street voice, not because he doesn't know enough to keep quiet but because he can't. "Then when? You ignored me at the dinner—"

Ashley cuts him off. "*That* I'm trying to forget."

"I'm sorry, I drank too much. It's just, seeing you there . . . with *him.*"

"I live with him, Andrew. I can't believe you're going for your master's degree but couldn't figure out when you accepted the invitation that he'd be there. Where did you think he'd be? Chowing down at Lot-a-Burger while you and I had a candlelight dinner?"

"I know, I know," he says quickly, under his breath. "I thought I'd be okay just being able to spend some time with you, even though we couldn't—"

Ashley shoots him a don't-even-think-about-it glance.

"—be close."

"Jesus, Andrew." Ashley fights back a scream. She looks into his eyes, which are shielded by a pair of Polo tortoise-shell glasses and a glazed look. "This just isn't going to work. It was never going to work. It just happened."

"But you said maybe . . ."

As Ashley retreats down the shelf, Andrew follows, nervously shifting his leather backpack from shoulder to shoulder.

"I never said anything, Andrew. You make out like I led you on, like I promised you I'd break up with Craig, but that's bullshit. It's all in your head."

"You didn't have to say anything. I thought your actions were speaking for you."

"Never trust my actions," Ashley replies bluntly, "only my nonactions. Like when I didn't call, like when I avoided you. That was me speaking." She chuckles even though she knows she shouldn't, thinking, *When I'm not talking is when you should listen.*

Ashley turns her head quickly, and the pencil behind her ear falls to the floor. Andrew picks it up and steps behind her. She turns slowly, discovering Andrew's familiar face only a few inches from hers. She can smell a faint trace of bad breath and wonders if it is his or hers. She looks at a strand of thinning brown hair drooping over his forehead, thinking he looks cute but forcing the thought from her head. Andrew leans in and gently places the pencil behind Ashley's ear, its thick pink eraser skidding on the back of her neck. He bends down at the knees, coming in for a kiss.

Ashley lets the moment go on too long and pulls away a second before contact, leaving Andrew to lunge forward and hit his head on a thick volume of bound newpapers from the '20s hanging a few inches out from the orderly rack.

"I'm sorry, Andrew. No."

"But how . . . why?" He becomes flustered for a second before telling himself to calm down. "Okay, if you don't want me, that's one thing. I'm not such an egomaniac as to think I'm the only man in the world . . ."

Ashley arches an eyebrow.

"But Craig? Jesus, Ash, you deserve better."

"Says who?" she asks, turning away from him and randomly pulling books off the shelf and putting them back quickly.

"Says who?" Andrew blurts out. "Says everyone who knows either of you. I mean, the guy's a washout. You know about him and Brook, don't you?"

Ashley stops in her tracks and spins around.

"What?"

"Brook told me that she knew Craig before—"

"How?" Ashley cuts him off, lunging forward.

"That's what I asked, but, mind you, this was after the dinner party, and we weren't exactly getting along. All she would tell me was that she knew him 'biblically,' which means she either slept with him or they were trapped in an ark for forty days."

"But he said . . ." She begins the sentence but lets the words trail off to the dead end she knows they lead to. "But *you* said she was pissed at you. She was just trying to get you riled up."

"No, Ash. She couldn't care less about me. In fact, she was proud of the fact, kept boasting about it like Craig was some sort of prize or something. I didn't tell you until now because I didn't want to hurt you."

"What do you mean you didn't want to tell me until now? This was all of twelve hours ago, Andrew."

"I was going to call you the second I got home but didn't. You know how hard it was to sit on this information all day? But now that it's out, what more proof do you need?"

Ashley turns away from him again and stares at the long row of books, interrupted by an open area that looks down on the children's section below. Nothing told her what to do about the man she could have sworn she loved, despite his (and her) mistakes.

"He cheated on you, Ashley. That's all you need to know."

"You think I don't know that?" she returns fiercely, admitting it for the first time. "And what about it, Andrew?" She spits out his name as if it were a piece of stale food, as if she'd bite it if she could. "I mean, look at you and me. Like I've got a leg to stand on?"

"Well then, break up with him." His hands waft up, pleading.

"I can't." She shrugs. The words creep from the side of her mouth. "I mean, I don't know, but we've got something worked out. That may seem fucked to you, but . . . it works. It still counts."

"But I—" Andrew begins.

"No, Andrew, you don't." She thinks for a second. "Maybe you do, but you *can't*. You see?"

"No, I don't see." He fights back a tear, thinking for a second that maybe he should let down his guard. Maybe that's what she needs to see. Maybe that's what she *wants* to see. He lets go and prepares for a riverful of sorrow but, stage-shy, the tears won't come.

"God!" Ashley scowls and shoves aside the gray stool and Andrew as if both were just items in her way. "For someone so smart, you really are stupid."

For a second after Andrew sees the look in her eyes and hears her voice until a full five minutes later, his nostrils are still sniffing for the faint traces of that perfume.

"Fuck."

6

Mark is confused. He sits up in bed, shakes out his hair, and wonders if it was all a dream. He turns over and sees Henry James's card on the nightstand, and realizes it was true. Realizes what kind of a choice he has to make and what kind of an opportunity he has. He thinks of calling Laura to ask her advice, only he knows that's not a good idea, that she would only tell him to be true to his heart and not to screw over Dave. Besides, he is still kind of pissed at her.

"Be true to my heart?" Mark says, his voice sore from the night before. "What in the fuck does that mean?"

Mark pulls on a pair of jeans and an old T-shirt. He leaves the house and goes to walk around downtown, trying to take his mind off the band and the decision, but his dilemma sits on his brain like a fog.

If I don't sign with Subterfuge, I know I'll be disappointed.

He kicks at rocks and pinecones in his path.

I'll see some shitty band that they signed instead of us, their dumb video on "120 Minutes," and I'll think, "Shit, that could have been me." I just don't want to regret anything.

He turns right on Euclid, passes Moore's Mall, and heads for DISContent.

And yet what happens if we do sign and these guys try to change us all around?

Mark sticks his hands deep into his faded Levi's pockets.

But why else am I doing this except to make a living off it? I mean, being true to Dave plus fifty cents gets me a cup of coffee. I'm twenty-

four. In a few years I'll be thirty and won't have a college degree. Am I supposed to take this job my father's shoving down my throat and keep it for the rest of my life? I just don't see how people equate signing to a major label with ratting on your friends to Congress.

"Hey, Mark. Good show last night," Larry yells from behind the cash register as Mark enters the store. "I saw the guy in the suit. Good luck."

Mark just sort of waves and goes over to the singles bin, flips through the B's. There's not one Bottlecap record. "Fucking Dave," he mutters beneath his breath. He spots a seven-inch by Bleeding Rectum, and following that is one by Bongwater. *This is how I want to spend my life, being lumped together with these pinheads?*

Mark turns to the rows and rows of CDs. DISContent is a pretty small store, but it still has probably ten thousand CDs. Mark imagines his Bottlecap CD stuck among all the rest.

So many bands, so many people, so many ideas. The numbers make Mark's head swim. *Most bands, if they are lucky, have one or two hits. Longevity, like R.E.M. and U2, is rare. But I don't really like either of those bands anymore anyway. I stopped liking them a long time ago. But then you get a band like the Kingsmen who have one smash, "Louie Louie," and they live the rest of their lives trying to live down a song that was pretty much a joke in the first place. And yet we would be lucky if that happened to Bottlecap. The Kingsmen may have one good song, but it's one more than millions of bands get.*

Mark knows he'd be a fool to turn down the offer, but accepting it would also be foolish.

"Wow, Odysseus back from the journey." Mark hears Jim say this as he enters from the stockroom carrying a stack of CD singles. Jim wipes a long strand of red hair off his pale face and looks a little too surprised to see Mark back in the shop so soon. "So how was the tour?"

"It's like going to Helen back."

"Huh?" Jim looks dumbly at Mark.

"Helen back. Hell *and* back? You know Helen? Helen of Troy? You just said— Oh, forget it. The tour was okay, I guess."

Jim eyes a suspicious-looking kid who has been loitering in the punk rock cassette section all morning, wearing a big, loose, heavy jacket even though it's pleasantly warm outside. The two long, thin airport-type security system posts do not go off, though, as the youth leaves the building, so Jim does not take chase, even though the kid sprints from the sidewalk to his car three spaces away and peels out of the parking lot.

"I've already started to see some reviews," Jim says coyly, pulling from underneath the counter a cheap-looking zine set in newsprint. A crude-looking logo reads INDIE FILE, CAROLINA'S MUSIC MAGAZINE.

"Jesus," Mark groans, leaning against a stand-up display for a Metallica home video. "For which show? Knowing our luck it was probably our worst show since those are the only ones reviewers seem to show up for. They have an uncanny knack for it."

"Um, let me see." Jim grins as he flips through the magazine. He knows exactly where the review is—he and every other employee of the store, most of whom are in bands themselves and are jealous of even the small amount of attention Bottlecap has been receiving. They had all read and gloated over the review many times already. A few had photocopied it and posted it above the cubbyhole-sized bedrooms they shared with other students or rented cheaply from families on the outskirts of town. This gave them some sort of perverse hope to keep going. "Ah, here we go."

"Which show?" Mark keeps asking. "Which show?"

"Um, some club called Rockafella's. Columbia, South Carolina."

South Carolina. South Carolina. That was just a few weeks into the tour, and the whole state is a little blurry. He can vaguely remember a drunken show at The Pier in Charleston, then piling into the van for a show the next day in Greenville. They didn't make it in time, but the bassist of a band called Margo Sells Cargo had put them up in an expansive house that was home to a number of punk rock squatters, until the next night when they played a party at the house and everyone got incredibly drunk and stoned. They didn't leave until midday the next day and were late for their Columbia show, and even though the capital city is smack dab in the middle of the state, Steve still could not find it on any maps or off any large highway, and it was only later that Gary pointed out in a whisper—

since Mark was still recovering from his heinous hangover in the back—"No, you idiot, *South* Carolina." They didn't pull into the parking lot of the red-brick club until close to nine and were then informed by a large, rude manager named Art that not only had they missed their soundcheck but a more prominent band had been booked at the last minute and Bottlecap would now be opening up for The Jesus Lizard.

"The Je-Je-Jesus Lizard?" Mark said, stunned out of his sleep when he heard Art growling such words inches away, outside the van.

"Oh, man, the best live band in the world," Steve kept repeating, wanting to find a toilet, "the best live band in the world."

"Stay cool, guys." Gary tried to keep the peace as he unloaded the van. "We're only going on *before* them, not *after*. It's not like we have to follow them or anything. So stay cool."

"Yeah, but their fans are rabid." By then Steve was biting all five of his nails at once. "You think they're going to want to sit through forty-five minutes of lightweight pop songs about paraplegic scientists sung by a lead singer who has the stage presence of a dead body compared to David Yow?" He glanced over at Mark and added, "No offense."

The South at that time was still coming off one of its infamously hot and humid summers, and the effect inside the club, stuffed wall to wall with kids, was of a steam bath. When Bottlecap took the stage to some judicious booing and "Come on, let's get this over with," not to mention chants of "Li-zard, Li-zard," kids were already running their hands through soaked wet hair.

When they were halfway through their set, the audience looked like an accident scene, a mass of contorted, sweaty corpses lodged together, bodies screaming their heads off and slamming into one another. By the time Mark sheepishly mumbled, "Thank you. Good night," a puddle was forming around the perimeter of the mosh pit.

"Oh, South Carolina," Mark says brightly, putting on a good face for Jim. "Yeah, sure, *now* I remember."

Jim grins before digging his long nails into the review.

"Of course this whole thing is mainly about the Jesus Lizard, but you do get a paragraph all your own." He mockingly clears his throat before reading, as if he were delivering a commencement address: " 'Virginia's Bottlecap, which has two singles and a CD out on the indie label Violent Revolution, looked frightened as they took the stage. For forty minutes they tried their best to convert the crowd of Lizard loyals, but to no avail. Toward the end this reviewer could barely keep his eyes on the band and his hands off the beer. The set ended not with the traditional encore but with the lead singer, Mark Perrion—' "

"That's *Pellion*. Sorry. Keep going."

" 'With the lead singer being hit in the head with a beer bottle. The band left the stage looking just as stunned as when they had gone on a little more than a half-hour before. A crucial sacrifice for the growling pyrotechnics of David Yow and Company or just another set of slackers with jangly electric guitars? You decide.' I guess in hindsight"—Jim is trying to hold back a laugh—"it's really not so bad."

All Mark can say is "I thought that beer bottle thing happened at the Wilmington show, at Mad Monks. Oh, well."

"So how's Laura?" Jim asks in a curious tone after putting down the magazine.

"Jeez, Jim, I don't know. I've only been back a few days after being gone for three months. You probably have a better idea than I do."

"Wha-wha-what do you mean?" Jim says nervously, beginning to blush, though it's hard to tell because his pale skin is always a bit pink. For a second Mark imagines Jim's pink cock going in and out of Laura the way it used to before he stole her away. Mark imagines that Jim is imagining the same thing he is. And he's right.

"Jesus, where's the Mel Tillis records?" Mark kids. "Take it easy, Jimbo. No need to get so flustered. We're playing another show at The Scene in a couple of days, if you can make it."

"Shit, man, another show? I thought you guys'd be burnt out on playing live for a while. I've been having Kitty High hipsters in here for the past eight weeks wondering when you're coming back, and I've been telling them you'll be out of sight for a while. Why two shows so soon?"

"The band's already burnt out, and, oh hell"—he drops one

of his hands back into his jeans—"I think *I'm* getting burnt out, too. It's such jacking off. Like we're going in circles, you know? This small town, small label. Something's got to give." He looks out the plate glass window of the store and sees Gary's Volvo, which he had borrowed for his daily errands, standing at the yellow curb, and beyond that he imagines his father's frowning face, and further beyond Laura, tainted by Jim, a frown on her face as well. "Something."

"Well, shit, if you don't feel like playing, why not just cancel the show? I'm sure Todd would understand," Jim says sarcastically.

"Yeah, right. Actually Dave planned this thing a few months ago. It's next Friday, and to be honest, another piece of the door will come in handy right now."

"Tour wasn't as monetarily satisfying as you would have hoped?" Jim raises a hand and rubs his fingers together as a visual aid.

"Yeah, you could say that." Mark mentally pictures the large cardboard box still filled with unsold merchandise. He tries to think of some use for it all: CD as coaster, T-shirt as shammy, seven-inch single as raw material for a house of cards for really slow children.

"It's like I've been telling you for years, Mark. It's tough for a small independent band to live off their music unless they're really dedicated to it."

Mark turns and looks Jim in the eyes. "You saying we're not?"

Jim returns with a dumb-looking face. "You saying you are?"

Mark sighs and shrugs. "You're right. When we started, it was just for fun. But now that we're trying to make a career out of it, it's like . . . it's just pulling us under. I don't know. My dad has offered me this cushy job that'll be easy money. I'd have enough to live on and begin to pay off my credit cards, but . . . I don't know. That would just feel like . . ."

"Like what?"

"Like giving up, I guess. Shit, I don't know. Maybe it's just time for a new city. You know, Charlottesville or Arlington. Or south, like Chapel Hill." Maybe Los Angeles? He fights the urge to mention Henry James's offer to Jim, fearing the gossip that Jim would disseminate like a gas leak. What Mark doesn't know is that Jim already knows and with every second that passes is biting his tongue, wondering how on earth this guy standing in front of him with the scraggly hair and minimal talent could possibly have such luck, first to have Laura and now this. "We met some nice guys in Philly, but Philly was basically a cesspool, so forget it. Aw, hell, I don't know."

"Well, look"—Jim pats him on the back—"no one is saying you have to decide this instant, right?"

Mark again imagines his father's voice booming in the air: "The deal." Then he thinks of Henry James's voice, certainly not as resonating but also dripping with an offer.

"Just take a break for a while and relax. Replenish your juices after your long tour. Okay?"

Mark turns and takes Jim's hand to shake it, but Jim's long guitar-playing fingernails dig into his palm, so he stops.

"Thanks."

"Oh, Mark!" Jim calls out just as Mark is leaving.

"Yeah?"

"Don't forget a copy of the review!" Jim is waving the dog-eared zine in one hand and pointing to the door with the other. "There's a whole stack of them right there."

"Yeah, thanks, Jim." He fakes a smile. "You're a real prince."

A few hours later, as Mark pulls into his driveway with a few bags full of groceries, he spots Laura's Galaxy 500 sitting there next to the enshrouded carcass of his car. She hasn't been invited.

"Great."

Mark enters the house cautiously, not knowing what to expect. Maybe she's waiting for him in bed, writhing seductively in black panties and bra, a come-hither look on her face, the way it's been all afternoon waiting for him to come home. Or maybe she's talked to one of the guys and found out about one of the dalliances that occurred on this tour or the others and is angrily tapping a foot against the hardwood floor like the fluttering of a hummingbird's wings.

"Hello?" Mark calls out, dropping the groceries in the hall.

"In here," Laura calls out from the back part of the small

house. "I'm taking a bath. Hope you don't mind. All I've got is a shower, and I wanted to relax. Is that okay?"

"Sure, that's okay," Mark mumbles under his breath as he goes out to the Volvo for another load of groceries. On the sidewalk he asks, "Yeah, why not? Don't bother calling or anything."

He grabs a carton of milk and a few frozen dinners out of the brown paper bags with WINN DIXIE on them, and puts them away in the refrigerator.

"So," he calls out, "what's the big occasion?"

"No big occasion," she answers back, her voice muffled due to the distance and the half-opened door. "Just a night out with the girls. Besides, this is more relaxing."

"Oh, yes, *must* be relaxed." He shoves a can of Pringles into the pantry. "Heaven forbid you're not relaxed."

"Huh?" she calls out. "What are you saying?"

"Nothing!"

He finishes putting away the puny amount of groceries, all he could afford with the twenty dollars he had left after the tour, and then walks down the hall to the gaping bathroom door.

"Is Jim going to be there tonight?"

He peeps through the crack and can see her legs pointing away from him, toes and the tips of her breasts poking out of the thin surface of bubbles. The back of her head is toward him but out of sight.

"Jim, no. I don't think so. Why would you ask that?"

"Because"—Mark throws the dark green jacket he was wearing over a long-sleeved T-shirt onto the bed—"he asked about you today. He still has a crush on you."

"Oh, you're crazy," Laura says, flicking her hand against the surface of the water.

"Then why are you blushing?" Mark leans against the doorjamb and takes a guess.

"I'm not." She tries to wipe the color off her face that Mark couldn't see anyway, even if he had a good view.

She rises from the tub and stands up.

"Well, what do you think?"

On her face is a thick, puttylike mask, dark orange in color and put on with heavy strokes like deep grooves of oil on a Van

Gogh canvas. She tries to smile, but the substance is too hard so she can't. Her just-shaven legs are riddled with cuts, one still bleeding right below the ankle, not to mention a few around the kneecap, all raised bumps and glowing purple. Her hair is filled with a gelatinous goo that is a conditioner with another twenty minutes to go on its treatment before it can be rinsed out. It gives her head a startling Medusa effect, her long curly locks stuccoed about her ears and neck.

"Wow . . . beautiful," he says sarcastically. "Where's the fucking zucchini for your eyes? Why not just stay in a hyperbolic chamber until it's time to go out?" He leaves the door of the bathroom and in the hall leans against a Warhol print of row after row of dollar bills. "Or just wrap yourself up in plastic and stay in a dark room all day? We'll just talk every once in a while on the Internet. It'll be fun."

She quickly grabs a towel and wraps it around herself, then stomps out of the bathroom in chase.

"What in the fuck are you talking about?" she asks.

"I'm talking about your getting all gussied up to see your friends when a few nights ago I came home from an exhausting tour and found you wearing one of my T-shirts, a week's worth of stubble on your legs and armpits, and your hair smelling like chlorine."

"Well, I was doing laps down at the— Look, that was different."

"How is that at all different?" Mark finds his voice rising. As he hears his shouts echoing through the space of the hall, he catches a glimpse of Laura, her eyes sad behind the mask like a crying child on Halloween. He has to look hard to spot the crumbling emotion inside, but it's there. He feels the anger pouring out of him, but only a small portion is earmarked for Laura; the rest is for Jim, the review, and his inability to make a decision about either his father or the record company. Not that he lets this revelation stop him. "Huh? Tell me!"

"Well, uh, I mean . . ." Laura stumbles.

"It's like you don't care about looking nice for *me* anymore. Just your friends. You come over here all the time in that same old ratty pair of jeans with the damn Inspiral Carpets cow scratched into the leg that you did with your dad's Mont Blanc pen at graduation four years ago, and you think that's *cool as fuck,* but when you go out with your friends, or Jim even, you get out your Betsey Johnson and Agnes B. dresses. I get your hair in curlers or in that fucking bun on top of your head like Janet Jackson when she was on 'The Jeffersons,' but the rest of the world gets you looking like a fucking supermodel. It's just not fair."

Laura's lower lip begins to tremble, and Mark notices thick streams of tears starting to flow silently over her caked-on, terra-cotta mask.

"For the whole fucking town you're this sparkling diamond, but all I get is a lumpy sack of coal."

"That's it," she screams, lashing out at him with the end of the hairbrush in her hand. She connects half a dozen times as Mark retreats into his bedroom, half-laughing and half-afraid as he protects his face and eyes with his arms just in case she gets in a lucky shot and blinds him. She continues swatting at him until her short burst of resentment peters away, and she leaves with a giggly Mark on his ass in the corner of his room, red cuts up and down his arms from elbow to wrist, some beginning to bleed.

Laura throws on her bathrobe and stomps out the door, leaving a trail of soapy suds and flakes of her face.

A Clean and Well-Lighted Kinko's

1

JABBERJAW.

Craig's not sure what this means, he only knows that it's a word he's seen in the background of the video for the song "Gimmie Indie Fox" that he saw on a cable access show the other day, painted-wood letters cut crooked, at odd angles, nailed to the wall in a beatnik-looking coffee house where the music of Further plays to a bevy of good looking riot grrrls.

"No I ain't your West coast babe . . ."

Craig feels for the headphones of his plastic, bright yellow Walkman, singing along with the song that he put on a compilation cassette earlier in the week, as he walks the long distance from the parking lot of Kitty Community College to the bookstore across the campus. He smiles at a young girl sitting on the lawn reading a textbook, only she doesn't smile back.

The song reminds him of SST-era Dinosaur Jr. in the whiny singing, the fuzzy guitars and the exploding solos, but it also contains hints of Sebadoh (who wrote the song from which the title "Gimmie Indie Fox" is based) and there's a general Sonic Youth haze in the Wharton Tiers production job, but Further has their own unique quality which is greater than the sum of their parts. Now Craig wishes he'd put the entire *Griptape LP* onto the cassette instead of just a few songs.

"Fuck," he mumbles as he trips on a crack in the cement, looks around quickly to make sure no one noticed, and keeps going, "I'd give my left nut to hear 'Greasy' right now."

"Open up my eyes East Coast girls, but West Coast blows them away." Craig turns the corner, turning up the volume.

He smiles, looking down at his blank, white T-shirt, reminded of the scenes in the video for "Gimmie Indie Fox," where all the girls line up for the camera, each clad in a shirt for an indie band while a group of four females pantomime on stage, Further in proxy. Craig tries to count off all the band-shirts he has, but loses track after a car honks at him at an intersection, and also because he quickly runs out of fingers. In the corner of the spare room back at his apartment he's got a whole dresser filled with nothing but T-shirts covered with band-names, mainly because three or four years ago it just wasn't fun for him to go to a show and not buy a shirt. But now that he's a little older and doesn't feel the need to be the coolest guy in DISContent while still shopping for vinyl (which, on its own, makes him cool), Craig feels content to wear a plain T-shirt, or even a polo, fraying at the collar, the Izod logo fallen off years ago, satisfied to know that, inside, he's cool.

"Hey!" Craig hears a voice shouting at him. He turns and spots Brook a few buildings away waving a Peachee and a long pale arm.

"What are you doing at this place of lower learning?" Brook says, slightly out of breath from the jog across the quad. "I thought you dropped out."

"Nah, you don't drop out from community college. You just sort of skip classes for a few years."

"Seriously, though"—Brook stifles her giggling—"you slumming?"

"Well . . ." Craig nervously digs his hands into his pockets. After the other night he isn't sure how to deal with Brook. Is she still pissed at him for spurning her, and if so, which time? "I was looking for a good book, and I figured this bookstore beats one of those crappy chain stores in the mall."

"What are you looking for?"

"Oh, nothing specific, just some good reading material." The more seconds that go by when Brook doesn't mention either the other night or the one-night stand a week ago, the more relaxed Craig becomes, and the closer his body revolves around her curves like a planet in orbit.

"You know, if you're looking for a book"—she's biting her lip—"why don't we go to the Novel Idea? They have tons of great books, and they're a hell of a lot cheaper. You could maybe get a nice hardback and even"—she winks and bumps him with her hip like a dance that was popular in another age—"a cup of coffee with a good-looking girl."

The comeback takes only a millisecond. "Sounds good. But who's the girl?"

She slaps him playfully on the back, and they both turn and head off campus, toward the parking lot.

"Is this one yours?" She points to his rusted Tercel with a fading Dead Kennedys sticker.

"Yeah." He pries his door open. "So?"

"Well, it's just that Andrew has a Saab."

Craig ignores her, gets in the car, and puts the key in the ignition.

"And not only that but—" Brook begins.

"Jesus Christ," Craig bellows. "Will you cut the Saab stories?"

Brook laughs at his joke while Craig smiles, trying to make it seem intentional.

On the way to the cafe they chat amiably. Craig finds himself laughing at Brook's jokes and staring at her legs as she twists around in her seat to point at the street where he should have turned. Craig regrets not trying to know her better because it seems she is worth knowing.

"Here, here, here!" Brook is shouting as Craig gets ready to circle the block again; he's eyeing the soft nape of Brook's neck and not the cafe on the corner.

Once inside, Brook orders them both some drinks and Craig looks over the shelves. He spots at least a dozen books he's read in the past couple of years, but if pressed today on what they were about, he'd have a hard time explaining. He fingers Fuentes's *Christopher Unborn*, thinking to himself, *Uh, Jesus, what was this one about?* A few rows down he comes across a paperback of *Skinny Legs and All,* and again Craig is hit with a literary déjà vu. *I remember I bought it because of that R.E.M. quote, but was this the one about the girl with the big thumbs? Or is this the one about the redheaded terrorist and the Egyptian cheerleader?*

He picks up a hardcover of Mailer's gargantuan *The Executioner's Song* but decides against it. *Ancient Evenings* is already being used as a doorstop.

He glances over at Brook who is concentrating as she carries two mugs, balancing a muffin on top of both. She motions with her head to a table underneath a garish oil painting, her red bangs falling into her eyes. Craig watches as she sits down, and he thinks, *I've fucked her, I've seen her naked, I've been inside her— and I don't even know her last name.* When Craig was a kid, he thought that getting laid would be the answer to everything. But now he realizes that what might seem like victory could also be defeat. What is macho and proud can also be sad and weak. He shrugs, knowing it is no victory to con some girl into thinking you care for her or that you will still be there in the morning even when you know full well you won't be.

Craig examines Brook as she smiles cutely at him. Even though their brief encounter had been mutual, the word *consecrate* flashes through his mind, but he's not sure what it means. *Consecrate.* It appears again. He thinks of Brook as a child with big wondering eyes, being held by her father. Daddy's little girl. He thinks how she once wore pink Peter Pan collars, her hair was in pigtails, two front teeth missing, bright red freckles on her cheeks standing out like a rash. Now she is a grown woman, and Craig has fucked her. What did that mean? *Consecrate.* The word appears for the last time as Craig crosses the room to join her.

"So did you find anything good?" She tears into the blueberry muffin.

"Yeah, I picked up a few things." Craig takes a sip of his iced mocha as he looks over his selections. "This copy of *Breakfast of Champions* isn't in bad shape. I also got a pretty good digest-sized *Crying of Lot 49*, which should be about only two bucks, and, hey, check this out—a paperback of *Camp Concentration.*"

"Ugh." Brook shrugs and sets down her enormous cappuccino mug.

"What?"

"You have got to be wary of any book Buddy Bradley would read, except *Confederacy of Dunces.*"

Craig sets the books on the floor.

"So is this place bringing back a flood of great memories for you?"

A puzzled look flashes across Brook's face. "Why? You and I never spent any— Oh, you mean Andrew, don't you? Yeah, real funny."

"No, really," Craig says, laughing slightly. Unable to hold back a bad joke, he holds up a small hardback, *Death Kit*, before continuing. "How is the old volcano lover these days?"

"I wouldn't know. I haven't heard from him since he unceremoniously dropped me off after the night at your place."

"Did he at least slow down?"

"Not funny," she says, her voice full of lead.

"What's the problem?" Craig counters, setting down the book and grabbing a small handful of the muffin. "I thought you didn't like him."

"I don't, but . . . still. He wasn't that bad." She thinks again of those K-Swiss sneakers. *Get those shoes and you'll be popular* was the theory. *Buy the shoes and people will like you* was the unspoken advice being passed around from kid to kid like a father's *Playboy. Nothing has changed,* she thinks, laughing to herself in the split second between words in her conversation with Craig. *I've traded a pair of white leather shoes for a person. Nothing has changed since fifth grade, only now instead of a pair of shoes, I'm searching for a man. Every time I get my hands on what everyone else has, they put something else on the shelf. The popular girls are still out there living lives I don't dare dream about, and the bullies haven't changed, except now they're my boss.*

"So what?" she continues. "He was a little boring in bed. Big fucking deal. It's a drag living alone. And my shitty job doesn't help. The only reason I'm in school *again* is to meet people. It's something to do. I couldn't give a fuck about what they're teaching."

"Brook, that's why half the town is going to that shitty school. They should fire the teachers, hire some bartenders, and turn it into a singles bar."

"Is that why your girlfriend goes there?" Brook says slowly, licking the back of her spoon for effect even though there is plenty left in her cup. "You know, I could have sworn I saw her and Andrew having some sort of fight in the library the other day. Of course, I could be wrong."

"No." Craig sighs and stares at a whirling ceiling fan, watching it go round and round. "You're probably not."

"What's wrong? Did I say something I shouldn't have?" Brook slouches in her chair. "I'm sorry. I thought we were just kidding around."

"No, no, it's not you," Craig tries to reassure her. "It's just . . . I've been depressed lately. This whole relationship is driving me crazy because I don't know what to do about it. I can't leave because I'm broke. I have no place to go. My dad's pissed at me enough as it is, and my mom, well, forget that. It's just . . ." He slams his glass against the table out of frustration. "Oh, fuck it."

"Well, let me ask you this: Are you happy?"

"I don't want to be happy," Craig says, adding quickly, "Besides, there's no such thing as 'happiness.' There are only varying degrees of ignorance. They only invented the term 'happiness' because head-in-the-sandness didn't look good on paper."

"Jeez." Brook laughs. "You can't be that cynical. You make Vonnegut look like Leo Buscaglia."

"Count on it." Craig chuckles as a young black kid in a wheelchair comes in surrounded by a group of friends

"I've seen him around campus," Brook whispers, pointing her head toward the handicapped customer. "He's really nice. Hangs out near the quad and talks to everyone. He's *really* friendly."

"Well, of course he is," Craig scoffs.

"What do you mean?"

"What in the fuck else has he got? He doesn't have the clout to have an attitude. You see what I'm saying?"

"So what if that poor kid"—Brook motions across the room where the youth in the wheelchair is now talking to a small group of people, obviously the center of attention—"spent his whole day pissed off because he couldn't walk but *you* could? Where in the hell would that get him? What's with this self-pitying crap? My God."

"You know what this is?" Craig asks rhetorically, ignoring Brook's last comment. "This is a prime example of the International Copenhagen Airport Method. Remember my trip to Europe?"

"No, we never got that far, Craig. We met, we fucked, and then you left. Nope. No Europe trip."

"Oh." He laughs nervously. *She meant that as a joke, didn't she?* "Anyway, in the airport at Copenhagen they have this huge mall where you can buy duty-free goods—you know, watches, sunglasses, booze, whatever. I was on my way to Amsterdam and had a stopover before catching my connecting flight, so I had a few hours to wander around and really check the place out." He takes a sip before continuing. "I kept racking my brain trying to figure out the exchange rate to see if I had enough money to buy a sandwich or something since all they served on the flight in was this tasteless hard boiled egg on a piece of fucking melba toast. So I was trying to figure out how many dollars there were to the crown or kroner, whatever it was. And finally in this little convenience store type place where they sold books, ice cream, and magazines, I saw all these people using different currencies to get what they wanted—you know, dollars, marks, crowns, pounds, yen, anything. And suddenly it struck me: 'Man, *this* is fucking life!' We're all trying to buy things, you know, get what we want, and we all use different methods to get there. Like, say a really good-looking guy wants to get a girl. Well, he uses his looks. That's all he has to, and, *bang*, she's his. Now that guy in the corner"—Craig cocks his head backward—"he's obviously stumped as far as that angle's concerned, so he has to be charming, witty, all of that to make up for it. It's like in Germany, right before World War Two, a loaf of bread cost a wheelbarrow full of money, whereas in America you could get a whole meal for a couple of dimes. You see? Some currencies are worth more. We put different amounts of value on different qualities. Get it?"

Brook stares at Craig, thoroughly unimpressed. She reaches into her wallet and pulls out a bill.

"No, no, the coffee's on me," Craig says, reaching for his own wallet.

"Relax, Craig. The coffee's paid for." She slaps the dollar bill into his hand. "This is for Ashley, for putting up with you. Jesus, you're a real gem, you know that?" She drains her cup. "But I never knew you went to Europe. How was it?"

"Well, let me say this about Europe"—he catches the eye of a waitress placing empty cups into a brown plastic tub—"there aren't enough long-haired, smelly college kids hanging out at train stations."

She laughs, glancing at her watch. "Oh, shit, I gotta catch a class." She picks up her backpack from the floor, throws it around her shoulder, then takes the strap and lets it slide off, as if it is the strap of a slinky gown. "Want to give me a ride back to campus?"

Did that waitress smile at me? Craig is thinking and barely hears Brook.

"Huh? Oh, no, why don't you go on. I have to, uh"—he clutches awkwardly at his cup—"finish my drink."

Brook leans forward, sees about four drops of liquid that Craig might be able to suck up with an eye dropper, but gets the point.

"Okay, take care." She gets up and leaves him with a generic "Call me."

"Yeah, yeah."

Brook exits the cafe, and Eileen goes in the back to empty the tub, returning even though there are no more cups to pick up. She takes a rag from her pocket and wipes off a table a few feet away from Craig although the table is already spotless. She glances back at Jess who is standing behind the counter, fidgeting with the stereo, trying to pry his beloved import copy of *The World Won't Listen* from the cassette player. Bored, Eileen moves a table closer to Craig.

"Problem?" Eileen says noncommittally, ready to walk away if he doesn't answer. The tone in her voice shows she hasn't invested much thought in what she has said and is not expecting a big return.

"What?" Craig asks, trying to act as if he was shaken out of a deep thought. "Huh?"

"Nothing," Eileen says, embarrassed. She looks over the room quickly, to the ceiling, the counter. Her eyes lock with Jess's for a moment; she tears away from them before setting them on the stranger again. "I asked if there was anything wrong. No big deal. I mean, I hardly ever . . ." Her words trail off.

"No, no." Craig speaks quickly as Eileen starts to move away, backing out of the conversation. "You're right, something *is* wrong. But how could you tell?"

"Well"—she slips her rag into her pocket and brushes back her bangs—"most customers drink the coffee, not stare into it."

Craig grins, glancing down at his glass.

"You're right. I'm not really in the mood for"—he pauses, grabs his almost empty mug, and then pushes it away—"whatever it was I ordered. I just needed a place to think. It's been a strange day." He laughs. "A strange month."

"Need someone to talk to? I have a break coming up, and if you don't mind, I could—" Eileen finds herself saying. *Why am I doing this?* she asks herself in the time it takes for him to answer.

"Sure, but I'd hate for you to waste your break on me," he says slyly.

"No, that's okay. My name's Eileen." She lamely offers her hand, feeling ridiculous the moment she does so. "Nice to meet you."

"Me, too." They shake hands. "My name's Craig."

Craig never knows what to do when he shakes a woman's hand. Shaking other men's hands is simple—it's like an unspoken arm-wrestling contest. Each opponent clenches as hard as he can without making it apparent to the other that at any second he fears his hand will fall off. And if the other man gives out before you do and relaxes his fist, leaving you with a pile of dead meat in your paw, then that man is not to be trusted. Simple. But when it comes to women, Craig will often grab a girl's hand, raise it to his mouth to kiss it, then realize it is just a coworker he was meeting and not the queen, and abruptly stop in mid-raise, leaving the recipient thinking she was some sort of pump handle the way he is jerking her arm up and down.

Eileen pulls up a chair beside him. From behind the counter Jess is watching it all like a car crash happening in slow motion.

"So what's wrong?"

Craig opens his mouth and pauses for a second, trying to think of something to say. What *is* wrong with him? He knows he is in a relationship that isn't working out, and yet the problem is mostly him, which is not the best way in the world to entice Eileen, by saying how much he fucked up this time. Instead he skirts the issue, telling Eileen a tale of friction at work, unrest at home, though skillfully dodging the question of exactly what home he is referring to. Eileen asks about the pretty girl who was sitting with him minutes before, but Craig skips the details, instead exchanging Brook's small talk for a meditation on Godard's question: "Am I not free because I'm unhappy, or am I unhappy because I'm not free?" Eileen leans back in her chair and sighs, "Yes, oh yes," slowly, like an orgasm washing over her staged only slightly better than Belmondo's final death scene.

Ten minutes later, and only after the conversation has taken more turns than a fighter in *Top Gun*, Eileen announces she had better get back to work.

"You sure?" Craig asks as she gets up. "I mean, I know you have to go back to work, but I was just wondering if . . ."

"What?"

"If I could see you again sometime?" Craig's lips blurt out.

"Like when?" she asks, massaging the back of her chair.

"This, uh, Thursday?" Craig's voice squeaks. "Maybe we'll get some dinner or check out a band at The Scene?"

"Sure," she says, blushing, all the old feelings coming back.

"Great. I'll see you then." Craig gets up quickly, as if Eileen might come to her senses and change her decision at any moment, which is what she is considering. "Bye," he says, grinning, and then saunters out of the cafe on his way home to Ashley.

Ashley? Fuck.

Eileen is just recovering from the buzz of her conversation (sometimes a good flirt is like a shot of vodka—liberating, and gets you flushed, makes you want more) when Jess stops her.

"Who in the hell was that?" he asks as Eileen slides underneath the counter.

"A guy." She has a smirk on her face.

"Wha-wha-what are you grinning for?" Jess asks. Eileen fishes a clean apron from the cupboard. Jess catches a glimpse of the curves of her body, French-cut underwear panty lines visible underneath old and ragged Levi's. His heart sinks as he remembers Eileen moving into bed, tossing her hair back, biting on his thumb, caressing in between his thighs. He almost can't believe it is the same person.

"What's your problem?" she asks, staring at Jess's frozen face as she ties the two cotton strings.

This used to be such a victory. . . .

She shrugs and begins to move on, but he stops her as she heads to a table in the corner where a balding man is holding up an empty cup and a chess piece.

"When can I see you?" Jess asks.

"What am I, a vampire? You're seeing me now." She shakes loose.

"You know what I mean." He tries again but loses Eileen to the crowd.

"Yeah, yeah," she says softly, facing the customers.

He stares at her as she gathers cups, her jet black ponytail, secured by a red rubber band, bouncing up and down. She puts in an order for a café au lait, and Jess takes two half-filled cups out of a bus tub, combines them, adds some foam, sprinkles some cocoa, and hands it to her. He marches into the supply closet.

"Jess." She follows him into the small space. "You'd better get out there. We've got customers, and"—she jiggles the cup in her hand—"I need a *fresh* cap."

"What in the hell was that out there?" he demands, his voice no longer shaky but forceful, full of anger. "Picking up on a guy right in front of my face?" He strikes out at the wall, an act he has been taught is forceful.

"It was me!" she roars, upping the ante by countering his rancor with her own. "Making a goddamn friend," she announces, slamming down a brick of coffee.

Jess eyes the bet and the cards on the table, and folds. He says nothing.

"I'm " she starts, but then stops, lets out a breath, calming down. Her voice regular now: "I'm . . . *allowed*, you know?"

She brushes past him.

"I know," he says, "I know."

2

"Maybe he is," Randy is singing off-key, his voice warbling. *"Maybe he's not."*

Chipp looks around, noticing heads turning their way.

"Look, Randy, will you keep it down?" he pleads.

Randy continues, oblivious, swaying back and forth as he lays out *Godfuck*, half the clientele of Kinko's looking on.

"Please?" Chipp nudges, whispering. "Quiet."

"Eyes in a socket," he's now shouting, *"so I'm going to sock it!"* He stops for a moment and then says plainly: "Chorus."

"What?" Chipp asks nervously, sweat forming on his upper lip.

"I said *chorus.*"

"I'm not going to sing the chorus, Randy." Chipp moves to the other side of the layout table, the whir of a copier in the background.

"Well, if you don't," Randy says in a singsongy voice, taping down the *Godfuck* logo, "I will."

Randy clears his throat, takes a deep breath, and shuts his eyes, making as if he's going to scream.

"Okay, okay," Chipp says quietly. "Here goes: *Ba ba ba da duh, debris slide!* You happy?"

"Yeah." Randy is grinning. He reaches for a new roll of tape. "I'm happy."

A group of kids come in and begin crowding around one of the copiers in the corner, photocopying their hands and faces, throwing attention off Chipp and Randy.

"Now we need to decide what to put on the cover." Randy is rolling his skull ring around with his chin, an old nervous habit. "I say we go with 'G. G. Allin: Death of a Scumrocker.' " He pulls out a photo of a chubby guy, pale white, covered in tattoos, dried blood, and feces, naked except for a studded dog collar, squatting on a stage. The trails of shit and flowing cuts on his bald head make it look like a cracked egg; the microphone is almost totally inside his mouth, which is surrounded by a scruffy brown goatee.

"I don't know." Chipp picks up the photo with the tips of his thumb and forefinger, as if it had cooties. He shuffles it into a pile of assorted photos. "Why don't we put my photo of The Deer Park on the cover? Then we'll put at the bottom, 'Interview on page three.' We'll put G.G. somewhere in the back."

"But—" Randy begins to protest.

"But what? You think the title of the magazine is bad? You think the logo's going to scare people? I mean, that's nothing compared to having that psycho on the cover. I mean, I sat through *The Cook, the Thief, His Wife and Her Lover* twice, but I still can't watch some of that G. G. Allin stuff."

"I just think"—Randy rolls his shoulders—"that 'Death' and 'Scumrocker' has a nice ring to it. But I guess you're right."

A few copiers away an old man, overweight, wearing gray polyester slacks, a white short-sleeve shirt and bright red suspenders, is sweating profusely even though it's not hot outside or inside. He sidles up to Chipp and Randy and tosses onto the layout table a raggedy shopping bag bursting with scraps of paper. Chipp's and Randy's eyes gravitate to his pudgy hands, which are taping together row after row of coupons, six to a sheet. He then waddles over to a copier, plugs in his blue meter, and makes about a dozen copies. He retrieves the warm pages and moves over to the paper cutter, where he haphazardly cuts them into sections, pausing between each slice for a breath. He sweeps them into his paper bag and waddles out, leaving his originals in the machine.

"Hmm, buy one, get one free at Paco's Taco."

"Randy, will you get over here? Now what about my suggestion?"

"Sure," he says. "Put The Deer Park on the cover."

"Hey, Randy." Chipp is going through the pile of material that Randy had spent the last couple of days typing into semi-straight columns.

"What?" He's laying down a photo, trying to judge whether it's crooked.

"You did a great job on these classified ads." Chipp thumbs

through the twenty or so ads that are a combination of personals, tape collectors, For Sale items (secondhand guitars and records, mostly), and pen pals. "Where'd you find all these people?"

"I made them up," he says out of the side of his mouth, his face an inch away from the table. He's trying to line up a headline: ROYAL TRUX VS. UNSANE: WHO SHOOTS MORE HEROIN? "God, I wish they had those light box thingys here. It'd make this much easier."

"They do, over in the corner. But someone's using it. Wait a second—you *what?*"

"Aw, you heard me." Randy stands up, cracking his back and noticing the expression of disapproval on Chipp's face. "Oh, come on. What did you expect me to do? This is our first issue. No one knows about us yet. I had to do something."

"That's what the flyers were for!"

Randy is silent.

"You did make the flyers, didn't you?"

Chipp groans and buries his head in his hands.

"Well, after the poetry thing didn't work out—" Randy explains, "I mean, we got only one submission, so I figured that flyers weren't an impressionable form of media in which to get our message across."

"But lying is?"

"Don't look at it as lying, Chipp. We're just being creative, that's all."

"So is there a letters column, too? All of our feedback from issue number zero? Minus one, the prequel?"

"Sure." He laughs. "There are a few."

"Jesus!" Chipp exclaims and actually reads one of the ads out loud: " 'Reality does not exist, only what is in your mind. Write to a vampire who believes in lust, love, and things that go bump in the night. No Christians, weirdos, or goths.' You dipfuck, that's *our* address! We're going to have every psycho in town stopping by!" He brings the paper closer to his face. "No, wait, you got the apartment number wrong again."

"Relax." Randy pats him patronizingly on the back. "I did that on purpose. I put the apartment number across the hall, so when we hear a knock, we can look out the peephole, and if it's

somebody weird or demented-looking—in a bad way, mind you
—we'll just let it go. And what is he? A schoolteacher?"

"Yeah, at the local parochial school."

"Well, whatever. We'll let him handle it. And if it's two busty
blondes, well, then we'll show them the way in and have the best
night of our young lives."

"Oh, this is great." Chipp ignores him, reading another ad:
" 'Bassist wanted for established Olympia band. Write to Calvin
Johnson at K Records.' Jeez, he'll love that." Randy grins as
Chipp reads another. " 'Pen pal wanted: I want to hear your
most bizarre sexual fantasy. Your explicit photo gets mine. All
letters answered.' " His eyes widen at the last sentence. "That's
my parents' address!"

"Is it?" Randy says innocently. "I got it off a scrap of paper in
the apartment. I thought it was Sarita's. Oh, well."

"Change it."

"But—"

"Change it."

Randy scratches out the address, mumbling under his breath,
"Change it, change it."

Chipp leans against a copier, and his ears catch a snippet of
conversation taking place behind the counter at the front of the
store.

"It doesn't matter if you're sending it to Alaska or to Atlanta,"
an employee explains to an old woman. "They both cost the
same."

Chipp looks over the four employees rushing around like
cockroaches behind the counter, one of them still trying to explain the confusing process of a fax machine to an elderly lady,
while another is hunched over a Macintosh in the far corner
under a big sign that reads TYPESETTING HEADQUARTERS, and the
other two keep closing and raising the tops of the industrial-
sized copiers.

"What are you boys working on?" a man in his late forties
asks. He has long hair, is wearing a tie-dyed T-shirt and cheap
sandals.

Randy pulls out the title page of *Godfuck*, covering up the
sensitive title but with the photo of G. G. Allin, which sort of
defeats the purpose. The guy only glances down, not noticing.

"A *zine?*" he says, *zine* rhyming with *line* instead of *lean,* like it's supposed to. "What's a zine?"

"Uh—" Randy readies a smart-assed answer but Chipp sees it coming and cuts him off.

"It's a school project, basically." Figuring that the only reason this guy asked them what they were doing was so they would ask what *he* was doing, Chipp plays along. "What about you?"

"Well, since you asked!" The guy reaches into a brown tube, pulls out a large poster, and unrolls it over the entire layout table. It's a black-and-white ink drawing of a large mountain, on top of which is a medieval castle, and surrounding the hill is a circle of elves, gnomes and waifs, all holding hands. The surrounding country is thick brush; a few animals sit in the overgrown grass and cattails, among which are a few unicorns.

"Uh, so?" Randy says.

"I sell these at a few places in town. It comes with a small batch of colored ink pens. People color them in any way they want to."

"But"—Chipp looks over the monochrome poster—"I don't see any numbers or anything. How do they know where to put the right colors?"

The stranger stiffens his arms at his sides and looks up at the ceiling. "That's what I'm trying to get rid of. This whole *rules* type of thing. It doesn't matter what color you— Oh, here's my ride." He points out the window to a girl with a billowy floral-printed skirt on a Day-Glo bicycle; a huge wicker basket is tied to the handle bars. He quickly rolls up his poster and rushes out the door, squeezing onto the back of the banana seat.

"Okay, that should be it," Randy announces, getting back to business and applying another piece of tape to a headline.

"Did you put in the disclaimer?" Chipp turns back around to the layout table.

"Disclaimer?"

"Yeah, you know, that thing I wrote about the views expressed therein are not expressly those of blah, blah, blah. I showed it to you the other day."

"Disclaimer? But why?"

"Randy"—Chipp looks him straight in the eye—"you offer a money-back guarantee that Six Finger Satellite is the worst band in the world and flat-out call them cocksuckers and also use, oh, I'd say half a dozen recognizable corporate logos. Why am I the only person here worried about getting sued? Doesn't the name Negativeland mean anything to you? Wake up, Randy, this is the nineties. Every American living today needs to be worried about being sued by someone."

"No, I didn't put in the disclaimer, since you're so curious. It's in that pile over there. Cut it out and paste it on yourself if you're so worried."

Chipp ignores Randy's snotty tone and searches through the pile of leftover material and clippings for the disclaimer. He grabs the third page and puts a small dab of rubber cement beneath the staff box, which reads simply "Chipp and Randy," preparing the space for the disclaimer. He grabs an X-Acto knife from a pile of office supplies in a clear plastic holder and cuts a box around the small square area of type. Rounding the last corner, the knife turns sharply and slides into his finger.

"Fuck!" Chipp shouts out.

"What? What happened?"

"I cut myself."

Chipp examines the cut, which is about half an inch wide; he pulls back the open skin, which looks like a gill on the end of his thumb. Blood begins to trickle down his hand.

"Aw, you got blood on the disclaimer. Now we'll have to leave it out."

"No, I didn't, you asshole." Chipp grits his teeth to stifle the pain. With his good hand he places the disclaimer, crooked. "Look, I'm going back to the apartment to wash this thing out. That hippy may have been using it. I'll try to find a Band-Aid and come back in a little while."

"Don't worry about it. All that's left is to make copies. It's all ready to go, and I can take care of that." Randy pats his backpack, which contains the extra meter.

"Good. I'll be back at the apartment. You have your own car, right?"

"Yeah, yeah," he mumbles as Chipp runs out of the building.

Randy looks around, making sure most of the Kinko's employees are busy in the back of the store, working on jobs behind the counter. He takes the meter he picked up as he entered the store and makes a few token copies of nothing, just to rack up a few numbers on the meter. He then sets it aside, glances around again, and pulls out the trick meter from his backpack. He quickly slips it into the machine, trying to cover up the counter with a folded piece of paper.

Randy takes the pages of *Godfuck* and, making sure they are in order and lined up straight, places them into the top document feeder of a large green-and-off-white machine in the corner. He hits the 2 SIDE button, then enters 200 on the keypad and slaps the glowing red START button.

The machine jams every few minutes as the hastily pasted layout sheets get caught in the document feeder. Whenever this happens, Randy curses loudly, stupidly attracting attention to himself and the growing mound of paper. He takes a few piles of pages out to his car, loading up the trunk and even the back-seat. As the machine is churning out the copies, Randy hoists himself up on the layout table and sits crosslegged, picking at his nails, yawning, contemplating a nap. A few other customers wander in and use the copiers, but half a dozen come and go while Randy is still there, dozing off, his feet kicking off bottles of Wite-Out, sending the caddy full of office supplies crashing to the ground.

After making a few poster-sized cardboard copies of the cover, along with some color copies, Randy shoves the layout sheets and the last of the pages into his backpack, along with the trick meter. Then he grabs the original blue meter, reading 00004, and walks to the cash register, sporting a grin.

He slaps it down on the counter, tapping his foot as if he is in a hurry.

"Okay," a short young girl with black hair says, stepping behind the cash register. She takes the meter from the counter and checks it. She is startled at the 00004, especially since Randy has been there ever since she came on her shift two hours ago. "Hang on a second, please," she says, and then goes to the back and has a brief word with an older man who, Randy guesses, is the manager. He starts fidgeting, tapping the counter over and over again. *What's going on?* He feels sweat beginning to form under his armpits. *What could be the problem?* After a minute or two of the employee and the manager shaking their heads and glancing over at Randy every few seconds, she returns.

"That'll be twenty cents, please."

"What?" Randy says, shocked. "Oh, yeah, twenty cents." He shakes down his pockets looking for cash, remembering he left his wallet at home. He switches the rolled-up posters from under one arm to the other, then checks his other pocket, mercifully finding a quarter. He plunks down the dirty coin and actually waits for his nickel as the girl goes in the back to get another roll of coins.

"Whew!" Randy says as he opens the Plexiglas door, holding it open for a cute-looking girl walking in. Just as he turns the corner to head into the parking lot, his eyes adjusting to the twilight sky, trying to find his car, he feels someone grab him by the shoulder.

"Excuse me, young man . . ."

Randy turns around and sees a tall police officer blocking out what's left of the setting sun.

"Can I talk to you for a second?"

3

Mark is pacing furiously around his small apartment, waiting for Gary and Steve to arrive. He walks around in circles, through the kitchen, around his bed, and back out into the living room. He sits down, turns on the stereo, Heavens to Betsy, gets up, turns the stereo off, and begins pacing again. In his hand is Henry James's card, nearly turned into pulp from the sweat of Mark's hand, which has been clutching at it for the past two days.

"I think your sound is something real and something new." He is remembering the conversation he had with the A&R man at the Chinese restaurant across from The Scene on Friday night. "And, hey, I could bullshit you, but the fact is, I want to sign Bottlecap." The A&R man went on to name some figures which made Mark choke on the sake.

"Knock, knock?" Gary sticks his head through the door.

"Yeah, yeah, come in. Fuck the pleasantries. We're going to be huge, so just get your sorry ass in here."

Gary enters the apartment, heads for the fridge, returns with a beer.

"Where's Steve?" Gary asks.

"I thought he was with you. Didn't you guys finish setting up the gear at the practice space today?"

"Huh, are you kidding?" Gary sits down on the couch, takes a sip from the beer, and begins rubbing his fingers, which are still sore from the past few months of touring. "He left all that shit to me. He spent all weekend with some chick he met last week, said he'd be here when he was finished—you know, wink, wink."

"Well, good, because knowing Steve, that'll be fifteen minutes . . . including foreplay."

"Ha! Say, thanks a lot for abandoning me on Friday while you went off and had a 'private chat' with your little friend."

"I invited both of you guys to come, so don't give me any of your shit."

"Who was going to tear down the set? Superchunk was supposed to go on in ten minutes. Todd was looking at me like he was going to strangle me. You know how he gets when we take too long and then the last band plays past curfew. The cops are just waiting for the kids to come out."

"Boo fucking hoo. Listen, I've got big news."

The doorbell rings.

"Steve, get your ass in here!"

Steve opens the door, makes for the fridge, returns with the last beer.

"Yeah, well, make it quick because I've got her idling back at my place." He has lipstick smears on his cheeks and neck.

"How old is this one? Twelve?" Gary asks.

"Huh? No, twice that . . . I think."

"Will the both of you shut up? Now, just take a look at this." Mark unravels the card in his hand, flattens it out on the table, and then passes it to Gary and Steve.

"Ugh, what'd you do, come on this thing?"

"Yeah, what's with all this moisture? I can't even read it. Is it a business card?"

"Yes, it's a business card, you morons." Mark snatches it out of Steve's hand. Sometimes he wishes two other people had answered his rhythm section want ad. "Okay, I'm going to start from the beginning." He sits down opposite Steve and Gary.

"This guy, Henry James, was in the audience the other night. He flew in from Los Angeles just to see us, okay?"

"But how did he know we were going to be playing? I mean—"

"Will you let me finish? He's like a scout for Subterfuge Records, and he wants to sign us. We'll be fucking rich!"

"Wait, wait a second." Gary protests. "What is it, Lucifuge Records? Like Danzig? But he sucks."

"Not Lucifuge, *Subterfuge.*"

"Never heard of them," Steve pipes in.

"Me, neither," Gary responds.

"And what does Subterfuge mean anyway?" Steve runs his hand over his three-day stubble.

"Who cares?" Mark yells. "What in the hell does Shimmy Disc mean? What does C/Z stand for? The point is, he's willing to pay us to make our music."

Steve and Gary are silent. They turn to each other.

"But what about Dave?" Steve says softly. "What about the label we're already on, Violent Revolution Records?"

"Gary, did you tell him to say that?"

"No, Mark," Gary says dryly. "I know it's hard to believe, but Steve actually thinks for himself sometimes."

"Anyway, fuck Dave!" Mark screams, getting up and pacing around the apartment again. "This is a MAJOR LABEL."

"But Dave is our friend. I mean, shouldn't we at least ask?"

"Look, you guys, sure, Dave's our friend. But we're not under contract to him. Hell, he doesn't even *have* contracts! What are we supposed to do, continue to have these pressings of five thousand when this guy wants to put out an entire record and have us make a video? With tour support? Do you *hear* what I'm saying? And what about when we did that single of the month for Sub Pop? You guys weren't so hot on sticking with Dave then."

"That was different. That got us exposure, which helped sell our other records."

"Yeah," Gary agrees. "It was a one off, you know that. Bruce Pavitt even talked about signing us for an album, and we all voted that down."

"He was never serious, though. Jesus, the guy has three bottles of Ballard Bitter, and you think he wants to sign us! He was just talking drunk talk, jacking you guys off who are too stupid to know any better." Mark turns and sees that the comment is not sitting well. "Well, you know what I mean. Look, I like Dave, and I know he gave us a chance when no one else did. Remember when Slap-a-Ham Records wouldn't even put out our EP but Dave did? Don't think I don't know that. But he's been talking about taking us to the next level for the past couple of years, and he can't even get his own shit together—waiting tables at the Whales Fin, give me a fucking break!" Gary squirms in his chair. "He's just another college dropout with a lot of big ideas, but he's missing the wherewithal to do anything about them. Throw a rock in any small college town, and you'll hit someone just like him."

"I think you're being a little harsh, Mark." Gary stops to take another sip of beer. "Dave's a good guy, and to bail out on him when we've practically committed to making another album with him would be bullshit. It'd be a dickless thing to do. But, hey, what do I know? I'm just the bass player. You're the leader, Mark, and I know that. Bottlecap's your baby, so I guess the decision is ultimately yours . . . but I'm against it."

"Come on, you guys. Give Henry a chance."

"Henry, who's Henry?" Steve asks.

Mark points to the balled-up paper.

"You mean the math teacher?" Steve erupts in laughter, finally remembering the A&R man from Friday night. "Jesus, that fucking square wouldn't know a good song if one bit him on the tip of his dick!"

"That's what worries me. Like what does he know about us?" Gary says. "One show and *bang*, he wants to sign us? Doesn't that seem suspicious to anyone else?"

"Look, at this point"—Mark throws up his arms—"I couldn't give a shit if this guy's a fan or not. If the Subterfuge check cashes, he's okay in my book."

Steve looks in Mark's clouded eyes but can't see what used to be there. He thinks back to the day he auditioned for Gary and Mark at their rehearsal space on the outskirts of town. Mark had this great batch of songs, and Steve was excited to get a chance to be part of something as good and genuine as Bottlecap, to make good music, to create something new—all this never seemed to matter. It never seemed to matter to Mark, either, but here he is, frothing at the mouth. Steve can't understand it.

"He needs an answer today."

"Why so soon?" Gary asks.

"Yeah. Besides, today's already over." Steve glances down at his watch. "It's almost eight o'clock."

"It's eight o'clock here, dummy. It's still five in California."

Gary gets up. "Look, I know things aren't perfect here in Kitty or with the band, but this just doesn't seem like the right solution. It's too much too soon, and just *too* damned suspicious. You do what you want and we'll go along with it, but you know how I feel."

"Me too." Steve follows Gary out the door.

Have they lost their fucking minds? Mark's thinking as he paces around the room at breakneck pace. He stops in his tracks, grabs the receiver, and dials the number he memorized earlier in the day.

"Subterfuge Records"—girl, cute voice—"how can I help you?"

"Uh, can I talk to Henry James, please."

"One moment."

The phone clicks, clicks again, and then starts ringing.

Mark feels sweat break out on his forehead. His neck becomes hot, his vision blurry, his ears afire. He fights the impulse to hang up, slam down the receiver. The ringing is driving him insane. Over and over again, the tone rolls like a drumbeat, stops on a dime, silence for a second, then begins again. Mark realizes now why Chinese water torture is so effective.

"Hello? Is anybody there?" the A&R man asks.

"Is, er, this Henry?" The name *does* sound funny. Mark never thought he could trust a man with a name like Henry. Maybe he could call him Hank?

"Yes, who's this?"

"This is Mark. Mark Pellion from Bottlecap."

"Well, Mr. Pellion, do you have an answer for me?"
Mark closes his eyes so tight he sees swirling colors.
"Yes, Henry. We're going to . . ."

4

Jess lingers for a few seconds outside the Novel Idea cafe, staring up at Eileen's window. He can't see her, but a shadow floating across the walls makes it seem as though she's dancing, the shadow alternately wide and then thin, as if its subject keeps turning, dipping, skipping happily about. Jess steps up on tiptoes to try to hear what is going on, maybe a snippet of conversation or a familiar voice from the television that would tell him what show she is watching. For some reason he thinks this would be important, neat, at least a kernel of knowledge that would make him feel closer to her. "Keith's gone, Alison"—a wimpy lisp. "I love you . . ." And Jess would nod, roll back on the heels of his shoes, and know: She watches "Melrose Place."

But instead he hears music, a song, unidentifiable, but it sounds like one of the those bands Jess isn't much a fan of but Eileen loves and is always popping into the cassette player in the cafe. And every time a customer points to the speaker and says, "Wow, who's that playing?", Eileen grins and Jess shrugs, another defeat. He played *Kill Uncle* the other day and was booed three seconds after the first few wailing strains of the second song, "Asian Rut." Eileen just shook her ponytail and put her tape back in.

Jess is approaching the building when a car rounds the corner, its spotlight in his face, making him feel guilty, caught.

"What in the fuck am I doing?" he swears at himself, feeling like a stalker. "This is ridiculous." He turns and walks away, down the sloping street toward his apartment, turning right at the corner, heading down Euclid Street, hanging a right at Swansea. He trudges over the lawn, trying to look into his next-door neighbor's apartment to see if she is home. In the hallway he checks his mailbox. A few bills, a few Dear Occupants, and a cable bill that should have been delivered two doors away. Jess grabs it all and tosses it on the couch.

He goes directly to the kitchen, checks the answering machine first; the little red light is staring at him, not winking. He grabs a glass of water, then sits on the couch and opens his mail. On the way back he turns on the stereo; Joy Division's "Closer" creeps out of the speakers. He starts with the Occupant mail, sets aside a few pizza and dry cleaning coupons he might actually use one of these days, and tosses the rest on the floor. He flips through the bills: gas, phone, credit card. He slices open Peter Tressle's cable bill, curious to see if he has basic or premium channels. It turns out Tressle has only the regular cable service but owes for the past five months; his amount due column is almost two hundred dollars. Jess slam-dunks it into the trash.

He sets his water on the nightstand and turns off the stereo, depressed by the melancholy music. He switches on the TV for a little white noise and goes into his bedroom. He lies on top of his covers, on his back, and begins wriggling out of his clothes. He throws his shirt across the floor, kicks his jeans toward the door, where they catch on the doorknob, leaving on only his socks and boxers.

Jess slips a hand inside the flap of his boxers, yanks and massages his limp penis, trying to get it hard. He closes his eyes, expertly rolling around the malleable flesh between his fingers, trying to think of Eileen: Eileen bending over, Eileen smiling, Eileen naked in this very room. His cock becomes half-erect, but the newscaster's droning voice from the next room makes it difficult to concentrate. The distraction only makes him shut his eyes more tightly; concentrating deeper, a voice inside his head tries to match Eileen's whispering come-ons: "I want you, Jess," and so forth. Just as Jess has mustered up a decent erection and is about to come, the phone rings.

"Aw, fuck," he shouts, his concentration broken immediately and his penis collapsing. He lies on his bed, staring at the ceiling, waiting for his machine to pick up.

"Hey, Jess, this is Jack. You there? Okay, guess not. I just want to let you know that the gang is getting together to play a game of Risk tonight. Called to see if you wanted to come. Uh, give me a call if you do. I'll be here for about another hour. Uh, okay, I guess that's it, so . . . bye."

Jess holds his limp penis in his hand, decides against working it up again, and instead pulls up his boxers and goes to his desk. He switches on his Mac; the bluish white screen lights up, showing a small cartoon icon of a Mac, and the modem chimes to life with a loud BEEP! He tries to log onto a local bulletin board, but considering that there's only one node for the 2,400 baud and one for 9,600, it's predictably busy. Jess shrugs, runs a hand over his bare shoulders, giving him the chills, before remembering that he should be getting some E-mail on the other board any day now from a kid called Kramer, who is in the Midwest and is a "Seinfeld" freak, not to mention someone named 2600% who is interested in buying the games Jess has in his closet for a buck a cartridge. He clicks onto his America Online folder.

He types in his password, presses Enter, and listens as the computer has his telephone dial a preliminary four digits, followed by another seven, connecting him to the network. *Connecting*, the screen reads, moving onto *Checking Password*. A few seconds later his password is confirmed, and the America Online logo pops up, on its right the special features that are switched daily but are never that entertaining anyway. *Adding* Time *Artwork, Please Wait*. He sits for at least a minute as the network downloads the information to his computer.

"The reason this takes so long," he mumbles as the computer finally frees up, "is that I'm paying by the minute."

At the bottom of the screen he sees the small graphic of an envelope, above which are the words NO MAIL.

"Aw, fuck." He clicks on the GO TO window with his mouse and, holding down the button, pulls down the menu, highlights LOBBY, and releases the button, which clicks as he does so. The America Online logo disappears and is replaced by a large window; at the top it reads PEOPLE CONNECTION—LOBBY B. Off to the left it says PEOPLE HERE: with a number that keeps fluctuating as people come and go. Below the title of the room are two lines: NOW ENTERING, which lists all the people coming into the room, and the exit, reading, simply enough, NOW LEAVING.

Jess's own screen name, Meat Is Mu (which should have been Meat Is Murder, but he was cut off after ten letters because he accidentally hit Enter) is shuffled down the NOW ENTERING line, sandwiched between VIK2000 and MSDEMEANOR. A few more people enter the room, and Jess is further pushed along until he's digitally dumped in. The NOW LEAVING line is just as crowded, six or seven people jumping ship every few minutes. The PEOPLE HERE counter keeps steady at around twenty or twenty-two. At the bottom of the screen is a long, thin box next to an on-screen button marked SEND. This is where Jess posts his replies to messages in the dialog box; he hits SEND, and a second later they are injected into the on-screen conversation.

Jess sits back for a second, wanting to survey the conversation before jumping in. The first person to post is someone who just entered the room. "Amateur," sighs Jess

Mike526066: Hi, y'all!

Anthony961: yeah, hi, mike, don't interrupt us. now, trekkie, how can you even stand up for that new generation show?

Trekkie113: Anthony, quit picking on me. Hey, Mike, what's up?

Trisha E703: What's happening in here?

Trekkie113: Hey, Trisha, this is the lobby. Where are you?

Rodeo043: Anyone out there from Texas?

Anthony961: texas sucks

MsDemeanor: good one, anthony. LOL.

Anthony961: :)

Trisha E703: Treeki, what's LOL mean?

Trekkie113: It's onlinespeak for Laugh Out Loud and my name's TREKKIE not TREEKI, stop or you'll hurt my feelings. :(

Even though there are now twenty-five people in the room, this is usually the way discussion goes: a few obnoxious people like Anthony961 dominate the conversation while people like Trekkie113 are their fodder and float from room to room as other people's bait. Names like Trisha E703 are picked by the computer whenever a screen name isn't chosen. The computer defaults to your own name, and the number behind the name represents how many others were already signed up with that name. One time Jess saw a Eugene 784 and couldn't believe so many people out there actually had that name. "Come on," he snarls at the glowing screen, "have some imagination."

Anthony961: hey, meat is mu, that's a real neat name . . . not!

A few other messages click by before Jess notices he's been singled out. Guys like Anthony961 hang out in the lobby all day and pick on people, choosing up a name from the NOW ENTER-ING list and asking some dumb question. From his use of all lowercase letters (which is easier to type, so it's faster getting out the message since you're held up only by your own typing speed), Jess can tell that Anthony961 spends a lot of time on the boards.

Ignoring the insult, Jess aims his mouse at the ROOMS icon, a square graphic of a scary hallway. The ACTIVE PUBLIC ROOMS window appears on top of the one he was just looking at, the scrolling conversation still seen on the bottom and sides. Inside the window is a list of all the public rooms, along with how many people are inside each one. Jess scrolls down the list. There are only two people in BEST LIL CHATHOUSE, nineteen in THE FLIRTS NOOK, thirty in ROMANCE CONNECTION, and eighteen in both TEEN CHAT and GAY AND LESBIAN. Yet despite whatever sort of themed room it is, people usually just ask the same sort of inane ques-tions, like "Where you from?" or "Anyone out there in South Dakota?" Real conversations are hard to find because talking in the computerized room is remarkably like trying to hold up a meaningful conversation in a club while a band blasts music from the stage, or in a bar where the clatter of everyone else's conversation seems to drown out your own. With so many peo-ple in a room and so many conversations being tossed back and forth, it is difficult to get into any subject deeply, since every two lines someone new to the room interrupts with "Hey, what is this? Where are all you from?" The only way to talk about any-thing substantial is, as in real life, to go to a private room.

Jess often laughs at the thought of how this electronic service is a lot like a real-life party: the way you're rushed into the room, rubbing shoulders as you enter with those who are exiting, and once in it's up to you to speak up and make a joke, say something interesting, or gravitate to a corner and stay there. On Friday and Saturday nights the boards are jammed, and users complain of trying to get on for hours, only to get busy signals (though for Jess, logging on from a small town, it is no problem). All across the country men and women squeeze onto the boards for conversation and information. There are at least four different lobbies you can wander in and out of, not counting all the other public rooms available. Instead of going out to a bar and having to look nice and pay for drinks, people stay at home and cruise the computer screens, gliding along the information highway rather than the smog-filled interstate, meeting people, chatting, getting out of the house even though they are still in their homes.

Yawning, Jess clicks onto a space entitled PRIVATE ROOM. Another dialog box appears over the other two, reading ENTER A PRIVATE ROOM, below which is a blank box and a button marked GO. He types in *Sex,* then hits Enter, activating the GO button.

The screen flashes back to the lobby screen of a few minutes ago, except at the bottom of the old conversation it reads, in bold letters: YOU HAVE JUST CHANGED TO ROOM "SEX." He glances at the top left of the screen—PEOPLE HERE: 12—and mumbles, "Hmm, not bad."

After a few minutes it is apparent that the usual lame discussion is taking place in the room, which consists mostly of some guys looking for girls.

Allen M: hey, how about an orgy in here?
Jun L16: You're all sick!
Doug E12: Car Toy, you M or F?
Sewarat: See you all later
Doug E12: bobbi?
Allen M: aw, who needs you
Crasher: me too, I'm leaving, I'm going to go write a book
Car Toy: sorry, M
Doug E12: fuck you, crasher, is there a woman in here or not?

Jess moves the arrow of his mouse to the PEOPLE icon, which looks like the back of the first Doors record, and clicks it. A window appears that lists everyone in the room, including those not listed on either the NOW ENTERING or NOW LEAVING lines, so you can check out the people shyly hugging the wall. Jess scrolls through the names, even recognizing a few (Don't I know you?) looking for a female. Near the bottom is the name Eros 69, which sounds good, so he highlights it and clicks the GET INFO button. A half-second later a profile of Eros 69 appears:

> Screen Name: Eros 69
> Member Name: Paul
> Sex: Male
> Occupation: Mortgage consultant, accountant

"Ooh, gross," Jess says as he clicks the box shut. He finds another name that could mean either, Bobbi Sex, again highlights the name, and then clicks the GET INFO box.

> Screen Name: Bobbi Sex
> Member Name: Elizabeth
> Sex: Female
> Marital Status: Divorced/separated

"Divorced *and* separated?" Jess asks himself as he sends Bobbi Sex an instant message. *Want to go private?* Jess resumes watching the lackluster conversation when his computer chimes, announcing he is receiving an instant message.

Sure, Meat Is Mu, I'll be in the Bobbi room. C-ya!

Jess clicks again onto the ROOMS icon, chooses PRIVATE ROOM and types in Bobbi. NOW ENTERING: Bobbi Sex, Meat Is Mu. People Here: 2.
"Perfect!"

Bobbi Sex: i like it like this
Bobbi Sex: all alone
Meat Is Mu: what are you wearing?
Bobbi Sex: you don't waste any time do you?
Bobbi Sex: nothing, how about you?
Meat Is Mu: naked

Jess slips his hands back inside the boxers he just lied about. A few seconds go by before Bobbi Sex answers. She is either waiting for Jess to say something or has been responding to somebody else's instant message.

Bobbi Sex: so now what, big boy
Meat Is Mu: i want to fuck you
Bobbi Sex: sounds good to me. how big's your cock?
Meat Is Mu: huge. almost ten inches. it's rock hard and i want to shove it into your pussy.
Bobbi Sex: :)
Bobbi Sex: tell me what you look like
Bobbi Sex: while i roll these big nipples around
Meat Is Mu: you tell me first
Bobbi Sex: okay. tall, long blond hair and very big breasts. you like big breasts?

Jess takes his hand off his penis for a second to type in a response.

Meat Is Mu: yes
Bobbi Sex: good. i'm running my hands over my big breasts right now, my nipples pointing straight up. now my hands are moving down my tan, slender chest. my fingers are running through my pubic
Bobbi Sex: hair, sinking into my wet cunt. i'm playing with myself, teasing my clit, waiting for your hard cock, my pussy juices running over my fist, onto
Bobbi Sex: the floor. ooh, this feels good. want some?

Jess begins to jack-off, eyes glued to his glowing computer screen, picturing this woman in his mind even though he is not sure that this Bobbi Sex is even a woman, and if so, probably nothing like she described herself. After all, Jess is clenching his own sexual organ that is just over half the size he claimed it was.

Bobbi Sex: my hot pussy lips, sinking my fingers
Bobbi Sex: inside, lick the juices

After stroking his penis for a few minutes, Jess finally comes in a lackluster orgasm that's a complete misfire. He feels the sperm rising up his shaft without any pleasure connected to it. It's like a sonic boom where he shot his wad first but the pleasure forgot to follow close behind. The hot juice fights its way up his half-hard cock, and Jess winces at the pain, feeling like a BB is being shoved up his penis. He gets up carefully, not wanting to drip on the floor. Once in the bathroom he grabs a long stretch of toilet paper and wipes the come from his hands and belly, dabbing at a spot on his shorts that is glistening wet with a warm drop. He throws the wad of tissue paper into the toilet, flushes, and then goes to sit back down at the computer.

   Bobbi Sex: hello? meat?
   Bobbi Sex: you still want
   Bobbi Sex: to fuck?
   Bobbi Sex: hello

Jess glances disgustedly at the screen, points his mouse at the QUIT command, holds down the button and drags the menu, highlights DISCONNECT, and releases the button in a *click!*

As his system logs him off, the computer says in a happy male voice, "Good-bye!"

5

Dave pulls up to Stacy's house, his car sputtering to a halt just as he reaches the curb.

"Perfect!"

Whistling as he gets out of the car, he shuts the door and contemplates locking it, but then figures *Why?* and leaves it un-locked. He leans down to check his hair in the driver's-side win-dow, only it's too dirty to reflect anything except Dave's allergy to car washes. He smooths a hand over his slicked-back hair and wipes the excess gel on his jeans.

"Ooh la la," Stacy greets him at the door, wearing a colorful print skirt she found at a thrift store and a baggy blue sweater. "I like the hair. Very"—she searches for the right word—"Italian."

"It's the International Male look," Dave says, walking inside.

"Does that mean you're wearing leopard-skin thong briefs underneath those faded Levi's?"

Dave grins and follows her into the bedroom.

"You'll have to wait to find out."

Stacy ducks into the bathroom for a few finishing touches. "I'll be ready in just a sec." She rakes a brush through her hair, then fishes around in the medicine cabinet for something.

"Oh, guess what?" Dave shouts out from the bedroom. "The good news continues. I got a letter today from a distributor for more Disappointed CD's and Deer Park singles than I have in stock."

"That's great!" Stacy says through her clenched teeth, a bobby pin in her mouth and her hands full of hair she's trying to put up.

"Yeah, sort of." Dave shrugs.

"Why are you so ambivalent about it? It sounds great."

"Well, it's like this." He sits down on her bed, scooting back to the headboard and then putting up his feet. "A distributor only *distributes* my stuff. They don't foot the cost of making it. I do."

"Yeah, so?"

"You see, they make money if I make money. And if I don't, well then, it's no skin off their nose, but it sure as hell is off mine because I'll be sitting with a roomful of records that *maybe* I could turn into guitar picks or something like that. I mean, sure, a distributor would be great for getting my stuff out to stores that I never could have even known about, but I pay the shipping and the cost of making the product. And even if they don't sell, to add insult to injury, they make me pay the price for shipping it all back to me. That's like having to pay the cab fare for a guy to come over and rob you. Hell, they even charge me for putting on a UPC code. Then I'm paid only ninety days *after* I've sent them all this stuff, if I'm to get any money at all." His eyes wander to a Keane painting on the wall and are sucked into the vacuous black pools of the subject's eyes. "It's a big invest-

ment, and right now I don't have the money for it. Jesus, who
am I kidding? I don't have the money for the phone bill let
alone make a thousand CDs. Oh . . ."

Dave leans his head back, slamming it into the fabric-covered
headboard. "But!" He stiffens up, his greasy head leaving a wet
spot. "I did get some really good news on Thursday. The used
CD war is over! CEMA and WEA and all them big boys are
backing down, which means DISContent can go back to handling my stuff. So with a few well-placed gigs in town—and if
that wimpy junior college radio station gets its act together—I
should sell enough stuff in a couple of months to press what I
need if I save up tips. I know a guy who says he can get me
credit at K-Disc—you know, pay some now, pay the rest later—
so I'd have to come up with only a fraction of the cost. Plus, if
the rumors I keep hearing about Bottlecap being snatched up
by a major label are true"—he cracks his knuckles—"I may be
out of the woods, so to speak."

Stacy is blowing on her still-drying red nails, patiently listening to Dave's story. She adds at the end, "Now why do I
doubt that for some reason?"

Dave plays with the radio as Stacy drives them to the multiplex
on the outskirts of town.

"Boy, you really know how to show a girl a good time, Dave.
You make me drive all the way out here, and you know I have
wet nails." Stacy is holding the steering wheel with her palms,
her fingers outstretched, her face in close, blowing periodically.
"And you keep trying to find the college radio station when you
know they have a range of about a ten-foot circle around that
piece-of-shit homemade transmitter."

"Look," he says, fiddling with the dial. "You're lucky I didn't
asked to be picked up, too. After all, I'm paying for the movie,
aren't I?"

"Yeah, yeah," she grumbles. "Dollar theater, big deal."

Dave finds what he knows is the college radio station, unless
the bevy of country music and oldies stations in the area all of a
sudden thrust Pansy Division's "Smells Like Queer Spirit" into
rotation. But the tune is coming in at half-volume, scratchy,

barely recognizable. Dave nudges the dial slightly to the left, and the tune switches instantly to clear and deafening classical music.

"Turn that crap off!" Stacy says with a look on her face that suggests she has bitten something sour.

"I'm trying," Dave reassures, adjusting the dial to the right, finding the song again for a brief moment before it disappears again and is replaced by monotonous talk radio. "Why don't you have one of those digital radios anyway?"

"Sorry. Besides, we're almost there."

Stacy turns off the interstate, winding around an off-ramp before being deposited at the mouth of a large theater complex. She circles the lot a few times before finding a spot in the corner.

"Jesus, look at all these fucking kids," Dave says.

"I know, and check out all the parents who are double-parked picking up little Susan and Joey from their first date." Stacy points to a row of station wagons and minivans driven by haggard-looking middle-aged women and men, parked next to the red curb with their hazard lights flashing. Teenagers are everywhere: sitting on the curbs, running in and out of the theater, circling the box office on rollerblades.

"Jesus, this town ought to have a seven o'clock curfew for anyone under eighteen. I mean, when you start paying state taxes, then you can be out after dark."

Stacy laughs. "I know. It's been so long since I've seen a movie out here. Thank God these kids hate to read, or else they would have invaded the Capitol Cinema a long time ago."

As they line up at the box office, Tim walks by, his arm around a young blonde who looks like the rest of the kids cavorting around.

"Dave, long time no see!" Tim calls out good-naturedly. "Why haven't you called me?"

"Tim, hey," Dave says nervously. Glancing over, he remembers the girl as Cherry, one of the females from the other night at the field. "Uh, busy. You know how it is."

"Yeah, so many fish"—Tim starts laughing before he can finish his own joke, barely getting out the punchline—"to fry . . ."

Dave gives a courtesy laugh, and Stacy just stares at the bimbo on Tim's arm.

"How's your mom, Tim. She feeling better? All alone right now, I bet?" Dave says, fighting back.

"Who? Oh, Mom. Yeah, she's fine. It was nothing, really. Just some minor palpitations. Anyway, I'll be in town for another week, so give me a call. You know the number."

Just as Dave turns to Stacy to start in on his what-a-geek speech, Tim halts in his tracks and turns back around, Cherry idiotically swiveling with him as if they were inseparable.

"Oh, one more thing, Dave. Cindy says hi. She said she can't stop thinking about you." Tim begins to laugh again. Cherry smiles as well. "Bye!"

Dave's face turns red as the line advances, and he inches forward, his head down.

"Who's Cindy?" Stacy asks. "Huh?"

"I told you about Cindy." He lowers his voice and whispers, trying to keep his private life away from the moviegoers.

"No, you didn't," Stacy says loudly, crossing her arms. An older couple in front of them turn around to see what the problem is.

"She's just a friend from, uh, the other week. Nothing happened."

Saved by the ticket counter, he whips out a twenty-dollar bill. He gets his change, then opens the door for Stacy and buys her a popcorn and a large Coke (totaling six bucks, which he could have used to order a whole meal at the Waffle House near the freeway). Dave, on his best behavior, opens the theater doors for her and begrudgingly sits in the fourth row even though he hates being so close to the screen. Stacy, in anticipation of seeing her favorite actor, has forgotten about Cindy and has moved on to Bill.

The lights go down. Stacy hungrily munches her popcorn, instantly devouring the first couple of layers, which are the only ones that have any salt or butter. She squints every other bite, the sodium flakes gritting between her teeth before dissolving into the cool Cola that washes it all down her throat.

The film begins with Bill Murray as a cranky weatherman for a Pittsburgh television station. He is forced to live the same day —Groundhog Day—over and over again in a small town. Stacy's eyes are fixed on the screen even though she saw this film three times in its initial release a few months ago. Every few minutes she nudges Dave in the ribs and whispers, "Isn't this great?"

Two hours later they're making their way to the lobby, caught up in a group of prepubescent teens.

"That was funny, sure," Dave says, cracking his back, "but it's just so implausible."

"What? Repeating a day like that? Haven't you heard of time locks? Or the Bermuda Triangle where—and this is a known fact—people have—"

"No, not the logistics. But the people all around that guy wouldn't have acted the same way every day."

"What?"

Dave grabs Stacy's arm and pulls her past a throng of kids sitting against a wall.

"What I mean is, I don't care if the same stimuli, or whatever you call it, is presented to people day after day, they're going to react differently every time. Like when he was in the lobby and the lady said, 'Will you be checking out today?' Well, she might have asked that a couple of times, but human behavior is so random. She might have been debating whether to say that to this total stranger: This time she said it, next time she'll just pass him by. Another time she might ask a different question, like 'Cold enough for you?' or something like it. People just don't act the same all the time. I mean, hasn't Harold Ramis ever heard of the chaos theory? But then I guess they wouldn't have a movie, would they?"

Stacy weaves to the right to let a couple go by, then catches up to Dave, wanting to rebut one of his points, but again she is interrupted.

"Hey, look, there's Jim."

Dave leaves Stacy behind and bolts across the lobby where Jim, holding a black purse, is standing against a Street Fighter II video game.

"I like the purse, Jimster," Dave says cheerily, "but I'm not quite sure it matches the outfit."

"Oh, hey, Rowland. What's up? No, this is my date's. She's in the bathroom." Jim looks around nervously. "So . . ."

"I heard some good news about the used CD war. The majors backed down, right? DISContent is going to go back to normal?"

"Uh, yes and no."

"What?" Dave asks, confused. Stacy comes up behind him but backs off when she hears the startled tone in his voice. "I thought the majors had—"

"The majors did, Dave. That's not the, uh, problem. You see, I had been wanting to make some changes at DISContent for a long time—I mean, you've heard about that new mall they're building near the outlet center? Well, I've heard there might still be some spaces available, and if so the owner's going to go for it, which would mean—"

"Goddamn, quit jerking me around, Jim. Which would mean what?"

Jim pauses for a second, searching the lobby. *What in the fuck is taking Laura so long?*

"Dave, I'm sorry, your stuff is staying off the shelves. DISContent's just not a mom-and-pop outfit anymore. If we're going to compete with the big chains, we've got to act like a big chain."

"A big chain? What in the fuck are you talking about? The only good thing about your fucking store is that you *aren't* a big chain. Who in the hell's going to go to DISContent to buy Michael Jackson records? Kitty needs—"

"Look, Dave, I'm sick and tired of hearing this from you and all the other little shits in town with their DON'T SUCK CORPORATE COCK T-shirts. Fuck what Kitty needs. What about what I need? I've been making the same salary since I graduated from high school. You think that's fun? You think I'm going to be thirty years old and still give a damn about what hot new group is on what label? Hell, no, Dave. And if you ever intend to grow up, you'll realize the same thing."

A poor kid nervously clutches a quarter, eyeing the video game, too frightened to approach it and ask, " 'Scuse me, you guys done?"

"Jim, DISContent is cutting its own throat if it gets a place in that disgusting mall. No one is going to go there, especially if you don't support the local bands and labels."

"Oh, we'll support local labels, all right, just not yours." Laura, emerges from the bathroom and takes her purse. "I mean, look, I've got to go. Our movie's starting."

"Laura?" Dave says, surprised. "Gee, how's Mark doing?"

"Mark's . . . I don't know," Laura begins, becoming flustered.

"Dave, leave us alone." Jim grabs Laura's hand and pushes Dave aside. "If you want to discuss this, stop by the store tomorrow."

Dave stands there in shock as Jim saunters away with his arm around Laura, who's trying to shield her face. Stacy approaches Dave and places a consoling hand on his shoulder, but he just knocks it away. He leans against the wall of the lobby; the air is filled with conversation and the aroma of percolating popcorn.

"Are we going to my place or yours?" Stacy asks, hanging a right out of the parking lot.

"Yours," Dave says, pissed-off, pouting.

Stacy makes a few rights and a left in silence. The only noise comes from Dave's insistent tapping on the dashboard and his muttering of something incoherent. She finally pulls alongside her apartment complex. Dave walks impatiently ahead of her.

"Want something to drink?" Stacy calls out from the kitchen.

"Something with alcohol," Dave shouts, making his way to the stereo. "Hey, when did you get this Guided by Voices CD?"

"The other day," she calls back. "At DISContent."

"From now on do *not* go there! We have to boycott that place!" She reenters the room, so Dave lowers his voice.

"Sorry." She hands him a jelly jar filled with orange liquid, adding, "Screwdrivers."

Dave takes a deep mouthful of the drink. The large amount of vodka floating on top stings for a moment. He gulps it quickly, can feel it going down warm, and almost instantly he feels numbed, relaxed, better.

"Jesus," Dave says under his breath, quickly taking another gulp of the drink that is almost already gone. "This CD has their entire last record, too, off Rockathon Records. *Rockathon.*" He laughs. "No wonder I missed that one. Some of these record labels are so small, one of the ten most wanted could be recording for them and still nobody'd ever find him."

"Probably no bigger than Violent Revolution," she kids, popping the CD into the player.

"Thanks," Dave says, soaking up the music. "Salt in the wound."

"It's the way you act, it's the way you look, when you're near me." Bursts of guitar fill the room, the lead like a sun ray, a beautifully delayed reaction, taking seven minutes to get to you, but it still makes you warm. *"It's the things you say, it's the things you do, go right through me."*

Leaning forward, Dave says, "How a girl with such great musical taste ever got such bad taste in comedic actors is a complete mystery to me."

"Yeah." She sips her drink. "Sorry. I'm not like your average college girls wearing black turtlenecks and Birkenstocks, pledging how much they like Bergman when in reality they stay up till four in the morning watching shit like *Better Off Dead* and *Sixteen Candles* on USA 'Up All Night.' I'm *me*, Dave. Sorry if I disappointed you."

"No disappointment," he says slowly, suddenly feeling very tired. A buzz takes Dave in either of two directions: It lifts him up or pushes him down. Right now he's rolling on the ground with his eyes closed.

"You are such a lightweight," Stacy says, noticing that Dave is drinking what's left of her drink. "Scratch that. I meant to say an alcoholic."

Dave sits up quickly and says in a comical tone, "Hey, I've got my drinking under control. I can quit any time I want to!"

They both begin laughing and then stop at exactly the same time, screaming out in unison, "YOU WANT TO BE COOL, DON'T YOU?"

They laugh for a few minutes before Stacy gets up to refresh their drinks, returning with a pack of Marlboro reds.

"Perfect."

Dave lights up a cigarette, taking note of the black-with-red-trim saucer that Stacy pushes toward him to be used as an ashtray even though her just-lit cigarette is sporting no ash. She pantomimes, flicking the imaginary ash into the center of the ceramic plate. Dave smiles, makes a mental note, and tries to blow a smoke ring, but it comes out looking more like a smoke boulder.

The songs are slower now, a lazy drumbeat hugging the

haze in the room. *"The history book has lost its binding, pages everywhere."*

"Want to see a jack o' lantern?" Dave asks, taking a sip of his newly refilled drink.

"Sure."

Dave takes out his lit cigarette and turns it around, placing the lit end in his mouth and clenching down on the shaft with his teeth.

"Ha ahh!" he says, trying to say *ta da*, but it doesn't come out right. He gets up to wave his hands in an abracadabra fashion, and the movement of his body knocks a pillar of ash onto his tongue.

Sssss.

Dave spits out the cigarette, and smoke in his mouth suddenly escapes. He scrapes his tongue with his hand and gulps the vodka and orange juice until there is nothing left but ice cubes. He takes one of the cubes in his mouth and rubs it over the dime-sized burn rising on his swollen tongue.

"Did you see that?" he asks Stacy, who hasn't stopped laughing since Dave's eyes clamped shut when he got up. She could hear the flame going out against his flesh.

She nods, still laughing hysterically.

"But was my whole mouth lit up? Like a pumpkin?"

"No," she manages to get out between subsiding giggles. "No."

"Then what did it look like?"

"Nothing . . . really. Just you with a cigarette turned the wrong way. Sorry."

"What in the hell did I do wrong?" Dave racks his brain for a moment before slapping his thigh.

"The worst defense is intelligence, the best defense is belligerence."

"It's supposed to be a match! Yeah! God, what a dumbass, right? Fuck, how could I forget?" Dave is rambling. "I saw it in a Cheech and Chong movie."

"Boy, and I just can't understand why they're not still around," Stacy says sarcastically. "And you rag on me for the movies I like? I've got two words for you: Corsican Brothers."

"Yeah, yeah, I know. But try telling that to a thirteen-year-old who thinks that big tits and pot jokes are the funniest thing in the world."

"Oh, yeah, I'm going to drive my car. Oh, yeah, I'm going to go real far. Beyond the shadow of a doubt, beyond the power of your clout . . ."

Stacy leans forward and lightly kneads the back of Dave's neck.

"Feeling better?" she asks quietly.

"What? Oh, yeah, thanks," he says absentmindedly. "It only hurt for a second. It's no worse than one of those pizza cheese burns."

"That's not what I meant."

He turns and grins. They kiss for a moment, and for both of them it feels odd and formal, more like a handshake, a gesture between friends who haven't been taught to express affection any other way.

"I see a face that used to cry. Where were you then?"

He pulls away after lightly biting her, licking the alcohol off her lips. As he thinks back over the night, anger begins to rise in him again.

"You know, fuck Jim. And fuck this town. I don't need either him or his damn record store." His voice turns lighter, filled with hope. "If I could just get eight hundred bucks together, I would press those Bottlecap singles the distributor wants. After all, when the word gets out that they might sign to a major, kids will come out of the woodwork to find out about them."

"But I thought you were selling a lot of records at DISContent?"

"I was, but that was before I was taken off the shelves—permanently, I guess. Jim was good for some hard cash every two weeks, I'll admit that. It's like pulling teeth to get money from some record stores who owe it to you, whereas I could go in DISContent and they'd give it to me in cash. That store was like a fucking automatic teller machine."

"Look," Stacy says, one hand still making circles on his back. "You need some money, right?"

"Yeah," he says, turning to look at her. "And?" he says brightly.

"Don't get any funny ideas about me." She slaps him. "That's not what I meant. Tonight was the first time in months I saw a movie that wasn't on TV. No, I had another idea."

"Shoot."

"Why don't you have"—she pauses, proud of her idea—"a benefit?"

Dave cringes.

"Like a 'We Are the World' thing? No, wait. How's this song." He starts humming the Band Aid theme: *"Does Dave know it's Christmas after all. . . . Feed David Rowland . . ."* His voice cracks under the weight of his thin falsetto. "No, wait. How about Hands Across Kitty?"

"God, you're a real asshole, you know that?" she says, laughing as Dave stands up with his arms outstretched and rocks back and forth. "What I meant was to have the bands on your label play a gig at The Scene, with all the proceeds going to Violent Revolution Records."

"I don't know," he says hesitantly, holding the glass a foot above his head and savoring the last drops. "Superchunk pulled in only around five hundred dollars last Friday night, and I need twice that."

"What was cover charge for Superchunk?"

"Four bucks."

"So charge six."

"First of all, if we didn't pack them in for Superchunk at four, we ain't gonna pack them in for my roster of nobodies at six." Dave begins part two of his explanation but burps instead. "Second of all, Todd would never go for it."

Now Stacy is excited about it. She slides close to Dave and unfolds her plan quickly, for fear it might evaporate before she can get it out.

"Superchunk packs them in in Chapel Hill because that's *their* hometown. So people would be willing to pay that much here if it was for their own hometown bands and also to help you out."

"Mmmmaybe."

"And as for Todd"—she pushes up the sleeves of her sweater to her elbows—"you tell him flat-out that if he doesn't do this show, then none of your bands will ever play there again."

"But that's total bullshit! Stoner fries fish all day. The only thing he has is the chance to jump around stage every couple of weeks. They'd play there *without* my backing. There'd be no way to stop them."

Stacy shoots him a dumb look.

"It's a bluff, idiot. Of course the bands will play there. You're just trying to scare him. Besides, he'll make enough on drinks to cover what he's going to give up at the door. He's been getting fewer and fewer bands these days anyway. Urge Overkill pulled out last week to play a bigger show up in Arlington. And that Amphetamine Reptile showcase gig canceled at the last minute. The only band available was The Dwarves, and they ended up playing for ten minutes. I heard Todd almost had a riot on his hands." She lightly taps her cigarette; ash drifts to the saucer below. "Don't worry, he'll go for it."

"But when?"

"Why not this weekend? Friday? That would give you a couple of days to get the word out. You know, put up some flyers. Get your bands together. It'd be a nice show of solidarity."

Dave blooms with the idea.

"You know, that's not a bad suggestion."

The CD ends, but Stacy presses PLAY, starting it all over again from the beginning.

Youth Culture Killed My Dogma

1

A key in the door.

Chipp, sleeping soundly on the couch, dreaming of being asleep, wakes up at the sound of the rattling doorknob.

Randy walks in, looking slightly rumpled, wearing the same clothes from the day before.

"Randy? Where have you been?" Chipp asks, jumping off the couch.

"I was in jail." He almost laughs. "They fucking arrested me!"

"What? Where? The last time I saw you was when I left you at Kinko's to make copies of the zine." Suddenly it hits Chipp between the eyes. "No, they didn't!"

"Yes! That fucking meter trick didn't work! Well, it worked up until I walked out the door. The next part didn't work so good." Randy crosses the room and collapses in a chair. Chipp goes to the fridge to get him something to drink, but the fridge is empty. He fills up a glass with tap water and thrusts it into Randy's slightly shaking hand.

"But I still don't understand." Chipp sits down opposite him on the edge of a coffee table still covered with leftover magazine clippings. "How did they catch you? Last I saw it was working perfectly."

"It was!" Randy starts, pausing to take a sip of the water. "I took a meter when I got there, made a few token copies, and then switched to the decoy. Well, this asshole who works there saw me take out the extra meter from my backpack, and he called the cops! Can you believe it? And the guy's our age! What a fucking traitor!"

"And they arrested you for making copies?" Chipp is trying to hold back a laugh. The image of Randy sauntering out of Kinko's and then being dragged away by Kitty's finest is too amusing for him to shove out of his mind. He wishes either this had never happened or that he could have been there to witness it. "Is Kinko's running their own internment camp these days? I mean, I know they're a big corporation, but give me a fucking break."

"Well"—Randy leans forward and lowers his voice along with his tired eyelids, his mood more serious—"for some reason they look at it as stealing. They added up how many copies were actually on the meter, and it came out to a couple of thousand dollars."

"What?"

"But I told them that some guy had given it to me with most of that already on there. I mean, there was no way I could have racked up that many copies in just a few hours. Thank God I had been taking the copies out to my trunk every half-hour because when the cop stopped me all I had were a few of the posters, maybe two hundred copies and some color copies. It was still about three hundred bucks, though."

"Three hundred dollars!" Chipp shouts. "We never planned to spend that much!" His tone turns sarcastic, "You just had to have those color copies of that Mono Men record sleeve, didn't you?"

"Have you ever seen that chick? She's hot!"

"But why didn't you call me? I thought you'd met some girl or something like that. At first I was all proud of you. Guess I should have known better."

"Let's put it this way: It's not like I *couldn't* have been having sex."

"Are you serious? They actually put you in a cell with other criminals?" Chipp nervously bites a nail.

"You'd better fucking believe it. And most of these guys weren't in there for stealing copies at Kinko's, either. One guy was in there for attempted robbery, another for stabbing a guy at a party. Oh, he was a fun one, let me tell you. Like one of those guys we see on TBS wrestling on Saturday mornings. A few of them wouldn't even say why they were in there, which a few of the boys later told me is not a good sign."

"Not too many pencil makers who refused to pay their taxes, huh?"

"Ha!" Randy laughs and takes the last swig of the water. "These guys consider punching a police officer civil disobedience. Though they'd call it 'fucking shit up.' "

Chipp gets up to go to the bathroom down the hall and takes a piss with the door open, shouting out to Randy over the splattering of urine against the toilet bowl water, "But how did you get out?"

"Oh." Randy shrugs and bends over to pick up an old copy of *Ben Is Dead* lying on the floor, open to an Ethyl Meatplow interview. "They weren't really going to press charges. The manager was just pissed off, and it was like a Scared Straight type of thing, although I've heard that people get killed like that sometimes. The manager came in this morning and said that I'm banned from Kinko's for life and to tell all my friends that Kinko's won't put up with that kind of thing anymore, blah, blah, you know the routine."

"And the copies?" Chipp asks, buttoning up his Levi's and tucking in his faded gray T-shirt.

"Well"—Randy drags out the word as if there were trouble behind it—"they're there, and we can have them whenever, but he's going to make us pay for them eventually."

"But three hundred bucks! That's a lot of money."

"I know, I know, but we should consider ourselves lucky. He was going to shred them all and then we'd really be fucked. But don't forget, I have enough in my trunk to make a couple of hundred issues. The stuff they got down at the store is just gravy —extra covers, posters, shit like that."

Randy slaps down Chipp's arms that are supporting his head, his hands wrenched deep into his furrowed brow.

"Hey, listen to me, Chipper. When this thing hits the street, they'll be no stopping us. We'll get so many ads for the second issue that we'll have *more* than three hundred bucks. Don't sweat

it." He scratches his stomach. "Remember, you're still thinking small." He looks out the window, then farther down the
street. A pretty girl walking her dog stops for a moment, then
turns and rounds the corner, out of sight. "But I'm looking at"
—a car drives by, red; the driver looks familiar—"the larger
picture."

"Well," Chipp muses, dollar signs rushing around his head
like rings around Saturn, "I guess."

"But!" Randy slaps his knees as he gets up and stretches for a
moment. "It gave me time to think. We have the pages for *Godfuck* all ready to go. But now what?"

"What? Oh, *Godfuck*, yeah, right. Jeez, I just can't get over the
fact you spent the night in jail. Don't you want a day or two to
relax, get your mind back in order? You're not tired after all
this?"

"Nah, I'm not tired at all. In fact, I'm wired. Fuck that lying
around shit. I've been sleeping my entire life. No more."

Chipp tries to hold back a grin and looks Randy over carefully. *Maybe something did happen to him in jail. He's not acting like
he usually does. I'm not sure I like it.*

"You sure?" Chipp tries to tempt him, switching on the TV.
"Sarita called and told me there was a 'Ren and Stimpy' mara-
thon on Nickelodeon today."

Randy slaps the remote out of Chipp's hand.

"Seriously, cut it out. We have work to do. I had a great idea.
Godfuck is all ready to go only we need to put it together, right?"

"Uh, yeah," Chipp answers, still stunned by the turn of events.
"So?"

"So? So if you and I sit here and put these things together one
by one, it'll take us three years. What we need to do is make like
a production line."

"A production line?"

"Yeah." Randy's eyes are sparkling. "Set out all the pages and
then just bribe a few friends to help us put it together."

"Bribe? How?"

"How do you think? I mean, these aren't the most demanding
people in the world. We'll serve them some beer, some mixed
drinks, a bag or two of chips—hell, anything salty—and, trust
me, the mindless fools will do whatever we ask them to."

"Oh," Chipp says, smacking his forehead with his palm. "You mean a collating party."

"I swear it will work."

"Sounds good to me. When?"

"How about Thursday? That way it won't conflict with anybody's weekend plans, like if there's a good band playing somewhere. And it's not like anyone we know has jobs that they care if they're awake for, or are hesitant to miss their Friday classes. Hell, people will thank us!"

"Sounds like a plan mamazram sam."

2

Dave staples shut the holes in his pockets.

From the living room he can hear the water starting to boil, the cover of the pan rattling as steam escapes around the edges. He pulls on the pants quickly, grabs some change and a few loose keys sitting on the counter, and shoves it all into his repaired pockets. He pogos to the kitchen. Nothing falls out. It works. Dave smiles and then ruefully shakes his head, remembering the night before, kissing Stacy good night at the curb and finding his pockets empty. Last night his fingers had fished through the soft cotton pouches to no avail until they stumbled on the rips in the corner of his pockets. He remembers the look on the locksmith's face as he met up with this tired looking guy at three o'clock in morning, standing next to a beat-up blue Honda.

Dave removes the lid of the pan and pours in the hard macaroni. As the small elbow noodles twist in the bubbles, softening and expanding, Dave readies the rest of his ingredients. He takes a tub of margarine from the mostly empty refrigerator and scoops out a large dollop with a wooden spoon, heaves it into a bowl. He grabs the small, dull gray pack of powdered cheese and empties it over the butter. He stands in awe of the marvel of powdered cheese for a second before moving on. He looks for the milk, the milk, the milk . . .

"*Shit!*"

He remembers his wallet, his tip money, two keys, and a grocery list, all gone. While he's pacing around the apartment wondering what to do, the noodles boil over. He pours them into a colander and rinses them with cold water before pouring it all into the big bowl with the butter and cheese mix. The box calls for one-fourth cup of milk, but Dave's growling stomach and lack of money or anything else in the house to eat leaves him rather optionally impaired and open to innovation. He stirs the ingredients, hoping milk is just one of those superfluous ingredients like eggs in a cake.

The mixture begins to grind like coarse cement. The scraping sound of the hard-as-sand cheese nearly drives him crazy, so he stops. He grabs a cup, fills it halfway with water, and splashes it into the bowl of crumbly orange noodles and cheese dust. Instantly the dish turns to watery mud, the liquid making a soupy broth with islands of cheese clumps.

"Aw, fuck it," Dave mutters as he grabs an open can of flat Coke from the fridge. He turns on "Saved by the Bell," which, thanks to cable and the local stations, is on five times a day in Kitty. He sits on the couch and begins eating his dinner.

"But Slater," Screech pleads, his prepubescent voice cracking on command, "if you're going to the prom with Lisa, who am I going to take?"

Slater, a thick-looking Mexican whom these rich upper-class chicks wouldn't let near their houses except to piss off their dads or to mow the lawn, pulls Screech in by a beefy arm. "Look, geek, if Preppy finds out, you'll be dead meat. You got that?"

The audience *aahhhs* knowingly, as if on cue. Dave figures it is either prerecorded or they have an AAHHH sign that flashes during moments of exceptional dramatic impact.

"Ha, ha." Dave laughs out loud, taking another big grinding spoonful of macaroni and cheese. "Hey, not bad."

Zack comes stumbling onto the screen wearing a dress in hopes of sneaking into the girls' locker room. The principal, Mr. Belding, sees the awkward young "girl" fumbling in the hall and approaches the new student. Zack pulls the wig over his face to conceal his eyes and speaks in a shrilly falsetto. *Jesus,* Dave thinks, *this principal spends every moment of his day with five students. Imagine how the other three hundred feel.*

In real life the phone rings. Dave wishes he had an answering machine. He is one of the few people left who don't. He remembers seeing a film once where this guy picks up the phone and pretends to be a machine.

"Hi, this is David Rowland," he says slowly in a slightly computerized voice. "I'm not home right now, but why don't I—I mean you, yeah—leave a, um . . ."

"Cut the shit, Dave, it's me. There's trouble."

Kelly and Jesse walk into the locker room to immense applause and howls from the guys.

"Look, don't tell Zack, but . . ." Kelly says as she gets ready for gym.

It's Mike, the guitarist for one of Dave's bands, The Disappointed. So far the group has remained somewhat of a local entity, even though they put out four singles and, recently, a full-length CD on Dave's Violent Revolution Records. Their records were sold only in DISContent.

"What is it?" Dave says, annoyed, trying to focus on the screen. Zack leans in to eavesdrop, and the wig falls off. He grabs it quickly but puts it on backward, looking like Cousin It. *Classic.* Dave roars.

"This isn't funny," Mike breaks in, his voice deadpan. "DISContent has stopped selling the CD,"

"Hmm?" Dave says, his eyes diverted from the screen by a boring commercial: *Flavor crystals? Try getting away with it in my class . . .*

"What is this about DISContent?"

"I was there earlier today to check on the sales of the CD, and there weren't any on the shelf. I asked Jim where they were, and he said they'd been taken off. Permanently."

"Jesus, Mike, sorry to tell you this way, but it's old news. This went down last week, but I'm working on it. In fact—"

"No, no, Dave, listen to me. He said it was *permanent.* I heard him joking with Larry about stringing you along, blaming it on the used CD thing, but that's just an excuse to clean house. We're out. *For good.* He said he was packing up all the Violent Revolution stuff and was going to return it to you."

"But . . . he can't . . ." Cheese-liquid dribbles down Dave's chin. He tries to fight a burp and loses. "Without DISContent, I mean, how are we going to sell any fucking records? You guys haven't even played past D.C. yet, and even that was a disaster."

"Yeah, yeah. But what are we going to do?"

"I don't know. DISContent had been moving about ten CDs a week. That's more than I've had from mail order in the past month. And I just got a letter from Blacklist saying they wanted only five more copies, and we won't see that money for three months." He looks around the room and sees boxes of CDs, piles of jewel boxes, a mound of four-color inserts. The food he bought with his windfall of cash the other day has already disappeared. The bills he just paid off—gas, phone, electric, rent, credit card—are suddenly coming due again. He marvels at how quick the fall can sometimes be and how short the ride was this time. For a second it disappears, and all he can see is red.

"And did you hear about Bottlecap?"

"Just the rumors. Why? What have *you* heard about Bottlecap?"

"I don't know, either," Mike says, his voice still shaky. "I just heard there was some A & R man from a major record label at The Scene the other night asking them a bunch of questions. Hey, you're not looking to sign a P and D deal that's not going to include us, are you?"

"Look, Mike, one disaster at a time. I don't know what in the fuck you're talking about. Todd was trying to dick me over about the guarantee that night, so as a solution I got very drunk and barely even remember the Bottlecap show. I tried calling Mark over the weekend, but he hasn't called me back. But if anything good happened, I'm sure he would have—I mean, why *wouldn't* he? And a production and distribution deal would benefit everyone, including you, okay? Because, as I've told all you guys over the years, if one of us makes it—"

"We *all* make it. Yeah, right. It looks good on paper, Dave, but I've just got this feeling that what's happening is that we're *all* being screwed."

"Look, let me go down to DISContent and talk to Jim, okay? I ran into him at the movies last night, and he wants me to stop by anyway. I'll make him listen to reason."

Dave ends the conversation and hangs up the phone. As he reaches for his shoes, he glances up at the screen to see Mr. Belding leading Zack away by the ear, and in his best *Fast Times at Ridgemont High* impression, slurs: "What happened?"

"This may sound strange to you," Jim continues the lecture he has been giving Dave for the past half-hour. His voice is tinged with a slight lisp that Dave never noticed before. Dave keeps his eyes trained on Jim's mouth, where his tongue repeatedly gets caught between both rows of teeth. "But this store sells records by groups other than The Disappointed, Bottlecap, and The Deer Park."

Dave is honestly astonished.

"Those sales actually account for a very small number of our profits. You see?" Jim points to a huge display of CDs by Janet Jackson, Aerosmith, Spin Doctors, and Garth Brooks. In the far right corner, near the wall, Dave spots the good stuff: Sebadoh, Polvo, Tiger Trap, Fugazi, Nirvana, Tsunami, Superchunk, and the new Bratmobile CD. *Bratmobile? When did that come in?* It's funny, but all Dave has ever noticed is that corner. Whenever he comes into the store, he always sort of floats toward it, as if pulled by some magnetic field. He notices his CDs are gone.

The manager continues: "If you compare the units of merchandise of the small independent records we sell to those of the majors labels, the number is quite small."

"Look, Jim, that's bullshit!" Dave's voice rises even though there are half a dozen customers in the store. "With the wholesale rate I give you, you're making a killing. I sell these things to you for six bucks, and you turn around and sell them for fifteen!"

"Sure, when I *can* sell them," Jim says, as if exhausted.

Dave waltzes over to the rack and pulls out a CD. "Hmm. *In on the Kill Taker* for sixteen dollars and ninety-eight cents? Jim, I know for a fact that Dischord sold this thing to its distributor for less than eight bucks! Hell, you can order it from them for eight, and that includes postage!"

Jim runs a hand through his hair quickly and over his eyebrows, the extension of an old nervous twitch, then waves Dave over. "Will you get over here?"

Before Dave returns to the counter, he picks up Nirvana's *In Utero*, replete with the six-month-old tag New Release and sixteen-dollar price tag, from its indie sandwich and places it alongside Rod Stewart's *Unplugged* and the *Bodyguard* sound track.

"Dave, we're talking units here, and I'll show you the sales for the last quarter if you'll . . ." He babbles on about the recession, shipping rates, returns, merchandise loss, and so forth. Dave stops listening.

Units? Dave scrutinizes the manager as he speaks in a silent film. *Sales? Fiscal year? What in the hell is this asshole talking about?* Dave notices that Jim is wearing a Sugarcubes T-shirt. *Traitor.* He wants to rip the ugly red shirt (which he had undoubtedly received free from Elektra) off his smooth pink back.

I've always noticed Jim at the cool shows in town, and now he's doing this. Why? How could he stage-dive onto a bunch of kids one day and shit on them the next? If I can't trust a small local guy like Jim, who is there for me to trust? Sure, Frontier Records warns me not to bleed when I swim with the sharks, but I could have sworn these waters were safe.

"Excuse me."

Dave examines the tall, tanned guy who has just walked in. He looks about Dave's age but is wearing Weejuns, brown Duck Head pants, an Oxford shirt, and a regimental tie.

"How can I help you, sir?" Jim begins.

Sir? Dave rages inside.

"Do you have that Marilyn Monroe song that Elton John sings, on a single?" the man asks in a deep baritone.

"Actually, that never came out as a single. It was originally recorded . . ."

As the manager and the customer discuss the lengthy discography of Elton John, Dave walks over to the rack of CDs and examines the new Bratmobile CD.

"Queenie"? But that was also on the Yo-Yo Studio compilation. God, can't you trust anybody?

He notices the customer has retreated to the back of the store, in the Easy Listening section, and is currently fingering a Harry Connick, Jr., CD. Dave returns to the counter.

"You still here?"

"Look, Jim, I bring a lot of business into this place, and you just can't do this to me, not now. Temporary is one thing, but permanent I will not stand for."

"Hey, I'm sorry you feel that way, but my hands are tied."

Dave feels his anger rising.

"Jim, one time I bit the hand that fed me. And do you know what? Do you know what?"

"What?" the manager lamely responds.

"It tasted like shit!"

"Easy, buddy boy," Jim says quietly. "I always knew you couldn't control your bands, but why don't you try to control your voice. Huh, big fella?"

"What in the fuck's that supposed to mean?"

"Oh, please." Jim laughs out of the side of his mouth. "You don't know?"

"Know about what?" Dave asks, suddenly feeling vulnerable. Two minutes ago he was in a tower pelting Jim with rocks, and now he's looking up as Jim readies a big one.

"Bottlecap."

"Wh-wh-what about them?"

"Jesus, you really don't know, do you?" Jim says more to himself than to Dave. Jim suddenly feels like folding his hand, burying his royal flush at the bottom of the cards, and forfeiting the game.

"Goddamn it, Jim, tell me."

"Some A & R guy from a major label passed through town the other night and offered them a big deal. Mark jumped at it, and, well, they leave for California first thing in the morning. You know, Los Angeles. Happy?"

"But . . . they would have told me . . ." Dave's voice trails off.

"Look, I'm sorry." Jim is getting uncomfortable. "It's done. They probably won't even be coming back. Try to forget about them." Now that Dave has been shattered, Jim just wants to sweep the pieces out the door. "And, uh, I'll send you your stuff. Really, there's nothing I can do."

"But, I still don't believe . . ."

Jim comes out from behind the counter and grabs Dave by the arm.

"Dave, you've got to be quiet. You're starting to scare the

customers. It's not good for business. If you continue to keep up with this I'll have to—"

"BUT HOW COULD THEY!" Dave screams.

"Larry," Jim calls out to a young kid wearing a Monster Magnet T-shirt (another freebie) who is restocking the wall with Dr. Dre CDs from a huge pile on the floor. "Take over at the register for a few minutes. Mr. Rowland and I are going to, uh, get some air." He winks.

Jim pulls Dave out of the store and around the corner to the parking lot behind the small row of shops. Jim sits him down on a school-bus-yellow curb.

"Why would they do this, Jim? I don't understand." A chill suddenly runs through Dave's body. "I helped those guys out when no one in Kitty wanted to hear them. They were so bad, people wouldn't even waste their beer throwing it at them. I let Mark sleep on my couch for a month when he couldn't pay his rent and the landlord locked him out, and Scott threw up all over my car one time and— I just don't understand *why*."

"Why do you think?" Jim says quickly, as if the answer is sitting in front of them but Dave won't lift his head to see it. "Money! There's no way you small guys can compete with the amount of dough the majors are throwing around these days. Especially small guys like you. Frankly"—he pauses for a second, examining his reedlike thumbnail—"I'm surprised any of them stay as long as they do."

"But that kind of money doesn't last! It's not even real. If the record doesn't earn it back, they won't release a second. Besides, in two years the majors will have moved on to the newest fad and left all these bands far behind. And then where do they go? They'll be like Vietnam vets stepping off the plane and no one will want to hug them."

"These bands don't give a shit about longevity or a career, Dave. They're no different than any other young kid today. They can't pay their rent now, fuck tomorrow. They're hungry tonight, don't lecture them about next week. They don't know who they'll be in the morning, let alone next year. None of *them* do."

Dave notices the emphasis on "them" as if Jim isn't counting himself in his harsh assessment. The world is filled with guys like Jim who resist generational tags for fear of being swept up in a mob that's a tenth of a degree less intelligent than they are. Jim belongs to the Jim Generation and nothing else. Generation J.

"But what about . . ." Dave begins whining.

"What about what!" Jim snaps. "The majors can do things for them that you can't."

"Like what!"

"Like pay them," he says ironically.

"Oh, yeah."

"Look, Dave, don't feel bad. Do you know how many small record labels like yours go belly-up after a couple of years? Tons. I see it happen all the time. They come and go so quickly, sometimes I don't even have an address to return the records. I've ended up throwing them away just to make room on the shelves." Jim sits down next to Dave on the curb. "Back when we were taking stuff on consignment from every little label from here to Arlington that had a four-track, guys would come into the store every day asking if we'd sold any of their records. They said they needed the money for food. Some of them looked homeless, but you could bet they still had their record collections, their instruments and equipment. They were like these . . . these techno-bums, just like you, broke all the time and living off Taco Bell and macaroni and cheese mix . . ."

Dave winces.

". . . and the sad thing is, a lot of them aren't into it for the music. They think of themselves as businessmen just waiting out the lean years. But the lean years never end, and by the time they figure that out, half their lives have gone by, and all they have to show for it is a stack of flexis in the closet. And to be really successful an indie label has to act just as scummy and stupid as a major. Like Sub Pop—you think those guys could give a shit about you or me? Those bastards would send out a press release saying their own mothers were dead if they thought it'd sell a few Les Thugs records."

"But Sub Pop!" Dave rises to defend the label as if it were a friend. "But they're . . ."

"A couple of jerks who are just out to make money, just like the majors are," Jim completes Dave's sentence. "The only difference between Warners and Sub Pop is the distortion. It's just a matter of time before they, too, make some sort of corporate pact with the devil and sign an agreement with—oh, I don't know"—he glances down at his shirt and says as a joke— "Elektra."

Dave begins to rise as if Jim had muttered fighting words. "Never!"

Jim starts to put his arm around Dave but pulls back at the last moment. Instead he stands up and kicks at a patch of loose gravel on the sidewalk. "Just don't go around thinking that everyone out there is as gullible—I mean, as *dedicated*—as you are."

Dave sits on the warm, hard pavement in a state of shock. After a minute and a half of silence, Jim scoops Dave off the sidewalk and leads him around the corner to the lot in front of DISContent. A few old ladies coming out of the Hallmark Hut and the Old American Store cast a frightened glance toward the two men, one with his arm around the other, who seems to be sobbing lightly.

"Go home and try not to take it so personally." Jim pats Dave on the back, thinking, *Dave will never buy enough CDs in his life from my store to deserve this kind of treatment.* "And don't forget, I'll have your stuff to you in the mail."

"Better send it to the P.O. box," Dave says numbly. "My landlord's been hiding my mail, 'cause I'm behind on the rent."

Jim gives him a final pat on the back, which he prays no one in the store can see.

Dave swallows the thick lump in his throat and turns to his car. He plunges his hand deep into a pocket for the key, fishes around for a second, finding nothing. His fingers sink into an open hole surrounded by staples. His car and house keys are gone. A breeze wafts up his leg and through the bottomless pouch.

"Who knows," Jim calls out from the entrance of the store. "Maybe they'll change their minds and not even go!"

3

"You shittin' me?"

James keeps asking this. One leg is tucked between the last cushion of the couch where he is sitting, his bare foot stuck deep down between the metal frame and the white padding, his toes scratching at the various debris—coins, lint, pizza crusts—while the other foot is perched atop a Santa Cruz skateboard, rolling it back and forth on the hardwood floor.

"No, I'm not shitting you," Gary repeats, shrugging.

"So you're telling me the truth?" James asks again even though Gary has already explained it twice. James looks across the room and sees the bags packed that were unpacked just a week ago. "You're telling me you're leaving again. This time for fucking Hollywood?"

"Well, Los Angeles. No, wait " Gary reconsiders, remembering what Mark had told him. "Yeah, Hollywood."

"No, no." James laughs. "You're shittin' me. Right?"

"Jesus," Gary moans. He thinks back over the past half-hour and remembers that he hadn't so much told James the situation as explained it to him. It was as if Gary were now part of some unforeseen phenomenon that James could not fathom. "No, not you" had been James's first reply. Immediately a sense of hostility filled the apartment. They had never been incredibly close to begin with, but Gary more or less considers his roommate a friend, so to receive this kind of shock as a reception to what is the biggest news of his life is a slap in the face.

"People around town are going to be pissed off," Mark had warned earlier on the phone. "I'd keep the news to myself and not tell a soul. People you thought were your friends won't be happy for you. They'll be jealous."

Gary had scoffed at Mark's prediction at the time, but throughout the day, over and over again, he saw it come true. And it depressed him. The first was his father, who seemed to

barrel past Gary's news with news of his own, that of his morning's activities of mowing the lawn, pruning the lemon tree, and
embarking on his quest to catch a particular squirrel that has
been terrorizing his garden. His father ended the conversation
as if it were any old exchange. "See you soon," he said lightly.
No, you won't, thought Gary.

Then there was Kelly, the girl he met the other night at The
Scene. Her reaction was "Like, it is so rad that you're going to
have a record out. No, seriously. Like, it's so cool." Gary asked
if she would miss him, to which she replied, the scratching
sound of her filing her nails in the background, "Yes, I will. No,
seriously. Like, I will." And now there is James, who still can't
believe it.

"And they're paying for everything?"

"Yeah, yeah. Airfare, hotel, recording. Everything."

"But for how long?"

"As long as it takes for us to cut the record."

Gary grins to himself. *Cut the record. Jesus, I sound like some
Hollywood schmoozer.* He wonders how long it will be before he
starts saying *Ciao* or *Let's do lunch,* and making that kiss-kiss
motion when he meets people. Normally he would have just
said *made* the record, but now he's trying to get James's goat.
He also knows that there has to be some limit on how long
Subterfuge is willing to foot the bill for everything. Bottlecap
is still an untested talent, and it's unlikely that the record company will allow them to squander a year and a half of studio
time like the Beatles working on their own *Sgt. Pepper's.* Gary
will be the first person to admit he is naive, but he at least knows
that.

"A-a-and then what?" James can't help but sound excited.
He's trying to play it cool. He keeps glancing down at his wrist
as if checking the time, as if there is somewhere important he
has to be, as if there are people waiting for him in some hot spot
in town.

"Who knows?" Gary raises his stubby nails to his face and
examines them. He pushes back a cuticle or two in a nonchalant
fashion. "The sky's the limit."

"What do you mean?"

"Well, they're talking about a tour, photo shoots, interviews,
videos—"

"Videos?" his roommate says excitedly.

"Sheesh." Gary sighs. "You didn't think there'd be videos? Oh, yeah. *Videos.* Like, for sure."

"Wow," James says more to himself. For the first time the facts, the ideas, and the concept that Gary is leaving are beginning to sink in, and he just can't believe it.

"Jeez," James says. "Won't you miss Kitty? Like, at all?"

Gary stops in his tracks for a moment. In the rush of excitement he hadn't asked himself this question. All during the tour his homesickness kept mounting like the tension in a Hollywood film, the audience members waiting on the edge of their seat for the climax. The farther away he went, the more clearly he saw his hometown, and for the first time appreciated it. The first couple of weeks on the tour were fueled by some killer pot and a wild adrenaline rush, and he was glad to get away from the dreary job he quit, but after the first couple of shows of booing out-of-state crowds, all he looked forward to was his familiar room and the bed that seemed carved to the outline of his body. To leave Kitty, the only thing he had been looking forward to for almost two months, seemed strange. But leaving this time has an eerie finality to it. Even Mark seemed to have the same sense and spoke of it on the phone in hushed tones, his hand cupped over the receiver, his voice muffled and almost disguised. Gary figured that Laura was either in the room or else close by.

"This is weird, man, but it's not like anything I've ever felt," Mark whispered. "This is like spooky."

"Spooky how?" Gary replied. He imagined Mark in the bedroom of his house, his fingers twisting over the mouthpiece while his head jerked back and forth, making sure the coast was clear.

"I feel like I'm being exorcised of this town. Like I'm getting it out of my system." There was silence on the line for a second before he added, "For good."

As Gary listens to his soon-to-be ex-roommate ramble on about something—not even he was sure what—Gary feels the same sense of . . . of . . . what *is* it exactly? Gary tries to put his finger on it, but the closest he comes to it is: *Going.* He sums it up like this: *From one place to someplace else, but I'm not sure where. Just . . . there.*

For the first time he considers that just because you're heading across the country doesn't mean you're not also somehow
going backward.

"No, no, no, no." James is grinning, his long bangs dropping
into his face as he wriggles his hand back and forth. "You're
shittin' me."

"Why are you taking so many CDs?"

"Huh?" Mark says absentmindedly, looking down at the blue
duffel bag in his left hand. Already he has put in about twenty-
five CDs and has another three in his clenched right fist.

"I mean"—Laura lightens her tone, trying not to make it
sound like an accusation—"you're going to be gone for just a
couple of weeks, right?"

In his mind Mark hunches his shoulders, rolls his eyeballs,
says, *Here we go again,* but his outward appearance is calm, col-
lected. He thinks of the advice that commercial is always giving
him: Never let them see you sweat.

"Well, honey, I don't know," he says sweetly, putting down
the bag of music and sitting next to her on his bed. The crumpled sheets are soft to his forearms. He always hated making his
bed, doing laundry, or even being neat in general. He made a
few concessions to past roommates and to Laura especially to
keep the toilet and bathroom and kitchen sinks clean, but everything else he let go, usually, to rot. The garbage was often overflowing, and the only sign that made him take the overstuffed
red plastic container to the curb was a trail of ants leading from
the baseboard to the wastebasket or else an overpowering smell
that drowned out even his most garlicky creations.

He brings one leg up the bed, tucking his left foot under his
right thigh. He turns to get a better angle to Laura, who, it
seems, is sniffling. *A tear or just allergies?* he wonders. *A good cry
because I'm leaving or just a reaction to all the dust in the room?*
Instead of examining her eyes more closely, he feels his powder
blue sheets. He can see various stains every few inches, some he
knows the source, others he doesn't. On his pillow is a large,
brown, sort of rashish effect that completely bewilders him. He
sniffs and smells sweat and the musty dryness of dust.

"I *told* you," he reiterates, placing his hand on her back, "that I wasn't sure how long we'd be gone for."

"Yeah, but all of these clothes you're packing." She points to a tremendous pile of jeans, T-shirts, underwear, socks, even a few button-down shirts and the only sports jacket Mark owns. "This is more than you packed when you went to Europe, and that was for two months!"

"Look, all I needed for Europe was a few pairs of shorts, shirts, good socks, and a safe, dry place for the traveler's checks and passport. This is completely different. I'll be going out, you know, doing stuff."

Inside, Mark is kicking himself. He has already crossed the fateful bridge, and there's no going back. He considers pushing on, moving forward, hoping Laura didn't notice, but she is smarter than that.

"Doing *what*, exactly?" Laura says on cue.

Mark gets up and nervously paces around the room, looking for something to do, but the only things that come to mind are more tasks that lead his life away from hers, transferring all his possessions and pieces of his life to another place, an inevitability he is already living with, perhaps, but one she has yet to even approach. He picks up an alarm clock sitting in the corner of the room, begins to toss it into a pile of magazines for the trip, but then decides against it.

"Doing just"—he searches his mind for the words that will cause the least amount of attention—"whatever the record company wants us to do. You know, they're going to be the ones shelling out the advance, so Henry said we'll be going to a few parties—you know, meeting some people."

Laura scrutinizes Mark as he darts around the room. Already she thinks of him gone. She talks to him like she used to speak to his ghost right after they first met when she was too shy to call him on the phone right after he'd dropped her off from when they'd just spent the entire day together but still she had things to say and so conducted strange two-way conversations underneath the shroud of her bedspread, with herself asking questions and then answering as Mark's proxy. Now he's trying to be subtle about weeding through the superfluous cards in his wallet, the ones for DISContent, the waiter job he held two summers ago, on the back of which was the manager's name that he could never remember, and he kept it just so he could list the job on applications. An old automatic teller card, a high school identification card held there partly by nostalgia but in equal parts by laziness. Laura watches as he tries to hide the fact that he slips out three photos, one of himself as a boy, one a family portrait—his mother at the head, his father to the left, and he appearing almost as a bud to the right. The last is Laura's senior portrait. He completes the act by getting rid of two old check stubs and a deposit slip to a checking account that has by now overdrawn itself into oblivion. His wallet is now properly slimmed down for California, sleek enough to fit unobstructed into a power suit and easy to open, waiting for the cards of agents, producers, and stars to crawl inside. Even fame itself if it could slip into a wallet.

"What *kind* of people?" Laura asks, just to hear what kind of answer Mark will pull from his hat.

"Oh, industry people, I guess."

"Are there girls in this industry?"

Laura says this as a joke, but Mark stops in his tracks and seriously considers the idea.

"Yeah, sure, I guess. Though I can't think of any off the top of my head, but yeah." He shrugs. "California is pretty progressive, so I'm sure there are women doing all sorts of jobs."

"That's not what I meant," she says dryly.

"Yeah, I know," he says slowly, alerting her that he may be smarter than she thinks.

"And I know we haven't been getting along lately, but that doesn't mean . . ." She stops speaking and begins looking for the well of his eyes. His head is darting around the room, scanning the horizon for objects he might need in the hectic upcoming weeks. Catching his glance is like shooting skeet, and so Laura gives up the chase. "I mean, do I have to be worried here that you're going to cheat on me?"

She's thinking, *I shouldn't have to be saying this. He should want to tell me this.* Tears quickly surge in her eyes. She hates that she has to say these things, to fight for herself when the battle could be won if he would just be honest. She feels she can live with the truth if only he would deliver it. Instead she's turning into one of *them,* those girls she has always despised and swore she would never be, those clingers, those hangers-on, the girlfriends who, months after it's over, still think their dead relationships can work even though their boyfriends are already with somebody else. "He still loves me," they kid themselves. *Why do they do it?* Laura always found herself asking when one of her friends fell prey to the syndrome. She's asking the question yet again, this time addressing herself.

"No, no." Mark leans in to assure her, one eye straddling both of hers while the other spots his overnight bag sitting squashed in the corner. "No, no, no, no." He stretches out again. "But I will be busy, so don't be freaked out if I don't call every day."

"Well then, when *will* you call?" Laura gives a slight nervous laugh, trying not to get pissed off.

"Oh, you know, when I get there. When we're making the record. The first day, I guess, and then, uh, whenever."

Mark zips up a brown suitcase that has been filled with clothes and shoves a few more things into the already overflowing duffel bag. After looking around the room for a few seconds, he goes to the closet and pulls out a black trunk. He drags it to the middle of the room, pops the lid, which groans; it emits a few moths and a spit of dust, and then he begins filling it.

"Look, Mark." Again the laugh creeps into her voice, trying to keep things light. "Just be honest with me. Are you even planning on coming back?"

"Sure," he says with a smile. "Of course," he repeats the sentiment. From atop his dresser he throws his house keys, cars keys, passport, birth certificate, social security card, and all the cash he received when he closed out his savings account earlier in the afternoon into the open lockerlike vessel. "You bet."

"What is *that?*" Phil asks, pointing to a ragged teddy bear with the unraveling tip of a hand-rolled cigarette.

"Huh?" Steve replies as he is shoving the bear into an already filled vinyl garment bag. The piece of luggage, with two side pouches already bursting, is black, with cotton handles, below which is a Lands' End patch and the words MY DEGENERATION in red, thickly embroidered letters.

"That, that," Phil manically says, little shreds of tobacco falling to the ground each time he says the word. "That mangy toy in your hand. *That.*"

"It's not a toy," Steve says by way of a defense. He's trying to shove the thing in quickly, to get it out of sight, hopefully derailing the subject. "It's a, uh, pillow."

"Pillow, my ass," Phil cackles, reaching into his back pocket for a plastic tobacco pouch. "That's a fucking teddy bear, and you know it. Wait, don't tell me. His name is Ted *E.* Bear, right? Oh, so clever, little brother. Oh, so clever. No, really, it's no wonder you're on the road to the big bucks."

"His name is Calvin, and believe me, we're not making that much money. So don't go thinking—"

"Well, no matter how much you're getting, I hope it's enough to soothe your guilty conscience. That is, if you even have one."

Steve stops packing for a moment and looks over at his brother.

"Guilty conscience about what? I have nothing to be guilty about. It's not like I was the one who house-sat for his little brother for a few measly months and while said brother was on tour, let all of his plants die, not to mention used his first-edition copy of *The Ticket That Exploded* as a goddamn coaster."

"Abandonment is what I'm talking about, Stevie boy. Abandonment."

"Abandoning who?" Steve laughs, trying to track down the cord to his electric razor.

"Who? Who do you think? Mom."

"Mom? Mom will be fine. First of all, she doesn't need me anymore, and second of all, she has you. Although, to think of it, she really doesn't need you, either."

His brother grabs a dark blue disposable lighter from Steve's dresser and lights his raggedy cigarette.

"You keep telling yourself that, kid, but you know that ain't the way it is."

Steve stops for a second, considering Phil's viewpoint for the first time. The truth is, he hadn't really thought about how his mother would react. He hoped she would be happy at the news, which she seemed to be when he told her the day before, but thinking about it in a long-term sense, nothing else seemed to change. He hadn't even seen her since he came back from the tour, and with his flight leaving in barely ten hours, it looks as if he won't see her before this trip, either.

"That's bullshit, Phil. Don't try to lay all this on me. Mom and I haven't been getting along for the past couple of years anyway. She thinks I'm a fuckup, and I know that. Hey, it's fine by me. Maybe I'll prove her wrong with all of this, although, knowing her, she'll just be pissed anyway."

Phil laughs abruptly, having to spit out a mouthful of smoke before he has the chance to suck it into his lungs.

"You got an answer for everything, don't you, kid?"

"Stop it, Phil. Just stop it. And why are you saying all this? You see how she treats me."

"Hey, don't look at me," Phil says, waving his hands in front of his chest, ash falling to the ground. "I'm not the one who blew up at Mom on Mother's Day just because she didn't know that DW stood for Drummers Workshop."

"Well, *jeez*," Steve dumbly responds. "How stupid can you get? Besides"—he turns back to his packing, mumbling under his breath—"I'd been saving up for that set for years. *Years*. And then she plays dumb, like she doesn't even know what I'm talking about. She thinks my music's a joke anyway."

"Oh, come on, Little Steven the Disciple with No Soul, what else is she supposed to think? For two consecutive birthdays all you gave her was some experimental music crap that was— Jesus, I don't even know how to describe it—but it sounded like you were banging on shopping carts and garbage cans."

"They were synthesized tape loops fed through a vocal effects processor. I saved up for months to buy the four-track recorder just for her birthday."

Phil picks up a pair of rolled socks from the ground and throws them across the room where Steve, reacting too late, takes them between the eyes; the cotton ball bounces off the bridge of his nose and back onto the floor.

"Don't bullshit a bullshitter," Phil says. "I know you bought that four-track for you and your little friends. Mark told me that was for your demos and nothing else. Hell, I bet my Christmas present of your fucking *Drumming Opera*, or whatever the fuck you called it—"

"*Percussion Symphony,* dummy, with the double-tracked cymbal parts and the breaking glass in the background, yeah?"

"Hell," Phil scoffs, kicking at a dustball on the floor, "I bet that was just outtakes."

"You're just not getting it, are you?"

"Not the way you do," he replies slyly. "Or at least *will* be."

Steve stops for a second.

"What in the hell is that supposed to mean?"

"Oh, please," Phil feigns frustration. "Don't act like I don't know. Like I don't know what all this is about."

"What? All what is about?"

"This." Phil sweeps his arms around the room, emphasizing the small pile of luggage on the floor, on which sits Steve's plane ticket. "Your trip and your—ha!—career."

"What about it?"

"It's just a way to meet chicks. I know that."

"What?"

"Look, little brother, don't make me give you my *River's Edge* 'getting so much pussy' slash 'glazed donut' routine because you know exactly what I mean. I can practically smell it on you now. Or maybe that's just suntan lotion." Phil sniffs comically. "Nope. I was right the first time. It's pussy."

"You really think that's why I'm doing this? Why I've been broke all these years, roaming the country in a fucking van while parasites eat my gut out and an inch of dust gathers on what little life I have back home? You think I like having the runs for three straight months and then coming back in a deeper hole than when I left? You think it's fun to watch all my friends graduate from college and get decent jobs while I'm still struggling to pay the rent every month? Huh? You think it's easy for me to watch MTV and see all these sucky bands who are younger than I am and richer than I'll ever be just because they've got some good management company who knows how to sell them?" Steve stops for a second, running out of breath. "You think this is all just for chicks?"

Phil leans against a black-and-white Charles Bukowski poster proclaiming FUCK HATE and says incredulously, "Why else?"

4

It gets cold almost overnight.

A river of cold air seems to float above hardwood floors in the morning, a layer of fog hitting you in the shins every time you place your trembling feet on the ground. To combat the tide of chilly air Ashley pulls out her thick gray wool socks with the snags at the ankle from too many washes with bleach (she always jokes that a dog has attacked her, and Craig always laughs, out of courtesy).

Ashley goes out to the living room where Craig is reading a book he bought the other day at a cafe in town.

"How do I look?" she asks, circling once and then curtseying.

"Great," he says in a deadpan voice, not even looking up.

"You didn't even look at me," Ashley says in a laugh, hoping to make the moment funny even though it's hurting her inside. A second before she'd pulled her hair back, applied a light touch of lipstick, wiped away the sleep that formed perennially around her eyes, and tried to make herself look nice.

"Ashley, I've known you for four years. I think I know what you look like by now," he says, not taking his eyes off the page. "Now, if you were Thomas Pynchon, then I'd look at you because, you see"—his voice is flat, like a scientist tediously explaining a formula to a class that should know it by now—"no one knows what *he* looks like. Whereas you, on the other   "

"What in the fuck is your problem?" she shouts, throwing a tube of mascara across the room.

For a moment there is silence. Ashley's sobbing doesn't make a sound. The tears stream down her cheeks, then slide down her neck before being soaked up by the cashmere turtleneck sweater. Finally the crisp sound of Craig turning the page breaks the silence, followed by the slamming of a door and footsteps in the apartment above theirs.

Ashley sniffs and wipes her eyes with the sleeves of her

sweater, which are pulled over her hands, and sits down next to him.

"Craig, will you at least look at me? Please? I thought I had to want to fuck you before you'd avoid me like this."

Finally Craig springs to life.

"Hey, do you want to keep it down? Please?"

"Why?" Ashley asks, to herself as much as to Craig.

There's a knock at the door. Craig gets up quickly, glad to be saved from any more of Ashley's caterwauling, picks up his wallet from the top of the stereo, and answers the door. He pays for the Chinese food and tips the guy five bucks out of jealousy because he gets to leave the apartment and Craig has to stay. Of course Craig could have left, too—if not tonight, then long ago —but the strings holding him back are more like suspenders that he fastens every day, pretending not to see. It is not that the binding is strong, only that he is weak.

Without words Craig shuffles to the kitchen, pulls two plates from the dishwasher, and scoops out equal portions of the food. He brings them to the table and mockingly coughs as a signal to Ashley that dinner is served. Ashley wipes a tear and joins him at the table.

"Did I get any mail today?"

A munching sound is heard between Ashley's small bites, but no answer.

"Hello?"

"Oh, what?"

Craig shrugs.

"Any mail? Did I get any mail, I asked, and you just sat— Forget it. Did I?"

A few seconds later, after Ashley has pushed a nugget of her sweet-and-sour pork to all corners of her plate, she answers: "No."

"Thanks." Craig shrugs again. "It's just, you know, I wrote a couple of letters to my friends in D.C. I mean, they should have gotten that package by now." Silence. "Don't you think?"

Instead of answering, Ashley pushes out her chair, gets up, and marches into the living room. Craig can hear her put a VCR tape into the machine, grab the remote off a nearby table, and then sit down on the couch. There is silence for a moment, then a buzzing of the VCR's heads, pulling the black sinewy tape in motion. Again, silence for a moment, then there is grand, sweltering music.

"*Casablanca?* Again?"

"Shut up," Ashley calls back.

Craig sits back down at the kitchen table. He stares at the Chinese food (ordered after he got home as a goodwill present). Craig watches it for a movement, expecting the chicken with snow peas to jump off his plate at any second. "Thirty bucks," Craig mutters. The unopened bag on the floor that contains egg drop soup, egg foo young, fortune cookies, and Ashley's favorite, fried shrimp, catches his eye. "Down the drain."

Craig angles his head so he can see the TV through the kitchen nook, the glare from the screen affording him a view of both Ashley and Bogart. Bogart's face is animated, talking, smoking, acting suave when all is chaos around him; Ashley's visage is that of a statue, carved, permanent, until a tear from her left eye drops unwillingly, with shame.

"Ash, what are we doing?" Craig asks, not able to stand hearing only Peter Lorre's voice fill the apartment.

"What do you mean?" she answers, emotionless.

Craig joins her on the couch.

"Look at us. What's happened to us?"

Ashley's eyes are still focused on Rick, not Craig.

"I mean, you've got to admit that things haven't been normal around here since . . ." Craig's voice trails off, and his own eyes become attracted to the screen, filled with the presence of the luminous Ingrid Bergman, shot through an inch of gauze.

"Since when? Since the night Brook was here?"

On the screen a poor woman is bargaining with a man for an exit visa out of Morocco, anything to get her out of her miserable situation. Craig wants in on the bidding.

"You fucked her, didn't you?"

He doesn't say anything, trying to get into the film.

"Didn't you?" she screams, slapping at him, kicking him off the couch. "I hope it felt good, asshole."

"Just as good as Andrew did for you, I bet."

"No, no," Ashley says quickly. "Don't pull that shit on me. I never would have cheated on you if you hadn't stopped loving me. I didn't want to . . ." She begins crying, every tear putting out the fires of her lie.

Can she be right? Am I just the world's biggest asshole about all this? I wish there were a referee here, blowing whistles, throwing flags, letting us know who's right and who's wrong. Why is this territory so uncharted? So many have been here before, you'd think someone would have drawn a map. I've got to get out of this. I've got to.

Craig rises off the couch and sleepwalks into the kitchen. Ashley watches him.

Can he be right? Am I just as bad? There's no way I can tell him that I was initially attracted to Andrew, but now I know it's not him I want, it's Craig. I know it's fucked. I know it's sick. But I just don't believe there's any right way to do any of this. We need to make our lives work any way we can, and I still think Craig and I can work. Which is more crazy: thinking it might work or wanting to try?

Craig begins to clean up the meal, retrieving the various cartons of MSG-packed food. Untouched vegetable fried rice leaves a small puddle of condensation on the surface of the glass table. Craig puts the box aside for a second, concentrating on the small circle of fog. He takes his finger and scribbles the word *love* in the steam. He stares at the word for a few minutes, watching it slowly disappear.

5

Out on the streets you can see the weather affecting the town: the crowd outside The Scene waiting for The Humpers show wears long black coats over their Black Flag T-shirts, and their combat boots may actually come in handy now that the recent rain has turned the gravel parking lot into a sloshy mud-filled pit.

The odor rising off the soaked streets is musky, like dust, but icy. The air is clear, the sky limitless, the stars sparkling like a million prickly points.

"Not like in Baltimore," thinks Eileen as she turns the corner from the thrift store, heading down a side street.

She thinks back to a few months ago when she was living in Maryland. How the lights of the city made the night sky seem orange, and the stars were like friends who never called, but you guessed they were still out there. She laughs, thinking of Ray, her strange landlord who was always borrowing money and who makes eccentric Brenda look boring and normal. She always avoided him, dropping the rent check through his faux brass mail slot, humming, *"It's a shame about Ray."*

Eileen gets sad for a moment, remembering the summer night when she and Don had a picnic in that oblong-shaped park behind the aquarium. After eating their chicken salad on fresh croissants, Don sang to her an old Violent Femmes song but couldn't remember the lyrics past *"Seven, seven is for n-n-no tomorrow,"* and they kissed awkwardly on the rigid stone steps, though neither of them seemed to notice how uncomfortable it was at the time.

The words of his letter are spoken by his voice in her head almost like a nightmare: "I want you back, and I'm coming to get you. Please, I don't know why you left, but I hope that you never leave me again. . . ."

Eileen spits to get the taste out of her mouth, hooks the last button on her sweater, and breathes into her hands, rubbing them together.

She approaches the Capitol Cinema, glancing up at the marquee as she walks underneath it. WEEKeND. All the letters are in bold black capitals except for the third *e*, which is in red and much smaller. As she approaches the box office, an older man, Thom, whom she knows just from town gossip, catches her glancing up.

"Sorry. Ran out of e's," Thom says as he takes the five Eileen hands him and gives her a one and a torn ticket stub. "The distributor also offered me *The Discreet Charms of the Bourgeoisie,* but there was no way I'd have enough letters for that *and* this one. Hell, when I had a triple bill of *2001, 2010,* and *THX 1138,* I had to borrow numbers from the damn gas station."

When he smiles, Eileen swears she can smell alcohol on his breath. She smiles back and quickly rushes into the theater, passing the abandoned condiment stand (if anyone wants candy or a hotdog, Thom has to close up the box office for a few minutes, but most people bring their own food. And Thom never cares, as long as they throw the wrappers away in the lobby instead of on the theater floor).

Eileen walks down the aisle looking for a good seat, NPR playing lightly in the background. The theater is completely empty except for her, but it's still a chore to find a seat since there are gaps in every row where chairs should be. She sits in the middle of the fourth row, but the chair collapses as soon as she rests her full weight on it. The bottom of the chair is completely unhinged on the left side, barely hanging on the right.

"Oh, fuck," she mumbles.

Eileen moves down a few chairs, testing the seat before she sits down.

Surely other people will be here tonight, Eileen is thinking. *I mean, just because this is a small southern town and this is an obscure French film doesn't mean there aren't a few intellectuals who want to— Jesus, where are all those pretentious types who hang around the cafe when you need them?*

Her thoughts are interrupted by the sound of footsteps near the theater's doors.

Thank God.

It turns out to be Thom, who's given up on the box office, shutting the window and heading up to the projection room.

"All set?" he calls out to the audience of one through the porthole in the cramped room.

"Uh, sure," Eileen meekly calls out, wondering what in the hell she's gotten herself into.

The film begins abruptly, no coming attraction trailers, no Please, No Smoking ads or plugs for the refreshment stand.

Large blue French words appear on the screen, eerily lighting up the whole room while their small white English translation follows a beat behind, spread out on the bottom: "A film adrift in the cosmos . . ."

After about ten minutes, when Eileen has at least a tenuous grasp of what's going on (the largest victory anyone can hope to make with Godard's films), she sits back in her chair and begins enjoying the film. She forgets the fact that she's alone in the vast theater, that the sounds are bouncing off the walls, echoing back into the lobby without a crowd to absorb them. Eileen finds herself laughing out loud, gasping, slapping her knee, even unselfconsciously talking back to the screen as if she were at home and watching the film on video.

"This is such a crazy movie," a character in the movie says to his wife. "All we meet are idiots!"

Ten minutes later the film jerks, at first, then slides out of view, finally breaking—the frame stuck in the projector melting against the hot bulb it's resting on. The theater is struck with silence.

"Uh, hello?" Eileen calls up to the projection room, not seeing anyone. "You okay in there?" She's hesitant to call out Thom's name because she's never been formally introduced to him and knows about him only through the scuttlebutt of the cafe. "Everything, um, okay?"

After another minute of sitting in the empty theater staring at the white screen (which finally begins to really creep her out), she gets out of her seat and goes into the lobby. Looking through the lobby doors (which, after trying them, she discovers are open) onto the street, she discovers there's not a soul around. It takes a full thirty seconds for a car to go by

"Hello?" she calls out again. No answer.

To the left of the men's bathroom, in the corner of the lobby, she sees a set of stairs leading up, she figures, to the projection room. She approaches them carefully, expecting Thom to burst out any minute, cursing at her for no apparent reason. She scales each step slower than the next, hoping that she'll hear the film continue so she can find her seat and resume the night without incident.

At the top of the stairs is a door. She puts her ear against it and can hear a regular clicking sound, almost like a beat, the reel flaying the wall with a strip of film over and over again. She warily takes hold of the knob and turns it slowly.

"Hello?" she calls out again, taking a hesitant step inside. "I was downstairs, you know, in the, uh, audience, and was wondering if . . ."

The room is a long rectangle stuffed with dozens of cans of film. The projector in the middle of the room is huge, the top wheel still spinning, the side covered in various switches. To the left is a small couch, covered with pizza boxes, fast-food containers, beer cans. Thom is lying on the ground, his eyes shut. Next to his head a receiver is off the hook from the phone screwed to the wall.

Thinking he might have had a heart attack trying to lift every single reel of the director's cut of *1900*, Eileen quickly puts her hand to his chest, checking for a heartbeat. She finds one but checks his sweaty neck and cold wrist to make sure. Both are normal.

"Passed out," she sighs in relief.

She tries to lift him off the floor and onto the couch, but he's too heavy and keeps sliding out of her hands, landing back on the celluloid-covered ground. Eileen begins to hear something over the strip of film's insistent rapping against the projection window, and she turns her head, trying to find the source of the sound. She zeros in on the phone, hearing not quite a voice but a mysterious sound. She daintily picks up the receiver, hoping the other person won't notice it's being picked up. She puts the phone carefully to her ear.

What she hears is a female voice, sobbing uncontrollably. There seem to be sounds in the background, like cars or conversation, as if the person is calling from a pay phone, though it's hard to tell. No words are even trying to be spoken, just a stream of continual crying as steady as the rotating film a few feet away. Eileen sets down the phone, closes the projection room door behind her, and leaves the theater.

Looking through the window of the Novel Idea cafe she spots Jess, as usual, behind the counter, filling orders, whipping up hot mugs of coffee. She also spots Brenda, who is (unbelievably) helping out by washing cups and plates. Eileen skips up the steps, switches on the TV, and hops into bed, her head suddenly filled with thoughts she doesn't want to have.

The night predictably drones on, and switching into her flannel pajamas and staring out the window, Eileen finds herself thinking of the stranger (Craig) who walked into her life the day before and then, just as quickly, walked out. She finds herself wondering why she's obsessing over a man she's exchanged only a handful of words with, and half of those were "Hmm" and "You don't say." Maybe it's the hole left in her routine of work, frozen dinner, work, frozen dinner, rent a movie, work, which begged for nearly anyone to crawl inside. And yet there have been others, such as Jess, men more than happy to share her bed and then maybe her life if the bed part worked out okay, but she had been refusing them lately, discovering men were often like running on a track: You always run around in circles, and the terrain never changes. She wasn't about to make the same trip again and be hurt.

But Craig . . . Without him actually in the apartment, farting, drinking beer, wearing a smelly undershirt, barking orders, it is easy for Eileen to idealize him in her head. He wasn't there to fuck up the image she had built up of him, the way most other guys seemed to compete in breaking the land speed record when it came to fucking up. Still, because he wasn't there to ruin his image, it also meant he wasn't there to hold her, kiss her; and his arms, even if perfect in fiction, might have been better when smelly, sweaty, and in person.

She thinks about calling him, but what would she say? How can she admit the truth that she doesn't know why she needs to be held? After three or four variations, her opening line still never sounds right, and so she drops the plan, further screwed up by the fact that she doesn't have his number. Maybe instead she'll heat up a Healthy Choice dinner in the microwave, catch the last five minutes of Dana Delaney chumming it up with Ricki Lake in a "China Beach" rerun on Lifetime, and then walk back down the hill to see if anything new has come out on video.

As Eileen climbs back into bed, the frame horribly creaking, she thinks of the way she approached Craig, sensed something was wrong, and moved in when normally she would go to the other table, wipe it down, and move on. Her act of random kindness seemed oddly like the one Jess had perpetrated the day he introduced himself to her, the day she took the job at the Novel Idea cafe and thus cemented her decision to stay in Kitty.

Jess. She laughs. *What a mistake.*

Eileen is now staring at the tired ceiling, missing her virginity. She used to think her virginity was something she could just get rid of, like the shrink-wrap from a brand-new CD, something you throw away and get rid of forever. But now it seems to her that it's more like a coast of land, and with every new person she sleeps with, her ship drifts farther and farther away. "A virgin seven times removed," she says with a laugh, stroking her thigh.

A noise downstairs, probably Jess closing up for the night, rattles her out of half-sleep. She turns on her side, raises the blankets to her chin, and again looks out the window onto the clear, cool night.

He's not here to fuck up his image—Eileen thinks back to Craig—*which is what Don did.* Super-gorgeous Don. She never thought for a second that she would become bored with that square jaw, those deep eyes, and Don's hair, constantly breaking to the left like a perfect sandy brown wave. Finally his utter perfection actually repulsed her. She now found herself attracted to men she never would have given a second look only because Don's looks had become old, staid, like a piece of art that loses its effect over time: No matter how powerful it once was, you find yourself unmoved by it after repeated viewing. Picasso's *Guernica* just doesn't pack the wallop it did on first impact.

By the end of the relationship, she hated looking into Don's sweet, deep-as-a-pool eyes. His eyebrows were constantly arched in a questioning fashion, wondering what had gone wrong, what the problem was, and what Eileen could say except the lame truth she felt, which was "I've gotten used to your looks. I'm bored. Give me something else." He couldn't.

In the room above the Novel Idea she holds herself tight, then alternately pushes away, plunging her hands against her chest and pressing down hard, pushing aside her breasts, going in for the real meat, wanting to plunge through the strudel-like layers of skin to rip out an ill-conceived heart. STUPID: the word appears on her brain like a fiery brand. She replaces this with YOUNG but then slaps herself with the answer: THAT'S NO EXCUSE. Again her thoughts turn to Craig. She blurs her vision, blurs it yet again, then clears it up, making it a different image each time.

until the next week. Meanwhile, Mark's alarm clock would go off and present a kind of Zen wake-up call of silence that was there but could not be heard.

"What time is it?" Laura asks, brushing the hair out of her eyes.

Mark glances over at the glowing digital clock face for a confirmation before answering: "Quarter to seven." He prods her limp body with his toe.

"Why so early?" Her voice cracks as she exercises it for the first time that day. Her eyelids are still only half-open, viewing the room as a thin horizontal rectangle. "I mean, it's even three hours earlier back there. And the flight is only three hours itself."

"Correction, four hours, and that's direct. But since when have you heard of our pitiful little town being a major hub for anything except chronic ignorance? Hell, every plane taking off from the Kitty airport still has propellers, and half of those are crop dusters."

"So then you fly into Dulles or National?" She sits up quickly and the covers fall back, exposing her bare chest. For some strange reason she pulls them back up quickly.

"No, actually we fly into Charlotte. We have a dinky little commuter flight down to there, and then there's a two-and-a-half-hour layover. Our flight leaves North Carolina at, like, one o'clock, and we finally make it to Los Angeles at about two or three."

Laura gets out of bed and begins to gather up her clothes like she's done so many times, but this time there's a resounding feeling of finality to the usually casual act. Before, if she couldn't find a sock or bra or even panties, because they had slipped under the bed or behind a door when Mark pulled them off, she would just leave the hunt for another day, figuring she would find the item the next time around. But this time she's filled with the acute feeling that she will never be back again, and she doesn't seem to mind.

"What are you looking for so hard?" Mark asks casually as he notices Laura rooting around in the garbage of yellow used bookstore books and cheap newsprint entertainment weeklies handed out free around town.

This Moral Coital

1

As Mark wakes up, shaken out of sleep by Procol Harum's seminal psychedelic song "Whiter Shade of Pale," the first thing that catches his eyes are his packed bags sitting in a neat pile by the door.

He moves to raise himself before noticing that one arm is pinned underneath the still-sleeping Laura, whom he's already forgotten about. He eases himself back into the soft comfort of his worn flannel sheets, fighting the temptation to sleep, lulled into a dream state by the lazy rhythm of the song.

"And the truth was plain to see," the half-spoken lyrics crawl out of the tinny alarm clock speaker.

Mark likes this song, and he laughs when he thinks that it reminds him not of the '60s, but of the '80s. Not Woodstock but *The Big Chill.*

"Huh? Wha'?" Laura begins to shake to life.

Mark rolls out of bed and turns off the alarm, but not before groaning as the opening bars of Deep Purple's "Smoke on the Water" begins to seep out of the radio's front. He generally hates the classic rock station the alarm clock is set to, but the only good station in town, the local community college radio station, is run by students and hence is too flaky to be counted on. At least once a week one of the DJs with the morning show will oversleep or have a test and so decide to shine on his slot

"Nothing," she replies innocently, even though she finds what she was searching for: the back to an earring she had lost three months before.

Mark reaches for the blue duffel bag bulging with CDs.

"You sure you don't mind giving me a ride to the airport?"

"No, no," Laura says with her back to him as she clasps the rear of her bra in the center of her chest before sliding it around and then putting her arms through the double satin straps. She turns and, facing him in the bra and a grin, says, "My pleasure."

Mark moves swiftly through the house, double-checking his pockets for his tickets and wallet. He takes a mental inventory of his luggage and its contents: toothbrush, comb, razors, couple of pairs of shoes, underwear, some jeans, T-shirt, one decent sports jacket, pretied tie from high school senior ball, condoms.

"I guess that's everything," he says brightly to Laura who is looking at him strangely. She examined his face as his lips trembled but uttered no sound; his cheeks blushed on the last item of the bunch.

"Wow, that's an awful lot of stuff," Laura says when she sees the combined pile of CDs, clothes, and guitar cases in the backseat of her old sedan, "for just a few, er, weeks."

Mark slams the front door.

"Look, Laura, I told you, I'm not sure how long we'll be gone. This may take longer than we expect."

"Or you may never want to come back."

Her words cut easily through the thin, icy air. Mark doesn't even answer, just stares back at her.

Poor kid, Mark thinks as he moves down the sidewalk and gets in the passenger side of the car. *I can see how much this is hurting her.*

Laura scrapes her feet as she moves across the sidewalk to the car, thinking, *Jesus Christ, it's cold out here.*

As she pulls out of the drive, Mark looks back over his shoulder, with the pretense of checking on his gear when he really wants to see his meager little home fade into the distance, as if he were leaving his entire past behind him, en route to bigger and better things. He lamely grips his acoustic guitar case, then his electric, switching a bagful of pedals, picks, extra strings, and cords to the floor, while secretly spying out the rectangular-shaped rear window as his life behind him gets smaller and smaller.

He tries to take note of the topography of Kitty, from its sloping hill, at the top of which lie the cafe and bookstore, and at the bottom, Moore's Mall with its fast-food joints and DIS-Content. He makes a mental note to remember the Hardees on the corner of Euclid and Maple, and Maurice's Piggie Park just kitty-corner to that. But then he thinks, *Why?* So instead of re-membering, he tries to forget. He takes every landmark pres-ently coming into his sight and demolishes it in his mind before he can commit it to memory. He glances away before the image is burned into his eyes and transferred to his mind, where, he's sure, the space should be left for more important things. He catches Laura's soft wrist as she gets on the highway and slaps her blinker, and he thinks, *Uh oh, better start forgetting her, too.*

"Here we are," she announces fifteen minutes later as they enter the long curved driveway that leads into the Kitty airport. On one side of the winding road are dense woods with bark-strewn dirt driveways leading to tin-corrugated supply shacks for the airlines, but on the other side is a man-made lake, at the center of which is a large red wedge used by water-skiers as a jump. A few floating orange buoys and red, white, and blue–striped flags remain from the Fourth of July fireworks ceremony held last summer.

Laura pulls up in front of the lone building and surveys the desolate parking lot and nearly empty terminal.

"Where are the guys? You are taking them, too, right?"

Mark twists his head quickly and speaks.

"What in the fuck is that supposed to mean? Of course they're coming." Small puffs of his breath in the chilly interior punctu-ate his abrupt words. "You think I wouldn't take them?"

"No, it's just . . ." She backs off from her earlier insinuation, figuring it's not worth it. "Forget it."

Laura gets out but merely stands by the curb as Mark unloads from the backseat and hands it to an older gentleman who is the airport's only skycap.

"Well," Laura grimly announces, "I guess this is good-bye."

"Sure, *a* good-bye but not *the* good-bye. You think my plane's gonna crash or something?"

For some reason a smiling Laura gives him a perfunctory hug. "In a way."

"Huh?" Another car comes into view, appearing from around the curve, and Mark recognizes it as Steve's.

"That's my cue," Laura says, pulling away from him and moving toward the car.

"I'll, uh, call you." Mark looks back and forth from the retreating Laura to the approaching Steve. Phil is behind the wheel. "Yeah, call you."

Laura just sort of nods, gets into the car, puts on a pair of sunglasses even though it's overcast and still very foggy, reaches a hand out the window, waves, and then pulls out of her space.

"Hey, man, you ready for the biggest day of your life!" Steve jumps out of the car as his brother pops the trunk from the inside. He reaches into the open space and begins moving a few bags from the car to the curb. "Fuck." Steve swats at his shoulders for warmth with his arms crossed over his chest. "It sure is cold, isn't it?"

Mark watches Laura's car disappear behind the bend.

"Yeah, it is."

2

Dave can always tell how big the crowd inside is by the number of cars outside. If most of the small lot is full (and none of those cars belong to employees), Dave groans as he pulls up, snaps on his novelty whale bow-tie, and just accepts that he is in for a rough night. On the other hand, a large crowd means turning your tables quicker and amassing tip after tip. But most of the time when Dave pulls into the parking lot, he prays for it to be empty so he can be cut early, go home, watch TV, listen to some records, eat a frozen dinner, maybe call Stacy, drift off to sleep.

"Oh, well." Dave shrugs, feeling ambivalent about driving over to the Whales Fin because he's not going there to work, just to make sure he's off on Friday for his benefit show.

Earlier in the day Stacy helped him put up flyers all over town, and even Jim from DISContent, trying to prove he wasn't all bad (though Dave is still unconvinced), weakly concurred with Dave's suggestion that he put the pile of flyers for the show at the cash register instead of at the back of the store along with all the others. Since Bottlecap hasn't returned his phone calls he expects the worst, and only The Disappointed and The Deer Park will be playing the benefit the next day. Both had their respective loyal followings, and Dave is praying it will be enough.

Dave taps the wheel as he drives, and finds his left foot pressing down rhythmically on the brake pedal at stoplights, causing the car to shake back and forth.

"This could be it."

As he pulls into the parking lot of the Whales Fin, he chuckles to himself, spotting Sasha's, Amy's, and Nicole's cars parked in the back. He walks up to the front door and enters the restaurant, feeling strange that not only is he not wearing his blubbery bow-tie, black polyester slacks, and white shirt, but he's also coming in the front door and not through the supply door in back. Once inside the lobby he sees a few couples standing around waiting to be seated by a hostess who is nowhere to be found. *Probably in the back with Dan,* he thinks. He stifles the temptation to shout out "Run while you can! Eat somewhere else! You don't know what they're doing to the food back there!"

Passing through on his way to the dining room, he spots the lobster tank sitting in a dark corner, with the same four or five lobsters from last March (can't even tell for sure how many because they're all huddled together). They're barely moving in the chalky, murky water, surrounded by pennies, nickels, and dimes that stupid kids toss in every couple of days.

As he walks around the tables, he begins to feel more and more uncomfortable. The waitresses see him and instead of saying "Hey, what's up?" they eye him suspiciously, as if he came in on his day off in street clothes to mock everyone who was working. Dave sympathizes because he himself is always suspicious of people who spend their days off lounging around the place they work, especially at a place like the Whales Fin. He remembers all the times Dan yelled at him while putting tomatoes on top of a salad or tried to distribute the dressing evenly so there weren't clumps of it in one place and dry lettuce in another: "Faster! Faster! You ain't making a work of art! Get it out there!" Or whenever Dave would try to send the food back, following the old waiter coda of "Don't serve anything you yourself wouldn't eat," and Dan would stop the plate as it slid through the window separating the galley from the assembly line and push it back in Dave's direction. "You're too picky, Rowland. Salmon is *supposed* to be slightly blue. Now get out there and move those tables!"

One day when they ran out of croutons, most of the salad dressing, and then the salad itself (to which Dan skitteringly gave this advice, "Uh, push the soup"), Dave wrote on the chalkboard where items of food that were in and out of stock were posted daily: 86 RATIONAL THOUGHT. When he reentered the alley a moment later, his joke was, as he expected, rubbed off and replaced by 86 ALL SOFT DRINKS, which unfortunately was not a joke. "Uh, push the bar drinks," Dan said, and Dave wondered if it hadn't happened on purpose.

Finally Dave spots Dan sitting at the bar, smoking a cigarette, a pile of papers laid out in front of him.

"Hey, Dan, how's it going?"

By way of an answer Dan takes a deep drag off the cigarette and calls out to the bartender, who is also nowhere in sight, "Hey, Pup Tent, give me another!"

"Uh, is that the new schedule?" Dave climbs up on a bar stool. "Because if it is, I need to make sure I've got tomorrow night off."

"Yes, it is," Dan says, adding quickly, "and no, you don't."

"But I told you over the phone that I need Friday night off. It's really important."

"And I told you over the phone that I would see what I could do. And I can't."

"But—"

"Listen, David, there's a big dance tomorrow night at the recreation center, and there are going to be a lot of hungry teenagers coming in."

"Yeah, either that"—Dave's voice is dripping with sarcasm—"or *thirsty* ones who come in here because we know we're so

desperate for business that we have orders from the management not to card anyone."

Dan shakes his head and taps his cigarette against the clam-
shell ashtray.

"Don't even try it, Rowland. You're working Friday, and that's
final."

"Dan," Dave pleads, changing his strategy, "I really need the
night off. Can't I just work the lunch shift instead?"

"Didn't look very close, did you?" Dan laughs.

Dave scrambles through the schedule for his name.

"A split shift? Oh, come on . . ."

"And don't forget," Dan says graciously, "for a double shift
you have to roll double silverware. Which at fifty rolls a shift
adds up to, hang on a second"—he pecks at the air with his
fingers, making computer noises with his mouth—"one hundred rolls! Hell, maybe you'll be here all night and will be on
time for your Saturday shift."

"Dan—"

"Dave! For the past two weeks you've been bitching at me to
give you a shift. Fine, I give you one—in fact, a good one. And
now all you do is whine about it and try to weasel your way out
of it. What's your problem, kid?"

"My problem is I need the night off. Bad."

"What for? Another great excuse like Sick to My Stomach is
playing in Chapel Hill and me and my friends are going down
for the weekend?"

"It was Sick of It All, not Sick to My—oh, forget it. I'll admit
I've fucked around in the past, but this is serious."

"Yeah, I bet," Dan says through clenched teeth, sucking in.
Before continuing he leans over the bar, trying to find the bartender. He shrugs, leans back, and turns to Dave.

"You think this is a shitty job, don't you?"

Dave is playing with a rip in his jeans, pulling on the inch-
long white fringe dangling at his exposed knee.

"Well, no need to answer because I know you do." Dan shakes
his head, says lightly, "You selfish little brat."

"What?"

"You know, you may not like this place, but it is your job, and
you and Carlos and Stoner and the rest of you fucking slackers

might like to remember that those checks you get every week and those tips that people leave on tables for you are for a reason. Because you work here. You don't just show up, look pretty, throw some fish on the table, and then spend the rest of your time in the bathroom fixing your hair or hitting on a hostess."

"Now look, Dan—" Dave begins.

Dan throws his arms up quickly, as if Dave's words were a physical presence he could ward off, like swatting a fly.

"I don't want to hear any more of your excuses—about how you're above this sort of work, how it's so demeaning." Dave notices that Dan is beginning to sweat. He shifts awkwardly on the bar stool to stare into Dave's bloodshot eyes. "Tell me, what's so demeaning about doing an honest job and doing it well? Huh?" The question is obviously rhetorical, but when Dave begins to give an answer, Dan steamrolls over it, moving on to his next point. "And do you know how many people would love to have such a *demeaning* job? Do you realize how many hurdles in life you and your little friends have already jumped over, and yet all you do is whine about what a shitty race you're in? You have homes and cars, and even if they're beat-up or old cars, there are *a lot* of people out there who don't even have that." Dan relents for a moment. He retrieves his cigarette from the ashtray. "How much were those shoes?" he asks, pointing to Dave's black Doc Marten Gibsons with the butt of his cigarette.

"About . . . thirty," Dave says, hesitating.

"Don't bullshit me, Rowland. I'm not a total loser. I know those must have been at least fifty," Dan declares, though still about fifteen dollars away from the amount Dave actually paid. "Jesus, you kids all got nice shoes. Horrible lives, but nice shoes."

"Look, Dan, spare me all your jealous generation-envy bullshit, okay?" Dave finally explodes, returning Dan's aggression with some of his own. "Just because your peace and love hippie shit didn't work out the way you planned doesn't give you the right to point a finger at me and my friends and say how lazy we are. You know how sick and tired we are of hearing that bullshit?"

"Hey, hey"—Dan waves his hands in front of his thick chest. "Slow down, kiddo. *Hippie* shit? Who you calling a hippie? I'm thirty-two years old, and I probably hate the hippies more than you do. I grew up on Aerosmith, Rush, Led Zeppelin, which sounds exactly like the same crap you're listening to these days."

Dave's mind races back to a few nights ago when he vaguely remembers saying the same thing to Chipp.

"So don't give me that line of bullshit," Dan continues. "What pisses me off is that I used to be a lot like you. I played in a band. Thought I was going to be famous. But guess what? It never panned out. Yeah, big fucking surprise. But by that time I was twenty-seven and scrambling for a decent job. I started as a waiter here and worked my way up. Does that mean anything to you? Work? I was also a busboy, a dishwasher, line cook, and food preparer before becoming assistant manager, and then it was a year of staying here till two in the morning counting fish, showing up the next day at five in the morning to start it all over again, and only after all *that* did I became manager."

"Yeah?" Dave is laughing, unable to control himself. "That's great. You sure work hard. After all, we're saving lives here, aren't we? Oooh, what you do is *real* important."

"Look, Dave, laugh if you want, but now I've got something, and so what if it wasn't what I always wanted, so fucking what? It's something, and that's more than you're going to be able to say in five years."

"Don't be so sure," Dave mumbles, thinking of the benefit. *Raise the cash, press some records, start to get some major distribution. From there it'll all happen. . . . It'll have to.*

"Look," Dan says calmly, putting out his cigarette, continuing to push the filter into the ashtray even though it has long since died. "Come in tomorrow, get some good tips, and you can start paying off some of those bills. You don't even know how nice it'll feel to get out of the hole you're in."

"Bills?" Dave says slowly. "Who told you about my bills?"

Dan is silent.

"Did Stacy say something to you?"

"Stacy didn't say to bump up your shifts, but"—Dan hesitates for a moment—"yes, she mentioned you were having some problems, so I just thought you could use a few shifts. That's all. No big deal."

Dave jumps off the stool.

"Look, Dan," Dave shouts. A few customers from the dining room now turn their way. "You can shove that split shift right up your own ass because I quit. And ask Stacy if she wouldn't mind keeping her fucking mouth shut!"

"Dave, calm down. Stacy really cares for you, and she wouldn't have said anything unless—"

"Fuck you, Dan. I quit!" Dave shouts, turning away and marching out of the restaurant.

As Dave drives home he finds himself shaken by the confrontation. While he playfully tapped out a tune on the steering wheel just twenty minutes ago, he is now clutching the wheel tightly, afraid to let go. His heart is beating rapidly, his limbs shaking, his eyes resisting a battle on all fronts to cry. He hasn't felt like this in years.

Dave absentmindedly takes a left down a street that doesn't look familiar. He bites his lip, only half-paying attention to the road and the mirrors. He puts on the radio, but there's only static. He leaves it on.

Dave parks his car and sort of stumbles into his apartment, his expensive shoes heavy on his soft feet, and as he marches through the dirty apartment, everything seems like a sign of failure, things to do, things he hasn't done, dirty dishes staring at him, appliances and emotions that don't work, an unmade bed.

He sits on his couch unable to cook anything because the gas has been turned off. A stale pot aroma is competing with rancid garbage for control of the air, his phone has been turned off, and he'll be evicted in three days if he doesn't turn up with the rent. His last salvation is electricity and cable. He turns on the TV, "Saved by the Bell," familiar faces, familiar universe, things are looking up.

The set is the same: the cheesy-looking hallway, the fake lockers, young but cute extras—only instead of Slater, Kelly, Zack, and the rest, it's a group of new faces. The characters remain: the geek, the schemer, the jock, and the pretty girls. As if in some sort of Menudo sitcom, the older actors have been forced into retirement and a fresh, new crew brought in.

"What in the fuck is this?" he shouts to the screenful of strangers. "What's happened?" As he throws down the remote, the TV changes channel and the little piece of plastic skitters onto the cluttered kitchen floor. The screen is filled with wavy lines, a black convoluted picture twisting, turning, and revolving, but the sound is audible. Dave winces at the scrambled HBO signal, still able to make out the final scene of *Home Alone*.

3

Randy grips the duct tape firmly and attaches the sticky side to one end of the doorjamb. He walks a few feet, pulling the tape along with him and it only grudgingly unravels, jerking his arm back and forth, coming undone in loud spurts. Randy brings the roll to his mouth, makes a small cut with his teeth, rips the tape, and seals it on the opposite side of the doorjamb. He does this twice more so that the entryway to his room is blocked off.

"What are you doing?" asks Chipp, who's been watching all this for the past five minutes.

"I'm making sure some drunk couple doesn't screw in my bed again. Remember the last party? I had to throw those sheets away."

"Oh, yeah." Chipp rubs his hand against his chest. "Did you ever find out what that purple stain was?"

"Nope." Randy makes a diagonal line with the tape, then another, forming an X across the entryway, along with the triumvirate of horizontal lines. "And it ain't going to happen again." He tosses the tape through one of the spaces of the sticky grid. "What's next?"

"Give me a hand with these drinks."

Randy follows Chipp into the kitchen where Chipp has a circular trash can and is lining it with a dark green trash bag.

"This for bottles or cans?" Randy asks.

"Neither," replies Chipp. He unscrews the top of two bottles of Stolichnaya vodka and pours them into the can. Once emptied, he takes eight packets of Purplesaurus Rex Kool-Aid mix, then adds four buckets of water and mixes with a frying pan. He scoops out a portion and hands it to Randy, who sips and squints.

"More vodka?"

"More water," Chipp croaks. "Ooh, nice kick, actually. That's really good. Maybe you should just leave it the way it is."

Chipp breaks two ice cube trays into the tub and then slides it into a corner. He moves to the fridge and pulls out a box of rainbow Popsicles and begins unpeeling them.

"What are these for?"

"The margaritas. Grab the blender and the tequila."

Randy plugs in the blender and fills it a fifth of the way with the golden-colored alcohol. Chipp drops in four Popsicles separated from their sticks, whipping it up for about five seconds. Randy scoops out a spoonful and swallows the fruity alcohol-soaked mush.

"Perfect." He takes a spoonful, then another.

"Easy. We have to leave some for the guests, remember?"

"Oh, them." Randy takes a suitcase of beer out of the fridge and places it in a cooler. Then he takes a block of ice and begins to smash it against the tops of the cans.

"Great, fizz 'em up. Real smart."

Randy stops instantly, the block of ice poised over his head like a boulder a caveman would throw to kill his dinner. He sets it down lightly, closing the lid.

"Maybe I'll just let it, uh, melt naturally."

"Good idea."

"Where'd you get all the dough for this stuff anyway? I mean, Cuervo? I thought you'd get that Piggly Wiggly brand of tequila where they spell it with a *K* and two *L*'s."

"I took a bunch of the promo CDs we got for *Godfuck* and traded them in for cash at DISContent."

"I thought they stopped doing that."

"They did, for a while, but they've started again. Don't ask me why. All I know is that they gave me fifty bucks for all of that crap, so I thought I'd splurge since our guests are going to help us out with the zine."

"Yeah, but Häagen-Dazs coffee-flavored ice cream swimming

in a puddle of Bailey's as a chill-out cocktail at the end of the evening?"

"Too much?"

"No, it's really nice, actually. I just doubt they'll appreciate it. I mean, last time we threw a party, I remember a guy drank some of my Nyquil, a vial of vanilla, and a spray bottle of hairspray some girl had left here, just because there was some alcoholic content. I think he was putting a bottle of rubbing alcohol to his lips when I caught him. Who was that anyway?"

Chipp throws the empty Popsicle box across the room, hitting Randy in the head.

"That was me, you asshole. And I was depressed. Besides, I caught a good buzz off all that. You're just lucky we didn't have any Scotchgard in the house. And don't give me any more shit about that because you're the guy who sat up all night frying bananas and trying to smoke them, listening to that Dead Milkmen song, so shut up."

Silence pervades the room for a few seconds: four eyeballs roll around, minds are set in motion, engineers in the brain yell for more power, the millions of tiny synapses half-pulse with lazy energy.

"I won't tell if you won't," Chipp blurts out.

"Deal!" Randy responds in a flash.

They both exhale and move on. Chipp pulls out a card table from a closet and nudges it against their large wooden dinner table. Then he drags his dresser out from his bedroom, aligning it with the other two, forming a long flat surface running almost three-fourths the length of the room.

"Where are the copies of the zine?" he asks.

"Hmm?" Randy says, scooping another dollop of mushy margarita into his mouth.

"The copies you managed to salvage from Kinko's? The piles of paper we're going to collate? Remember? That's why we invited all these people over here tonight?"

Both of their heads swivel slowly to Randy's taped-up bedroom door.

"Shit!"

After trying unsuccessfully to slither acrobatically through the largest hole of the grid in the lower left corner, Randy carefully takes off the tape and cusses as he marches into the room. He takes out the six brown Kinko's boxes, stacks them on the card table, and then reattaches the long strips of black tape. This time they are sagging, like the strips of cotton on a muscleman's sliced T-shirt.

"I think we should"—Chipp reaches into one of the boxes, pulls out a stack of pages 1 and 2—"start here and make it go in a *U* shape. So you have to follow it around the table since it's wide enough to fit two pages. Rather than have you try to zigzag, which would just confuse people, especially after they've had a few beers."

"Sounds good," Randy says, placing the pages on the table. "But what about the covers?"

"Never mind the covers until tomorrow. Then we'll sit down, put the covers and backs on, and staple 'em."

It takes them about ten minutes to arrange all the pages in ascending order, lining up each stack straight, evenly spacing them so no one will get confused. Chipp slices the black tape into thin strips and makes arrows on the floor, pointing in the direction people are to walk.

"So who'd you invite?" Randy asks, rummaging through his records, picking out good party material.

"The usual gang of idiots, I guess: K.K., Jason, Heather."

Randy groans, inspecting a lamination crack in his new Silver Jews LP.

"What? What'd I say?"

"Heather? Is she going to bring Jen, her psycho roommate, with her?"

"Yeah, I guess anyone who'd date *you* would have to be psycho." Chipp places saucers, bowls, and coffee cups around the room as ashtrays. "Except that she dumped you, so she must have some brains."

Randy slips the record back into its colorfully painted sleeve, laying it on top of his Heavy Rotation stack. "Looking back," he says, "I think I may have been a bit insensitive about all that."

"Randy," Chipp says, stopping in his tracks, "by way of an explanation for why you cheated on her with her cousin, you only half-legibly scrawled down the lyrics to 'How Silly Can You Get?' on a bar napkin and left it on her doorstep."

"Cold?"

"Um, frozen," Chipp replies, spotting Randy pulling out some of his records.

"No, no. You put all *my* stuff in my room. I'm not going to have some drunk asshole slide the needle across my purple vinyl Pavement bootleg. No, no." Randy relents, setting the records aside. "And no more Fudge Tunnel. The last time you played that crap you cleared the room, but keep your Man Is the Bastard/Bleeding Rectum split LP close by in case we actually *want* to get rid of people."

Randy drops a stack of LPs and singles onto the ottoman. "I need your help deciding the order in which to play my ultimate collection of groups with the prefix 'Super' in their name."

Chipp eagerly looks over the bunch. "Hang on, I'll need a drink for this."

He goes into the kitchen and scoops out a glassful of the purple vodka–laced concoction, scooping out another cup for Randy. They both take large gulps and wince; the warm liquid coasts into their empty stomachs unobstructed, and they feel its wonderful toxicity only seconds after. Randy lights up a cigarette using a Teenbeat Records matchbook.

"Okay." Chipp drains the last of the drink and tosses the cup onto the floor. "Start out with the big guns."

"Supercharger?"

"Super*chunk.* Leave Supercharger for later. I'd say the *Tossing the Seeds* LP ought to do it—after that slap on the Supersuckers' record with the Dan Clowes cover, but only for a few songs since that's pretty annoying. Then, keeping with the Sub-Pop mood, throw on Supersnazz's *Superstupid.* By this time people will have a good buzz, so *now* you throw on Supercharger's Estrus record and then maybe that seven-inch on Bag of Hammer Records, if people are digging it. Slap on that pink vinyl Supersport 2000, then that Superdrag single on Dragola. After those, hit side two of Superconductor's *Hit Songs for Girls.* Then I'd put on the Supernovices—no, wait, the Superkools' *Love Turns Gray* EP, *then* the Supernovices. That new Superstar seven-inch is okay, and follow that with the Superkollider record, but it's probably too heavy for mass consumption. Around now I'd play that Super Thirty-One CD. Start winding things down with some

Superball '63 and feel free to work in Superheroine or Super-
nova at your discretion. Oh, and if those old guys from the
comic book store show up, play the 'Logical Song' by Super-
tramp."

"Now I know why I put up with all your crap," Randy says,
admiring his roommate.

Chipp blows on his nails, then brushes them against his flannel
shirt in a *Who, me?* fashion just as there's a knock at the door,
announcing the first guest of the evening.

" 'This group winds dissonant pop songs around layers of distor-
tion-drenched guitars, sinewy bass playing, and a tribal drumbeat, and give it sugar-coated lyrics and the perfect mixture
of melody and aggression—combining the best lo-fi aspects of
groups like Trumans Water and Sebadoh with the lush harmonies and aural soundscapes of British bands like My Bloody Valentine and the Cocteau twins. The whole album has a fuzzy feel
to it, the end effect soft and surreal, underscoring the temporal
aspects of beauty. You get the idea there's a brain behind the
stare or maybe a plane behind the little fluffy clouds where with
other bands there's just an empty sky.' Jesus," Heather groans,
setting down the page, "you said *that* about the Swirlies?"

Chipp stops the blender, noticing he forgot to take out the
wooden stick from the Popsicle. He switches from BLEND to PAR-
FAIT and adds another shot of tequila.

"Yeah, so?"

"Is that what you really think?"

"Sure, I mean, the Swirlies kick ass."

"But this," Heather says, repeatedly pointing to the page with
the long neck of a wine cooler, leaving a stain every time it
touches, "this makes them sound like the second coming or
something."

"Ahh, what's the big deal?" He pours the slushy mixture from
the blender into a plastic cup that has already been used. "You
exaggerate here, hyperbole—uh—lize, there. It's a good record.
So maybe it's not *that* good. Who am I to say?" He hands
Heather the cup with a smile. "Drink up."

Dropping the stack of papers to the table, she takes a sip.

"Hey, not bad."

Heather moves into the living room, then plops down on the armrest of the couch, bullying her way into a conversation. Lake, a guy with a master's degree in English who is working as a bag boy, is reading a sheet of paper, holding up the line. Collators have to walk around him, reach past him for the requisite pages. Jason, drunk, just skips that page altogether.

"Don't *read* it, for God's sake." Chipp slaps Lake's hand. "Just collate."

"Not read it?" replies Lake, burping. "Then what did you do this for?"

"Well, read it, yeah"—Chipp stumbles, leans back, catching himself before he falls—"just don't read it *now.*"

"God, if I have to look at this picture of G. G. Allin one more time, I'm going to puke," shouts K.K. "I've been around this table eight times, and I swear, he's like *staring* at me!"

Chipp rushes over, shoves a few more sheets into her hands.

"No, no, he's not staring, he's just, ahh, oh, will you fucking grow up! The man is dead! Just make a few more issues!" K.K. bites her lips, numb to the verbal thrashing, her eyes still focused on G.G.'s own glazed-over eyes.

"Dead, right? Really dead?"

Chipp shrugs and glances at his watch: 12:13 A.M.

"He's dead, I assure you. I have a picture from *Flipside* that actually shows him in his casket wearing his famous 'Eat Me' jock strap. Okay?"

K.K. sniffles, closes her eyes, and reaches for another sheet, moving down the assembly line.

"Sarita, you're going backward." Chipp spots Sarita biting on the lower rim of a plastic cup so that it covers her nose, making it look like a beak. Chipp grabs her by the shoulders and turns her around as she places page 18 underneath page 20. "This isn't the Koran. Now put them back and start at the other side."

Sarita drops the papers, burps, and moves to the other side of the table.

"No, Sarita. Put the copies under, not over. Jesus, it's turning out the same," Chipp screams.

This has been the scene most of the night. The partygoers

and reluctant collators discovered the high-octane vodka punch before they stumbled upon *Godfuck,* and three hours later it is easily the vodka that is winning the war. All night Chipp has been corralling people around the table with the sheets of paper, urging them to collate a few issues, *then* have another drink. He would steal Jen or Jason away from their conversations in the hallways, living room, or even the bathroom (where he found K.K. talking to herself in the mirror), promising the other half of the conversations that they would be back in a minute. Half the time people left out a page, put them in backward or upside down, or just ridiculed the material.

" 'Primordial sludgerock thicker than mud from the bowels of hell?' You said *that* about the Melvins?"

"Yeah. You got to make it interesting or else no one will read it." Chipp wades through the crowd, spotting an unfamiliar face in the corner who is making paper airplanes out of pages 7/8.

"What's my address doing in here?" K.K. shoves a sheetful of classified ads in his face.

"What?" Chipp says, distracted.

"Right here!" She points to the paper. "Under the heading of TATTOUED, PIERCED, SCARRED, OR OTHERWISE BODILY MODIFIED. And there's *my* address."

"Look"—he fends her off, backing up—"don't ask me, ask Randy. He's the one who handled all of those."

"Well, where is Randy?"

"I don't know." Chipp screams over the wailing of the Supersuckers, sound flooding the room, walls practically vibrating. Above the din of the music is the equally loud sounds of voices in conversation, screaming, laughing, yelling.

"Chipp." Sarita runs up, her green eyes livid. "There's some guy named The Cleaner who's guarding the cooler and won't let anyone have a beer."

"The Cleaner? Who in the hell's that?"

"I don't know. He's wearing a beret and speaking in a French accent. He said something about throwing acid in our faces if we 'botch the job.' Someone said he sat through *La Femme Nikita* four times last weekend at the Capitol Cinema, and Thom finally had to throw him out when he began shouting at the screen."

Chipp tries to find the person in question in the sea of people in his tiny living room. Where in hell did all these people come from?

"Tell The Cleaner I'm looking for him," Chipp says, putting the matter on the back burner.

"*Oui,*" Sarita says direly, wading back into the crowd.

"Goddamn it, Chipp." Jen comes up to him and grabs him by his shirt. "If I have to hear this goddamn Supersuckers record one more time, I'm going to burn this whole place down!"

Chipp wriggles his way free. "What? How long's it been on for? Goddamn! I told Randy not to play more than one or two songs."

"And have you met The Cleaner?"

"No, but I just heard about him."

"Now he's raving about Bridget Fonda, calling her a 'mealy-mouthed plucked chicken.' What's he mean by that?"

"I don't know, but I doubt it's a compliment."

"Well, where's Randy? Have him get rid of this guy."

The question also strikes Chipp: Yeah, where is Randy?

Chipp pushes Jen aside, telling her to play anything she wants. As Chipp approaches Randy's room, he hears his *Jimmy Smokes Crack and I Don't Care* bootleg hit the turntable, where it plays for five seconds, then stops abruptly with a loud scratching noise, the needle being dragged over the grooves.

"Randy?" He slides through the sagging tape. "You in here?"

He spots something under the covers, moving around slowly.

"Hey, you okay? You sick or something?" Chipp says quietly but loud enough to be heard above the music, which has roared up again. He puts his hand on the lump underneath the covers.

"Leave us the fuck alone, man!" shouts a guy emerging from the sheets. Chipp can make out a mouthful of white teeth, a chest, and a head of long blond hair.

"Yeah, okay, sorry," Chipp mumbles, quickly backing out. He turns around in the hallway, faces his own door, notices a small bar of light shining through the space between the floor and the closed door, which has a homemade KEEP OUT taped to it. He eases it open.

"Randy!"

Randy is sitting up in bed, reading an issue of *Penthouse* magazine, stolen from a small stack that Chipp keeps under his bed.

"What in the hell are you doing?"

Randy folds over a corner of the magazine, the cover reading CLAUDIA SCHIFFER TOPLESS. Chipp can see a naked female torso on the triangle of paper and the slightly cropped head of another female who is licking the other's nipple.

"I ducked in here to get away from the party." Randy tosses the magazine to the floor. "That's what sucks about having a party at your own house. There's no way to escape it. And I'm not about to leave the premises to come back and find this place razed to the ground."

"No shit." Chipp picks Randy's feet off his sheet, and places them on the ground. He sits down. "I looked for you in your room, and, uh, let's just say there was a couple in there doing, well, you know."

"Trust me," he says, "I know. I tried to duck in there first and was told to get out. I told the guy that it was my room, but he just snarled something and threw a motorcycle boot at me."

"Who's in there anyway?"

"I don't know, but I'm going to let them finish."

"Meanwhile"— Chipp leans back against the wall, vibrating from the pulse of the music—"there's some guy named The Cleaner holding everything in the living room hostage."

"Great. But how many copies of *Godfuck* finally got collated?"

"Actually, most of them. There are a few pages left over and a whole stack of pages fifteen and sixteen, which doesn't make sense, but there are almost two hundred made."

"Cool." Randy takes a sip from a beer can lying on his chest. "In the morning we'll staple on the covers and then cleverly deposit them around town."

"I don't know," Chipp groans. "That's going to take some time, and I doubt either of us will want to wake up early to do it. Besides, we're going to have to clean up the apartment first anyway just to make some space to work. Why don't we wait till Saturday?"

"Because if we wait till Saturday—" In the living room a body is knocked against the wall behind Chipp and Randy. Both stop for a second, then they hear another small thump, then laughing. Randy continues: "If we wait till Saturday, we won't get them out till midday Saturday, and half the shopping crowd will be gone. Who cares if there's a big stack around for Sunday because Sundays are dead around here. You know that. We need to have them in the shops first thing Saturday morning because that's when we'll get the biggest initial push. Then they'll trickle away throughout the next couple of weeks. But Saturday morning is when we'll move the most copies."

"Yeah, sure, but the major places we're gonna put them, like DISContent and a few spots around the JC campus, close at like six tomorrow night. We'll never have them ready by then."

Randy sits back, deep in thought, while Chipp listens to Heavenly's *P.U.N.K Girl* ten-inch on K Records being played on the stereo, another disc he could have sworn he hid under the couch so no one would touch it.

"I've got it!" Randy announces, the lightbulb in his head shattering due to the enormous power surge. "Why don't we bundle them up—you know, like they do with the stacks of newspapers they deliver in the middle of the night—and set them outside DISContent and places like that. And when they come in first thing Saturday morning, *voilà*, they'll be ready to go. What do you say?"

"Bundle them up? You mean like tie them together?"

"Well, I guess not. But you know, a stack here, a stack there."

"Hmm." Chipp weighs the decision. "That's a good idea. We'll snag a shopping cart from the Winn Dixie and load it up and then just put copies all over town. Then we'll take the remainder to The Scene since there'll be a big crowd there for the Violent Revolution benefit."

"Hopefully."

There's another slam on the wall, this time louder than before. Chipp looks at Randy, who looks away, glancing at a pile of dirty laundry in the corner.

"Come on, Randy, let's get out there before somebody gets killed."

"Yeah, yeah."

They exit Chipp's room.

"Hey, K.K., what's going on? What's all the racket?"

K.K. looks around quickly for the voice calling out to her, finds out it's only Randy, and, relieved, runs over.

"Two guys were headbutting each other, but they knocked each other out. Now they're sleeping in the corner."

"What happened to The Cleaner?" Chipp asks.

"Oh, he's better. Now he's just sitting there telling Jen how his band's van broke down tonight, and they may have to cancel a tour next month."

"I don't get it," Randy says, looking to Chipp for answers. "Mr. Clean is a *band?*"

As Chipp marches through the crowd, he hears K.K. behind him rebuking Randy, "Not *Mr.* Clean, *The* Cleaner!"

"Stoner?"

Sitting on the couch, wearing a dusty black beret and speaking earnestly with Sarita in a horrible French accent, is Stoner. After a few seconds he spots Chipp, smiles, takes off the beret, and drops the accent. He gets off the couch and leaves a bewildered Sarita alone.

"Chipp!" Stoner embraces him, throwing his arm around Chipp's thin neck. "I've been looking for you." His voice is now normal, slightly slurred, but definitely in English.

"Yeah, Stoner?" Chipp is trying to work his way out of Stoner's grasp, but since Stoner is bigger, drunker, and higher, he keeps a tight grip on Chipp. "I wanted to ask you about something you wrote."

Stoner pulls out a crumpled piece of paper from his pocket that Chipp recognizes instantly as one of the pages from *Godfuck* featuring his interview with The Deer Park.

"Hey, Stoner, did you hear there's a Luc Bresson film festival on Bravo right now? If you rush home, maybe you can still catch that Roseanna Arquette scene with the—"

Stoner cuts him off, pulling him into the kitchen.

"What did you mean by this? This . . . this . . ." Stoner is searching the long article for the quote that offended him hours ago when he was still sober. "Aha!" He leans back, knocking over an empty bottle. Back in the living room Chipp hears something crash, tries to see what it is, but Stoner is blocking his way. "What in the fuck do you mean that The Deer Park—by the way you misspelled *Deer* three times—" His words suddenly explode into a loud burp.

"Well, you see, Randy actually, uh, typed the whole thing up. I think he's right over there if you want to tell him."

"—that we sound like"—Stoner burps again before continuing, quoting the magazine—" 'a bunch of crazed banshees, assaulting their instruments like the bastard stepchildren of Iggy and the Stooges, distilling from the past of the MC5 and the future of the Dischord scene, a groove and style all their own!' Huh? What's that supposed to mean?" He pushes Chipp against the counter. "Is that even good? Why, I should just"—he staggers back—"break your little—" He twirls to the right, mumbling the word *face* as he passes out and falls onto the rickety card table sitting piggyback to the kitchen table. It collapses instantly, sending Stoner to the ground along with a handful of beer cans, a dozen plastic glasses with varying amounts of booze inside, two mugs used as ashtrays, and a few pages of *Godfuck*.

"Whew." Chipp wipes his forehead. "That was close."

4

Craig reaches for a tie, his hands finding only the empty steel hanger on a hook on the back of his closet door. He looks around for a second, then finally to the ground where seven ties lie like sleeping snakes, two partially covered by a pair of blue-and-green-plaid pajama bottoms. Craig kicks away the flannel pj's with a polished shoe and picks up all the ties in a clump. He throws them down on his overcrowded drafting table and tosses a *Rock Guitar Fake Book* and a Martin Amis novel onto the floor. He pokes his hands through the ties, trying to measure the best one for the clothes he's wearing—old faded Levi's, worn denim shirt, blue socks, black belt, black Kenneth Cole Unlisted shoes (made in an area code far, far away). He chooses a tie with a brown background and colorful flowers in the foreground. He slides it, pretied, over his head and tightens it up, gulping as he always does, as if allergic. "Jesus, I've done this twice today. It just ain't fair.

"Ashley!" he calls out, her help in the matter finally available. "Come here, I *need* you!"

She appears a minute later, wearing her glasses pushed up on her head and the top of Craig's plaid pajamas. But in the time it takes her to take out of her mouth the pencil she always clenches while studying, put down her book, and come into the room, his collar, for once, has laid down flat, on command, the first time.

"You needed me?" she asks brightly.

Craig is standing stiffly, as if caught even though he invited her.

"No, sorry," he says plainly, without time to think. "I don't."

"So," she says a moment later, "a night out with the boys, huh?"

"Yeah," he says awkwardly.

"Who, exactly? Bryant, Roger, the usuals?"

"Probably," Craig says quickly, laughing self-consciously. "You know, *office* people." He pictures Eileen's face, soft and elegant, and compares it quickly to Ashley's, who is just as good-looking, if not more so. *What in the fuck am I doing? Rip this tie off, tell her you love her, and end this shit right here and now. You still act like a kid. You think everything is so important. After only twenty-three years, everything that you think is a dent is really just a scratch. There's a lot more to go.*

"Well, have fun," she says, turning but then stopping quickly. "Oh, you think you'll be *real* late? I just want to know if I should wait up for you."

Craig shifts in his tracks for a moment, faces the full-length mirror but turns away quickly, choosing a face with which to answer.

"Don't stay up," he says, grabbing the ball of the tie and yanking it down violently until the noose is undone. He edges it out of his collar, like he used to extricate the onions out of onion rings when he hated the vegetable but loved the batter. He tosses the tie onto the floor, untied for the first time since the day after he bought it nine months ago, thinking, *Eileen probably wouldn't like the tie.*

Craig steps on the pedal. He crushes it. He stamps it to the ground until it's merely a bump in the smooth floor. The speedometer slowly reaches 50, waving back and forth between 45 and 55 every few seconds. "Fuck," he mutters. "I have *got* to get a new car."

On the way across town to the cafe his mind returns to the

first time he saw Ashley, walking through the campus bookstore, her books held tightly against her chest. A schoolgirl, he thought at the time. He followed her around until she picked up a title he knew something about. "Oh, Faulkner's *The Fable*. You know, he never really was in WW One, even though he bragged to the whole town that he had been a flyer. He even came back with a fake limp. The townspeople called him 'Count No Count' because he tried to pass himself off as royalty, but they all knew he was full of shit." He sighs. The moment seems infamous to him now. *What would have happened if I never said anything?* he asks himself regularly. *Who else would I have met? What would they have been like?* From here his mind boggles with the endless variations his life would have—no, he dwells, *could* have—been. He finds his life mutating into other men's lives. He slaps the wheel of a wheezing car, saying out loud, "But *no.*"

Instead, he did meet Ashley, and after they both graduated and moved back home, she continued to take courses (for some insane reason, Craig always thought) at the community college. He got the office job where he's been ever since, which he took because he was bored and poverty just didn't seem so bohemian anymore.

He thinks of Ashley tonight, right now, looking very cute, in her face all the moments of happiness they have ever shared in the past couple of years. Why were the bad times now like a tide that seemed to float in every couple of days? Couldn't they move farther inland? He laughs, knowing that instead of cursing the hand of fate, he should chop off his own hand, the one that still derives childish pleasure out of unbuttoning strange skirts, caressing unfamiliar necks, feeling breasts never touched before. Tonight Ashley was herself; no hint of the fight from two nights ago, like everything could be forgiven if he'd just . . . what? Propose? Get a lobotomy? Castrated? Tonight was great, sure, but what about tomorrow? "What about tomorrow," Craig says out loud, wondering where his dick is going to end up tonight.

He hangs a right, goes past the cafe, sees Eileen just stepping out onto the sidewalk. Looking in the rearview mirror he can see her running a hand through her gorgeous black hair. His chest starts thumping; all the old feelings come back, the machinery creaking but holding together. "Come on, baby," he whispers his best Hans Solo, "hold together."

He stumbles getting out of the car, hoping she doesn't notice but she does. She is stifling a laugh as he approaches.

"Wow, you look great," Craig says on cue.

"Aw," she feigns, like she's supposed to. Looking in the mirror just minutes before, Eileen was thinking, "Damn, I *do* look good." She's wearing a black tank top, black shoes, and gray herringbone slacks.

"So . . ." Craig says awkwardly.

"So."

After thirty seconds Craig suggests, "Want to get a bite to eat?"

Bite to eat? Craig chides himself. *What am I? An agent in Beverly Hills?*

"Sure," Eileen agrees. "Where at?"

"I don't know. What do you feel like?"

"Anything, really."

As Eileen waits for Craig to be a man and make a decision, he's waiting for the same thing.

"How about this Thai restaurant that just opened up?" Eileen finally suggests. "My boss says it's good, but I've never been there. It's even within walking distance."

"Thai?" Craig says with a straight face. He hates Thai food. "Sure."

They begin walking down the hill away from the cafe, striking up various bonfires of small talk.

"It's been so cool lately."

"God, I'm glad that humidity's gone."

"Yeah"—fake laugh—"you're telling me."

As they turn a corner and Craig falls back a step to let Eileen walk ahead of him, he notices the tight-fitting slacks and the straight line her waving hair makes across her back. He can smell her rosy perfume wafting in the air. He drinks it up, catching a buzz.

"Here it is."

He opens the door for her, only to be met with another set of doors a few feet in. He knocks into her, racing for the brass handle before she touches it, only barely managing to reach it in time. They are shown to a table by the window, overlooking Cedar Pine Road.

"This place is nice," Craig says.

"Yeah," Eileen replies, "nicer than I thought. I thought it'd be like a Chinese take-out joint. This isn't too elaborate for you, is it?"

A young waitress comes up and hands him a wine list as two busboys regally unfold their napkins and place them in their laps. A third approaches, places a fresh rose in the vase near a dish of dark sauce, and lights a candle in what looks like a stand carved out of jade. Looking down he sees that a glass of the house chablis is five bucks. "No, no," Craig says, beginning to sweat. "It's fine."

"Mmmm, I don't know what to get." Eileen's eyes are running over the items quickly. "That *mee grob* really looks good. Or how about that *tom yum koong?*"

Craig is totally baffled by the menu. Left to his own devices his regimen would consist of Taco Bell and Pizza Hut—or an exotic combination of the two. The only reason he agreed to Thai was to seem like a casual guy, but right now he's leaning on the window, the golden arches of the McDonald's in Moore's Mall almost visible. He gulps.

"What would you like?" the waitress asks. After Eileen orders *pla kong* with a side order of *koaw noodle,* Craig rambles off the name of one of the few dishes that has chicken in the title, thinking, *How bad can it be?* To avoid looking like a total cheapskate he orders two glasses of wine.

"So how long have you been in Kitty?" Craig asks.

"Is it so obvious I'm not from here?"

"It's a small town," he says.

Eileen takes a breath before launching into the expurgated version of her life story.

While she's talking Craig finds himself getting hot, not because of his attraction to Eileen but because of his thick denim shirt and the lack of cool air blowing inside. He can feel the sweat forming under his arms and on his face. *Can she see? Is it obvious?* He excuses himself to go to the bathroom, and once inside wipes his face with toilet paper. He splashes his face with cold water, but some drips onto his shirt, and his bangs look cheesily slicked back. "Fuck!" He slaps the hand dryer and holds his shirt under it, then the front of his head.

"Everything okay?" Eileen asks, noticing Craig's hair sticking up an inch higher than before.

"Yeah," he says, his ears still warm. "Why?"

The food arrives, and Craig is even more perplexed than before. The menu said B.B.Q. Chicken, but they have delivered half a chicken, bones sticking out, leg still attached, all a light pink, along with some rice, a pasty brown sauce, and a tortilla-like pastry. For a second he picks up the chicken to eat it like a piece of Kentucky Fried but thinks better of it and takes knife and fork, beginning the battle for chunks of meat.

Delighted, Eileen tears into her dish of grilled shrimp mixed with mint leaves, savoring each bite. With some of the awkward small talk and inevitable, patented first-date-brand exposition out of the way, she becomes relaxed, orders another glass of wine, begins enjoying herself. She looks at Craig, obviously not happy with his meal but afraid to do anything for fear of looking bad in front of someone he's trying hard to impress. The waitress could have brought raw pork chops, Eileen figures, and Craig would have taken them, said thank-you, and tipped big, just because he didn't want to make a fuss or even hint at the possibility that he wasn't a man in total control. She can't help but be attracted to this boyish quality, his rosy cheeks, his slightly goofy demeanor.

"So you know all about my life, but where do you live?" she asks.

"Uh, other side of town. Near Kitty High. Well, across from it, sort of." He fumbles his words.

"Do you have a roommate or live alone?" She dips the tip of the pitalike pastry into the small dish of peanut sauce and delicately pops it in her mouth.

"R-r-roommate."

"Do you guys get along, or is he a jerk or what?"

"We, um, get along . . . most of the time," he answers, failing to clarify.

"That's cool, because I've had so many horrible roommate situations in the past couple of years. And it's so sad because you go into it as best friends, thinking it's just going to be the best thing in the world, and you usually come out hating each other."

"Yeah," he mumbles, trying to saw a bone in half with his butter knife. "I know the feeling."

After a few more minutes of Craig wrestling with his plate and Eileen cleaning hers, the waitress again approaches the table.

"Any dessert or coffee this evening?"

"Ugh." Eileen shudders. "I just today got that coffee smell out of my nose. No, thanks." She turns to Craig, who has a speck of food stuck to his cheek. "But do you want to maybe split a dessert?"

"Um." Craig is quickly adding the bill in his head, trying to remember how much his entree was, and hers, and how many glasses of wine she ended up ordering. He only brought sixty bucks, and he seriously doubts that'll cover it. "None for me, thanks. Stuffed." His voice cracks. "But feel free to order some for yourself," he says, using his mental powers to sway her decision into voting in the negative.

"I think I'll . . ." Eileen rolls her eyes, her brain making that crucial decision. "No, I've had enough, thanks."

"Just the check." Craig lets out a huge breath.

The check comes to $56.35. Craig gulps. He throws down three twenties and then hurries Eileen out of there, fearful that the waitress will return, spot the skimpy tip, and demand an explanation.

"Come on, let's go!"

"Okay." She is laughing. "All right. Boy, you're crazy."

As the evening wears on, Eileen feels herself filling with emotion for Craig, and she wants to stop it because he still a relative stranger. They walk around the neighborhood, the air cooler than before, the night sky completely black. The conversation flows more smoothly, and Craig becomes more himself and Eileen lets down her guard.

It's funny, she thinks, how we give our hearts to those who haven't really earned the right yet. And then later we wish there was a more discreet distribution policy. But with Craig's bright eyes filled with clouds, and his warm hand creeping around her waist, what can she do? There's plenty she can do. Like go home and watch "China Beach" on channel 15. Or do her laundry.

But the warmth of another person is like that overgrown, mysterious road you can't help driving down. It's been a dead end before, but maybe this time it will lead someplace exciting or someplace you've never been before.

Eileen breathes in, puts her chest out, tries to make herself attractive. She feels as if she's selling herself, as though she should wear a sandwich board that reads GOOD COOK! LOW MILEAGE! A STEAL! Craig needs her as some sort of fucked-up antidote, and in her own camouflaged way, she needs him right back. It is amazing how many times a day this sort of thing happens over the world.

"Want to come up?"

"Sure."

"This is a *real* nice place," Craig says, walking around Eileen's cluttered apartment. "I especially like the jeans-on-the-floor look. I think I saw Todd Oldham do something about that on 'House of Style' the other day."

"Sorry." Eileen pushes past him, gathers up the dirty clothes from the floor. As she scurries around trying to pick up the cotton debris on the floor, she forms a triage system of priority in her head. *First: the panties and bras. Second: the dirty socks and T-shirts. Third: fast food containers and . . . Wait, no! First: Tampon box!*

Craig saunters over to the window, ignoring Eileen as she runs back and forth to the bathroom, burying something underneath the pillow and sliding everything on top of a dresser into the top drawer with a sweep of her arm.

"Nice view," he says.

"Yeah, I guess it is," she responds, slightly out of breath. "Late at night the moon passes right over and really lights up the room. Sometimes I just sit in bed and read by it."

"I never even knew Kitty *had* a view. I thought the closest thing we had was being intellectually nearsighted, but this is really great."

Craig turns away from the window, looks furtively around the room, then at Eileen, whose own eyes lock with his. Somewhat embarrassingly, he pulls away. The room is quiet except for the not-so-faint rumbling of discussion and clanking of crockery in the cafe below. To mask some of the noise, Eileen pops a cassette into her stereo. A second later bluesy music with whispered female vocals gently fills the room.

"Opal," she says.

"Nice."

"Thanks."

"Hey, I hope I'm not intruding here," Craig says sincerely. "I don't mean to keep you from anything. I mean, if it's getting late . . ."

"No, no . . . don't be silly." She motions for Craig to sit down in a chair. "I just wasn't expecting to show off my new apartment so soon. I guess I never realized how messy it was."

"So this was . . . unexpected?" Craig asks slyly.

"Yeah, I guess," Eileen admits, blushing.

She lights a few candles before joining Craig on the couch.

As they talk he gently puts his arm around her. He tells a few jokes and she laughs, relaxing, the night and the wine and the half a Valium she swallowed while in the bathroom numbing her body.

Looking at Craig as the light of a candle hits his face, illuminating a few acne scars and even a wrinkle, Eileen thinks, *The big leagues*. She feels old, an adult, and now it no longer seems cute to drift from bed to bed or relationship to relationship. Somewhere along the line the rules changed, but her reaction to all the input she received has not. They aren't two kids experimenting anymore, just out to have fun. By now both partners know more, they know better. And yet they continue on, like those Apache Indians who put on tribal gear and keep the rituals of their ancestors alive. Craig plants a quick kiss, his tongue bobs underneath her earlobe, and Eileen's hand runs through his hair, frizzy and curled at the ends.

"Mmmm." Craig makes noises. "Mmmm hmmmm." Not words or even a grunt, just a queer buzz of sound, coasting his lips across her bare neck.

Craig unzips her pants and takes her top off over her head. With her arms stretching above her head, she is flooded by the memory of her father putting on her pajamas when she was a small child. The image leaves her cold, queasy, and she strikes it from her mind.

Eileen reciprocates, unfastening Craig's belt, pushing down his pants, and a second later the belt buckle clanks against the floor.

"Sorry," Craig says a second after Eileen startles at the touch of his cold hand against her back.

She's nervous. She tries to pull up this awkward feeling every time just to keep herself from feeling jaded, numb. Only it's always artificial, and inevitably sadness creeps in, the YOUR NAME HEREness of it all, the geometry of filling space, and the realization that the tools can really be found anywhere.

"You feel nice." Craig delivers a stock line, his pants at his feet in a puddle.

"Thanks, um, so do you," Eileen replies, as if returning a weak serve.

They fall onto the bed, and it squeaks like a baby being strangled.

"Jesus, what's that?" asks Craig, pulling away for a second.

"It's the bed." Eileen laughs. "Sorry, I should have warned you."

Craig laughs it off, trying like hell to concentrate and keep a flailing erection.

They continue to kiss, shedding their clothes, until all Craig is wearing is a pair of plaid boxers and Eileen her black underwear. They try to ignore the awful noise of the bed as they roll around kissing and hugging, but it finally becomes too much.

"Jesus," says Craig in a whisper, the bed still shaking. "I'll bet they can hear this downstairs," he jokes.

"I know," Eileen says. "I'll bet they're all looking up here wondering what the hell—" She stops, thinking of Jess. "Look, let's . . ." She was about to say "stop" when Craig beats her to it.

"Why don't we try the floor?"

"Sure."

They slide onto the cool hardwood floor. Eileen winces as she lies down; the cold floor feels like a burn on her warm back. After a few seconds her skin becomes numb, then finally adjusts, her own warmth soaking into the floor.

Craig clumsily climbs on top of her, his penis poking through the flap in his shorts. As if doing a repetition of one-handed push-ups, he supports his weight with one hand while easing off her bra and then panties with the other, switching every few seconds before the arm becomes too tired.

I've got to get in shape . . . and get a new car.

Following his lead, Eileen tugs at his shorts, then pulls them off with the big toe of her right foot.

They kiss for a few more minutes, rolling around on the floor, wincing as they stray away from the small patch of floor they've warmed with their bodies. Craig scoots off and sits up for a second, reaching over to his jeans to pull out a condom, hoping it doesn't look too staged that he had brought one with him. *This was just in case,* he thinks of saying. Or maybe, *Didn't know they were in these jeans.* Surely anything was better than the truth: *I brought this because I hoped we'd fuck tonight.* Followed by a lascivious, *Heh heh.*

He rips the package in half, pulls out the vanilla-colored condom. Instantly the sterile hospital-room smell hits him, and he tries to figure out in the half-dark which side is up. He places it, like a beanie, over his erect cock and begins to roll it down, only it's facing the wrong way, so after thirty seconds of struggling it's still in a flabby disc. Eileen is now whistling a song, trying to remember if she has to work the next day, cursing when she remembers: yes, early. Craig turns it over and rolls it down, a snug fit as always, clamping down tightly at the shaft. The ends of a few pubic hairs caught in the hem are pulled out as Craig turns around and gets on top of Eileen. He winces.

"What's wrong?"

"Nothing."

She guides him into her. Both of them breathe easily after it's through. He begins to move slowly, trying to become accustomed to this strange body when he is already so used to Ashley's. He tries the same tricks he uses with her, that exact wiggle of the hips, one hand under her pelvis, girding his midsection into hers, but none of it seems to be working. As he blows in Eileen's ear, Eileen wishes like hell he would stop.

His knees, firmly anchored on the hardwood floor, crack with each stroke; his bony elbows are propped up on the firm floor. Eileen's coccyx rams into the floor bluntly every few seconds. Craig stops, and they both laugh mildly at what has become a painful situation.

"This hurts so bad, it's almost kinky," Craig says, delivering a tiny kiss between her eyes.

"I know." She tries to lift her head up but brings it down on the hard floor with a thud. "Someone should start humming 'Venus in Furs.'"

They both laugh, the tension of the moment breaking. Craig starts moving again, and Eileen starts concentrating, moving her hips against his. After fifteen minutes both of them come, Eileen a few seconds before a surprised Craig who had no idea she was that close.

Cool, he thinks quickly, rolling off to remove the condom before he loses his erection.

Both of them sit up and lean against the bed. Craig puts his arm around Eileen, who is watching the shapes their shadows are making on the walls and ceiling.

"That was really—" Craig begins before she cuts him off.

"Look, don't say it, okay? You don't have to."

"Say what?"

"That it was 'so good for me.'" She mimics his deep voice.

"Well, it was." He shrugs, kisses her hair.

"Aw, it's just such a cliché. I'd think you were saying it just to say it." She stops herself. "Jeez, I'm cynical. Isn't that sad?"

"Sad?" Craig scoops her in his arms. "I think it's kind of . . . cute."

Eileen laughs, feeling comfortable in this stranger's arms even though she is completely naked in more than just a physical way. She thinks, *Maybe this one's different.*

"Well." Craig fake-yawns. "I should be going."

Then again, maybe he's not.

As Craig find his clothes from the various corners of the room, Eileen walks to the bathroom and returns in a white terry-cloth robe. Craig grabs her and holds her tight.

"Call you tomorrow?"

"I have to work. Why don't I call you?"

"You'd better not."

"Why?"

"Tell you what, why don't I just stop by on Saturday and say hi? Maybe we'll plan something to do then?"

"Oh," she says. "Okay."

"I really had a good time tonight. I mean that." He looks into her eyes.

"Me, too."

He kisses her on the lips, both cheeks, and the neck before leaving.

Eileen walks slowly to her bed, sits down softly, greeting the squeaks like language, voices assuring her she did the right thing.

Seconds later there is a knock at the door that wakes Eileen out of half-sleep.

"Craig?" she calls out. "What is it? What'd you forget?"

The door opens. Don walks quickly into the room, a harried expression on his face.

"Who in the fuck is Craig?" The words come quick, his chest moving up and down. "That asshole who was just in here? Huh?"

"Don!" she shouts. "What? How? When?" She has so many questions, she can't decide which to ask first. "What are you doing here?"

"I came here to see you, just to say hi . . . but instead I find . . ." His hands rush around in front of his chest. His eyes become accustomed to the dark, spot a familiar pair of underwear in the corner, a pair of pants he used to love. In the air hangs an aroma of stale sperm and latex that does not go unnoticed by Don.

"Jesus Christ!" he shouts, his voice soaked with tears. "What in the hell is going on with you, Eileen? Just three months ago you were screaming out as we were making love that I was the only one, and now it turns out I was just the next in line."

"Look, I don't know what to tell you . . ."

The words trail off, the tail of a comet, smaller and smaller until finally there's nothing.

"What do you mean? Tell me what in the fuck is going on. What are you still doing in this shitty little town?"

"Trying to"—Eileen gets up and paces around the floor— "get away for a while."

"Get away from what? From me?"

"Yeah, I guess." She shrugs. The answer doesn't sound right to her, either. "You, my parents, my old life, everything."

"But why?" His voice is shaky. His hair falls onto his exhausted face, which even under the strain is still shockingly handsome. "I don't understand."

"You think *I* do?"

"Come back with me tonight." Don wipes away tears with his sleeve. "We'll send for your stuff. We'll leave right now. In my car."

"Don't make it seem like you're rescuing me, Don. Fuck, that's one of the reasons I left. I don't need a goddamn hero. I can leave whenever I want to."

"But your mom said that your car— "

She twirls the excess length of the robe's belt in circles and falls onto the bed. "That was just an excuse. I mean, yeah, the car did break down, but I had it fixed a week ago. It wasn't a big deal."

"You mean you actually want to stay here?"

"Yeah, and do you know why? Because for the first time in my life this is something that I've carved out for myself. You didn't hand it to me with a ribbon around it, and Mom and Dad didn't buy it for me."

"Look"—Don swallows, making a pained face—"I'm willing to forget about this guy if you'll just get your stuff and—"

"Guys," she mutters.

"What?"

"It hasn't been just that guy. I've been seeing a few guys." Eileen regrets the words the moment they leave her mouth. She was getting mad, but she could see that every syllable she spit out at him was like an anvil falling on top of him, that after each sentence Don appeared an inch shorter.

"You used to be a virgin!" he shouts.

"We all did! I mean, Jesus, you act like I've been cheating on you. No! We've been broken up for three months. I'm getting on with my life, so don't act like I've done something wrong!" Eileen shouts, only she knows it's not the truth. Jess's face appears as an apparition, floating in from the open window: *But I love you, too.* She slams the shutter.

"Okay, okay. You wanted some time alone. Fine. You got it. You got it out of your system." Don, shaking, points at the door. "Now pack your bags because I'm taking you home."

"Bull-fucking-shit, Don! You're not taking me anywhere! Quit acting like I'm Blanche Du Bois and that you're doing this in *my* best interest. You just can't face the fact that I'm living alone and doing what you've been doing all these years."

Don flinches, as if someone has shoved a hat pin through the back of a voodoo doll bearing his likeness.

"Oh, so that's it, is it? You got to be a womanizer all those years, sleeping with every lameass lit major from Georgetown to William and Mary, but heaven forbid I see what life is like out there."

"And?" Don roars. "Did you like it?"

"Don." Eileen starts to cry. "Why don't you just leave?" She chokes.

"Marry me," he says quickly, as if he just thought of it.

"What?" She dangles her feet over the side of the bed, flaking pink nail polish catching her eye for a moment.

"You heard me," he says with renewed enthusiasm, as if he can't believe he hadn't thought of it before, as if what was so irrational before now made complete sense. The thing is, it *had* made sense to *her* before, but not to him. "Marry me," he says again.

"Don." She swats at the air, the suggestion only making her angrier. "No."

"But . . . why?"

"I'm not marrying you. I'm not marrying anyone. I've got to . . . figure some things out first."

"Like what? Like how to fuck even more guys?"

Eileen shakes her head slowly, looks Don over.

"Just get out of here," she says, now more tired than anything else. "Just . . . leave me alone." The words fall out of her mouth.

Don looks as if he's about to speak, his eyes plaintive, his upper lip bearing down on the bottom as if about to separate and spew a roomful of knowledge. But it just doesn't come. He pours the pot but nothing comes out, not even a drop. Whatever it was that fueled him on the drive down from Baltimore has boiled away, evaporated into the cool, clear night.

Don turns and walks out slowly, each step down the staircase echoing up the dark hallway. Eileen lies on the bed and begins crying, feeling Craig between her legs, Don in her heart, and

Jess still somewhere in the building, wondering where she's supposed to fit in.

Now how does this work again?

On the street below Don runs into Jess, who is staring up at Eileen's window, wondering where the other figure just went. Jess has been hearing cries and shouts all night and has barely held back the urge to run up the bare stairs to her rescue.

Don storms down the street, notices Jess, and puts the puzzle together.

"Hey," Don says, nudging Jess in the side, "you football or baseball?" His voice is scratchy, about to disappear.

"What?" Jess says at first, shaken out of thought. He tears his eyes away from the window and trains them for a second on the stranger. "Oh, I'm sorry. Uh . . . neither," he finally answers. "I don't play contact sports."

Before Don turns to walk away, to begin the long drive home, he says sadly, "Wanna bet?"

D. I. Why?

1

Ashley wakes up early after tossing and turning all night. She turns and sees Craig, who wasn't there when she went to sleep. She stumbles out of the room, though not as quietly as she thinks, knocking her knee against the side of the door, slamming the bathroom door, and bumping into Craig's alarm clock. He wakes up for a moment, just as Ashley is leaving the room, and pretends to be asleep; he watches her body leave, a blurry image through half-closed eyes.

Ashley gets out a mug and puts in it a packet of Earl Grey tea. She searches the countertop for the silver-and-black kettle, then the cupboards, but it's nowhere to be found. Finally, in the cupboards next to the refrigerator (the ones that open up only halfway because the fridge is too big for its space), she spots the kettle shoved way in the back. As she reaches for it, something bright catches her eye. She pulls out the object that glints off a ray of light as well as the kettle.

The object that attracted her attention is a photo of her and Craig that certainly is no secret (in fact she noticed it was missing last time she cleaned but couldn't find it). She figured it had been misplaced the way things are always being randomly lost, like half a pair of socks or car keys, scissors or phone numbers written on scraps of paper. But what is new to her is the thick crack that runs down the length of the photo, separating the two of them like the work of a guillotine.

Did he do this?

She knows where he was the night before, or at least has an idea and is fairly positive it is not where he said he was. A few names present themselves—Brook (as Andrew had been suggesting) or that new receptionist in his office—but nothing really concrete. She can just feel him . . . away.

It isn't as if they are drifting apart and Ashley is plainly losing him. It's more than that. Or maybe less. They are just so bored with their lives that they interpret this as being bored with each other, and so they fuck around, trying to add some spice to a meager existence, trying to give romance a purpose once again since they have found domestic life—and its prequel-like feeling to marriage—not wholly unsatisfying but just plain boring. Faced with what life was going to be like for the next fifty years, they rebel in the only way they think there is. The more they try to drive away their feelings for each other by being with others, the more they find themselves oddly drawn to each other in the most fucked-up ways imaginable. If only they could admit that they cheated on each other, then they could say how much they hated it. They would both agree that it was a hollow, useless experience, and they could put it down as just another item in a long line of things they had in common.

After two weeks of hardly a word to each other that wasn't either shouted (usually Craig) or whispered in tears (almost always Ashley, unless Craig stubbed a toe, and even then he held back from crying), Craig and Ashley search their exhausted minds for answers. It has gotten to the point where she doesn't even give him good news anymore, and she isn't even sure why. She received a great grade in school the other day, the chances of getting into graduate school are looking better all the time, and yet it just seems such a struggle to tell him, as if the exposition alone, "Well, first there was this test," would wear her out, not to mention having to muster up excitement for someone who can't bother to be excited back. And the thought of gloating, of shoving her own good fortune into Craig's increasingly drooping face has never entered her mind, either, but not because she deemed it cruel or unfair but because it was just too much of an effort as well.

Ashley sips her tea, and a pattering of footsteps in the hall outside their door reminds her of when she and Craig first moved in with each other two years ago. They were so excited. Every weekend they scoured flea markets and garage sales for an end table, a lamp, an endless string of useless bric-a-brac to decorate their empty apartment. They pooled their money together and bought a used color TV whose color leaned a little on the green side, and for the first season of "Melrose Place" Craig thought everyone was sick but still good-looking. The VCR had been donated by his father, and when recording a program, the screen would often become gray, and only slapping the machine repeatedly in a certain section in the lower left of the unit restored the picture. (Ashley proved better at this than Craig, and it was only after Craig gave it a few valiant but fruitless swats that he stepped aside for Ashley, who always got it on the first try.) More than a few times they came home to watch an episode of "Saturday Night Live" that they had taped using the timer (another feature that only Ashley could figure out), only to rewind the program to find what appeared was a dull gray screen with the sound track behind it. One night, after returning at four in the morning, they opened another bottle of wine and watched the show sans picture, trying to figure out what was going on, laughing outrageously loudly at jokes that were—aided by the alcohol—funny.

A month after they moved in, the quiet pair of female roommates upstairs moved out; they were replaced two months later with what Craig and Ashley then considered an "old" couple. The man seemed about twenty-nine and the girl pushing twenty-seven. As Craig and Ashley are now only a few years away from those twilight times themselves, they don't consider them so old, but still Craig always smirked to himself when the guy was home alone and blasted The Clash or Elvis Costello, thinking, *Give it up, old-timer.* This couple, while charming at first, on occasion fought like cats and dogs. One morning Craig and Ashley woke up when the man was searching around in the bushes outside the apartment complex, the girl calling out in a deeply southern-twinged voice, "I'm sorry, Patrick. I don't know where I threw 'em!" For a year and a half, every couple of weeks or so, the couple yelled and screamed and shouted death threats at each other while Craig and Ashley downstairs were discovering cute little things about each other that had somehow escaped their notice during courtship: "Oh, you like ketchup on your eggs? How cute!" "You don't brush your teeth before you

go to bed? How, uh, cute." There were at least a dozen nights
that Ashley lay in bed listening to the couple upstairs toss their
hate back and forth like a beach ball on fire, while Craig, the big
oaf, slept soundly next to her. She would curl up next to her
lover, burying her head deep in his chest, twining her legs and
arms through his as if he were a trellis and she was a sinewy
vine. Then she would cry a thankful tear that *she* was not like
that and that *they* were happy and always would be.

And now, just a few years later, she finds herself getting
strange looks in the laundry room from the young girl who lives
below them.

Ashley starts crying, staring into her mug. The reflection staring back at her is blurry, undulating, wavering like her own
stance. She hears a rustling behind her as Craig shuffles into the
room, the bottom of his slippers making a scratchy sound
against the hardwood floor.

"Want to, uh, go downtown?" Craig says, his eyes darting to
the various corners of the room. "Do some shopping?"

"Yes."

2

Randy's slightly blurred vision stares at the black-and-white
photo of The Deer Park on the cover of *Godfuck.* The photo was
taken with a shaky hand by Chipp with one of those disposable
cameras that you just aim, click, and then throw away. After
being developed and blown up at Kinko's and then run off
hundreds of times, the copy of a copy of a copy of a not-so-great
original is dark and soaked with shadows, unclear, shitty. Randy
tries to think positive: evocative, moody. Even if someone were
to point out that you can barely tell who it is, that the photo
looks as if it were drawn by a child and then washed in black
water, Randy still wouldn't listen or care. "This is cool," he says
softly. "I did this."

As he looks over the magazine, a smile grows on his face. It is something he can point to that is a concrete example of his *work*, something he'd *done*. Usually the only things around that he did are mistakes, like getting kicked out of college, Jen hating him, used condoms, empty bottles. But this was something he looked at as a victory, even if it did scare people.

He turns the page, not even reading but just glancing at the way the type fits in with the photos and the crude line drawings he made at the last second while Chipp was freaking out about the cover. He reaches the end, closes it, and begins again from the beginning. He's been staring at the only copy of *Godfuck* in existence for the past two hours. It looks better than he expected, and it doesn't really matter about the sections that were done at the last second (stuck down with large gobs of glue or Scotch tape), where you can easily see the marks of the tape or where the rubber cement dried in dark clots that showed up as black dots, because the *spirit* is there. Randy sneers at the thought of those computers with expensive programs that lay the whole thing out for you, typesetting the entire magazine into some trendy Emigre font in a matter of seconds, reversed headlines, bold, italic, et cetera. That's so cold, sterile, so removed from blood and sweat and human emotions. It's like that music he can't stand that's created wholly by computers, synthesizers, samples. There isn't a human element involved except for the lone forefinger and maybe a thumb to turn the things on and off. In the pages of *Godfuck* he can see himself, the hours, the work, the decisions, even the struggles. He smiles, looking into the rough pages as if into a mirror.

"Jesus, Randy," Chipp mumbles, his voice gravelly. He rises off the couch where he passed out at about four the previous night. "What time is it?"

Randy takes another sip of water, further putting out the alcohol-fueled fire in his brain.

"It's almost two."

"In the afternoon?" Chipp asks incredulously.

"Yeah." Randy laughs, closes the magazine, turns it over, and starts again.

Chipp pries his heavy eyelids apart, can see Randy sitting at the kitchen table. Around him are strewn paper cups, cigarette butts, beer cans, and a few trodden pages of *Godfuck* here and there.

"Got to get . . ." he mumbles, trying to get up, but the headache forces him back down. "The Cleaner . . ."

Randy laughs, goes to the kitchen, fills up a mug with water, and hands it to Chipp along with a Goody's Powder packet. Chipp takes the small folded piece of paper with the white medicine in it, empties the dust on his tongue, and washes it down with a large gulp of water. He grimaces as he forces the chalky substance down his throat, takes another sip to get the residue and aftertaste out of his mouth.

"They taste like shit," Chipp groans, "but they work."

After a few minutes of easing himself up slowly, like a diver rising to the surface gradually, Chipp gets off the couch, avoiding the hangover bends. He sits at the table with Randy.

"Hey, is that a copy of the zine?"

"Yeah," Randy says proudly. "The only one."

Chipp drains the last of the water from his cup.

"And? What do you think?" he asks.

His roommate sort of shrugs, tries to decide how much to tell him. He doesn't want to appear wishy-washy, to say he feels great, that this marks a turning point in his life, which it actually did, because to turn onto one street is to admit you were once on another, and Randy isn't ready to divulge information like that, especially to Chipp.

"It's . . ," he begins, hesitating, ". . . okay."

"Just okay?" Chipp says, surprised. "Hmmph. I thought it turned out pretty good." He snatches it out of Randy's hands, who hates to see it go, and flips through it. "I mean, considering we threw it together in a few weeks."

As Chipp flips through the magazine, Randy returns to the thoughts he's been engrossed in since he woke up.

"Do you ever think about us getting jobs again?" Randy asks. "I mean, what in the fuck are we doing?"

"Well . . ." Chipp says, amazed, as if he's been ambushed. He expects this sort of thing from his father, but from Randy? The most serious chastening Randy has handed down in the past few months was when Chipp passed on seeing Red Kross in order to see the Afghan Whigs instead. "You know the, uh, job market is tough out there. The, you know, the economy's so bad. There's that—what's it called?—oh, yeah, recession."

"Oh, that's bullshit." Randy slaps his hand down on the table.

"I was with you when we walked past the Wal-Mart and they had that big hairy NOW HIRING sign out front, and we just kept on going, hoping we weren't late for the opening band, trying to pretend we didn't see it. Jesus, Chipp, let's just be fucking honest. There may be a recession out there, but for two decent-looking white guys like us, you know we could get a job if we wanted to. We can talk and write . . . usually. You know why we walked on by Wal-Mart pretending that it didn't exist?"

"Why?" Chipp dumbly asks.

"Because we could never imagine ourselves working in a stupidass place like that. We could never picture ourselves wearing one of those godawful name tags on those aprons they make you wear. You know? Heaven forbid."

"Oh, and where's all this coming from? Since when did you get so high and mighty? I remember when Todd was looking for someone to help out at the door at The Scene, and the job included working three nights a week, seeing all of the shows for free, not to mention being able to snag beers off the bartender who's too dumb to notice, and *you* turned it down. Why?"

Randy folds his arms, remembering full well but wishing to push past it.

"I'll tell you why, since you must have obliterated that memory file sometime last night. You said that you didn't want to work late on the weekends because that dumb Siskel and Ebert show had just been moved to nine o'clock on Saturday morning, and you wanted to be able to wake up in time to see it. Sound familiar?"

"That was six months ago, for Christ's sake, and Todd also said I was going to have to mop up the sweat off the floor after the shows, and that just grossed me out."

"See!" Chipp shouts. "You're just as bad as I am, so don't get all righteous with me just because I think I could do a little bit better than working at the Kmart, Target, or whatever."

"Sure, you could, but do you try?"

Chipp starts to say something but then stops, the words shoved out of his head by a dull, throbbing pain.

"Did you ever look into registering at the JC?"

"Oh, fuck community college," Chipp says with a scowl. "That place is like goddamn day care. I know people who are still going there five years after they graduated from high school. And anyway, junior college, college, even those pinheads getting their master's degree or even their doctorate, it's all just an excuse to stay out of life, *real* life. I mean, can you imagine being, like, twenty-six and walking around a campus with a backpack on, schlepping to class every day? Not me. And you show me a fucking philosophy graduate student, and I'll still show you a guy who reads *Penthouse* just like you and me. And these are the people who are doing it right? Excuse me, but that's the same damn routine we've all been following since kindergarten. College is just a big excuse to live off loans, avoid a real job, and lie on lawns all day *reading*. Only in graduate school you write thoughtfully in the margins. Ten years before that you scribbled on the cover with crayons." Chipp moans audibly. "Big fucking difference."

Randy looks over at his ranting roommate and laughs. He examines his eyes, his thin face, remembering the first time he saw him in his freshman science class. Chipp was across the room with some kids Randy didn't know, cutting up, making jokes, laughing loudly, disrupting class. Randy got mad and wanted to tell Chipp to shut up, wait for him after school, and shove his faded Converse All Star high-tops, which had been crudely converted into low-tops with what must have been an ax, down his skinny little throat. The next day the seating assignment was changed, and they ended up sitting next to each other, forced to be lab partners. By the end of the week they were best friends, stealing the stretchy plastic tubing from the Bunsen burners, tying one end, and sticking the tip of a ballpoint pen in the other, filling them up with water, and creating a crude fire-hose device known as a Water Weenie.

Since then they had been through a lot, and Randy could point out several places where Chipp's face had changed over the years. Where his head used to be more round, anchored with sheaves of baby fat around his cheeks, it was now slim, almost gaunt, his cheekbones jutting out of his head. His scrawny arms were still scrawny, but he had put on a few bands of ribbony muscle around his shoulders and had grown a few inches, but not many. While Randy shot up to a little above six feet, Chipp stayed almost exactly where he was that first week in Mr. Fox's science class at Kitty High: five-six.

Randy grins. He would like to tell Chipp what he's thinking, but he's afraid Chipp would misread him, call him a wuss.

"The point I'm trying to get across," Randy says, "is that every three weeks or so we drink a shitload of beer and get real sentimental, talking about how we want to direct music videos or open up an all-ages club in town or something. But when the morning comes we've totally forgotten it, like our goals in life are just some hangover we take a pill to get rid of. It's always just bullshit."

"Those are pretty strong words, especially coming from you." Chipp counters Randy's attack with some ammunition of his own. "What was that great idea you had about writing a novel from the point of view of the 'Full House' twins? Or that book about the psychological dichotomy of a D.C. drive-by murderer, entitled *Doppelgangbanger?*"

"I still have the notes for those!" Randy insists, whipping out his finger like a conductor's baton. "I'm just waiting for some, you know, time."

"Look, we're carving out our own niche, and, well, I'm completely happy with the life I'm leading. By the way, you didn't throw out that half-empty box of stale Saltines, did you? I was planning to have them for dinner."

In the moment of silence that follows, both sets of eyes gravitate (after looking over the bra in the corner) to the copy of their zine, *Godfuck.* They both realize, even though the words are not spoken, that their zine is the first thing in months, almost a year, that they finished. That they worked on, created, been proud of.

"Let's get to work." Randy points to the table.

Chipp gets up, the pain again swelling in his head, but he pushes it aside.

3

"There's nothing I can say that would convince you to stay?" Brenda asks, twirling her stout glass so the ice cubes are dancing, weaving in and out between a slice of orange and the cool orange juice and vodka.

"No," Eileen replies, stuffing a few more T-shirts into a gray duffel bag. "Sorry."

"But why?" Brenda asks, moving aside a pair of blue jeans on the bed, making room to sit down. "I don't understand."

"I don't understand, either," Eileen mumbles, cleaning out the medicine chest. She picks up the Sucrets pillbox, which rattles as she grabs it, and swallows the last Xanax. "I mean, I've got to go. I'm sorry if I'm letting you down."

"I guess I can find yet another waitress. It's just"—Brenda holds back a burp—"I thought you liked it here."

"I do," Eileen says, thinking for a moment before amending it to: "I mean, I *did*."

"Well, what happened?"

Eileen pauses for a second, debating whether to unleash on Brenda the sordid events of the previous night: Don barging in with the scent of Craig still in the air as Jess's lovelorn ghost stalked the halls and whispered "Call me." Eileen decides against it.

"I just need a change."

"Now I know I don't know your entire life history, but I thought *this* was a change." Brenda waves her arms around the room.

"Well, then"—Eileen stops for a second and glances around the room—"another change." Eileen clumps across the floor and sits down on the couch. "I just hope I'm not leaving you in the lurch like this. I mean, I know employers like two weeks' notice, not to come in to find their employees packing up to leave. I really am sorry."

"That's okay. I won't lie and say I'm glad to see you go, but we'll manage around here. After all, Jess was practically handling it all around here before you, and—oh shit, have you told Jess?"

"No." Eileen shakes her head. "And I don't plan to."

"But he has a crush on you."

"That's just it. Why do you think they call them crushes? Because they end up squashing you."

Brenda laughs. She looks through the open door down the hall, to her own bedroom door, a list forming in her head of things to do that day: shopping, laundry, put out that damn HELP WANTED sign again.

"But it's not his fault," Eileen continues. "I guess I led him on. He's really a nice guy, it's just—"

"Not your type?"

"Yeah." She shakes her head, repeats the phrase: "Not my type."

"Boy, I don't know what it is with you kids," Brenda says.

Eileen's ears perk up at the mention of "kids."

"Kids? What kids? Who are you calling a kid?"

"You!" Brenda points at Eileen with her glass. "And Jess and every person who comes into my damn cafe with those bright eyes and dirty clothes, thinking they're going to change the world." She laughs.

"Well, they are going to change the world. That's a fact," says Eileen. "We're just not sure if it'll, um, be for the better."

Brenda laughs again, drains the last of her drink, and hopes she has more waiting for her in her apartment.

"Don't go, Eileen. I like having you around. You're funny. You're different. Come on, stay. What's so bad about Kitty you have to run away like this?"

Run away. Those two words hadn't appeared to her until now. *Run away.* They strike like lightning, causing her brain to blank, to rethink the entire situation. All morning she's been coming up with terms like "new beginning" and "fresh start," even borrowing one from *City Slickers:* "clean slate." But the concept of "running away" hadn't manifested itself until Brenda was kind enough to bring it up.

Eileen sits back, remembering how fast she used to be able to

run. How she felt awkward and out of place in P.E. class, so tall
and gangly, her long legs shooting out of her shorts like bean
stalks. How she could run around the track three times in the
time it took the other kids to do it only twice. One day at lunch,
around the fifth grade, she challenged Tommy Puljiz, the most
popular boy in school, to a race. He accepted, and a small crowd
gathered by the swing set to watch. Somebody yelled "Go!" and
they took off, around the baseball diamond, through the porch
off the library, and through the sand pit. The entire time
Tommy was lagging far behind Eileen, his short legs no match
for her. She seemed to leapfrog the distance in no time, and
when she crossed the makeshift finish line (some kid's blue
jacket covered in baseball teams' patches), Tommy was still far
behind, a small figure on the horizon trying desperately to keep
up with her.

"This is your last chance," Brenda jokes, getting off the bed
to head back to her own room.

Eileen watches her leave and closes the door behind her, another door closed, another world left behind.

4

"Knock, knock?"

Laura shakes herself out of a thought and looks up to see Jim
poking his orange head through her half-open front door, his
right hand in the air, his fingers curled, and his wrist jerking
back and forth as if rapping against a door.

"Anybody home?" he asks even though he's now staring right
into Laura's eyes.

"Yeah . . . sure . . ." She hesitates, trying to remember, *Did I
invite him over?* "I was just sort of . . ." She tries to make an
excuse but then forgets it.

"Thinking?" Jim suggests, letting himself in the door and
plopping down on an off-white recliner that's missing the footrest.

"Not really." Laura runs a hand through her hair, surprised to find her scalp is sweating. "More like worrying."

"About Mark?"

Bingo.

Laura doesn't want to let on too much to Jim, an old flame who in his mind has simply been turned on low, while Laura could have sworn she blew out the pilot years ago. And yet she never really forgot the fun they had together in high school, how with him she really felt free, like an equal, as opposed to Mark, where she felt more like a sounding board for his songs, words, tunes, ideas, and—during sex—his body. She and Jim met on everything halfway, while with Mark she was forced to traverse the entire length just to get his attention. But in high school that's what she wanted, or at least *thought* she should want. She was through with boyfriends as best friends and wanted someone to sweep her off her feet, the big-time romance she had been led to believe was happening out there all the time, so why not to her? But by the time she realized that the closest Mark would ever come to a white horse was the primered Mustang he borrowed for the prom from his pal Joey, Laura had already found enough reasons to fall in love with him, and Jim was relegated from back burner to that dusty corner of the attic with the web in front. But now? She looks across the room at Jim, his longish shock of red hair slightly frizzled, his crooked but white teeth continually curled into a smile, and the long, bamboolike fingernails on his right hand that he grew to La Toya Jackson length in order to finger-pick the guitar.

"Still thinking?" Jim says as he pulls a large green apple from his coat pocket. "I mean, *worry*ing?" He takes a deep bite of the apple, and for a second the flesh of the fruit fights with him and his teeth stay locked in the tougher-than-usual pulp. He tries to look cool as the sweet white juice dribbles down his chin, and he smiles, the piece of fruit like a boxer's mouthpiece clenched between his teeth and jutting out his cheeks.

Laura laughs for the first time all day. *Yeah*, she thinks, *Jim's not so bad.*

"So, Mark left yesterday?"

Laura nods her head in the affirmative, trails of her wispy ponytail bouncing off her neck.

"Yeah. I thought he was flying straight to L.A., but Phil, Steve's brother, called and wanted to know the number of Gary's friend in Charlotte where they were spending the night. I guess they're staying over for the night and will head out to California today. Jeez, dishonest right to the end."

"You know, a lot of people around town are asking me what happened. You know how small Kitty is, and, hell, that damn A & R man stuck out at the show last week like a sore thumb. Is it okay if I tell people what's going on?"

"What, with Mark?" Laura says curtly, shifting her weight on the couch. "Hell, tell them anything you want. After all, I'm not his fucking agent." She laughs to herself. *At least not anymore.*

Jim lets loose some churlish laughter. He twists the apple in his hand, examining it, looking for a new excavation site. Around the stem he finds a stretch of cherry skin, round, full, free of bruises. He goes in for the kill but stops quickly, thinking, *The stem.*

Trying to act inconspicuous, he grabs the thin brown root with his thumb and forefinger and begins twisting the apple around. *A, B, C, D* . . . he recites quietly in his head, adding small footnotes to each. *A, not A, please not A, not Amy, I dated her once and couldn't stand her. Shit, here comes E. Man, if it's Ellen, forget it, I'll do it over.*

Laura is going on about how Mark was trying to act nervous and sad at the airport when in reality she knew he was excited and didn't want it to show, and that he said he was leaving for no more than a couple of weeks.

" 'Go,' I said. 'Have fun.' But he kept insisting, 'I'll be home for Christmas,' you know, in that whiny voice he can sink into sometimes. 'See you soon. I love you.' Sheesh. Give me a fucking break." She is speaking more to the wall than to Jim, who is now up to G.

Gloria, not Gloria. She's not what you'd call the marrying type. In fact, she's not the type you'd call.

"Why couldn't he just be honest with me is what I'd like to know."

J . . . K . . . L. L. Jim grins. *For Laura.* He tugs harder at the stem than he has for any of the other letters, but it won't come. *L.* He thinks again, cheating. *L . . . L . . . L.* He keeps pulling at the stem, twisting, jerking, trying to pry it out, his long finger-nails digging into the skin, juice dripping onto his hooded gray sweatshirt. In a last desperate attempt to extricate the stem from the apple, Jim places the stem between his teeth and, gripping the fruit like a grenade, jerks his arm at the shoulder. The stem and apple separate, but he loses the grip in the gushing juice and sends the piece of fruit flying across the room. Laura glances over at him as he smiles with the brown stem lodged in the crack between his two front teeth. "Heh heh," he mutters, sucking on the vaguely barkish taste of the stem before scuttling across the floor to retrieve the mutilated apple. "I'll go wash this now." He picks up the apple from the floor, noticing the stem-less opening at the northern pole of the apple.

L. He grins and heads into the kitchen.

Laura contemplates the silence in the room, already thinking of Mark away, out of the picture. This isn't because she never loved him or wanted to get rid of him as Mark's paranoia had suggested, because if she had had her way, he would have stayed in Kitty and they would have gotten married and stayed in the small town and been relatively happy together. But with Mark in the air, already far away and getting farther, her pragmatism is kicking in, and she thinks, *I've got to get on with my life.* She ponders this further after Jim returns and wrestles with another portion of the rinsed apple, not learning his lesson. He's now try-ing to rip off the lower quadrant, including a quarter of the core.

Mark didn't want any of this. She glances at her surroundings. *Correction, Mark didn't want any of me. Why should I mourn him like my uncle who died last year, who was cut down by forces inescapable to anyone? Mark was whisked away by a smarmy A&R man he's too stupid not to naturally distrust. My uncle never had a choice, but Mark could have said no. In fact, he should have said no.*

"So what are you doing tonight?" Jim asks, his voice strange, something behind it.

Reflecting on her newfound freedom, she answers, "Nothing, why?"

The second he sits down he senses trouble. The couple sitting next to him, an older Jewish man and woman, are already fight-ing, and the plane has yet to even taxi.

"Mort, did you order the kosher meal?" the woman says in a Brooklyn accent that Mark has heard only in movies.

"Yes, dear," the man replies with an accent as thick and a voice almost as deep as hers. "Yes, yes," he repeats, almost as a mantra, as if he would still mumble it at regular intervals even if she were not by his side. "Yes, dear, yes."

"And how about the extra blankets?" Her hands are on her hips even though she's sitting down and confined to the nearly chiropractic chair.

"Not yet, dear, but I will. I will, dear."

The man keeps saying the word *dear* over and over again, and Mark suspects that when he says it in his head, he's really thinking of something else, as if he were the only one wearing rose-colored glasses and only he knows that the sky for him is pink, not blue.

"Yes, bitch, yes." Mark grins, mumbling softly to himself. "Sure, stupid. Anything you say, moron."

Two rows away another older Jewish couple, obviously friends of the two sitting beside Mark, begin shouting idle chit-chat back and forth across the cabin.

"So, Mort, cold enough for you?" The man, who is a full ten feet away, asks.

Mort shrugs, the only real reply to a question that's obviously half-rhetorical and half-idiotic.

"Hey, Shirl," the man's partner calls out to the old woman sitting next to Mark. "You looking forward to California?"

"Oh, shoo-ah, shoo-ah." She raises her arm and then drops her hand limply. "Who wouldn't?"

To take his mind off the cackling of his neighbors, Mark reaches down to the mesh basket on the back of the chair in front of him and takes out the soft blue pillow. He buries one ear in the stiff back of his chair, reclines it as far as it will go, and holds the other pillow over his exposed ear, trying to drown out the latest argument between his neighbors. It's no use.

He sits forward and tries to cross his legs, but it's impossible in the small quarters. In trying, his knee knocks into his tray table, sending his stout plastic glass and miniature Coke can to the brown-and-blue-carpeted aisle.

As the passengers get settled and the flight attendants walk up and down the aisles securing the latches on overhead compartments, the couple continues to fight, quibbling over who gets the extra pillow, tugging at the spare blanket, debating whether to invest in a pair of headphones, and she hemming and hawing over whether to switch seats.

"Jesus Christ," Mark moans to himself. "Thank God I'm through with all of that shit."

Glancing over at the arguing couple, still bickering over something while the plane taxis down the runway, hanging a sharp right turn on the tarmac, he thinks of Laura and the not-so-good times. He remembers staring her in the eye, this woman whom he once loved, and thinking she was some kind of alien sent to this planet to make him miserable. His fond remembrance of Laura is slowly replaced with a "Whew, that was a close one" feeling.

He thinks back to the past couple of days, how she thought the trip to California and the major label deal would change him, and he knew it would. It's funny, but he's already thinking of her in the past tense: "She was great" and "She could be a good cook when she wanted to be." It's been only half a day, just a handful of hours since he last spoke to her, and already their life together seems a million miles away.

As the engines begin to rev up, a supersonic caterwauling underneath the wing, Mark starts humming the first few bars to Teenage Fanclub's rendition of Alex Chilton's "Free Again."

As the plane takes off, he glances to his left, to the old couple who are no longer arguing. The man puts a pink liver-stained hand on his wife's tray, which is not closed up as it should be. She joins his with her own hand, and they both clench, forming a union amid the shaking and the intermittent illumination, Mark thinks it's just one fleshy *Greg Kihnesque* appendage joining both of them. Mark reaches out his own hand for something to hold but returns empty. He thinks of Laura, how her hand is always there, now all turning to memory.

The plane lifts safely off the ground, and the lights come back on. The captain turns off the FASTEN YOUR SEAT BELTS sign, and passengers begin getting up and going to the rest rooms. Flight attendants push down the aisles large silver carts overflowing with soft drinks, liquor, and oversalty peanuts. The old couple are still holding hands.

"Her hand always *was* there," Mark corrects himself as the giant plane coasts in and out of the clouds. *"Was."*

"Remember this?"

Laura twists her head to look out the dirty windshield of Jim's faded red Aries K car, switching her concentration from the cement curb she had been following that turned after regular intervals from gray to yellow and finally red.

"Hmm?" she says absentmindedly, bringing the familiar-looking parking lot blurrily into view and trying to squirm out of her thoughts.

She is thinking back to the dinner they just had at an Indian restaurant down the road from Moore's Mall. Her mouth is still smoldering from her plate of spicy vegetarian noodles, and her head is still a little woozy from Jim's flirting. Or was he flirting? Laura is trying to think back to the battering eyelids and fumbled attempts to order for two, trying to pry out her crib sheet of criteria from the closet of her mind of what constitutes "coming on" and what is just normal friendly behavior.

Laura and Jim have remained close friends since their mostly mutual breakup five years ago in their junior year of high school, and now Laura is using those years as a yardstick for tonight.

Jim has never opened the door for me, at least not since our first date, and even then he launched ahead of me in line and grappled unsuccessfully with a locked plate glass door when we saw Chinatown *at the Capitol Cinema.* Laura is thinking back to all those cafes au lait and iced mochas they had shared at the Novel Idea cafe in the afternoons when he was taking a scarce break from DISContent and she had free time between a couple of classes at Kitty Community College, and she distinctly remembers them paying dutch for all their tabs. He even stiffed her once or twice, leaving her to contend with the three- or four-dollar check alone. But tonight, as soon as the small-boned waitress with the authentic Indian accent dropped the check—and this after appetizers, entrees, two glasses of wine each, and a split dessert with coffee—Jim had pounced on the bill like a predator and insisted he pay. When Laura objected and offered to pay her own way,

Jim's pale face became flustered, he became embarrassed and uncomfortable, and then perhaps a little pissed off, as if Laura wasn't playing by the rules of the game, that she wasn't paying attention.

"Remember this?" Jim repeats, pulling his Dodge neatly into a parking space even though the lot is completely empty.

"Jesus Christ," Laura says, shocked, looking up and seeing a set of goal posts, an oval track, and to the far left a set of bleachers. "Our high school?"

"Yeah." Jim grins, tucking a long strand of his hair behind an ear.

"But why?" Laura asks, not wanting to leave the car.

"I don't know. I just thought"—he shrugs as moonlight invades the car—"it might be fun."

"Fun? We spent four years trying like hell to get out of this place, and now we're going to break back in?"

"Break in?" Jim's eyes open wide. "What do you mean?"

"You really don't get out of the record store much, do you? *Sheesh.* Two years ago they put a six-foot fence around the entire campus."

"Even the quad?" Jim asks as he looks out the window, noticing the moonlight glinting off the ominous black fence that he is seeing for the first time.

"Yes, even your beloved quad."

"Hey, don't say it like that." He gets out of the car, slams the door, and then lifts the handle to make sure it is locked. Little chips of silver paint flake off on his fingers. "Spinning those records during lunch in my senior year was the only fun I had in high school, and that's counting all four years."

"What do you mean, 'records'?" She gets out of the car and joins Jim for his stroll down memory lane, if for no other reason than to make sure he doesn't get lost. "I stuck my head in the student center a few times to say hi, and all it was was a two-bit public address system with a cassette player attached."

"Yeah, yeah." He grabs Laura from her petrified stance and begins to drag her toward the fence. "I spun them at home and put them on tape. Big deal."

"You wanted to be a real DJ so bad"—Laura starts laughing at the memory as they make their way toward the main gate—

"that you actually sat there and recorded a record skipping and skipping."

"Hey, don't laugh. It worked. This one jock shouted out, 'Buy a new needle!' Not that anyone cared—about the music anyway."

They both approach the main entry of the school where two large pieces of black fence, hinged at opposite ends, meet. Between them are a few thin chains held together with rusty bike locks. There looks to be enough slack to slide through.

"You first," Jim says, opening the gates as much as possible.

Laura slides through, leading with her head, an easy fit.

"That's not true about the music. No one caring, I mean," Laura says from inside the school grounds. "I know that a lot of people got turned onto some cool bands because of your show. Mark even said it made him want to start a band. He said that in a small town like this he never would have heard of groups like The Wipers, Half Japanese, Big Black, or Beat Happening."

"Yeah, but"—Jim makes the mistake of leading with his feet through the gap and, not paying attention, bangs his chin against a cylindrical padlock as he pulls his head through— "that's one guy. Those jocks wanted to kill me, wanted to know why I wasn't playing Van Halen or something."

She offers her hand, guiding him behind a large red-brick building that houses the principal's and counselor's offices. The touch of her hand sends a chill down his spine.

They walk between the various buildings housing classrooms, lockers, and an auditorium. On a stretch of grass leading into an open lunch area, a wooden sign stuck into the ground with two rusting posts reads IF YOU CAN READ THIS, THANK A TEACHER. Laura and Jim remember this artifact from their own tenure at the school, only now it is layered with several coats of colorful graffiti, as well as riddled with smart-ass remarks carved on the top, back, and sides.

On the far wall of the cafeteria, one of the newer buildings on campus, a sign reads KITTY HIGH SCHOOL in large metal letters painted black, and below it where it used to say HOME OF THE COUNTY CHAMPIONS 1990–1991, there is now a cutout from the cover of *Gent* magazine stating, HOME OF THE D-CUPS, and even this has been defaced to read HOME OF THE D GRADES.

"Gee," Laura says tentatively, "things sure have changed."

"No shit," Jim says, slightly agitated, "and not for the better."

As Laura and Jim walk behind a large square building with a large sign over the arched entrance—ROOSEVELT WING—she remembers years ago when she overheard one student say to another, "I hear this building is named after some old guy who used to be president," to which the other wearily replied, "President Wing?"

Jim moves off the sidewalk and stands on tiptoes to look in the window of a ground-floor classroom. The door is open, and the light left on in the hall seeps through the room, each shiny desktop a reflective puddle, and the glow-in-the-dark numbers and hands on the rectangular clock in the corner stand out like traffic lights in the fog. Above the blackboard (which is pool-table green and not black at all) spans a paper cutout alphabet chain that seems redundant. This teaching aid is flanked on one side by the infamous photo of Einstein, with his hair a wild Warholian shock of gray sprouting up in every direction, and his tongue, like a limp banana peel, dropping out of his mouth. On the other side is a somber black-and-white photo of Woody Allen.

Jim eyes the various objects in the room, all familiar (except the computers lining the opposite wall), and it brings back his adolescence in an overwhelming rush. He imagines he hears voices, the chatter of his fellow students waiting for class to begin, rooting for a sub, film, or assembly of any kind. He remembers the notes passed back and forth, catching naps on the back of backpacks and tilting one's head at just the right angle to spot an answer or two from the person sitting next to you. It's hard for Jim to believe it was all so many years ago. He blinked and almost half a decade has passed. He smiles, thinking, *Jesus, what a fucking cliché, but it does feel just like yesterday.*

"Let's head down this way." Laura pulls on the sleeve of Jim's sweatshirt, leading him between the gym and locker rooms, around the equipment shed, to a small grove overlooking the various playing fields, while the indoor swimming pool is to the right and half a dozen tennis courts flank the parking lot to the left.

"You know," Jim begins, looking over the empty terrain, the

sounds still alive in his head, "my mind works so much better now than it did then."

"It'd have to," Laura says, unable to resist, but looking over, she sees that Jim is serious, so she adds, "Uh, what do you mean? How?"

Jim sits down on a short hill that slopes gently and leads to an overgrown baseball diamond.

"Like the other day. I was in that Eckerds across from DIS-Content buying some, er, notebook paper, yeah. And, uh, I just happened to find myself in the toy aisle."

"By accident." Laura grins.

"Yeah, well, anyway . . . And the thing is, I saw all of these toys from when I was a kid, things like the Fidget, superballs, Pocket Connect Four, Uno, that paddle-and-ball thing that I could never keep up for more than one or two whacks." Jim stares into the black night, looking past the fields in front of him, thinking back to the scene in the drugstore. "And I picked up one of those little games where there's a bunch of plastic tiles with a number on each one, and they're all scrambled up and you have to, you know, slide them back into numerical sequence."

"Yeah, yeah," Laura says brightly, imagining the device in her hand, the first time she's thought of it in years. "One of my brothers had one of those."

"So," Jim continues, "I picked it up and started going at it, you know, trying to solve the puzzle. And it was tough at first, like it always was. I was never too good at that sort of thing, but after a few minutes it just got so easy. These patterns just began developing. Like if the number you wanted to switch was below an incorrect number, all you have to do is drop the row two tiles away, slide the row above horizontally, push up the correct number, move the piece that was sitting to the side of the correct number into the new vacant spot, then the wrong number into the new open space, and then push back the two numbers you moved in the first place. It was so fucking simple, that pattern, it worked in every situation. All you have to do is alter it to each specific case and, *voilà*. It was a piece of cake. Before they kicked me out, I was polishing that baby off in thirty seconds, whereas, as a kid, I'd struggle with it for days."

"Well, yeah, you've gotten smarter," Laura says wryly, stating the obvious. "At least, let's hope so."

"Yeah, but . . ." Jim stumbles for the right words to verbalize the feelings coursing through his brain to explain how staring at that completed puzzle seemed more of a defeat than a victory. "But if I could know now"—Jim surveys the baseball field, the taunts and insults still ringing in his ears—"what I *didn't* know then."

"Oh, come on, Jim." Laura nudges him. "Don't tell me you're going to start singing 'Glory Days' and reminiscing about those good old times."

"That's the problem. They weren't glory days." He turns to her and looks her in the eyes. "Do you know that I was one of those kids who always got picked last to be on teams?" He waves his arm toward the field. "The other side used to come in from the outfield when I was at bat. They'd sit down on the bases, take off their gloves, turn the other way, or even close their eyes."

"Didn't get too many hits, huh?"

Jim barrels past the obvious. "And whenever I was in the outfield, make that *right field,* and the batter would hit me a flyball, which usually is an easy out, they'd keep on running because the whole team, *both* teams, knew the chances were pretty good I wouldn't catch the ball. And you know what?" Jim picks at a clump of earth and throws it against the night.

"What?"

"I almost always did drop it. And even when it didn't ricochet off my toe and roll into the girls' soccer game, my throw was so weak, the ball'd drop out of the sky like a rock only halfway to home plate."

Laura stifles a laugh.

"You think that's funny?"

"No, Jim." She wipes the smile from her face. "I'm sorry. It was an assholish thing to do, laughing at you like that."

"No, it's cool. It is funny, sort of. I mean, even I can laugh at it now . . . but back then, as a freshman who felt awkward enough anyway, believe me, it hurt." He thinks of the small black-and-white plastic hand-held puzzle now mastered so easily. *If only I knew now . . .* He gets up quickly and wipes the dirt and blades of wet grass clinging to him and offers his hand to help Laura. "Come on."

She puts her hand inside his and springs to her feet. They move down the hill and circle around the wire-mesh backstop of the baseball diamond. The hexagonal squares in the wire are now rounded from holding baseball bats and the toes of those who climbed over the apparatus like spiders on a web whenever the teachers weren't looking.

The abandoned fields before them, and the school like a skeleton in shadows behind them, are eerily silent, no sound present except for the light whipping of a breeze from the East. The just-watered lawn glistens under the blanket of moonlight, overgrown in some places, bare in others. At the edge of the football field white boundary lines drawn in chalk the day before have turned to mucky paste in the recent sprinkling. Laura glances down at her cotton sneakers, the toes dark with wet spots and surrounded on all sides by shreds of yellow dead grass.

"Over here," Jim says, pointing to the perimeter of the fields where four pieces of training gear stand casting long shadows over the end zone. Each one has a broad steel platform that on one end sprouts into two single posts, set at an angle and covered in padding with a leather exterior. There are worn areas in the middle of the blue pads where the heads and shoulders of countless students have rammed, rushed, and banged into them, the white sword and legend KITTY CAVALIERS worn and fading.

Laura leans against one of the posts, the apparatus creaking and shifting slightly as she does so. She looks into the night sky and tries to find a star but can't. Too many clouds.

"So I guess high school wasn't exactly a very good time for you," she says.

"Not really." Jim laughs. "But I didn't try too hard, either. I was sort of, you know, hedging my bets."

"How?" The cushion behind her is slightly wet and makes a squishing nose as she puts her full weight on it. She figures the insides are soaked as well because it has a rotten, dank, musty odor.

"They told us that high school was going to be the best time of our lives. And for those jocks, it was." He looks across the parking lot to Cavalier Stadium. He imagines the screaming, cheering, and clapping for the young sports stars. "The whole town loved those guys. What was that quarterback's name who was hot shit when we were in school?"

"Polcyn, Kevin Polcyn. Number twenty-five. They used to call him The Pulse."

"See? His name still rolls off the tip of your tongue and you haven't ever spoken to him, *ever*, and me, a supposed good friend, gets a birthday card every year in May."

"So?"

"My birthday's in June."

"Yeah, but . . . do you know what that Polcyn guy's doing now? He's selling insurance for his father. He got kicked off the team at Duke and then dropped out because his grades were so bad."

"Sure, because once he got with the big boys he couldn't handle it. But he's still regarded as a legend in these parts, whether he turned pro or not. He had four years at the reins, in control."

"But all those guys end up like Al Bundy, fat slobs, stupid, 'married, with children,' forever droning about 'way back when.' "

"Exactly." Jim kicks at the soft soil under his feet. "They bought into the 'Play Now, Pay Later' plan. Me, I was always more for the 'Concentrate on the Rest of Your Life' plan. I always thought that some sort of happiness would be there later, and if I hooked up with it later, it'd last." He takes a large chunk out of the ground with his heel. "Don't ask me when the good part's supposed to start, though, because I've been wondering about that myself."

Laura clutches herself in her arms for warmth, drawing the long sleeves of her shirt over her fists, clumping the cuffs into a sweaty ball in her palms.

"You know, that's what I always thought about you, too," Jim says, his tone different from the minute before.

"Me?" Laura asks. "How?"

"Sort of that you'd be there . . . later. That we'd hook up in a couple of years," Jim swivels back and forth at the hips, hiding his blushing face in the shadows. "That we'd . . . get back together again."

"Really?"

"Yeah. Like when we split up in the eleventh grade, I never thought it was a big deal because I was sure we'd get together again somehow." His voice lingers in the night air. "Some way."

Jim is silent for a second before continuing. He wonders if he should just drop it, leave the topic alone, quit while he's ahead, but he's been looking forward to this for a long time and has had this conversation in his head more than once, with his mind playing both parts. He decides, what the fuck.

"And when you hooked up with Mark, I didn't think it was a big deal then, either. I thought you guys would go out for a few weeks, prom that year, senior the next year maybe. But four years? I would never have thought."

Laura kicks the cold steel machine as if kicking herself.

"Me, neither."

Jim continues: "I don't know, maybe it was stupid to let you go like that, but I always hoped . . . But now that Mark's on the brink of becoming a big shot"—he laughs, although he doesn't believe it will really ever happen—"I guess there is less hope now than ever. Right?"

Laura's tries to decide how honest to be. The truth is that with Mark bullshitting her about the trip along with all the other fights lately, she doesn't know what to think. And the fact remains that she, too, never really forgot Jim, her first big romance, her first real lover, and the first man she ever felt really comfortable with, in and out of bed. Thinking back over the years she realizes that she and Jim had similar hopes, or at least she always entertained the idea of them ending up together somehow. It rarely manifested itself, but when it did, it was usually in the form of petty jealousy on being introduced to one of his new girlfriends. Seeing Jim and another girl never failed to make her feel somewhat nostalgic, a little ticked off, and the memory of being held in Jim's arms came back even while being held by Mark.

Laura looks at Jim, who is shyly bopping his head to some tune he's nervously humming, his sloping red bangs obscuring most of his face, his pale skin almost glowing in the moonlight. Laura bites her lip, figuring that she never forgot about Jim the way he never forgot about her.

"Oh, come here," Jim says quickly, as if forcing the words out of his mouth. He puts his arms around Laura's waist, the leather skin of the training device wet against the back of his hands. He pauses before moving in for a kiss, giving her time to react, to perhaps make the first move or else scream, yell, resist. Much to Jim's chagrin, Laura does neither. Her own feelings are just as much a mystery to her as they are to him. On the one hand, she's thinking of Mark, their life together and her own past inexplicably bound with his forever. And yet Jim's hands currently warming the small of her back are like an aspirin that soothes the headache of present-day Mark.

Jim's heart is beating rapidly. His eyes begin twitching, so he closes them. Going for broke, he leans in slowly for a kiss, still leaving Laura precious seconds to see what is coming and to kick him in the groin if she feels she must. Laura watches as Jim's head, his whole upper body, hinged at the hips, gravitates toward her like a domino falling in slow motion.

The wind meets her lips first and dries them, then Jim, over-puckering, plants his pursed mouth onto her relaxed lips. It not only surprises her that she kisses him back, but that she wraps her arms around his broad back and lets him pull her closer, his hands raising from below her breasts to her shoulder blades.

He kisses her softly three times before daring to open his mouth and offer his tongue, which she accepts willingly.

5

Dave walks up to The Scene, pausing a second before opening the door. He takes his hands out of his pockets and runs them through his hair, lifts his shirt an inch or two off his chest, then drops it back down and rotates his shoulder counterclockwise. "One, two, three," he counts, then rushes into the club.

"Ta da!" he shouts.

"Fuck ta da, Dave," Todd says, standing at the bar. "Where are the goddamn bands? Where's the crowd? Where is everybody? You're the only person I see and you're the only one who doesn't have to pay tonight. Now *that's* fucked-up."

"Wh-wh-what?" Dave stutters, noticing the empty club.

"I said"—Todd's tone becomes more menacing. He slams a fat fist onto the bar, hitting a plastic ashtray filled with black THE SCENE, THE PLACE TO BE SEEN matchbooks—"where's the fucking crowd? And where's the fucking bands to play to the crowd, which isn't here but should be?"

"Th-th-the crowd?" Dave says slowly. Suddenly it hits him that no one was waiting outside. Where was the line that usually wound around the corner whenever there was a good show? On Fridays and Saturdays you could see kids swarming around this place two blocks in any direction. They were hanging out at the Subway, being driven away by the irate manager of the Circle K, or spitting Coke through straws at each other in the parking lot of Burger King. There would be cars lined up and down the street, and the timid townsfolk would recoil in horror at the macabre-looking kids waiting to get in, either rolling up their windows as fast as they could or else cursing their automatic windows for not closing fast enough. But not tonight.

"I-I-I-I put up flyers," Dave say meekly.

"Great!" Todd shouts sarcastically. "When?"

"Today?"

Jack comes in through the back door that leads out into the alley, where the bands pull up to unload their equipment. Todd and Dave turn their heads instantly, hoping it is Stoner or someone from one of the other bands with a high hat or an amp in their hands, a sign that more are on the way.

"It's just me," Jack says, noticing the attention. "Sorry."

"Yeah, today," Dave says, sitting down on a bar stool. "So?"

"*So?*" Todd says mockingly, then turns to Jack who slides underneath the bar. "Jack, why don't you tell him what a shit-brained idea it is to put up flyers when there's a storm headed this way."

Jack transfers a few beers from a wooden case into the freezer, keeping his mouth shut.

"Storm?" Dave pipes up.

"Yeah, storm. Haven't you been watching the news?"

Dave winces. He had been sleeping most of the day.

"No. Why? What's on the news?"

"Okay, forget the news. So you're not McNeil *or* Lehrer. I figured that out already. But did you see all those gray clouds in the sky, Dave? Those little wet things falling out of the sky? Those are called raindrops." Todd's voice is gentle in a smart-assed sort of way, as if he cares when he really doesn't. Well, he cares all right, just not about Dave. He cares about business, how much beer he sells, what the action was at the door. Todd looks at Dave and sees right through whatever problems he has, trying to use his X-ray vision to see how much Dave has in his wallet to spend.

"How about those big gusts of wind?" His voice changes back to its usual gruffness. "They're gonna blow any goddamn flyer off any goddamn telephone poll or campus kiosk you put it on, man."

Dave hadn't noticed the wind, either.

"Come on, Todd, easy." Jack stands up and unexpectedly begins defending Dave who is too numb to do it himself. *Where are all the bands?* he keeps thinking. *Where's the crowd? Where are the dozen people, my friends? I spoke to them on the phone not more than an hour ago. They assured me they'd be here. Where, at the very least, is Stacy?*

"What?" Todd shouts back.

"It's a Friday night. We get a crowd in here no matter who's playing. I mean"—he's trying to joke—"as long as somebody's on stage. And I'm sure one band will show up."

The phone rings, and Jack rushes to answer it. Out of habit he grabs the phone with his left hand and plugs an ear with his right, blocking out both the band and the crowd that was always making noise, but not tonight.

"The Scene. Huh? Yeah, he's right here."

Todd reaches his hand out in expectation of the phone being placed in it any second. Instead, Jack rolls his shoulders, untangles the long, black, twisting cord, and hands the receiver to Dave.

"Hello?"

"Dave? Hey, this is Mike." The voice is scratchy, half-awake. The Disappointed's guitarist is trying to read some pornographic graffiti scrawled in the corner of a phone booth.

Dave turns his back to Todd and crouches over, covering the mouth of the phone with one hand while he whispers into it, "Where are you? At home? Get your ass over here now! Todd is getting pissed and—"

"No, Dave. We're not in Kitty. We're in Augusta," the voice says simply, as if this was a superfluous aside in an everyday conversation.

"*What?*" Dave says, his voice filled with horror. "You're still in fucking Georgia? Why?"

"What do you mean, why? We played that gig at the Masquerade Club."

"I know, I set it up for you. But that was Wednesday. This is Friday. Why haven't you guys come back?"

"Well, there was this guy there who's a big fan, and he introduced himself after the show and he had a bunch of killer weed and we've been partying at his house for a couple of days. . . ." Mike's voice trails off in laughter, as if he just thought of a really funny story to tell, only he is positive Dave wouldn't think it was funny.

"Okay, okay," Dave says quietly, noticing that Jack has stopped restocking the beer and Todd is leaning over the bar to eavesdrop. "I don't care about any of that. Just get your ass here by midnight. That gives you a couple of hours. You got that? All is forgiven . . . just *get* here!"

"Well, you see. That's why I called. We're not coming. We took a vote and decided to leave from here to go to New York, considering the CMJ New Music Seminar starts on Monday, and we have a showcase at CBGB's on Tuesday night."

"Goddamn it, Mike, I don't give a fuck about CMJ." Dave has now stopped whispering and is standing up, yelling into the receiver. "You get your ass here and play a goddamn set because if you don't, I'm going to go down the tubes. You hear me?"

Instead of a response there are a few clicks, a slight bit of static, and then Mike comes back on the line.

"Look, Dave. I'm sorry. I'm out of quarters, and the operator is being a real bitch and won't let me"—a few clicks cut him off again, but he returns seconds later—"real sorry—" and then there's just the dial tone, running on and on like a series of periods on the electronic headline in Times Square.

Dave sets his head down on the bar, still clutching the phone. The even buzzing of the dial tone is the only sound filling the air.

"I take it that was *bad* news?" Todd leans over and plucks the phone out of Dave's hand, which is still clutching it.

"Uh, the Disappointed's having, er, car trouble. They're going to try to make it to fit in what will be a somewhat—how can I say this?—*truncated* set."

"Jesus Christ!" Todd shouts. The little veins on the side of his head are percolating.

Just then the back door opens, and Johnny comes in with a bag of cymbals and a silver stand, followed by Ben who is carrying an amp, a gig bag around his neck, his guitar on his back like a pack of arrows.

"Yes!" Dave shouts, running down the length of the club. "You see?" He turns around and shouts to Todd, "I told you The Deer Park would play. And they're the band people really want to see!"

"Well, uh, not exactly," Ben pipes up, tossing a ball of cords onto the stage.

"What do you mean, 'not exactly'? Where's Stoner? Where's the other guy? Your rhythm guitarist *du jour?*"

"If you're referring to Fame Throwa, he moved back to Texas," Ben says. "Anyway, that's not a problem. We've been a three-piece before. It's just we're missing Stoner. He can't make it."

"But why?" Dave shouts. "I talked to him yesterday, and he said sure, he'd love to. What's happened since then?"

"He got a promotion at work, and tonight's his first night at his new job."

"Wait a second, *promotion?* He works at the fucking Whales Fin! I thought the only place to go there was down. What is there besides a line cook? Busboy?" Dave's lips clamp shut as it suddenly hits him. "Wait a second!" He screams, his voice echoing off the brick walls.

"Jesus!" Todd sighs back at the bar, elbowing Jack. "Put on a CD or something. I can't bear to hear this asshole whine anymore."

"Stoner got my job?" Dave asks, barely able to control his rage.

"Yeah, you know"—Johnny shrugs—"he always hated working behind the grill, boiling lobsters and sweating like a pig. Being a waiter's where the easy money's at anyway."

"But that was *my* job! The only reason I quit was so I could be here tonight where he should be!"

"Look," Ben says matter-of-factly, tossing a bass drum onto the stage. "All you have is Johnny and me. It won't sound as good, but we'll make it through our set."

"What do you mean 'make it through our set'? Don't you fucking guys see? If we don't get some people in here, I'm dead! I'm going to debtors' prison or have to move in with my parents or, well, fuck, it's all the same thing but . . ." Dave approaches the stage, pushing the bass drum a few inches. "Just guitar and drums? What are you guys, the fucking Spinanes? I'm sorry, but you wouldn't look half as cute in a dress. You couldn't have found some amoeba in town and taught him the parts to a few of your songs?"

"Now look," Ben says defensively, "*my* songs have complicated structures, time changes, and it's just too much for someone to learn all in one night."

"Oh, please, your three-chord bullshit and caterwauled vocals make The Dwarves look like a fucking rock opera."

Ben is biting his lip, holding back the rage, trying to think of a comeback.

"Oh yeah?" is all he manages. After a few more seconds of shaking in his place, like a rocket trying to launch but stuck to the pad, he motions to Johnny to stop setting up the drums and says, "Let's go."

"No, wait. I'm sorry," Dave says halfheartedly as Ben and Johnny exit through the same door they entered only a few minutes ago.

After a few minutes, when it's apparent they are not coming back, Todd pipes up.

"Oh, *great*, Rowland. Why don't you scare away the crowd, too."

Crowd? The word rushes through Dave's head like a bolt of electricity. He turns around quickly, only to find Stacy sitting at the bar, lighting a cigarette.

"There you are!" Dave runs over to her. "Where have you been?"

"Sorry I'm late," Stacy says. "Dan made me stay from the lunch shift to, uh, show a new guy the ropes."

"Stoner?" Dave says disgustedly as he hops up on a barstool next to her.

"Yeah, how'd you know?"

"Don't ask."

"Anyway, Dan was trying to con me into staying for the dinner shift, but I told him I really had to have the night off. He was real understanding about it. You know, he's not such a bad guy after all."

"Yeah, you two have been awfully close lately."

"Uh, Todd," Jack says, taking off his apron and tossing it under the counter. "Mind if I take off? Looks like you won't be needing me tonight after all."

"Yeah, yeah," Todd grunts.

"What's that supposed to mean?" Stacy whispers, raising her hand to her head as a shield.

"Did you tell Dan about how my bills were piling up? How I was broke?"

"Oh, jeez," she says, rolling her eyes. "I may have mentioned something, but I didn't tell him anything that was private. What's the big deal anyway?"

"The big deal is he probably got a huge laugh out of it. After all, it's his fault I have no money. He only gives shifts to his *girl*friends, like you!"

"Now that's not fair, Dave. I only said something because I was worried about you."

"Yeah, yeah," he mumbles. "Bullshit."

The door to the club opens. Chipp and Randy enter, bumping into each other, wiping the dewlike drizzle off their arms and faces.

"Wait, maybe you'd better not go," Todd says to Jack who is reaching for his jacket on a hook on the wall. "We've got a rush!"

"Jesus, it's you two!" Dave raises his arms and turns away from a flustered Stacy. "All my problems are solved."

"Hey!" Randy elbows Chipp in the ensuing silence. "What's his problem?"

"Beats me."

Chipp and Randy pass Dave and Stacy and walk up to the

stage. They can see that there are only a few scattered parts of a drum set and some cords lying on it, without anything else waiting in the wings. Obviously, something's gone wrong. They keep nudging each other, wanting to leave but not wanting to make it apparent. Chipp whispers that they'll stay for just a drink or two and then slip out. They hop on some bar stools a few feet away from Dave and Stacy. Chipp orders two beers, and while Todd is in the process of drawing them, Randy turns to Dave and asks, "So how's it going so far?"

"Fuck this shit!" Dave yells, heading down the bar and exiting through the door leading out to the alley. Stacy shoots Randy a nasty glance before going after Dave.

"What'd I say?" Randy asks innocently.

"Shut up and drink your beer," Chipp chides.

Outside, in the alley, Stacy catches Dave just as he's about to round the corner heading out to the street.

"Dave! Stop. Where are you going?"

Dave halts momentarily, then walks back into the alley, nervously pacing, kicking at the puddles on the ground.

"Stacy, don't start in on me. My whole life's going down the tubes, and it's all your fault."

"Now wait a second. . . ." She rises to defend herself. "Just because it was my idea doesn't mean I'm responsible. You're a big boy, you know." Thunder cracks open the sky, and a few seconds later rain begins pounding the alley. "Why don't you take some responsibility once in a while!" Stacy has to shout, competing with the sounds of the rain splattering against the various junk on the ground: tin cans, bottles, an old shopping cart. "You blame *me* for tonight and *Dan* for your fucked-up money situation, but where does *Dave* fit into any of this?"

"Aw, don't give me any more of your shit!" he screams, slamming his hand against a dumpster.

"This is just like *Groundhog Day!*" Stacy shouts. "But instead of being trapped in the same *day* day after day, you're trapped in the same life, the same problem, only you refuse to conquer and move past. You act the same way to everything, from running away to college to telling Dan off. Give you the same situation, and you act the same way every time. Why don't you try to conquer it for once in your life?"

"What do you want me to do?" Dave rages, his tone softening into tears within a second. *"No*body showed up."

"Well then, fuck 'em!" she shouts back. "Don't give up. Go back to Dan and ask for your job back."

"Fuck that shit! There's no way I'm going to ask that fat asshole for anything! That's just what he wants!"

"Well then, get another job, anything, but just do something else rather than get more pissed off, or else you're just going to explode into a fireball of anger by the time you are twenty-five."

"But nobody showed," Dave says again.

"Jesus Christ, Dave, learn to deal with it. You think life is rough? That everyone's ganging up on you? Give me a fucking break."

"What the hell are you talking about now?" he groans, brushing her aside to lean against a wet brick wall.

She grins, wondering what example to use since she has a drawer full of them.

"Okay, remember when you told me about how when you were a freshman in high school and that teacher was being disrespectful to you, or so you thought? Chewing you out in front of the class when you really were caught cheating on a test and *deserved* to be chewed out. Remember? And what did you do?" She crosses her arms, waiting for an answer.

"I told him to fuck off!" Dave shouts, half-laughing. "Because he was being an asshole, and I wasn't going to stand for being treated like that."

"The way you refuse to be treated by Dan? By the customers? By your fucking father, for God's sake? When's the last time you talked to anyone you're related to instead of these shitheads in a band? Why don't you try listening to people who love you for a change, instead of your goddamn records all the time?"

"Like who? You?"

Lightning illuminates the sky for a split second. Dave stomps away, explosions of water rising up from his feet. He stumbles out of the alley and onto the sidewalk, Stacy following shortly behind him.

"Come on, Dave. Let's go home. *My* home." Stacy tries to force a laugh to lighten the situation. "I'll make some chicken soup. Come on, we're both getting soaked."

Dave pulls back when Stacy steps forward, as if she is some detective trying to talk him off a ledge, and the closer she comes, the more he wants to keep backing up until there is nothing left.

A car drives by, slams on the brakes, then backs up.

"Well, hey, buddy!" Tim is leaning over Cherry, who is sitting in the front noticeably smacking on a wad of bubble gum. "If this ain't fate, I don't know what is." He pulls back for a second, allowing Cindy to push her bouncing blond head into view. "You see? This is perfect! Hop in, ol' buddy. We're just heading out for a drink!"

The door to Tim's Iroc swings open.

"Dave, please don't," Stacy says softly.

Tim revs the engine, the loud roar filling the empty space in front of the club.

Dave ignores her and lunges at the car. Stacy stands on the sidewalk and watches as Dave disappears into the bright red interior. Tim pulls away before the door is even closed, and two high-pitched female voices burst into laughter.

"Well, if Dave's leaving, there's certainly no reason for us to be here!" Randy shouts as the front door to The Scene slams open.

Stacy, startled, hustles off down the sidewalk, heading for her own car, and sniffling in the damp air.

"Jesus, look at this rain," Chipp exclaims as the hard sheets of water slam against him. "It was only drizzling before, but now it's . . ." His words trail off as he's shaken by a horrible thought.

"Hey, look!" Randy says brightly. "All the copies of *Godfuck* are gone. Isn't that cool? But wait, how could they be?"

Just as it sinks in, Randy feels something bumping into his toe. He glances down as a few bloated copies of *Godfuck* float in a foot-deep puddle. He looks down the block and watches as another five are washed down a storm ditch, another three are stuck behind the wheel of an abandoned car, and a dozen are scattered around the sidewalk, turning to shredded mush.

"But . . ." Randy blurts, followed by a "fuck!" that sounds more like a grunt than anything else.

Randy pushes Chipp aside and sprints to the first of the dozen stores they placed stacks of *Godfuck* in front of. The rain starts coming down even harder, and Chipp watches as Randy disappears frantically into the night, only the yellow stitching on his shoes still visible like taillights fading into the distance.

Chipp shrugs. He knows there's no hope, that they're all gone and that there's no money to ever make them again. They're both in debt as it is, and tomorrow it's going to rain even harder. Instead of worrying about it, he flips up his collar, buttons up his coat to the top.

As Chipp walks down the street, trying to stay under a tin awning with many holes in it, he bumps into an attractive redheaded girl in front of the Love Is Christ thrift store, apologizes, then stops for a second, pondering whether or not to start up a conversation, but he pushes on, knowing that *Godfuck* is a total waste and so would trying to pick up this girl, who is a few years older and way out of his league.

Brook glances at the guy who bumps into her, swearing in her head, and after Chipp turns the corner, she resumes her window shopping.

Half a block down, Andrew, who is coming back from grabbing a few things at the drugstore, spots Brook staring intently into the thrift-store window. He stops at the corner, his house a few streets off to the left. He glances down the side street filled with quiet homes, the barely audible laugh track of a TV breaking the silence and now and again a dog barking or a car driving by.

Brook runs her hands through her hair, wiping her long burgundy mane out of her face. The action makes Andrew swallow. The slender curve of her buttocks is visible through the shimmering blanket of rain and mist. For a second he can't believe he actually slept with her, that this person just fifty feet ahead of him had, at one time, been naked in a bed with him, clawing at his back. At first it makes him happy, makes him want to rush her like a bull at Pamplona, grab her in his arms, and request a follow-up performance. But then he's embarrassed. His face turns red, his ears get warm.

Andrew thinks of Ashley, out there somewhere with Craig. Perhaps they were rolling around naked on the floor, across the very spot that Andrew sat cross-legged a few days ago and

longed for Ashley from a distance while Brook babbled on about
a rabbit she used to have, her thick voice grating against Andrew
like a high-powered sander. He suddenly feels empty and
clutches uselessly at the brown paper sack in his arms, nothing
in it able to make him feel better: a bottle of aspirin, envelopes,
toothpaste, Scotch tape.

Andrew steps off the curb, but before his foot lands, he pivots
with the other, a piece of gravel grinding into the sidewalk,
letting out a squeal. He turns left down the quiet side street,
away from Brook, squinting as a VW Bug drives toward him.

Eileen swerves to avoid the guy, haphazardly crossing the
street, with the bag of groceries and weird expression on his
face. Her hand rushes to the horn, but then she decides against
it, turns the corner, passes the thrift store, having to swerve
again to avoid a redheaded girl. Eileen thinks, *Jesus, doesn't anyone in this town have any brains?*

She's driving up and down the streets of downtown Kitty,
momentarily lost. She sees a couple standing outside a red
Dodge and stops to ask for directions to the freeway, but as soon
as she slows down, the couple begins hugging, so she keeps
going.

"That's what I get for walking everywhere," she says, making
a right onto a street that looks familiar. "Wait a second, I've
already tried this street."

Out of the corner of her eye Eileen catches the glimpse of a
car that seems vaguely familiar. She twists her head quickly as
Craig's Tercel roars by in the opposite direction with Craig at
the wheel and a blond Eileen has never seen before clinging to
his side. In an instant Eileen's right hand jumps from the golf-
ball-sized stick shift and reaches across her lap for the latch to
open the window, but she is too late. Craig turns the corner,
leaving a vapor trail, the blond's face hanging in the night.

As Eileen pulls up to a stoplight and fumbles with the broken
stem of the windshield wiper, a car of kids pulls up beside her.
Even though both sets of windows are closed, she recognizes the
song blaring on the cassette player, a song by Superchunk that
Don had put on a mixed tape for her over a year ago:

"This is my life, this is my voice. It is stupid, it is my noise!"

As the light turns green, the driver, a young boy, maybe eighteen, maybe younger, glances over, spots Eileen, and, recognizing one of his own, nods his head in acknowledgment before speeding off.

Eileen sits there, watching the Merge Records insignia vanish into the misty night, thinking, *I don't profess to know you.*

She slaps the car into first, gently releasing the clutch, and steps on the gas, sending the car sputtering into motion. After two lefts and a right, she finds the highway on-ramp, and not even noticing in what direction she's going, gets on. At the top of the ramp she merges with traffic, slides into the fast lane, slips the car into third, fourth, and then fifth, and relaxes, trying to find something good on the radio.

Weaving into the slow lane for a second to pass a stubborn truck unwilling to give up its position, Eileen glances over her shoulder and catches a glimpse of her hastily packed bags spilling over from the backseat onto the floor. She sighs and eases back into the fast lane.

Eileen cracks open a window; the cold air slaps her in the face. Her head reaches through the open space, and keeping one eye on the road, she looks up to the sky. Through breaking clouds she can see the moon and, beyond that, billions of worlds caught up in action more chaotic than her own: fireballs explode, suns burst, expand, and then recede into black holes where not even light can escape its ferociously unfathomable grasp.

Every one of us wants to be some sort of star, Eileen thinks, *but instead we're just ending up satellites that don't call home.*